ME AND MISS M

JEMMA FORTE

ISIS
LARGE PRINT
Oxford

Copyright © Jemma Forte, 2009

First published in Great Britain 2009
by
Penguin Books Ltd.

Published in Large Print 2010 by ISIS Publishing Ltd.,
7 Centremead, Osney Mead, Oxford OX2 0ES
by arrangement with
Penguin Books Ltd.

British Library Cataloguing in Publication Data
Forte, Jemma.
   Me and Miss M.
   1. Private secretaries - - Fiction.
   2. Motion picture actors and actresses - - Fiction.
   3. Large type books.
   I. Title
   823.9'2–dc22

ISBN 978–0–7531–8664–0 (hb)
ISBN 978–0–7531–8665–7 (pb)

Printed and bound in Great Britain by
T. J. International Ltd., Padstow, Cornwall

Prologue

In life, there are a handful of days when we experience key moments that either determine or fulfil our destiny, depending on what you believe in. I call these days "destiny days". These days have two things in common. One is that at the time they seem utterly ordinary and it's only ever with the luxury of hindsight that you realize that you've had one. The other is that you never, ever forget them.

To understand me, in even the smallest way, you need to know about one of my "destiny days".

It was the mid eighties, I was nine years old and on the surface it was a completely average Saturday for the Massi household. My brother, Daniel, had left for football practice and Mum and I were looking forward to watching the afternoon movie in peace. Outside, the light from the lamp-posts was bleeding into the grey November gloom and it had started to drizzle. I thought with some satisfaction of my brother, who'd be shivering as he ran up and down a soggy pitch in the freezing cold. The smell of cooking wafted through from the kitchen.

"Film starts in a minute," said Mum, as she sat down next to me on the sofa.

"What's it called again?" I asked, taking her elegant hand and placing it in my own.

"It's called *It's a Wonderful Life*. They usually show it at Christmas time and it's about a man called George Bailey who finds out what life would be like if he'd never been born."

I digested this information solemnly.

Dad came into the room, sat down in his chair and put the glasses that hung round his neck on his nose so that he could see to do the crossword. At the time, he was still head chef at the local Italian restaurant that nowadays he owns and manages, so having him home at the weekend was a rare treat.

The overture began and the sound of sweeping strings filled the room. I swung my legs up on to the leather pouffe so that I could gaze down lovingly at my white jazz shoes, pinstripe jeans and maroon leg warmers. I sighed contentedly. Then I got my first glimpse of James Stewart as George Bailey, and I didn't think about anything else until the film was finished.

Years before, when I'd first watched Gene Kelly in *On the Town* managing the incredible sartorial feat of making a sailor suit look cool, my love affair with stars of the silver screen had begun, but until now a love affair was all it had ever been. However, this film affected me so profoundly that my passion turned into more than just a crush and became something far more serious. Ambition.

As it drew to a close, I wept.

George Bailey's redemption was complete and I had never been so moved by anything in my entire life. Tears spilled out of my big brown eyes and down my cheeks.

"That was such a happy film, but it made me feel so sad," I sniffed.

"I know, sweetheart, I know," soothed Mum, hugging me tight. "I'm so glad you liked it."

And she was. But she was also blissfully unaware of the cogs that were turning in my young brain. I would be an actress, and one day I would move people as much as Jimmy Stewart had just moved me.

Seconds later I declared, "Mum, I need to go to stage school."

Mum ignored me and got up to put the kettle on. But the maelstrom of thoughts that were swirling around in my head didn't abate and one hour later over supper I was still stuck on the same subject.

"But why won't you at least consider it? I want to go to stage school — pleeeeease?"

Mum rolled her eyes. "Francesca, we are not sending you somewhere where you will become horribly precocious and then out of work and miserable for the rest of your life. How many times do I have to tell you? Nothing in the world of acting is guaranteed and, for the last time, we can't afford it."

"But I really want to be an actress," I whined.

Dad sighed. "Fran, stop this nonsense, please. You're not going to stage school, so you may as well forget about it."

3

"But you're being so unfair," I wailed. "I neeeeeed to go to stage school. Everybody said I was brilliant in the school play, didn't they?"

At this point Daniel, who was home from football, felt compelled to speak up.

"Oh, shut up, will you? You were crap. You were completely over the top and Mum and Dad are just too chicken to tell you."

"Now that's enough, Daniel," said Mum sternly, putting down her fork.

I glared at my mother meaningfully, waiting for her to deny what Daniel had just said, but seemingly she had nothing to add. I was furious.

"Yeah, shut up, Daniel. Just cos Michelle dumped you," I lashed out.

I'd hit a nerve and Daniel gave me what could only be described as a death stare, grabbed his plate and headed upstairs as fast as his lanky legs would carry him.

Dad looked like his patience was wearing thin but I decided to chance one last try. "Dad, you've got to understand . . . I want to be famous."

"But why, Francesca?" asked Dad frustratedly, looking totally bewildered.

Why? Why did he think? Because it would be the best thing in the whole wide world. I tried to stay patient with my dense father. There was nothing for it. I'd have to spell it out.

"I want to be famous because it will make me happy."

4

Mum shook her head. Her little girl, who wasn't so little these days, had a lot to learn. Sadly, it looked like she'd have to find it all out for herself.

"Fran, how can you possibly know what it is you want to do now?" said Dad wearily. "I mean, only the other day you were telling me that you wanted to be a writer for *Cosmopolitan*."

Disappointment coursed through my young veins. "Well, I don't any more. I want to be an actress," I shouted.

"Now that really is it, young lady," snapped my mother. "I will not put up with this foul behaviour or this ludicrous idea that fame makes anybody happy."

The rest of the evening was spent sulking in my bedroom.

I scrabbled through my collection of cassettes, took one from its box and placed it in my tape recorder. As the machine clunked into action, I reached over to my bedside table for my precious diary and, to the strains of the soundtrack from *The Kids from Fame*, I scribbled defiantly. Like many nine-year-olds, I was prone to exaggeration.

I hate my parents. Mum and Dad are sooooooo mean and they don't know anything. Being a famous actress would be the best thing in the whole wide world. I just know it.

Years later I have come to accept that my parents may have had a point.

Twenty Years Later

CHAPTER
ONE

"And cut," the director shouted. "That's a wrap. Thank you for a great week, everyone, and I'll see you all on Monday."

Leading lady Francesca Massi breathed a sigh of relief as Richard Carrington finally peeled himself off her. She'd spent most of the afternoon being enthusiastically mauled by him and was covered in a thin film of his perspiration. Understandably, she was desperate for a shower.

"Here you are, Miss Massi." The wardrobe lady handed Francesca a dressing gown and she wrapped it round herself gratefully. Now that a crew of eighty had all had a good gawp at her considerable charms, it was important to protect what small shred of modesty she had left. Francesca headed for her dressing room but, as she did so, her heart sank. Lecherous producer Geoff was striding towards her, a look of intent in his pale blue, too-close-together eyes, arm casually slung round the neck of latest girlfriend Stacey. He'd been harassing Francesca for weeks about starring in his next project and no matter how many times she told him she wasn't interested, he just didn't seem to get the message.

"Ah, there are you are," he said. "I'm so glad I've found you. I really need to talk to you about a matter of crucial concern . . ."

"Francesca, I've only gone and dropped the ruddy hole punch again. Would you think it awfully beyond the call of duty to grab the dustbuster and have a quick go round my desk? There are little white bits bloody everywhere."

I immediately stop typing and spin round in my chair. "Will do, Geoff. I can do that now if you want?"

"No, no, not if you're busy," Geoff says, wafting his hand around airily while blatantly eyeing up Stacey, who's just returned to the office. She gives him a little wave and flicks her highlighted mane over her shoulder coquettishly. Stacey knows only too well the effect her blonde hair and long legs have on Geoff, and uses his lust unashamedly to her advantage. I'm not keen on Stacey, to say the least, and the feeling is completely mutual. In fact, out of the fifteen or so people working at Diamond PR, the only person I consider to be a true friend is Raj.

Raj sits opposite me and is lovely-looking, super intelligent (when he's not stoned) and, to the horror of his strict Hindu family, a complete hippy who dyes his hair all the colours of the rainbow and wears nail varnish. He's also our office manager and in the mornings he tackles his job with gusto. However, his enthusiasm tends to run out by about lunchtime, which is invariably when he goes out on to the balcony to smoke the most enormous joint you've ever seen. After that he's good for nothing, although to be fair he does have a very high score on Tetris.

The fact that most afternoons the only thing our office manager is capable of managing is talking rubbish and maybe a large kebab, seems to have bypassed our boss, Geoff, completely, but that's because he spends large chunks of the day safely ensconced in his members' club.

I'm not complaining. Having a boss who leaves the office to run itself works brilliantly for me too and is the main reason why I've put up with my crap salary so long, for I, too, have a habit that Geoff knows nothing about. A habit that I can't seem to shake, that I've been hooked on for years and that ultimately doesn't seem to be doing me any good. That habit is going to auditions and in order to feed it I need to be in a job where I can easily sneak out for an hour or so, when my agent comes up with a casting. My plan is, and always has been, to stop working as Geoff's PA as soon as one of these castings affords me my big break.

Geoff stalks away from the vicinity of my work station and heads for Stacey's. I start breathing again and return to my story. It's terribly difficult to concentrate properly in such an open-plan office but I've got good at zoning out.

"Good meeting, Stace?" enquires Geoff, straining to get a better look at her cleavage as she bends down to stow some Topshop bags away under her desk.

"Brilliant, thanks, Geoff," she coos, kicking the last of her bags out of sight with her foot. "I'm just sorry it took so long — there were terrible delays on the tube coming back."

I hear Raj mutter under his breath, "And my name's Doris."

"Don't worry about it, babes," says Geoff, smiling patronizingly while walking all the way back to his desk backward, which he must imagine looks deeply sexy but actually looks like something health and safety would be very concerned about, and is a hazard to himself and all inanimate objects in his path. However, sadly (and quite impressively), he makes it right back to his chair without tripping over or bumping into anything at all, and he even manages to sit down in one fluid reverse movement, still gazing all the while at Stacey, who's manfully trying to act as if she's comfortable with such protracted eye contact when I know she isn't. Reasons for me not liking Stacey are as follows:

Stacey is the sort of girl who thinks that anybody who eats a biscuit or a cake is repulsive and weak, and who would gladly relinquish all her worldly possessions just to be in *OK* magazine. She is, in short, not a girl's girl. Naturally, men love her and she has the whole of the male race wrapped round her little finger. Women see bitch from hell. Men see misunderstood/needs to be taken care of. The thing that irks me most about her though, and this is hard to admit, is that Stacey and I actually have a few things in common, which I think partially explains our strong distrust of one another.

Like me, Stacey is only biding her time by working at Diamond PR, and views her job as a mere stepping stone on the path to what she really wants to do. Also like me, what she really wants to do is act, although I suspect Stacey would be happy to present, sing, read the news or take all her clothes off and run naked round Trafalgar Square with a banana shoved up her bottom if it made her famous. The final nail in Stacey's personality coffin is that she reciprocates Geoff's flirting, which isn't pleasant to watch and is something that we all have to endure on a daily basis due to the open-plan nature of our office.

My fingers fly over the keyboard.

Despite Miss Massi's annoyance at having to chat to Geoff after enduring such an intense day, she couldn't help but stifle a giggle. Today Geoff had simply outdone himself and was wearing what could only be described as a truly nasty grey leather jacket. As he mooched towards her, Francesca could tell that he thought he looked wonderful. In fact, he looked like a Bee Gee. Not that Stacey would be letting him know — she was quite happy to allow him to make an idiot of himself as long as he kept on subsidizing her very expensive lifestyle . . .

"I tell you what, Fran," says Geoff, clearing his throat. "If it's all the same to you, let's have that tidy up now and then we can have a debrief at the same time. That way I'll have time to take Stacey out for lunch and she can fill me in on all these meetings she's been having to recruit new clients."

"No problem," I say, trying not to laugh as I watch Stacey's face fall. I'm only thankful that Stacey is the main object of Geoff's affections and not me. Geoff considers himself to be God's gift to women and there's something about him that is really creepy. He's always struck me as the sort of man who would play Luther Vandross if he was trying to get you into bed.

I save my writing, reduce it so I can come back to it later and make my way over to his desk, dustbuster in hand. I bend down to vacuum round his large feet, which today are encased in a pair of hideous shiny loafers with tassels. They're probably designer and really expensive but they look like cab driver's shoes to me and are totally wrong with jeans. Geoff's dress sense is amazing and I say that in the most sarcastic sense of the word.

Tasks that are definitely not part of my job description over with, I straighten up to give my boss the latest Diamond PR headlines.

"Right then," I say. "Firstly, you know that girl band you met with last week?"

"Yes?"

"They've decided to go with another company."

"Bugger," says Geoff, trying and failing to snap a pencil in half.

"But, on a more positive note, Shanice from *Big Brother* phoned," I hastily add. Geoff looks blank, so I fill him in. "Shanice wouldn't be a dream client admittedly — she was in *Big Brother* last summer and got kicked out for assaulting another housemate — but she'd love to meet with you to discuss how she can change the public's perception of her, with her ultimate and, let's face it, rather predictable goal being to become a glamour model."

Geoff gets up to go and lounge on the banquette seating in the corner of the office. "Blimey, now I know exactly who you mean. Gosh, we'd have our work cut out getting the public to like her, but she's certainly worth a meeting as far as I can remember," he says smarmily, while making inappropriate hand gestures. "Book it in, Fran."

"Right, will do," I say.

It's only now I notice that Stacey, who has been earwigging from her desk, has turned an extraordinary shade of puce.

"You're such a cow, Fran," she splutters across the office tearfully. "You know how much I love *Big Brother* and I happen to think that Shanice is bloody amazing. Why didn't you let me deal with her? You don't even watch *BB*."

I stare at her, completely dumbfounded. What a freak.

"Oh, babes," says Geoff eventually, with one long leg splayed straight out, the other bent at the knee like some ageing page-seven fella. "Listen, I can tell it would mean a lot to you, so why don't you go ahead and set that one up? I'm sure Fran won't mind."

"Oh, Geoff, thank you, you're such a sweetie," simpers Stacey. "Anyway, it is more my area. I mean, I am supposed to be the client liaison, whereas Fran's just your PA."

Silently I count to ten.

"Anyway, Geoff," I continue, "I've come up with a few ideas for your pitch and I've also mocked up a press release that you could show Shanice as an example of the kind of thing we do."

Stacey looks daggers at me and flounces towards my desk. "Well, I'll take a look at that, seeing as I'm going to be handling Shanice from now on. And, for future reference, you may think you're the only one capable of writing anything around here but, as it happens, you're not."

I wait for Geoff to pull Stacey up on her downright rudeness, but he doesn't. He just gazes at her indulgently as if she's being a bit silly as opposed to vile.

At this point I can't work out who I'm more cross with and find myself glowering at Geoff. When this finally registers, he does at least have the good grace to shift out of his month-of-April pose into a more sensible position. The next minute, however, I definitely lose the upper hand.

"What the fuck is this?" shrieks Stacey from across the room, causing everyone to look up. A terrible thought bursts through the swing doors of my brain and I instantly feel nauseous. No, no, no, no. This can't be happening. But it is.

"Geoff Harding was a man with an inflated ego and little brain," Stacey reads in a voice loud enough even for those at the other end of the room to hear. "While he may have made a name for himself making action films in the eighties, that didn't excuse his recent turkeys or his chronically dire dress sense . . ."

16

Stacey mouths a few more sentences to herself, her eyes skimming the page at a rate of knots.

"Hang on a minute," she says, changing gear from gleefully outraged to blinking furious. ". . . Geoff's bimbo of a girlfriend, Stacey, satisfied every cliché going when it came to men of a certain age and their inability to spot when a girl was more infatuated with their bank balance than their personality. In fact, Stacey was such a gold digger she was even prepared to overlook being with someone who wore skinnier jeans than she did . . ."

"What the hell is this, Fran?" asks a baffled-looking Geoff.

"Nothing, Geoff, honestly, it's nothing — just a bit of fun," I say, dragging myself away from the spot that I seem to have frozen to and lurching towards my computer. "Stacey, please stop reading that right now — it's private."

Stacey gives me a look that chills me to the bone and I know then that for the first time ever in my life I am going to have to physically defend myself. Sure enough, Stacey lunges towards me and the next five minutes pass in an undignified blur of elbows, nails and hair. A small crowd gathers and at one point I even hear Hazel from accounts yell, "Get her, Fran," which is very out of character, although her support is appreciated none the less.

What happens couldn't really be described as a scrap or a fight, but more of a pathetic tussle, during which Stacey scratches me so hard she draws blood. At this point I'm ashamed to say that out of sheer desperation

I resort to giving Stacey a Chinese burn and only then does she finally back off, muttering obscenities.

Show over, everyone drifts back to their desks (seemingly disappointed that Stacey and I hadn't ended up rolling about on the floor with our skirts round our waists) leaving a furious Geoff in their wake. Fairly understandably, by now he's fuming and informs me that he and Stacey will be deciding what is to become of me over lunch. Needless to say, I'm ecstatic that she is to be included in the decision-making process.

The two of them leave the office in a cloud of indignation, Stacey dramatically clutching her perfectly all right wrist.

I turn round and fifteen pairs of eyes swivel downward. It occurs to me that only a bloody good PR could get me out of this one, so sadly I'm in the wrong place. In urgent need of some friendly reassurance, I turn towards a stunned-looking Raj, but I don't get any.

"What on earth were you thinking, Fran? Why would you leave that on your desktop?" he says.

"Oh don't, Raj. I can't bear it. I'm an utter, utter prannet. Do you think I'm going to be sacked?"

"I don't know, Fran. I bloody hope not," says Raj, shrugging weakly.

I take his reluctance to commit either way as a very bad sign.

"Oh, shit it," I say, feeling really panicky. "Now I'm horribly late for my lunch with Carrie Anne, so I'm going to have to run, but I'll see you later."

"See you later," says Raj, who retreats out on to the balcony where no doubt he'll smoke an enormous joint, purely for stress-relieving purposes, of course.

CHAPTER
TWO

I hurry through Soho, worrying about what will become of me and mentally beating myself up. How could I have been so foolish? I may not love my job all that much but I bloody need it, and I also feel terribly guilty in case I've hurt Geoff's feelings, which was never the intention. I picture my best friend and flatmate Abbie's face as I break it to her that for the foreseeable future the rent may be somewhat of an issue. It looks pissed off.

On the corner of Wardour and Old Compton Street, while waiting for an opportunity to cross the road, a van only narrowly avoids soaking me as it races through a puddle. It's the end of February and the weather is foul, which matches my mood completely. As I make a fairly risky dash for it across the road, I remember that I'm seeing my boyfriend, Harry, tonight. Damn, now I'll have to tell him what's happened and when I do I know he'll show no mercy. Instead of doling out sympathy, he'll simply view my latest drama as an opportunity to take the piss out of me royally. Like he needs any more ammunition, I think wryly.

By the time I finally reach Bruno's Cafe, having sprinted the rest of the way, a justifiably irritated Carrie

Anne is already seated at our usual table. "Where've you been, babe?" she asks. "I've got to get back for a meeting, so I've only got another twenty minutes."

"I know, I know. I'm so, so sorry. It's just been one of those mornings," I explain, panting as I take off my coat.

"Well, you're here now, so sit down and tell me everything. I feel like I haven't seen you for ages."

Carrie Anne and I first met ten years ago on a film set, which probably sounds more glamorous than it actually was. I never did make it to stage school, so at eighteen I decided to get myself a job as a runner on a film. That way, I figured, I could learn about the industry that I still so wanted to be a part of. I did indeed learn a lot. I learnt how over eighty people took their tea and coffee, and that starting work before six in the morning can make one feel actually physically sick. I learnt that it's hard to survive on a wage of one hundred pounds a week and that if you eat a cooked breakfast every day for ten weeks you will put on weight. More significantly, I also discovered that though some may claim to find hanging around on a film set incredibly dull I loved it, even if the very obvious hierarchy didn't escape my attention. As a lowly runner, I was at the bottom of the pile. At the top were the actors, who were treated like royalty, their every whim catered to. Although, having said that, royal people do spend a lot of time doing things they'd probably rather not, like attending dull functions and talking to politicians, while actors don't.

Anyway, Carrie Anne was third assistant director on the same film and the minute I spotted this voluptuous redhead chatting up the sparks, laughing like a drain and responding to the crew's lewd comments with much cruder ones, I knew we'd hit it off and become firm friends.

When filming finished, I was more determined than ever to try to become an actress, whereas Carrie Anne wanted to stay in production. She has since gone on to become head of production at the biggest film company in the UK, Great British Films, and the contrast between our careers has always been a rather marked reminder that her plan was probably a bit more sensible than mine. She's in full-time employment, in demand and in the black, whereas I've spent years juggling various jobs along with the rather disheartening process of finding an agent and going to castings, and though I have occasionally got the odd acting job here and there (odd being the operative word), any small successes I've enjoyed have only slightly sweetened the sourness of a great deal more rejection.

"Thanks, darling," says Carrie Anne to Bruno as he delivers two mozzarella and tomato paninis to our table. "So come on then, Fran, give me the headlines. Have you had any more auditions recently? How's Harry?"

"Um, right, well, I've only had one audition recently and it was for a sanitary pad commercial, so that kind of says it all, and Harry's fine, but the rather more scandalous breaking news is that my little time-killing habit of writing at work has probably just cost me my job," I say, launching into the morning's events.

When I've finished, Carrie Anne looks gobsmacked. "Fran, I hate to say it but how could you have been so stupid? Why on earth would you not have changed the names?"

I can't answer. I feel sick with embarrassment and fully comprehend exactly how foolish I've been and don't need it pointed out any more. Carrie Anne quickly realizes this and takes pity on me.

"OK, listen, it's happened and there's no point going over the 'what ifs', so instead what we need to do is work out how best to handle the situation."

I sigh. "To be honest, Carrie Anne, even if Geoff doesn't sack me, which is highly unlikely seeing as right now he'll be having his ear bent by the person who hates me more than anyone in the world, I don't see how I can stay now anyway. It's just all too hideously mortifying."

I stop talking briefly to take a large bite out of my sandwich. "Besides, I've been doing a lot of thinking recently and I've decided that at the age of twenty-nine it's probably time for me to start facing a few facts."

"What do you mean?" asks Carrie Anne calmly. She's used to my dramatics.

"Well, though it pains me to say it, I'm starting to think that I just might never make it as an actress. I mean, I've put so much energy into trying to make it happen, but it's so bloody hard and so competitive," I say, munching away. "I haven't been seen for anything decent in ages and it's got to the point where if I really want to work then pretty much my only option is to do fringe theatre for no money. Obviously I can't afford to do that, so I'm stuck in limbo at Diamond PR. And what's even worse," I continue, really getting into my stride now, "is that any casting directors who were taking me vaguely seriously have stopped doing so ever since my advert came out. In fact, thinking about it now, I probably couldn't even do fringe theatre if I wanted to." This last depressing thought causes me to slump back in my chair, utterly defeated.

Carrie Anne tries not to but she can't stop herself and lets out a hearty chuckle, almost choking on a stringy bit of mozzarella in the process.

"Oh, babe, I know I shouldn't laugh but I can't help it. I finally saw your ad for the first time the other day and I nearly pissed myself," she says, throwing her head back as she laughs at the memory.

Carrie Anne knows I'm always up for a healthy dose of self-deprecation and we've never minced words with each other. Still, she could tone it down a bit.

"You were hilarious," she says, wiping away a tear.

I give her a rueful smile and sigh. I can never quite bring myself to point out to people that I wasn't supposed to be funny. This is what I'm up against.

Recently I did an advert for a women's car insurance company called Claims for Dames. When I got the job, I was ridiculously excited. Simply getting an audition had provided a very welcome boost to my wilted confidence and when I found out that I would be getting two thousand pounds for one day's work my joy had known no bounds. My friends and family were so pleased and relieved for me, mainly, I suspect, because they knew it might shut me up for a while. Even Geoff was chuffed. At least, he was until he began to question when I might have gone to the audition . . .

Of course, there was one person who wasn't so pleased for me and that was Stacey. Try as she might, she couldn't hide her jealousy and outright disgust that I'd been chosen, which at the time was an excellent bonus. When the call sheet came through, with my name right at the top under the heading "Artistes", it felt as if my luck had finally changed . . . and then I filmed it.

In the commercial I'm dressed as a gangster's moll. Claims for Dames, you see? I'm a fairly curvy but slim size twelve, so I looked quite fetching in the pencil skirt, fitted jacket, fishnet tights and little gloves they gave me. However, according to the make-up lady, my long, wavy brown hair simply wouldn't "behave", so after half an hour of fiddling about with it she just gave up and stuffed it all into a beret that she then clamped to the side of my head at a jaunty angle. I remember her telling the director that she thought it made me look a bit "Bonnie and Clyde", to which he replied, "Looks more Frank Spencer if you ask me, but it'll have to do."

Just to cement my total loss of dignity forever, I had to sing the ever so natty, terribly catchy jingle straight to camera. The advert was badly shot, tacky as hell, cheap-looking and terribly lit, and when it started to air it didn't take long for me to start wondering if my performance in it might actually be more of a hindrance to my fledgling career than a help.

Possibly for all these reasons, it seems to have caught the public's attention and has become one of those ads that people love because it's so bad. In fact, my agent even rang me a couple of days ago to tell me that they're planning on repeating it over the summer, although they won't be giving me any more money due to the way he drew up the contract last time . . .

On the bright side, at least I can finally say that — like my hero, Jimmy Stewart — a performance of mine has moved someone to tears. Only difference being that the tears are my own and they're tears of embarrassment. As for everyone else who's seen it, tears of mirth would be more accurate. Now, with my day job hanging in the balance and my acting career at a humiliating standstill. I can practically see my life's meter running and know that the only person who can change my situation is me.

"I'm going to give up trying to be an actress," I declare, testing the waters and secretly hoping that Carrie Anne will persuade me not to. However, to my chagrin her facial response is an expression of delighted relief as opposed to regret.

"That's brilliant news. I hate to say it, but you know I've always thought you'd be better off writing than acting. I'm so glad you're going for it."

"What?" I say, looking as puzzled as I feel.

Carrie Anne blinks. "Your writing? If you're giving up on acting, which — let's face it — is a dog's life unless you're one of a tiny, elite group, then I guess you'll finally be giving your writing a go, which I've always believed you have a genuine talent for."

"Carrie Anne," I say frustratedly, "I can't go from one ridiculously ambitious daydream to another. I do love writing, always have, always will, but it's a hobby and not one that I want to be judged by other people." I take a deep breath. It's been a long day already, but my friend is only trying to help. "After years of rejection I think it's probably time to stop putting myself on the line. It looks like my stint as Geoff's PA is about to come to an end, so I think what I really need now is a relatively interesting job that I can try to make a proper go of. So, what I was really wondering is, are there any jobs going at Great British Films? I know it's a long shot, but if I'm not going to be an actress then I can't think of anywhere I'd rather work and, honestly, I'd be willing to do absolutely anything if it means getting a foot in the door."

Carrie Anne fixes me with her big green eyes and smiles at me affectionately. "Not anything, I hope! Listen, Fran, of course I'll keep an ear out, but I hope you know that you could be wasting your best asset without even realizing it. You've never given writing a chance and if I do hear about any jobs at Great British Films then they're only going to be boring office jobs."

"Well, they couldn't be any more boring than the one I've had for the last couple of years and at least I'd be a part of the film business in some small way," I say, struggling not to let my voice sound shaky.

Carrie Anne gives my hand a little squeeze as she starts to gather her things together. "Babe, I've got to dash, but I want you to believe me when I say that the film world isn't all glamorous like you think it is. Yes, it has its moments, but even after all these years of slogging my guts out I still work ridiculously long hours and spend stupid amounts of time dealing with people whose egos are completely out of control."

"Like who?" I say, my curiosity instantly ignited. I love Carrie Anne's tales and, despite what she says, they are anything but mundane.

"Fran, don't get me started or we'll be here till midnight," she says drily. "Now, I've got to go, but send my love to that lovely boyfriend of yours."

"I will," I say, feeling sad that our brief lunch is over and worried that I've spent the whole time talking about myself. "I'm seeing him tonight, actually, so I'll say you said hi."

"You see," says Carrie Anne, buttoning up her coat. "That's another downside of my business. I've got no time for a love life and shall probably end up a lonely old spinster."

As she says this, though, she's grinning and we both know that no matter how much she protests, she loves her job with a passion and wouldn't have it any other way.

I get up and give her a big hug. "I'm sorry I was late and that I've spent the whole time waffling on about myself. I know things aren't that bad really and you're right, at least I've got Harry, which is one thing that's going well, so I'm very grateful for that," I say, pulling away and looking her in the eye. "But please do consider me for anything that comes up. I really mean it — I'll do anything."

Carrie Anne heads back to work and leaves me staring thoughtfully into the remnants of my lunch. I order a cappuccino — anything to avoid going back to the office where I suspect I am about to be unceremoniously sacked.

CHAPTER
THREE

I have precisely one week left of gainful employment. Any small thimble of hope I'd had left that I might get to keep my job vanished the minute Stacey staggered through the door with Geoff at five thirty. I'd seen the victorious glint in her eye and knew then and there that it was game over.

"The thing is, Francesca, I was almost prepared to overlook things because you are actually a ruddy good PA in many ways," an awkward-looking Geoff had said, his face flushed from lunchtime drinking. "But I simply can't be seen to tolerate violence towards other staff members."

At this point Stacey quickly remembered to clutch her wrist again. I considered pointing out that quite a lot of my skin was still under her acrylic fingernails but thought against it. I know when I've been beaten.

"Plus, Francesca," Geoff continued, "as Stacey quite rightly pointed out, in PR we are the holder of many secrets and I can't have someone writing about people behind their backs because, at the end of the day, trust is of tantamount importance to our clients."

Stacey grinned in my general direction, making no effort whatsoever to mask how much pleasure she was gleaning from my downfall.

Now I've left the office and I'm heading for Leicester Square, the tube and ultimately Harry's house, feeling thoroughly disillusioned, stressed out and anxious.

Getting on the tube does nothing to alleviate my mood. It's packed and oppressively stuffy and, as I stand all the way, sweating in my thick coat, I wonder what on earth I'm going to do with my life. I fight valiantly to hold it together by thinking positive. Maybe this is exactly the kick up the bottom that I need? I can start concentrating on the achievable as opposed to the impossible, and surely there must be plenty of things I can do if I put my mind to it. I just wish I could figure out what they are. At this point, much to the dismay of the man whose armpit I'm squashed against, I give up trying to be brave and burst into tears.

By the time I arrive at Harry's flat in Hammersmith I'm surprised by how much better I feel. Crying can be good and, having sobbed pretty much all the way down Hammersmith Grove, I'm now feeling less keyed-up, purged of stress.

As I ring the bell, I make a decision. There's nothing to be gained by infecting Harry with my doleful mood. After all, as Carrie Anne pointed out, I should be making the most of the one thing that's good about my life right now. So instead of feeling maudlin I decide to treat Harry to a nice dinner that I can't afford now I've been sacked. I gulp and ring the bell again, feeling full of determined, slightly manic, jangly anticipation for the evening ahead. We will have a good time.

"Hiya!" I say over-brightly when Harry finally opens the door. "I hope you're feeling hungry because I've had a really lousy day, so I need to go out and drown my sorrows."

"Your eyes are all red and puffy," is his sympathetic greeting.

My bottom lip wobbles dangerously and a stray tear escapes. I really am a woman on the edge.

"Oh, Harry, I lost my job today and I just don't know what the hell to do about it."

Now Harry looks completely mortified and the hug that I so need is not forthcoming. I barge past him so that I can at least conduct my misery behind closed doors. I stand in the hallway sobbing while Harry just looks around, almost as if he's hoping that someone will pop up and instruct him on how best to handle the situation.

"Shit, Fran. I don't know what to say," is the best that he can eventually come up with. I make a supreme effort to compose myself, aware that he is uncomfortable with such an outpouring of emotion.

"Right," I say, trying to sound upbeat again. "Well, don't say anything then, just agree to come out with me tonight for dinner, although you might have to change your T-shirt so that foraging out of dustbins isn't our only option."

Harry works for a small record company where they're amazingly relaxed about what you wear to work. Today, however, Harry is in serious danger of crossing over from the realms of laid-back and a bit scruffy (which I'm all in favour of), to smelly-looking and faintly trampy. His crumpled T-shirt looks in urgent need of a boil wash, there's a hole in his sock where his big toe is poking through and he's got a good four-day growth going on. Fortunately for Harry, underneath his complete lack of care for his general appearance, he's naturally quite sexy. Or maybe his sexiness stems from his complete lack of care for his general appearance, I'm not sure.

"Look, I'm really sorry about your job," says Harry, seemingly determined to ignore my suggestion of going out, like a closet agoraphobic. "What happened, anyway?"

"Stacey happened," I reply, not feeling brave enough to talk about it yet. "So are you up for going out or not?" I can't help noticing, not for the first time, that when I'm wearing heels I'm very nearly the same height as Harry. I'm not that tall; he's just quite short.

"Um, not really . . . I had quite a big lunch," is Harry's rather lukewarm response.

Finally I am forced to acknowledge that Harry is acting strangely and that we still haven't even made it out of the hall.

"Harry, are you OK?" I ask.

"Yeah," he murmurs, shuffling down the corridor towards the kitchen.

I follow him through, starting to feel distinctly annoyed. I've just lost my job and then had to battle through the rush hour to get here and I'm the one asking him if he's OK. I sigh.

"Do you want a cup of tea?" Harry asks, as he flicks on the kettle.

"Um, well, I was hoping for a glass of wine, but I suppose a cup of tea will do for starters. I'd also like a hug, please."

I don't get one.

"Where's Wayne?" I enquire.

Wayne is Harry's flatmate and I'm very fond of him. I could do with seeing his funny face right now. A dose of his sardonic humour might well alleviate this slightly strained atmosphere.

Harry doesn't look me in the eye. "He's gone out for a bit. I asked him to."

A cold knot of dread appears in the pit of my stomach and intuition tells me something I don't want to consider, so I choose to ignore it and decide that Harry's just in a bad mood for some silly reason that I can't fathom right now. Harry and I have been seeing each other for about six months, having met through mutual friends, and although I'm aware that we're not exactly love's young dream, I think we get on really well. We always have a laugh and both enjoy doing the same kind of things and then, of course, there's the added bonus that I fancy the pants off him. He's pretty laid-back, which means he gets on with most people and we're very relaxed in each other's company. Or, at least, we usually are. Today Harry is about as relaxed as someone who's just run the London marathon wearing nothing but a pair of flip-flops.

We stand in silence, waiting for the kettle to boil.

I can't cope with this weirdness and want everything to be normal. I try going in for a bit of a kiss and a cuddle, but Harry responds with the sort of peck on the cheek that would normally be reserved for someone with a cold sore, which only seems to confirm my fears. I feel vaguely nauseous.

"All right, this will cheer you up — guess what I found out the other day?" I say, in the manner of a stand-up comic who's having a bad night. "My advert's going to be repeated this summer."

Harry looks nonplussed, then shrugs and makes a weird noise. Something between a weak laugh and a whimper.

Right, sod him. What the hell am I playing at anyway? After the day I've just had I should not be the one trying to cheer him up. I set about making the tea, banging mugs around, noisily rummaging in the cutlery drawer and opening every single cupboard as I search for the sugar. I slosh the milk into the cups, add sugar and then put the sugar in the fridge and the milk in the cupboard.

"Fran, you're making a right mess. Do you want me to do that?" offers Harry.

"I am capable of making a cup of tea, thanks all the same," I say, stirring vigorously.

Concerned that I'm going to drill a hole through his Chelsea football mug with the teaspoon, Harry eventually broaches what's on his mind.

"Fran, listen to me."

He takes the mugs, puts them in the sink, gently takes me by the arm and guides me to the sitting room, where he sits me down and utters the inevitable clichéd words.

"We need to talk."

Shit. Shit. Shit. Shit. I don't want this to happen. Not today.

Harry seats himself in a chair on the opposite side of the room and it strikes me that he couldn't physically put any more space between us unless he moved his chair out into the garden. I am about to point this out when I think again. It's time for Harry to say his piece.

"Look, the thing is, Francesca ... I think you're great and I know my timing is probably a bit off ..."

"A bit?" I say sarcastically.

Harry's body language is awkward and shifty, but I don't feel like making things any easier for him. I wait for the "but".

"But I just think that we should stop seeing each other."

This bit positively speeds out of his mouth at ninety miles per hour and Harry, glad to have got it over and done with, finally looks up. He is visibly relieved.

Fuck it. Fuck, fuck, fuck it.

I'd accepted from the start of our relationship that Harry probably wasn't going to be "the one", but that didn't stop me from liking him and I certainly feel that there is a lot more mileage left in our fling. Obviously the feeling isn't mutual. Why isn't it?

"I think you're such a great girl. I mean, you're funny and gorgeous, but ..."

There's that word again, "but". The word that tells me that I'm not quite gorgeous enough. Something occurs to me and I interrupt.

"Are you seeing someone else?" My voice comes out smaller than I expect it to and I realize to my horror that I am on the verge of tears again.

"No. No, honey. I'm not seeing anyone else. It's just, well, I suppose at the moment I just want to be single and I don't feel ready for getting into anything too heavy."

I rally. "But we're not heavy. I mean, we just have a laugh and I don't pressure you."

"I know," Harry says, looking pressured. Then he changes tack and says hopefully, "Look, come on, Fran, don't make me feel bad. You're not really that into me anyway. I mean, you're always blowing me out because you've got a casting the next day and you want to 'prepare' and — what was the reason you couldn't see me this Sunday?"

"It's the Oscars," I mutter.

Harry can't help himself and grins broadly. "You see," he says triumphantly. "Now, while personally I'm delighted that you're finally getting the recognition you deserve for Claims for Dames, don't you think that the Oscars being on is a bit of a flimsy reason for not seeing somebody?"

I am not about to start justifying why I want to stay in to watch the Oscars or why it's important to prepare for auditions, for that matter. Why should I?

"Don't you dare lay all of this at my door, Harry Robinson. How unfair of you to turn things round to make out that you are finishing things because of how *I* feel, when I happen to be perfectly happy with how things are, if you must know."

At this point Harry has the decency to look uncomfortable.

"Now, why don't you at least have the balls to tell me the real reason you're chucking me," I demand.

"All right, all right," he says, looking defeated and a tiny bit sulky. "I suppose . . . I just can't make a commitment to anyone right now," he says, running his hands through his mop of tangled, curly brown hair. The hair that I'll never be able to touch again because once you've reached this point there's no going back. For what is blatantly clear is that Harry has simply gone off me. I swallow. Determined to come out of this with some dignity, I decide it's time to go. Otherwise I'm in danger of flinging myself bodily upon Harry's ankles, rugby-tackling him to the ground and begging him for another chance, which — let's face it — would not be the best move.

"I'm going to go now," I say, wanting desperately for him to persuade me not to.

Harry rises to his feet. "OK."

In my head I am the wronged heroine, spurned by my handsome lover who is about to realize he has made a terrible mistake. In reality, Harry looks pretty happy with his decision.

"Francesca, before you go — I am really sorry that you've had such a shitty day and that I've gone and added to it, but if it's any comfort I know you'll find another job in no time."

My face remains mutinous.

"I really didn't want to hurt you and I absolutely meant it when I said that you're great and I hope we can stay friends."

"Sure, whatever," I reply, not feeling particularly friendly at this point in time. I don't usually feel like punching my friends in the face.

"Actually, Harry, before I go I will just say one thing and that is that, to be perfectly honest, your timing is completely lousy. I mean, I know you didn't plan it this way but, quite frankly, losing my job and my boyfriend in the space of one day feels like the start of some seriously shite chick flick and I'm not particularly happy about being cast in such a crappy role," I finish indignantly.

I look at Harry and to my huge irritation I see that his face, which up to a second ago was creased with concern, is now making a concerted effort not to laugh.

"What?" I demand snottily.

"Nothing, nothing . . ."

"*What?*"

"Well, talking of crappy roles, all I really want to add is, 'If you've had a prang or a major bang, make sure it's your fender that's dented and not your pride. Don't be scared to tell your gangster, be a doll, get on the phone and be his moll and call up Claims for Daaaaaaames.'"

"Oh, just fuck off, Harry, will you? You can't take the piss out of someone and split up with them at the same time," I say, having a major sense-of-humour failure. I have to leave, have to get home where I can lose my composure.

Without further ado, I brush past him, grab my coat and hurry out of the door, out of his flat and into the street. Today has not been a good day.

CHAPTER
FOUR

Desperate to get inside my flat, I lunge my key in the vague direction of the front door. Abbie has heard me from the inside though, opens it before I do and only narrowly avoids being stabbed in the face.

"Oh my God, Fran, you could have taken my bloody eye out, you nutcase," is her initial greeting, which is a shame as we haven't seen each other for a few days.

Abbie is the manageress of a pizza restaurant in Clapham and works different shifts every week, so I'm never entirely sure when we're going to catch up next. Now, despite nearly having caused her grievous bodily harm, I'm really pleased she's in and as soon as she takes in my forlorn expression and tear-stained face her cross look is replaced by one of concern, which of course precipitates a fresh set of tears. Without another word she leads me through to the kitchen for tea and sympathy and, after listening to my entire tale of woe, gives me a huge hug.

"You poor old thing," says Abbie gently. "You have had a day and a half of it, haven't you?"

I nod, feeling absolutely drained.

"OK, Fran, please don't get cross," says Abbie hesitantly, "but I've got to say it, just once, and then it'll be off my chest forever. How could you be such a doughnut and not change the names or be more careful?"

"Oh, Abs, I don't know," I answer flatly. "I suppose I've got away with writing at work for so long now that I've become blasé and careless. I've been such a pillock."

Abbie gets up to get a glass of water. "Well, it wasn't all your fault. Bloody Stacey didn't have to dump you in it like that. Honestly, what a cow. And why on earth did Harry finish with you? What reason did he give?"

"He said he couldn't commit to anyone right now," I say in a small voice, knowing full well this sounds just like the feeble excuse that it really is. For reasons that I can't be bothered to analyse right now, I decide to omit the bit about me not seeing him for the sake of auditions or watching the Oscars.

"Well, I would have credited Harry with a bit more imagination than that tired old chestnut," says Abbie.

I can't answer and don't have the energy to dissect things any further. From out of nowhere I am overcome by the strongest urge for the most enormous yawn. It's only eight thirty but I feel absolutely shattered. Abbie's not my best friend for nothing though and she immediately takes charge.

"Listen, why don't I run you a bath and then if you feel like chatting we can, and if you don't then we can just watch a nice movie together," she suggests.

I nod weakly. "OK. Are you working tomorrow, by the way?"

"Yeah, but only the evening, so we can hang out all day, and then on Sunday I've got a day shift."

Abbie goes to run my bath and over the roar of the taps shouts down the corridor, "Sod Harry and his stupid curly hair, Fran. Forget about the idiot. He's obviously a wanker if he doesn't appreciate you anyway."

I smile faintly. "Thanks, Abs."

I have my bath, and then shove on my pyjamas and an old sweatshirt. I'm tempted to find my diary and put pen to paper but a rather nasty headache is starting to develop, so instead I find some headache tablets while Abbie scouts through our DVD collection. I settle myself on the sofa, piling all the cushions up around me for comfort.

With her head and part of her body actually in the cupboard, Abbie's muffled voice calls out, "*Casablanca . . . Singing in the Rain . . . On the Town . . . Kramer vs. Kramer?*"

"Ooh, no, I couldn't handle that tonight. Too heavy."

"*Grease?*"

"Maybe . . ."

"*Top Gun, Dirty Dancing . . . It's a Wonderful Life?*"

"*It's a Wonderful Life*, please."

Abbie rolls her eyes affectionately but indulges my choice anyway. She knows that, no matter how many times I see it, I will never tire of my favourite film and it will always be guaranteed to make me feel better. I fall asleep on the sofa, way before Clarence the angel has had the chance to even begin sorting George Bailey's life out.

By Sunday night, having had around forty-eight hours to digest everything that's happened, I'm slowly starting to get a better sense of perspective on things. While still not exactly thrilled by my newly enforced single, unemployed status, at least I no longer feel as if the end of the world is nigh, and deep sorrow has been replaced by a calm level of acceptance and some manageable misery. Admittedly it's taking all my willpower not to phone Harry but, just as my resolve is close to crumbling, Abbie arrives home from work and I determinedly switch my phone off.

I may be gutted and miserable but that doesn't change the fact that tonight it's the most fabulous, most glamorous night of the year and I refuse to let anything, including thinking about Harry, taint my experience of it. I've been looking forward to tonight all week and a heady dose of escapism is probably exactly what I need. Tonight it's Oscars night.

A few hours later and it's about to begin. Here we go, my all-time favourite showbiz bash. Bliss.

"Look at you, all excited," says Abbie, flopping down on to a big cushion on the floor and getting to grips with opening a bottle of wine.

"Mmm," I say, transfixed and wanting to hear the very first bit of commentary. This is the best bit — all the stars arriving on the red carpet in their finery. Abbie and I start to give everybody marks out of ten for their outfits. Catherine Zeta-Jones looks amazing; so does

Julianne Moore. There's the gorgeous Carson Adams with his girlfriend, Caroline Mason, closely followed by my favourite, Jennifer Aniston, and then Johnny Depp and Vanessa Paradis.

"Tell me, Fran — Carson Adams's girlfriend, is that Caroline Mason or Marina Madson? I always get the two of them confused," says Abbie.

"I know, they do look quite similar, but Carson Adams's girlfriend is Caroline Mason. She hasn't done much for a while, but she was in *Baby Don't Leave Me* in the eighties. Marina Madson is the one who used to be married to James Reddington, who obviously you know played James Bond for a while, and she stars in *The Love Story*," I explain quickly, loathe to miss even a second of the action. (Sometimes I even surprise myself with how much celebrity trivia I have stored in the recesses of my mind. Years and years of watching documentaries, films and, more recently, E! Entertainment has built up my collection.)

Joan Rivers and her daughter, Melissa, are on hand to deliver their acerbic commentary and the usual fashion pundits are wheeled out to give their opinions on all the frocks, although most of them don't appear to be in a position to judge when they look so awful themselves. I love it.

"God, I'd love to go to the Oscars and wear a beautiful gown like that," I say wistfully as Kate Hudson arrives looking sublime in gold. "The dizzy heights I've reached, eh?"

Abbie, who has just taken a big gulp of wine, looks at me incredulously.

"You can't compare yourself to A-list movie stars, you nutter."

I frown at Abbie. If she only knew the extent of the ridiculous dreams I've harboured since I was a child, she wouldn't be laughing. She'd be too embarrassed.

"Fran?" says Abbie, heaving herself off the floor and joining me on the sofa.

"Yes?"

"When you said yesterday that you might give up acting, did you mean it?"

"Er, I think so, yes," I say. "Why? What makes you ask that?"

Abbie looks faintly awkward, as if she's worried about what my reaction might be. "Oh, I don't know. I suppose I just hope you do think about it seriously because with acting being so competitive I can't help wondering if all the stress is really worth it."

Nicole Kidman's just arrived on the red carpet.

"Her dress is a ten out of ten, don't you think?" I ask.

Abbie gives a thumbs-up to confirm she agrees, but she still looks worried.

I turn to face my friend, giving her my full attention. "Abbie, listen. I was serious but only because I don't have much other choice. In an ideal world I still can't think of anything that would make me happier than earning a living as an actress."

"Really?" says Abbie. "Because you didn't seem that happy when your ad came out and everyone was giving you stick for it."

"That wasn't proper acting," I say, feeling a bit touchy. I watch the screen in silence for a few minutes before adding, "I know you must be worried about the rent, but I promise I won't let you down. I'll sort myself out with a job as soon as I can and in the meantime I'll temp."

"I'm not worried about the rent, Fran," she says. "I'm worried about you."

I smile gratefully at my friend. Then, pleased at the distraction, we both fall respectfully silent until the God that is George Clooney has made his way past the press.

Abbie tucks her short brown hair behind her ears. "I suppose what does bother me sometimes is that I've never really understood why this notion of being 'someone' or 'something' is so important to you. I mean, I enjoy working at the restaurant but I don't love it — it's just my job and that's fine," she says, her hazel eyes flashing against her pale Scottish skin.

I concentrate on the television screen, glad again that it gives me an excuse not to reply right away. I'm not completely deluded. I know my limits and I'm never going to make it to the Oscars, but I'd happily settle for just a tiny bit of the glamour that I was so seduced by as a child; just a small slither of the fame pie would make everything worthwhile. I glance at Abbie. I'm pretty sure that the chat we've just had is one of "those" chats that the girls have decided needs to be had, and that she's been nominated for the job.

"I know what you're saying, Abs, and I can't explain why I am the way I am, but — if it helps — I'm sure I'm on the verge of growing out of it," I fib.

"OK," says Abbie, smiling and seeming almost as relieved as me that the lecture can now end. "As long as you know what a nutjob you are, which you clearly do, then it's all right you being one."

"I do," I agree. "I know I'm a deluded freak whose biggest claim to fame is being in the most rubbish advert known to mankind. Now look at Helen Mirren — she's bloody good for her age, isn't she?"

An eternity seems to pass before the ceremony itself begins and during this lull Abbie eventually goes to bed defeated. She stops at the door.

"You know I only said everything earlier because we care about you, Fran, and because we think it's such a shame that your stories and stuff go to waste."

I knew it. "We" means Abbie, Sabina and Ella, my closest friends, and this *was* one of "those" chats. I was elected to have one with Ella last year when she'd been on the Atkins diet for six months and showed no sign of stopping.

"Abbie, if you think acting's competitive then I should imagine writing's even worse. Now don't stress about me any more, I'm fine," I call as Abbie retreats to her room.

And for now I am fine, more than fine. I'm in showbiz heaven. Even so, my eyes are trying to close so I will myself to stay awake. I am always surprised by how dull and overlong the ceremony part is, but I enjoy it none the less. I love the glamour, the speeches, the glimpse into life in Tinseltown. I love showbusiness and all its shiny allure. I am hollow-eyed when I finally crash out in the early hours of the morning.

CHAPTER
FIVE

On Monday I plod to work, completely shattered after not nearly enough sleep (my own fault entirely) and dreading the day ahead. This week of working out my notice is just a form of sadomasochism if you ask me. I decide to phone Harry for a quick chat and then I remember he's not my boyfriend any more, which puts even more of a dampener on things. God, I need to sort my life out.

When I arrive at the office it's a hive of activity, as most of the team are running around, frantically preparing for a visit from Shanice later on in the day. By contrast, Raj is slumped on his desk.

"Morning, Raj," I say, slipping off my coat and hanging it on the back of my chair.

"Hi, Fran," Raj replies.

Today Raj's hair is striped like a tiger and his head is face down on his desk. His voice is croaky.

"Geoff in yet?" I wonder.

"No," comes the muffled response.

"Brilliant. I'm going to send out loads of my tapes and letters this morning. May as well give my acting one final push, just for a laugh, and then I'd better get on to some temping agencies. Are there any of those padded envelopes in the cupboard?"

Nothing.

"Raj, are you all right? You look like you've been here all night," I joke.

"I have," comes the reply. "I was in town last night with some mates and I popped in here for a smoke. That last joint was a strong motherfucker."

Fair enough.

Three hours later and Raj has only just about managed to peel his face off the desk. I, on the other hand, have been much more constructive. I've scanned the pages of *The Stage*, sent out tapes to various casting directors and even have some temping work lined up for next Monday. As of next week I shall be filing in the accounts department of a company that sells stationery, which sounds thrilling, doesn't it?

I make Raj a strong coffee with two sugars, which he gulps down gratefully.

"I can't believe you're going, Fran. It's going to be so shit here without you."

"Thanks, Raj," I say dolefully. "I'm going to miss you too. Hey, you won't be able to escape me completely though. I forgot to tell you, Claims for Dames is coming back on this summer."

Raj spews half of his coffee out across the desk. "Hee hee hee . . . ha ha ha . . . Claims for Dames. That still cracks me up, even now . . . Hee hee." Then, noting my expression, "Shit, sorry, Fran. I mean, that's really great."

* * *

By the afternoon my eyes are starting to feel strained
and dry, but I still can't drag them from the screen.
With Geoff still out of the office, I'm using all my
powers of concentration and am hard at it.

Raj has introduced me to Tetris and any minute now
I'm going to beat my highest personal score. There's
something about the atmosphere here that just seems
to sap you of any life energy. As a result, any get up
and go I was experiencing this morning has got up and
left. Now the only thing I can be bothered to focus on
is this game of Tetris, and getting through the rest of
this week.

The blocks are starting to fall at the most incredible
rate and it's taking all my concentration to guide them
into the right position in time. My fingers are tapping
so fast I'm sure I can feel the onslaught of arthritis in
my joints, but nothing matters apart from winning. In a
matter of seconds I'm going to reach the score I've
been aiming towards all afternoon. My mobile rings.

"Raj, would you mind getting my phone?" I yell, my
frantic fingers rat-tat-tatting like fire from a machine
gun.

Raj emerges from the stationery cupboard where he's
been for a good hour doing . . . who knows what.

"What did you say, Fran?"

Bugger. I've lost it. Game over.

"Nothing, don't worry about it. Hello?" I say, picking
up my phone.

"Hi, sweetie, it's me, Carrie Anne. How are you
doing? Did you get the big heave ho?"

51

"Yes," I say. "And not just from work either. Harry dumped me that same evening."

Carrie Anne gasps. "You're bloody joking? Oh my God, babe, I'm so, so sorry. Why?"

"Who knows?" I reply. "But you've spent far too much time listening to me moaning recently so, honestly, please don't worry. I'm absolutely fine and, you know . . . onward and upward and all that."

"Oh, good for you, babe. Listen, I don't want to sound callous but as ever I'm in a tearing rush and can't talk for long, but I just thought you might be interested in a job that's come up."

"Too right I'd be interested," I say excitedly, straightening up at my desk and swivelling round in my chair, away from Stacey's nosy staring. "I'm up for absolutely anything, Carrie Anne. Filing, general slavery, anything."

"Well, don't speak too fast, Fran, because you never know, there might well be an element of slavery in this job. There's a well-known American actress who's going to be here for a while. She's going to be doing a play and she's also in talks with us about possibly starring in one of our films next year. Anyway, she's been in touch because apparently the assistant who's been looking after her isn't working out and she wants to replace her. She wants to find a new PA soon as. The pay is five hundred pounds a week."

Five hundred pounds a week!

"Who's the actress?" I ask breathlessly.

"Well, I'm not supposed to say but, seeing as it's you, I will — just don't tell anyone."

I'm puzzled. "Why all the secrecy? Why aren't you supposed to tell me?"

"Oh, you know what actresses are like. They like to shroud everything in mystery because it makes them feel important."

Despite wanting to be one myself, I don't know what proper actresses are like, but I take Carrie Anne's word for it seeing as she has worked with the likes of Renée Zellweger and Keira Knightley.

"OK, well, tell me, I'm dying of suspense."

"It's Caroline Mason."

"Ooh," I say, flicking through the celebrity Rolodex in my head; all that leafing through *Hello* and *OK* does come in handy sometimes. "Wow, Caroline Mason, how weird that I was watching her turn up at the Oscars only last night?" I say, flustered beyond belief.

"Oh, I know. She flew back to the States especially for the event just so that she could support Carson, but she's flying back later today."

I love how casually Carrie Anne pops the names of über-famous stars into the conversation. I mean, Caroline Mason and Carson "I'm so unbelievably gorgeous and phenomenally handsome no woman in the world could resist, wouldn't kick me out of bed if I farted, puked or possibly even soiled myself, I won an Oscar last year" Adams.

Bloody hell.

I gulp.

This could be the most fantastic opportunity. Carrie Anne was offering me the chance to work for the very thing I've always dreamed of being myself: a movie star.

It would be the most amazing new challenge and would give me time to reassess and to figure out what it is I really want from life. Earning five hundred pounds a week would be incredible and for the first time in my life I could actually save some money. It would be so glamorous, even if only by proxy, and so much more stimulating than filing in the accounts department of a stationery company, I think gleefully. Then again, sitting in traffic would be more stimulating than filing in the accounts department of a stationery company.

I come back down to earth.

"Carrie Anne, it sounds amazing — thank you so, so much for thinking of me. Is she doing interviews? How many people is she seeing? When does it start?" I say, practically frothing at the mouth.

"Oh my goodness, babe, calm down," says Carrie Anne, laughing at me. "Honestly, you might end up rueing the day I ever told you about it. These actresses can be quite tricky, I tell you."

We talk for a short while longer and, feeling exhilarated, I beg Carrie Anne to put me on the top of the list and to put in a really good word for me, which she promises to do, and then she has to go.

I get off the phone and swivel jubilantly back round in my chair, reminding myself of Geoff as I do so, and scan the office in search of Raj.

"Lover boy's gone to get munchies," says Stacey, eyeing me suspiciously. "Anyway, what's got you so flustered? Had another brilliant idea for a story, have you?" she asks cattily.

Very, very slowly and very, very deliberately I flick Stacey the V sign. Childish, I know, but extremely satisfying. Stacey responds aggressively with an action that makes use of both arms and that I've only ever seen employed by Italian drivers before.

When Raj finally arrives back at the office along with a baked potato, a strawberry milkshake drink and a packet of space dust that he pours down his throat in one, I'm literally bursting to tell him what's just happened.

"Oh my God, Raj! I've got something to tell you," I whisper across our desks. "Carrie Anne just phoned and Caroline Mason is looking for a new assistant and, to cut a long story short, any day now I may well be going for an interview with her," I finish, a bit disconcerted by the strange crackling sounds that are emanating from Raj's throat.

"She was well fit in *The Love Story*," says Raj, who is literally foaming at the mouth.

I am just wondering whether or not I should bother correcting him when the buzzer goes and somebody shouts, "Posts everyone. It's the boss man and Shanice."

After we have been graced by the presence of the new, non-aggressive, totally Zen Shanice and her almighty bosoms, the office returns to its usual state of inertia, and Raj and I are chatting outside on the balcony in the damp and cold. It turns out that, while he's obviously heard of Carson Adams, he can't quite place Caroline Mason and had initially thought that I was talking about Marina Madson, but then he's probably not as much of a movie fan as I am and the fact that Caroline Mason and Carson Adams have never married means the public have never been subjected to any wedding hype. They're intensely private about their relationship, which as far as I'm concerned only serves to make them all the more intriguing. I really hope I get to meet them. I daydream about how this could be the best thing to ever happen to me. Caroline Mason and I could become lifelong friends, I could pay off some off my credit card bills and, even more importantly, I might finally feel like a somebody, a feeling that I've been craving for as long as I can remember. I have to get this job.

CHAPTER
SIX

Over the next few days I'm forced into a strange state of limbo. According to Carrie Anne I am definitely on the list of people whom Caroline Mason would like to interview, so at some point I should expect a call from someone called Suzy. However, Carrie Anne hasn't been given any indication as to when that might be.

By Friday, my last ever day at Diamond, I still haven't heard anything and I'm worried sick that Caroline Mason may have changed her mind about seeing me or filled the position already. It's got to the point where every time the phone goes I jump out of my skin. However, fortunately for my blood pressure, on this particular afternoon my phone only rings once. When it does I pounce upon it, only to find that it's Harry on the other end.

"Hi, Fran. How are you doing?" he says and the concern in his voice makes me want to slap him.

"I'm fine, thanks. In fact, I'm great and I'm just waiting to hear about a new job," I say, trying desperately to sound blasé and cool but failing miserably.

"Oh wow, that's great. Really great . . ."

There's an uncomfortable silence and it suddenly strikes me how odd it is that, when it comes to relationships, things can shift so quickly and so irrevocably. I mean, one minute putting someone's private parts in your mouth feels perfectly acceptable; the next, merely conducting a phone conversation with them feels awkward.

"Look, Fran . . ."

"Harry . . ."

We both speak at the same time.

"You go . . ." I say. It briefly crosses my mind that Harry might be ringing to tell me what a dreadful mistake he's made.

"OK. Well, I know you're probably still a bit cross with me and of course you have every right to be cross, but I just wanted to make sure that you were OK and to say that I really do want to be friends . . ."

Clearly not then.

"Apart from anything else, Wayne and Briggsy will kill me if we don't stay mates because they love you and Abbie to bits."

A wry smile passes my lips. I think I'll miss Harry's two best mates, Wayne and Briggsy, almost as much as I'll miss him, but then they are two of the funniest characters I've ever come across. I'm touched that they feel the same way, although a cynical part of me is now wondering if Briggsy might have put Harry up to this phone call. I've always suspected that he has a major soft spot for Abbie, much to her complete horror.

It's all rather confusing because I feel as if I should still be terribly upset with Harry and yet only one week after our break-up I'm already grudgingly beginning to realize that — though my pride is still smarting — I might be missing him more as a friend than as a boyfriend, which means that his decision to terminate our affair was probably a sensible one. Rather than comforting me, this realization is a bit worrying. If things weren't right, why wasn't I the one to figure that out?

"Harry," I say calmly, "we will be friends I'm sure, and tell Wayne and Briggsy that they're not getting rid of me and Abbie that easily. But can you just give me a bit of time? I'm not exactly broken-hearted but I am upset and probably not quite ready to be 'bezzy mates' just yet."

"That'll do for me, Fran . . ." Harry says.

We get off the phone and, rather than feeling upset, my thoughts revert within seconds to willing the phone call that I really want to happen. I think this is probably quite telling.

At five o'clock Raj and I sneak on to the balcony for a cheeky farewell can of lager and a spliff.

"You're the only thing I'm really going to miss about this place, Raj," I say sadly. "Well, you and my wages."

Raj grins dopily and offers me the joint, and for some unknown reason I figure what the hell and take it.

Half an hour later, to the extreme misfortune of a couple of tourists, I am very sick over the balcony, although I can't remember much about it. In fact, the joint is so strong that I can't remember much about anything, including getting home or indeed much of the next day. And so it is that my time at Diamond PR has come to an end, as have my days of smoking pot. I'm not sure whether the fact that I'm not going to miss much about either of them is incredibly sad or incredibly good.

A few weeks later, another long, tedious day of filing over with, I'm at home idly wondering whether or not it might be possible for a person to actually die from boredom when my phone rings.

Just when I'd started to give up hope and had begun to resign myself to a life of poverty and tedium, my prayers are answered. It's the infamous Suzy, who utters the most eagerly anticipated words I've ever heard: "Would you be free to come and meet Caroline tonight?"

As I look at my plate of baked beans on toast and the chimney stacks on the TV that indicate that *Coronation Street* is starting, adrenaline is already starting to swoosh around in my system.

"Yes, that should be fine. Where should I come to?"

"You'll be meeting Caroline and myself at her house in South Kensington. I'll give you the address."

I flap at Abbie, who's hopping about with excitement, and make frantic writing gestures. Ten minutes later I have a famous movie star's address in my hand and have whipped off my jogging bottoms and transformed into a polished and professional-looking PA to the stars. It's amazing what you can pull out of the bag when the pressure's on and your best mate's on hand to help and style. We decide on a black pencil skirt with a plain beige shirt and smart black heels. I whirl round the flat, destroying everything in my wake.

"Bag, phone, house keys, car keys, coat, lip gloss . . . shit."

"I wouldn't take that in your bag if I were you, Fran. Might not make a good impression," says Abbie, chuckling at her own wit.

"No — shit, I said I might pop round to Ella's later. Can you ring and explain what's happened and tell her I'll call her later or tomorrow?" I yell, already heading for the door.

"Course I will," replies Abbie, her mouth full of my abandoned beans on toast. "Good luck!"

I'm grinning as I slam the door behind me. I can't believe I'm about to go to Caroline Mason and Carson Adams's house. This was going to satisfy my nosy nature on so many levels.

I arrive incredibly early, so I sit in the car and gather my thoughts. Ever since I initially spoke to Carrie Anne, I have become increasingly aware of Caroline Mason's presence in London. Previously unnoticed photos in the tabloids now leap out at me everywhere and she seems to be adorning the cover of pretty much every magazine going at the moment. For all self-respecting actors the current trend is to do a stint in the West End for which they are paid comparatively meagre wages. However, what they gain in kudos and publicity is priceless. Caroline Mason is no exception.

I've done my homework. In a couple of weeks' time Caroline Mason starts eight weeks of rehearsals for her much-hyped play, which opens in June. It's a heavy piece about love and betrayal, written by the playwright *de jour* John James. The plan is that the play will project her back into the limelight, which she has been out of ever since she gave birth to Carson Adams's son six years ago. (I can only presume that she must have given up work to be a mum for a while.)

When the play finishes in December, she's hoping that she'll go straight on to working on her movie in which she'll be playing the part of a psychologically damaged woman who has deluded episodes — not exactly a laugh a minute, but it sounds very interesting. Great British Films are making it, but it won't be one of their big commercial projects. It's more of an art-house movie that has been languishing in development hell for years and has only finally got the go ahead because the hot young director Thomas Anderson wants to make it and is now attached to the project. According to Carrie Anne, Caroline has always wanted to play the lead and has been angling for the part for ages, so it's something I should wax lyrical about. Carrie Anne has also strongly advised me not to utter the word "comeback" in her presence.

Other information I have gleaned is that, despite never having married, Caroline and Carson Adams are thought to have one of the strongest relationships in Hollywood. Their son is called Cameron and they own houses in Los Angeles, New York, South Kensington and Bermuda. While her career may have taken a back seat, Carson Adams's has been in the ascendant for some time now. In fact, his A-list stature was recently confirmed when he appeared alongside Tom Cruise,

Brad Pitt, Ben Stiller and Jim Carrey on the cover of *Vanity Fair* underneath the headline "Hollywood Heavyweights". They are a gorgeous couple and there were audible gasps when they appeared on the red carpet for this year's Oscars.

It's time. I check my appearance in the mirror, add a fresh bit of gloss and quickly send a group text to Sabina, Ella, Raj and my mum: "Just about to meet Caroline Mason . . . at her house! Wish me luck. Fran x". I grin, knowing the effect that my short message will have.

Dusk has fallen but I can still see that No. 47 is on a beautiful street that's lined with trees. The house itself is a huge double-fronted Georgian house with steps leading up to the porch, which is flanked by white pillars. I ring the bell.

Suzy opens the door.

"Hi, Francesca, come in. You found it all right then?"

"Yes, thanks," I say in answer to this obvious question that we all ask for want of something better to say, and smile warmly.

I follow Suzy down the wide hall, trying to absorb every detail for re-examination later: original parquet floor, an achingly stylish mixture of antique and modern furniture and what looks suspiciously like an original Damien Hirst spot painting on the wall.

"We're going to chat in the kitchen where it's comfortable, if that's OK. Caroline's been at meetings all day so she wants to be relaxed."

"Yes, of course," I say. "Suzy, are you her current assistant?"

"No, no, I'm another actor's personal assistant. My boss is a friend of Caroline's so I said I'd help her out with the interviews. She doesn't want to tell Louisa that she's no longer required until she's found someone to replace her," she says, half whispering this last bit in a very cloak-and-dagger manner.

I'm dying to ask Suzy who her boss is, but manage to restrain myself.

As we come to a halt outside some tall wooden doors, Suzy suddenly stops in her tracks as if she's just thought of something and says, still in a low voice, "By the way, apologies for not getting in touch sooner but Caroline was out of town for a while and then she decided to give her current PA one last chance."

I nod and murmur, "Oh, it's fine, don't worry about it," while simultaneously adopting an expression that I hope conveys *think nothing of it. I totally understand. I've been so incredibly busy myself with my hectic schedule of filing I hadn't even noticed.*

"OK, good luck. Now just be yourself and — word of advice — don't mention the word 'comeback', OK?" whispers Suzy.

I nod, wondering what would become of me if I did.

"Ready?"

"Ready," I reply.

Suzy pushes the doors open to reveal my fantasy kitchen. It's absolutely vast. The units are made from mahogany and topped with marble surfaces. All the appliances are chrome and shiny and, judging by their size, probably imported from the States. In the middle is an island, which has pots and pans hanging above it, and at the back is a huge wooden table next to French windows that lead out on to a leafy London oasis. At the end of the table, with a large glass of white wine in her hand, sits Caroline Mason.

"Hi," she drawls in caramel tones. "You must be Francesca. Thank you so much for coming to see me."

Her long, wavy, dark hair tumbles down her back and her eyes are heavily made up, huge and tragic. Her cheekbones are high and her nose curves upwards, which gives the impression that she is ever so slightly looking down on you.

She gets up and crosses the room to the island to fetch her cigarettes and lighter. Her body is lithe, lean and toned and her movement is catlike. She is wearing a camel-colour Juicy tracksuit (the cashmere version), and a diamond ring the size of a small child glints on her finger. Her presence is such that I can't stop staring at her and I now understand why some people are deemed stars and others merely celebrities.

"Hi, it's really nice to meet you," I say, feeling terribly star-struck but trying not to look it.

"You too," she replies, tilting her head coquettishly as she makes her way back to the head of the table and sits down. "Can I offer you a glass of water before we start?"

Her voice is incredible and I have to agree with one fawning journalist who described it as a lake of honey and milk flowing over a rocky riverbed. Except I would have said "deep and sexy".

"No thanks, I'm fine," I manage, feeling rather overwhelmed by the whole situation.

Caroline smiles at me, displaying very white American teeth, and appraises me.

She motions at Suzy and me to sit down.

"So, Suzy has filled me in on much of what you talked about on the phone, but why don't you start by telling us a bit about yourself?" she says.

I will myself to stop staring at her and to act naturally, but it's hard. I've been drip fed her image so much over the years in papers and magazines and yet somehow she looks different in the flesh. Smaller, thinner, and her face is a little harder. Just to distract me further, I have noticed a framed picture of her and Carson Adams on one of the shelves in the kitchen. It's not your average casual family snapshot. They're standing on the red carpet at the Golden Globes with Robert De Niro and Martin Scorcese.

I drag my eyes back to where they're supposed to be looking and I'm alarmed to note that, from out of nowhere, I suddenly feel drenched in nervousness.

"OK, well, when I left school I started working in production in various capacities and then I became a PA at Diamond PR . . ."

Caroline interrupts. "What made you decide to switch from working as a freelancer in production to being in full-time employment as a PA? Did you always want to be a PA?"

"Well," I begin, "at first I just needed to get something full time, because I was dabbling in acting a little bit. Nothing very serious, I hasten to add, just the odd play here and there . . . and, anyway, I needed to get something full time that would still enable me to

. . . go . . ." I feel myself blushing profusely. What am I saying? Nerves have got the better of me and now I feel excruciatingly embarrassed. Mentioning that you quite fancy yourself as an actress to someone who actually is one, but at a level so far removed from your own, is painful and I don't know why I ever set off down that path. I need to recover.

"Anyway, that's irrelevant really because I've spent the last few years working as a PA, which is . . ."

"Do you still want to be an actress?" she says, cutting in. Caroline Mason, it seems, is nobody's fool. "Is that what you really want to do?"

I could kick myself for being such an idiot. I know exactly what she's getting at and feel that my answer will be crucial.

"Being completely honest, I'm very disillusioned with the whole acting thing and very unsure as to why on earth I even mentioned it," I say hesitantly. "It hasn't really worked out and now what I want, what I really want more than anything, is a new challenge and one that . . ."

I'm in danger of rambling again, so I pause, take a deep breath and call upon all the acting techniques that I've been taught over the years at various classes for banishing nerves. I knew they'd come in handy at some point. Focus.

"If I were to get this job, I would be over the moon and one hundred per cent committed," I say much more calmly.

"Good," says Caroline. "Because I can't have an assistant who's going to be going off for auditions and who only wants the job to further her own career. I need someone who wants, first and foremost, to look after me. I need a personal assistant, not an apprentice." I notice that she considers every word before saying it and the result is very measured and has maximum impact.

I nod. "Don't worry, I totally understand and I promise that you would be my absolute priority. As for going for auditions, I wouldn't worry as I never seem to get seen for anything anyway," I joke.

Nothing.

I glance at Suzy; her expression is pained. I think quickly.

"Miss Mason, my feeble attempts at acting really are totally unimportant and I'm so embarrassed that I even mentioned them, to you of all people. The only thing I should have told you about is the fact that I've spent the last few years working as a PA, which is what I really hope to continue doing and what I am by definition."

Caroline stares at me for a while but her expression is impossible to read. You could hear a pin drop, and then she takes a sharp inhalation of breath and says, "Right, well, I think the best plan is if Suzy asks you a few questions now." She looks pointedly at Suzy, who's had a startled expression on her face ever since the interview began.

Suzy starts flicking through some notes and while we're waiting for her to take over proceedings I study Caroline's face, searching for clues as to whether or not

I've managed to redeem myself, but she's still giving nothing away. I pray I haven't stuffed things up.

Caroline reaches out a manicured hand for her lighter and elegantly lights a cigarette. A long, slim, white-tipped one that I bet you can't buy in the UK. I've never been inclined to smoke but they almost look worth a try.

Suzy finally finds the piece of paper that she's looking for and I'm surprised to note that her nervousness is resulting in making me feel more at ease.

"Right. The first question is, what would you expect being Caroline's personal assistant to entail?"

I pause before answering. It's hard to know who to address, so in the end I focus on Caroline.

"Well, I imagine that it would be a case of making your life as easy as possible while you're here in London. I suppose it would involve taking care of your diary for both work and social purposes and also making sure you have everything you need at the theatre to make your life run smoothly."

Caroline remains deadpan but Suzy listens to what I'm saying very intently and looks visibly relieved when my answer seems to be along the right lines. Wide-eyed, she nods encouragingly and looks at Caroline for her reaction.

"Yeah, I like that," she considers. "It is about making my life as easy as possible. But it's that and more really . . . I think Suzy will be better at giving examples than me." Once again, she hands the reins over.

"Well," begins Suzy, clearing her throat, "you would be speaking to and liaising with many different sorts of people on a regular basis. There is Caroline's UK publicist and agent, as well as the contacts at the theatre and Great British Films. However, you would have to be just as adept at organizing a plumber or a caterer, for instance, if the need arose."

"That's right," says Caroline. "I mean, one minute you could be speaking to . . . Spielberg, and the next I might need you to organize . . . the loft being insulated." She studies me for any naff star-struck reaction to her name-dropping, but I am too busy thinking how unlikely both these examples sound.

"That wouldn't be a problem. I'm very confident and would feel just as comfortable in both types of situation."

"Good," says Caroline. "I suppose really what I need is someone who's going to totally nanny me because the parts that I'm taking on, both in the play and my movie, are extremely demanding and quite dark. This means that I won't have time to think about day-to-day stuff. I am going to have to go to a dark place in my head and I need someone who will alleviate all the day-to-day running of things so that I can solely concentrate on my acting."

"I understand," I say, although it all sounds a bit dramatic. Still, I adopt what I hope looks like an understanding expression. "You are here to do a job and therefore won't have time to cope with mundane matters and need someone who's going to get on and deal with things."

Caroline gives Suzy a look as if to say *this girl might actually be on my wavelength after all*. Suzy smiles back in quite a patronizing fashion.

"That's precisely right," says Caroline, blowing smoke out but still managing to look like a sultry and gorgeous woman rather than an old fish wife.

Suzy interjects. "One very important part of your job while the play is on would be the organization of house tickets. Caroline will have four tickets a night allocated to her and everyone will be clamouring for them. They have to be paid for and sometimes Caroline will cover the cost and other times you would have to get the credit card details from the recipients."

I nod sagely. I think I could handle that.

Caroline picks up the reins. "The other thing I feel I should warn you is that the job won't all be glamorous. I need somebody who isn't going to mind doing some menial tasks. For example, I might ask you to get me some Tampax or maybe pick up a few groceries sometimes."

"That's fine," I reply. "I would expect that totally. I mean, how could you do those things yourself when you're going to be in rehearsals all day, working?"

Caroline is starting to look more and more positive and keeps widening her eyes at Suzy, who is still nodding away. My terrible start is beginning to feel more like a thing of the past. According to Carrie Anne, they've already seen and rejected a few other candidates and I'm starting to think that they must have been right idiots, as it seems pretty obvious to me the kind of thing that Caroline wants to hear.

Buoyed by their encouraging body language, I decide to add something. "I'm not precious at all and if you wanted me to do a bit of cleaning or to help pack your cases and things, I'd be more than happy."

Now I think my confidence may have been premature because Caroline retracts her smile and looks anxiously at Suzy. Suzy opens her mouth to speak but Caroline interjects.

"I have a cleaner so I wouldn't require you to clean, but I would most certainly expect you to pack my bags for me as and when." Her tone is challenging.

I have obviously made a major boo boo and need to make up for it fast. "Of course, and apologies. What I said probably didn't come out right at all. I would, of course, expect to pack your bags . . . and then carry them for you too," I add jokingly.

Nothing.

Caroline sits back. "OK, Francesca, do you have any questions for us at all?"

I'm glad she's asked me this because I do have a very important question and it has been playing on my mind ever since my conversation with Carrie Anne.

"Only one, really. Why didn't your current assistant work out?"

Caroline stares at me before leaning across conspiratorially. "Francesca. I feel I can say this to you."

She pauses for effect.

"The last few weeks have been a nightmare. The girl I've had basically hasn't got a clue."

She stubs her cigarette out emphatically and leans further across the table, giving me an eyeful of quite an impressive cleavage. She's not wearing a bra.

"The simplest thing and Louisa gets it wrong. The other day was the last straw. She booked me in for an appointment somewhere, but failed to tell me that I was supposed to be somewhere else having an interview."

This does sound a bit dozy. I make a mental note to write everything down in a diary as soon as it comes up . . . if I get the job.

Caroline seems to consider something before adding, "To be honest, there was also a bit of a personality clash, and the other day I just felt that she was downright rude and not aware of my needs at all."

Suzy nods in fervent agreement.

"Anything else, Suzy?" asks Caroline.

"Oh yes, um, do you have a car, Francesca?"

"Yes I do, although I tend to get the tube everywhere, what with parking being so horrendous in London. Why? Would you need me to drive you about?" I enquire, suddenly worried about the state of my rusty Fiat Punto.

Caroline looks appalled. "I have a driver, but you might need the car for errands sometimes."

"Oh sure, fine." I'm annoyed to find myself blushing again, something I do far too easily.

Caroline seems bored now by the finer detail. "It's not important anyway. You can always get cabs if need be."

The interview seems to come to a natural end as Caroline stands up and says, "I'm going to read my script now. Rehearsals start soon. Make sure my car's coming at the correct time tomorrow to take me to the Mandarin Oriental, will you, Suzy darling?"

"Of course, will do," she says, nodding away.

I wonder if Caroline's going to walk out of the room without saying goodbye to me directly, but as she reaches the door she turns round and drawls in her dulcet tones, "Goodbye, Francesca, and thank you. I think I'm going to sleep well for the first time in a long time," and with that she's gone.

Suzy gulps and her shoulders visibly relax once Caroline has left the room.

"Well, I think that went very well, Francesca. She obviously liked you."

I'm grateful to Suzy for not mentioning my ridiculous faux pas at the beginning and, despite myself, I can't help but feel rather chuffed that I've been approved of. I'm practically grinning as Suzy sees me out. We say goodbye and she promises to let me know as soon as she does. I head out to the car.

I drive round the corner and park up. I know that my friends will be waiting to hear what happened, but which of them will appreciate the gossip the most? After a nanosecond of debate, I phone Sabina. She picks up after only one ring.

"Fran? Oh, thank God it's you. I've been literally dying of suspense ever since I got your text. Tell me, tell me, tell me," says my excited friend.

"Well," I say, savouring my audience. "She's absolutely beautiful and I think it went OK. I don't think she's the sort of person who would end up

74

becoming mates with her PA though. She seems very . . . businesslike, but on the whole it was fine."

"What happened with the girl who's been working for her?" asks Sabina.

The line is beeping.

"Hang on a minute, I've got call waiting. It's probably Abs. I'll just get rid of her . . . Hello?"

"Francesca, it's Suzy here."

"Oh, hello . . ." I'm taken aback. I wasn't expecting to hear from her so soon.

"Hi there, Francesca. Well, I won't keep you in suspense. I'm delighted to say that Caroline has decided that she would very much like you to be her new PA."

"Oh wow, that's brilliant. I'm really pleased." And I am. I'm delighted, thrilled and in danger of wetting myself.

"Fantastic, she'll be glad you're so excited. Now, I won't keep you for long because we can have a longer conversation tomorrow, but what I do need to know is would you be happy to start in a couple of weeks' time? You would have been needed earlier but Caroline's decided to pop to Bermuda for a while until rehearsals begin."

"Oh, that's fine," I say happily, privately feeling frustrated that I won't be able to jack in the temping just yet.

"Also," continues Suzy, "are you aware that the job, although initially only up until Christmas, could be ongoing if things go well and her film gets green lit?"

My head is spinning. Everything's happening so fast. I'm more than delighted to commit until December, but a tiny part of me wonders how I'd feel should any acting opportunities crop up after that. Then a bigger part of me tells me not to be so bloody stupid, that the likelihood of anything cropping up is minimal and that I would be a fool not to grab this chance with both hands.

"I am aware of the time span involved and that's absolutely fine," I say firmly. "As far as it being ongoing is concerned, that sounds fantastic too."

"Fabulous," says Suzy. "Well, I'll ring you soon with all the finer details then."

After we've said goodbye, I'm surprised to find that Sabina is still waiting on the other line.

"Jesus, Fran, I hope you kept me waiting that long for someone important."

"I got the job," I tell her excitedly, beaming from ear to ear.

"Oh my God. That's brilliant, well done!" screeches Sabina. "Well? Come on, don't keep me in suspense any longer. I want detail. What was she wearing?"

"Oh, um, a tracksuit, but she still looked so gorgeous and elegant. Not at all footballer's wife."

"Wow," says Sabina. "Did she mention you know who?"

"No, but there were framed photos of him around and Carrie Anne said he's bound to come over at some point because he's just wrapped on his latest movie."

"Just wrapped, eh?" teases Sabina. "Fran, I'm so jealous — it's going to be so exciting."

"I know, it's going to be amazing," I agree, feeling slightly dizzy as all the implications start to sink in. Maybe this is the big break that I've been waiting for all my life. Part of me almost wishes I was still working at Diamond PR just so I could see the look on Stacey's face when she hears that I, Francesca Massi, am going to be Caroline Mason's personal assistant.

I drive home feeling happier than I have done in ages and optimistic that I'm going to have a brilliant summer. Speaking to Sabina has already given me a small taste of what it might be like to have a job that people are actually interested in hearing about and it feels good, really good. Finally something big is happening to me and pretty soon I am going to be hanging around with genuine superstars and not just as some hanger-on, or fan, but as someone who will be playing an integral part in the fabric of their lives. I am going to know what happens on a day-to-day basis at Carson Adams's house! It's going to be so refreshing to have a job where I might actually have to engage my brain a bit and I briefly worry if I'll be up to it. I must phone my parents.

It's funny, but if you'd told me a week ago that I would have just been to Caroline Mason's house I'd never have believed you, but then that's the thing about life — it's impossible to predict. I turn the volume up on the stereo and drive home, singing all the way.

CHAPTER
SEVEN

This morning I am due to meet Louisa for a handover, a prospect that I'm not particularly relishing, but want to get out of the way none the less so that the rest of my life can officially begin. Punctual as ever, I arrive at Caroline's house fifteen minutes earlier than instructed by Suzy, so I take a stroll up the street. It's early spring and the branches on the trees are laden with blossom, which is swirling around in the breeze like confetti. The general effect is all a bit Mary Poppins and I find myself fantasizing about which one of the beautiful houses I would buy if I happened to take up with a Russian oligarch until it is ten o'clock exactly, at which point I climb the steps to No. 47 and ring on the bell. The door is answered by a dark-haired, quite plain-looking girl who looks less than overjoyed to see me.

"Hi, you must be Francesca. Come in," she says in a monotone voice.

"Hi," I chirrup brightly, overcompensating for the weird situation that we're in. "I take it you're Louisa?"

She nods imperceptibly by way of response and slouches down the hall, then takes a left into a room that turns out to be the study. It doesn't take me long to comprehend that she's not in the mood for small talk and once I have stopped my fruitless attempts at conversation the whole process becomes less painful.

Louisa hands over the diary she's been using for Caroline's schedule, her keys to the house and keys to a safe that contains all Caroline's personal documents and bank cards, and gives me a brief précis of everything I will be expected to do. Then, without giving me a chance to digest anything, she starts to take me through the numerous files and folders that are littered around the room.

She hands me the first file. "This one has all Caroline's personal details in, such as doctors and whatnot."

And another. "This one is business that is pending."

And another. "This is miscellaneous."

And another. "And this one is just stuff that I haven't had a chance to talk to her about yet. So that's about it, apart from this one, which is stuff she wants done as a priority." She hands me this last file, which is by far the most full, and I feel rather panicked as Louisa picks up her bag and starts putting on her coat. She still hasn't looked me in the eye once.

"Caroline has a housekeeper called Lorna who comes in daily; your hours are ten till whenever Caroline has finished with you and you'll be paid by cheque which you'll write out yourself and get her to sign. I've left you a sheet of notes of my own on the desk and a set of keys. The alarm code is on my notes, so make sure you shred them soon."

I nod and regard the mountain of files that I am being left to decipher and feel more than a little concerned. I know it's an awkward situation but this is not my idea of a thorough handover.

"Is there anything else you can think of that I need to know before you go?" is my last-ditch attempt at extorting information from the inscrutable Louisa.

"Yeah," she says, already halfway out the door.

"Oh, good. What?"

She looks me in the eye for the first time and is on the brink of saying something, but then seems to change her mind.

"Just . . . just good luck."

And with that she's gone.

I am now officially Caroline Mason's personal assistant.

I sit down and contemplate the mound of paper. I decide to tackle it in a minute; first, I want to absorb my surroundings.

One thing I will say for my new boss is that she has fantastic taste. The study is painted in a deep shade of crimson and the desk is dark wood and obviously an antique. Despite the colour of the walls, the room is still incredibly light due to its size and the huge bay window that looks out on to the street. More original artwork hangs on the walls and amazingly glamorous framed photos litter the shelves. It's silent apart from the ticking of a grandfather clock that stands imposingly in the corner.

It's quite eerie being in this huge house all on my own. Caroline is obviously incredibly trusting. I slink round to the other side of the desk to peruse Louisa's notes. Not only am I alone in Caroline's house but, according to Louisa, I've also been left with all her credit cards and their pin numbers. I will be responsible for giving Caroline cash as and when she needs it and will also be in charge of paying all of her bills, both household and personal. She's lucky I don't just rob her house, clear out her accounts now and flee the country.

From down the corridor I hear a key in the lock and I jump out of my skin.

"Hellooo," calls a singsong Irish voice.

"Hello?" I call back, realizing that this must be Lorna the cleaner whom Louisa mentioned. At least, I hope it is.

I leave the study and wander into the hall.

"Hello, you must be Lorna," I say, approaching the little lady who I would guess is in her late sixties.

"Yes, that's right, dear. And what's your name?" she says in a strong southern Irish accent as she takes off her raincoat, one of those plastic rain hats you find in crackers and some quite trendy pink sunglasses that are totally at odds with the rest of her appearance.

"I'm Fran."

Lorna looks me up and down. "I just bumped into Louisa outside. It seems a shame she's gone because I was just getting to know her, but I'm sure you're very nice too." She turns and heads for the kitchen. "Do you want a biscuit? I'm just going to put the kettle on."

"I'm fine, thank you. I was going to make a start at going through all the stuff that Louisa's left me."

"All right then, love, but just holler if you want anything."

I like Lorna already.

I go back to the study and methodically start to make my way through the copious sheets of paper. Most of them seem to have been faxed over by Caroline and Carson's US assistant, Jodie. I can't help but think that Jodie, who I've been instructed to "make contact with later", must be very anal. Why half of this information should be relevant to me I shall never know and I start to organize it accordingly. I make three piles: stuff I think I probably do need to know; stuff that looks genuinely important and looks like it needs dealing with straight away; and stuff that looks like a load of unnecessary crap.

In the "unnecessary crap" pile goes the longest list of doctors I've ever seen. It's ludicrous and, according to the list, Caroline has a different doctor allocated to each separate part of her body. She has a doctor for her veneers, an eye doctor, a dermatologist, a chiropractor and so the list goes on and on and on.

Half an hour later and I have figured out that there is an army of people who all play a small part in the military operation that is Ms Mason's life.

For starters, there is Jodie, who must have far too much time on her hands because she has also typed out detailed lists of things like friends' birthdays, florists to

82

use in the UK and restaurant maître d's, and then actually laminated them.

Then there is Steph, who is Cameron's nanny. Again, Jodie has excelled herself and provided me with photocopies of Steph's driving licence, which at least means I get to see what she looks like. She's pretty in a mousy kind of way and I also discover that, like Lorna, she is Irish. I have been given personal details for all Caroline's staff, including social security numbers for her housekeeper in Los Angeles, her trainers (UK and US), her nutritionists and her gardener. Although why I need to know her American gardener's fax number I shall never know.

Caroline has told me that I can start properly tomorrow, so I resolve to swot up on my notes in the meantime. Now, though, I decide to take Lorna up on her offer of a cup of tea but only after I've had a closer look at some of the pictures that are dotted around the study. Sabina would wee herself. There are pictures of Caroline at various dos, such as the Golden Globes and the Tonys, looking radiant and stunning. In some she is on the arm of Carson who is just simply one of the most beautiful men alive. In fact, he pipped Brad Pitt to the post in a recent poll of the world's sexiest men, so that really isn't an exaggeration, and I haven't quite got my head round the fact that at some point it now seems highly likely that I'm actually going to meet him. How will I cope? I do a quick count. There are two small pictures of Cameron, three of Carson and twelve of Caroline.

That evening I write in my diary what will undoubtedly be the first of many entries about my new job.

7th April

So far so good. Tomorrow I start officially and I can't wait to get to know Caroline Mason properly. The interview seems so long ago now, but I remember thinking at the time that she seemed a little intense, which is probably only to be expected after such a bad experience with this Louisa girl. Once she's got to know me, however, I'm sure she'll lighten up. I was starting to panic about whether or not I'd be up to the job but after today I reckon it's bound to be not only a glamorous and interesting job but an easy one too. I mean, how much can there really be to do? Pick up a bit of dry-cleaning, organize a few dinners. It's going to be great.

CHAPTER
EIGHT

Nobody is answering the door. I've rung the bell a couple of times now and definitely heard it ring inside, but no one's come. I've even used the big brass knocker that is shaped like a lion's head and now, on what is my first official day, I've been standing waiting on the step for what feels like an age, feeling nervous and wondering if I should knock or ring again. I'm in two minds because Caroline might already be on her way to let me in, in which case I don't want to appear annoyingly persistent. Then again, maybe she's out and I should just let myself in with the keys that Louisa gave me? I doubt it though. Suzy told me that Caroline isn't needed at rehearsals today and that she would definitely be here to greet me. I suddenly realize that I'm holding my breath. I exhale, make a decision and knock again. Two minutes later, after having knocked again and rung the bell twice, I am starting to feel concerned that I might have got the wrong day or, even worse, the wrong house, and I'm starting to perspire. I take a step back. No, this is definitely the right house, No. 47.

I am just about to ring Suzy when my mobile goes. "Hello?"

"Francesca?"

"Yes?"

"Why aren't you using your keys?"

I am momentarily astounded to hear Caroline Mason's voice coming through my phone but pull myself together quickly.

"Oh, good morning, Caroline . . . um, I suppose I thought that what with it being my first day and everything, I didn't want to just assume and barge in."

"Right," says Caroline steadily. "Well, now you can assume away. That is, after all, why you have a set of keys. You do have them with you?"

"Yes," I reply, but she's already put the phone down.

It's not quite the start that I'd anticipated but, putting this thought to one side, I do as I am told and let myself in.

I venture into the hallway and, taking a deep breath, peer into the study. Caroline is sitting at the desk and appears to be engrossed in reading something. It looks suspiciously like *Heat* magazine, but I could be wrong. I stand there for a while, hoping that she'll look up. She doesn't, so then I decide that being wet and woolly isn't getting me very far and I clear my throat. Caroline looks up slowly.

"Good morning, Caroline. Sorry about that," I gush. "I just really didn't want to be presumptuous and . . ."

"Hello, Francesca," says Caroline, interrupting my torrent of apology and bestowing a dazzling smile upon me. "How are you?"

"I'm . . ."

"Great, great . . . Now come through to the kitchen and we can make a plan for the day."

Caroline gets up and slinks round the desk. She's wearing a tiny halter-neck top and looks lithe and suntanned.

"Did you have a lovely holiday, Caroline?" I enquire politely, but I don't think she hears and then I can't decide whether or not I should repeat the question, which as far as my ears are concerned is still hanging in the air. In the end I don't bother and, blushing faintly, I follow Caroline's incredibly pert, Armani jeans-clad bottom down the hall and through to the kitchen, where Lorna is clearing away what look like the remnants of breakfast.

"Morning, Lorna," I say.

"Oh, good morning, Francesca. How lovely to see you again. Sorry I didn't let you in . . ." She says this last bit while wrinkling up her nose and pointing at Caroline behind her back, as if to tell me that Caroline hadn't wanted her to let me in. I don't know where to look and certainly don't want to be caught making faces at my new boss on day one, so I just smile weakly and pray that Caroline doesn't look round.

"Would you like a cup of tea?" asks Lorna, having finished gesturing.

"Oh, thanks very much, that would be great. Just milk, no sugar, please." Much safer ground.

Caroline reaches the table, where she sits down and lights a cigarette.

"Wonderful. I'll have my coffee now too, please, Francesca?"

"Oh . . . OK. Um, how do you take it?" I say tentatively, scuttling sideways in the manner of a crab in the direction of the kettle and feeling slightly thrown.

"No. My coffee," Caroline repeats patiently.

I stop scuttling. Am I missing something, I wonder? My expression must say it all.

"My Starbucks, Francesca? I have it every morning. My assistant always picks it up on the way and then, if it's not warm any more, pops it in the microwave for me. I don't function without my venti quattro decaff skinny latte with a hazelnut shot."

I feel completely mortified. Bloody Louisa.

"Gosh, I'm so, so sorry. I didn't know anything about it. I'm pretty sure Louisa didn't mention anything about getting your coffee. Would you like me to go and get one now or shall I just make some instant and start getting them tomorrow?"

Caroline's smile remains fixed but she doesn't blink as she says, "No, I think go and get one now. Like I said, I have it every morning."

I feel like such an idiot and now my cheeks are flaming as I scuttle back out of the house in search of the nearest Starbucks.

Later on that evening I'm lying on the sofa, feeling grateful for once that Abbie is on an evening shift. It's not that I don't want to see her, but more that I don't have the energy to talk. I'm writing in my diary.

8th April
My first day as Caroline Mason's PA got off to a slightly

inauspicious start. She seemed quite pleased to see me but made it clear from the beginning that she likes things done in a very particular way. When I arrived, I was ringing on the bell for ages and in the end she rang me on the mobile to tell me to use my keys. You'd have thought it would have been easier just to let me in, but I guess she was in the middle of something. Anyway, it was rather disconcerting and made me feel like a bit of a prat. My second mistake was not bringing her coffee with me, which apparently I'm to do every morning. Still, I raced off to find a Starbucks and, fortunately, due to the fact that you'd have a harder task not to spot one, I managed to return within ten minutes, fervently praying that I'd got the order right. I had, thank goodness, so at least that was one thing in my favour. Despite these little hiccups, Caroline remained pretty unruffled, although she was certainly eager to get on with the working day. In fact, when I got back with the coffee I hardly had time to take my coat off before she started giving me lists of things to do. I guess she's just really keen to make up for any lost time that she's had without an assistant.

So, all in all, a good but slightly stressful first day. And now I'm off to bed. I'm exhausted and my brain is aching from taking in so much information — I need a good night's sleep so that I'm ready and raring to go for day two.

CHAPTER
NINE

Day two continues in much the same vein as day one. It's busy, slightly scary and begins with a conversation with Caroline that leaves me feeling wrong-footed once more. A conversation that starts while I am sitting on the toilet, having only literally just finished a wee. My instinct to take my phone in with me was obviously a good one. She's calling from rehearsals and there's not even time for social niceties.

"Get Lorna to prepare some lunch for me. I want a salad with rocket and watercress, pomegranate seeds and walnuts, with a side of cold roast chicken."

"OK," I say, hurriedly pulling up my knickers from round my knees. I urgently need to get a pen, so have no choice but to drip dry.

"Are you coming home for lunch then?" I ask, racing to the study. I find a pen and start scribbling. *Chicken, rocket, watercress . . .*

Caroline sighs. "No, Francesca, I am not going to abandon rehearsals so that I can pop home for lunch on a whim."

Pomegranate seeds, walnuts.

Right. Now I'm confused. Considering it's only day two, there's already been a lot of guesswork involved in this job.

"So you want Lorna to make the lunch and . . . put it in the fridge for tomorrow?" I suggest.

Caroline sighs in such a way that I know what I've said is not only wrong but stupid too.

"No. I know actresses have a reputation for not eating, Francesca, but I think I might faint if I skip lunch until tomorrow. Lorna needs to make my lunch and then you need to order a bike to bring it to me for one o'clock."

"Oh, right. OK, no problem," I say, privately thinking that her green credentials could certainly do with a lot of work.

"Normally I would get you to bring it, but I need you to find some bedlinen that I need for the house in Bermuda. Phone my housekeeper there and get the exact detail of what we have now because I want to replace it with exactly the same make and design . . ."

And so the list goes on and on and on, until I have enough to keep me busy for the foreseeable future and that's not taking into account the fact that I still have items on my list left over from yesterday and that my phone is ringing nineteen to the dozen from all sorts of people who seem to have magically acquired my number overnight.

"Hi, it's Leticia, I'm a friend of Cas's and I need you to make sure she has a lunch I'm hosting at mine in aid of women in film booked into her diary . . ."

"Hi, it's Claus here. I'm Miss Mason's voice coach and I need some face-to-face time with her . . ."

"Hi, it's Ralph Fiennes here. I'm in town and would love to take Caroline out for dinner. When is she free?"

That last one was rather thrilling, I have to admit.

Anyway, these calls take time and all leave me with something new to address, so I metaphorically roll my sleeves up and set to work, determined to accomplish a lot and to start creating a great impression on Caroline. A few hours later, however, I come across a stumbling block that I really can't do very much about.

At twenty to one I ring Caroline on her mobile, expecting it to be off and for me to able to leave a message. She picks up.

". . . hang on one moment, darling. It's my assistant, I won't be a moment," I hear her say smoothly.

"What?" she hisses, somewhat less smoothly once out of earshot.

"Um, I just wanted to let you know that your lunch is on its way . . ."

"Well, I should freaking hope so by now."

"Yes, er . . . well, the other thing is, I'm afraid the linen that you're after for Bermuda has been discontinued, although they have produced a design that's really similar and . . ."

"What do you mean?" says Caroline calmly.

What does she mean, what do I mean? "Well, they're not making it any more, so I've printed out a picture of the new design for you to look at and . . ."

"Not good enough, Francesca," she says icily. "Not good enough at all and, frankly, I'm disappointed. I expect my assistants to be proactive, to come up with solutions, not problems, and it certainly does not sound as though you have tackled this with any thought whatsoever. If I say that I need a certain design of linen, a particular design, then I am not saying it for my own enjoyment . . ."

I can't quite believe what I'm hearing. It seems very unfair to take umbrage with me about this and I can't figure out why it's such a big deal.

"You have to understand, Francesca, that when someone is as busy as me I don't have time to hear the word 'no' or to come up against any negative energy . . ."

This isn't so much shooting the messenger as talking it to death, and now that she's made her point I wish she'd let me get on with things as I'm rather anxious about how much I still have to do. Still, maybe I need to think more laterally and if I want to keep this job, which obviously I do, then I probably need to get with the programme. (A phrase I can imagine Caroline using.)

I abandon the rest of my list and spend much of the day on the phone to someone in the office of a factory in Milan where said linen was once produced. Begging them in pigeon Italian to consider reproducing the design that they stopped manufacturing more than five years ago is proving (unsurprisingly) to be a pointless mission and I don't know who thinks I'm more insane, Luigi in Milan or my dad, who I have to ring at the restaurant to ask for a few key phrases that I'm having trouble with. To my eternal shame, I have pretty much forgotten all the Italian that my father taught me when I was little and can now only remember very basic phrases like "Where's the disco?" or "I'd like a kilo of pears", neither of which are proving very helpful right now.

I waste the remainder of the day googling and surfing various international bedlinen websites and I'm just about to give up and call it a day when Raj calls. Hearing from him is such a pleasant surprise that I'm suddenly swamped by the urge to see a friendly face, especially one that has never given any thought at all to the subject of bedlinen. I can say that with some authority, as he once told me that he only changes his sheets when he can see the outline of his body on them. I persuade him to meet me at mine in three quarters of an hour.

Rush hour ended a long time ago, so I have the tube carriage completely to myself. I sit worrying about how I'm going to break it to Caroline that I have failed in my bedlinen task. Tonight she went straight out to dinner after rehearsals with her friend Leticia, so I managed to avoid telling her, but now it's looming over me until tomorrow. I feel absolutely knackered. In order to learn how everything should be done so that it is to Caroline's liking, I have to absorb a lot of tiny detail, which is quite exhausting for a brain that hasn't done so much exercise in years. Overall, though, I am finding the challenge thrilling, as opposed to off-putting. It's just that the change of routine is a shock to the system and by comparison I've been working at the pace of a sloth for the last few years. I'm also rather concerned about the fact that I haven't yet won Caroline over. I feel very much as though I'm on trial to a large degree and that in some way she's waiting for me to fail. This could simply be a symptom of having had lots of useless assistants in the past. (Although, frankly, her behaviour on the phone today can only really be described as dodgy, and I'm reluctant to come up with too many excuses for it.) This is a shame as I can see how the job has the potential to be really fun if only she'd just be a bit more friendly and relaxed. As it is, she's quite the task master and there is a very marked line between employer and employee. Still, call me the eternal optimist but I feel like if I can hang in there, once she's gained my trust she might just lighten up a bit and take her foot off the slave-driving pedal.

When I get home, Raj is already waiting for me outside and it's lovely to see him. Twenty minutes later and we're sitting on my sofa, eating scrambled egg on our laps (well, on trays on our laps), and chatting nineteen to the dozen about what we've been up to since we last saw each other. While we're talking I feel faintly distracted by something but I can't figure out what it is that's niggling me. All I do know is that there's something different about him. This must be how my dad feels when Mum's been to the hairdresser's. Finally it comes to me.

"Raj?"

"Yes, Fran?"

"You're not stoned."

"Ah, that noticeable, eh?" he says, looking rather sheepish. "Yeah, well, to be honest I was starting to get a bit paranoid about stuff and then one day I left my passport at a travel agent's, nearly burnt my mum's house down making myself a snack and thought that giant spiders were coming to get me, all in the space of three hours, so I decided to knock it on the head."

"Right . . ." I say thoughtfully. "Well, if you don't mind me saying, the fact that I can't remember the last time I saw you this 'normal' probably means it's for the best."

Raj nods and suddenly his abstinence seems so obvious. His pallor is the healthiest I've ever seen it, the whites of his eyes are exactly that for once and he's more animated and making a lot more sense than usual. He blushes to the blue tips of his newest hair colour. Then, clearly not wishing to be scrutinized any more or to dwell on his reformation, he changes the subject.

"So, tell me all about the new job."

I start to fill Raj in on what my daily life now involves and at one point, as I re-enact the first-day coffee saga, I find myself impersonating Caroline and Raj laughs his head off. With the benefit of hindsight, I realize that it is a very funny story and Raj's reaction is so rewarding that I get on a bit of a roll. Ten minutes later, Raj is still giggling about my ludicrous phone calls to Milan and I make a mental note to write all these stories down so I don't forget them. Only two days in and so much to tell already, I think, suddenly feeling quite proud of myself.

CHAPTER
TEN

It's exhilarating to have been jet propelled out of the comfort zone that I've been mouldering in for so long, and over the next fortnight I get a grim thrill out of working such long hours and so hard for a change, and the days begin to simply roll into one another.

As I become immersed in everything Miss Mason, my life changes beyond recognition and the only contact I seem to have time for with my friends and family is by phone. I don't even have time to write my diary very often. Still, when I do there's an awful lot to say.

28th April

I'm slowly starting to learn how Caroline's complicated life operates and I'm gradually getting to know the woman herself a little better. She's certainly formidable. On a good day I'd describe her as a woman who knows her own mind. On a bad day I'd have to go for bloody demanding and hard work. However, I know she's not the first actress in the world to be a little highly strung and I accept that it's probably part of the territory. In fact, for all her apparent faults, Caroline Mason is unquestionably an intelligent woman and deep down I think that on the days when she's, shall we say, a little short with me, she knows only too well that she is channelling her frustration unfairly. How much this actually bothers her I have yet to figure out. Sometimes she really can be quite rude and it may not be a valid excuse but I suspect that from what small glimpse I've had into her life so far, nobody ever pulls her up on her behaviour. As a result, over time she's probably convinced herself that foul moods are just a by-product of an artistic temperament. Taking them out on her staff is entirely understandable. Needless to say, I don't agree.

Despite all of this, I do feel that underneath it all there is potential for me to be, not friends exactly, but maybe a confidante of some kind. I still haven't fully gained her trust but I'm a long way from giving up.

The next day it's ten thirty in the morning and Caroline and I are sitting in the back of her chauffeur-driven car on the way to rehearsals.

Number 34, I scribble. Buy Lancôme cleanser and eye make-up remover (light blue not dark blue).

"Then I want you to call my bank and tell them I need another five thousand pounds transferred into my current account."

Number 35 . . . Oh, hang on. I look up. "Will I be able to do that? I mean, am I authorized, that is?"

Caroline looks irritated. "Oh shit, I suppose you won't be. OK, I'll phone the bank and tell them that you're authorized."

It occurs to me that if she's going to have to phone the bank anyway, then she may as well organize the transfer herself, but I wisely keep this logic to myself. Besides, over the course of the last fortnight or so, one of the many things I have learnt is that actors love creating extra telephone calls wherever possible. For example, instructions will often go along the lines of this:

"Will you call Mr Harris's assistant and tell her to call Mr Harris and say that I would like Mr Harris to call me?"

"OK, what is Mr Harris's assistant's number?"

"I don't know, but I'll give you Mr Harris's and you can call him and ask him."

. . . I know. But then I suppose if you're paying for the luxury of having a personal assistant who will do everything for you then a lot of your time becomes full up with thinking of things for your personal assistant to do. Are you with me?

"Then I need you to pick up a couple of cartons of cigarettes and some more of that coffee I like that you get from Harvey Nicks. Four tins should do."

I dutifully scribble. Four tins. Jesus, no wonder she's so highly strung. Caffeinated beverages have been a running theme from the start of this job and sometimes I feel like a runner all over again. In fact, I have decided that Caroline Mason may well be single-handedly keeping Starbucks afloat.

"Can you stop the car at a Starbucks, please, Terry?" she asks her driver. Ah, the timing.

On my side of the back seat I am surrounded by various bags, dry-cleaning and a set of plates that Caroline wants me to take back to Harrods. While I'm at Harrods I'm to purchase twelve sets of near identical bedlinen to the one she originally wanted, which she's finally agreed "will have to do". It took a while but I finally got her to see that defeat had to be conceded. A few minutes later when the car pulls over I automatically put my pad away and struggle out of the car to fetch her latest complicated beverage. My mobile starts ringing and I can see that it's her publicist, Kenneth. Caroline remains in the car, smoking. I answer the phone and I'm still listening to her publicist drone on about a forthcoming shoot for the *Sunday Times* style section when I get call waiting. The coffee is handed to me as I change lines. It's Caroline calling from the car.

"I want some gum, eight tins, and when you get back add to the list that I want some new socks for the gym. I need you to phone my trainer and tell him that I have to change our session . . ."

Trying to listen to and remember a list of instructions while simultaneously paying for and carrying coffee and eight tins of gum was always overambitious. With the phone tucked under my chin, I lean on the heavy glass door with my shoulder in order to get out and drop everything. I scald myself severely and suffer minor burns to my hands. Caroline can see all this from the car window but doesn't react or draw breath. In fact, it is Terry, her driver, who leaps out of the car with some wet wipes.

"Are you all right, Francesca? Ooh, that looks terribly sore."

Truth be known, I'm in agony, but embarrassment always tends to dull pain, I find.

Caroline's window slides down. "Seeing as that one's gone, will you make the next one the same but a frappé? I'm a bit hot."

Hands throbbing, I scurry back into Starbucks. I don't think I've felt this anxious or stressed in years. It seems ironic that having originally judged Jodie as being anal and neurotic I've now come to understand she is only that organized for very good reason. The reason she provided Louisa with so much information was not for fun, as I had first suspected, but because Caroline fully expects whoever is working for her to have the minutiae of her life at their fingertips at all times. Needless to say, all the papers that I'd earmarked as unnecessary crap have in fact been highly useful and if I'm unsure of anything or can't make head or tail of Caroline's instructions then I know that Jodie will always have the answer. I've come to see her as my saviour and to rely on her heavily. I ring her every day as soon as I know that New York is awake and I don't know what I'd do without all Jodie's help and all of Lorna's cups of tea.

I make my way back to the car and hand Caroline her frappé. She takes it and we resume our journey.

One thing I can say in Caroline's favour is that she's extremely adept and practical at working out arrangements. Last night she decided that this morning we should meet at her house so that we could travel in the car together because we have an unusual amount to discuss and also because a journalist is meeting her at the theatre for an interview for the *Standard* and she wants me to be there. This is more the sort of thing I

101

had in mind when I originally heard about the job, so I'm really pleased. I'm also terribly excited because being allowed into rehearsals means that I will witness first-hand one of England's most famous theatre directors, Sir Richard Brocklebank, at work. Still, now that my daily list has grown to such epic proportions I'm beginning to wonder how on earth I'm going to get it all done this afternoon.

I glance sideways at my strange boss. Her hair is tumbling over her shoulders and she looks stunning, except that if you look closely you notice that her mouth is pursed and her nose, as ever, is firmly in the air, which isn't so attractive. Her mobile goes.

"My darling, how are you?" she yells like the true actress she is. "What, you're cracking up, what? . . . Oh, I've got you again. So are you going to be around for my birthday, sweetie? . . . Really? Brilliant. No, I'll probably hire the penthouse at the Met or Brown's or somewhere and we can party . . . Fabulous. Yeah, Carson's coming and all the usual crowd, Leticia et cetera . . . No, not that bitch, she's not coming anywhere near it. Aha, well, Carson's working with Julia on his new movie, *The Reporter*, so if they're both here doing promotion then she'll be coming too . . . OK, sweetie, call me soon, *ciao ciao*."

She snaps her phone shut and sighs contentedly. It seems that even grown-up movie stars get excited about their birthdays. No small gathering at Pizza Express for her though. I try to remember every word she just said so that I can relay it to my friends later. They're all getting a disproportionate amount of pleasure from hearing about my daily goings-on, which they hear mainly via Abbie as I'm too busy and knackered to see them. To be honest, I actually get quite a thrill from being the purveyor of so many insights into such a famous household. Sad but true.

Minutes later we arrive at the theatre and Caroline leaves all her bags in the car, so I presume she doesn't need them. I follow her through the stage door and up the grimy back stairs that lead to a decidedly unglamorous room. Inside are a few people sitting around reading, drinking tea and chatting. I recognize three of them as being actors I have seen in one thing or another. It's all rather exciting.

"Morning, Cas," says one chap who I know was in an advert recently although I can't remember which one, and I'm sure I've seen him in something else too. I'd guess he's in his forties and he's tall with a hint of a paunch. He has dark hair and a beard and, try as I might, I still can't quite place him. I grin at him and he grins back, but Caroline ignores him and motions to me to come and sit next to her on the other side of the room.

She whispers out of the side of her mouth so that only I can hear, "I can't stand it when people I don't know call me anything other than Caroline."

This aside is real progress as far as I'm concerned. It means we have moved on from civil exchanges and work chat and have entered the far more entertaining arena of gossip and idle banter. I'm determined to make the most of it.

"Yeah, really annoying when people do that," I agree, solemnly nodding at her.

"Francesca, where are all my bags?" she asks, spoiling the mood completely.

"Um, in the car," I reply.

"Well, what the hell are they doing there? I need them. Go and get them, will you?"

I hate myself for blushing and I take the stairs two at a time, muttering to myself. Outside, the fresh air cools my face.

"You all right, love?" asks Terry.

"Yeah, fine. I just forgot her bags."

"Oh, I'm sorry," says Terry, looking apologetic. "That's probably my fault. I usually take them up for her but I just thought that seeing as you were here today . . ." He trails off, looking faintly shamefaced.

I reassure him. "Don't be silly, Terry, it's not part of your job description to carry her bags. I personally don't understand why she can't carry them herself." Oops, that is the first time I have openly said something negative about Caroline. I wince as I wait for Terry's reaction, but it's fine because he grins and chuckles to himself.

"Go on, you, you'd better get in there before she starts sending out a search party."

Terry is just helping me to load the last of her bags into my arms, taking special care not to crumple her garment bag which is draped over my shoulder like a toga, when my mobile rings. We both laugh because we know even without looking exactly who it is and in that instance we bond and become comrades. Terry takes my phone out of my pocket for me and holds it to my ear.

"I'm on my way, Caroline. Yes, I've got it . . . No, I haven't disappeared."

I reach the rehearsal room puffing and panting, laden with all her stuff, but Madam makes no move to assist. Today she is wearing Rock & Republic jeans, a vest top and a really cool poncho-type thing, but apparently I have committed some kind of offence in assuming that she would be wearing this for the interview.

"I mean, what did you think I brought the garment bag with me for, Francesca? Fun?" she says, as I go about hanging things up on a rail at the side of the room. "Do you think I enjoy having to spend so many of my waking hours thinking about what kind of image I need to portray, day in and day out?"

Halfway through this rant Caroline becomes aware that her fellow cast members are listening to her every word and tries adjusting her tone mid sentence to one that sounds light and breezy. She might be one of the most well-known actresses in the world but she doesn't pull it off. The actor who I have just worked out was in *Heartbeat* and is called Jeremy unadvisedly decides to offer his twopence worth.

"Hey, Cas, lighten up, sweetheart. You've got more important things to worry about than what you're going to wear, like our big scene, for instance, which I believe Richard wants to rehearse again today. In fact, I think we're up next."

At this point I feel terribly sorry for Jeremy.

105

Caroline turns very slowly on her heel in order to bestow upon him an unbelievably withering look and says slowly and clearly, in a voice so steely it almost makes me shiver, "Believe me, Jeremy, when I say that I am extremely worried about our scene for many, many reasons. As for 'lightening up', well, that may occur when you can actually be bothered to remember my freaking name, which for your information is Caroline."

"Oh, well, I . . ."

"Not sweetheart, not Cas, just Caroline."

"Oh, sure, but . . ."

"And while I appreciate that remembering words isn't your forte — at least, that's if our latest line run is anything to go by — surely remembering one little name can't be beyond even you?"

The stunned silence that follows is deeply uncomfortable. Jeremy is (finally) lost for words and I gaze at the floor as if it's the most fascinating thing I've ever seen in my life. One actress, who plainly can't handle the situation, clears her throat before scuttling out of the room. Others mutter something about going to get a cup of tea and splinter off. Those that are left stand stock-still and seem to stop breathing. It truly is a tumbleweed moment and only the sound of a church bell tolling or a baby crying could make it any more awkward or unsettling. I steal a surreptitious glance at Caroline and am amazed to see that she's actually looking ever so slightly unsure of herself. She must have realized how badly she has just come across and that it's probably a bit early in the day to be upsetting the rest of the cast, even by her standards.

Suddenly she pipes up. "Oh, don't look so shocked, Jeremy. Can't you tell when someone's joking?" she says, a forced, maniacal smile plastered across her face.

Jeremy, who's clearly uncertain of how to proceed, remains rooted to the spot for a while, looking thoroughly suspicious. However, when he eventually comprehends what is expected of him, he quickly rallies.

"Ah, ha ha, good one, Caroline. I love it," he says with forced jollity and the rest of the cast start breathing again. "Caroline it is from now on though," he says. Then, as an afterthought, "In fact, from this point onwards there'll be no more terms of endearment and 'Cas' officially no longer exists. Yes, ma'am," he adds, clicking his heels together in a "Herr Commandant" fashion.

Too much, I think regretfully.

Caroline's fake smile vanishes as fast as it appeared.

CHAPTER
ELEVEN

Watching rehearsals take place is fascinating and at this moment in time I honestly believe I've got the best job in the world. All thoughts about buying gym socks and linen and taking things back to Harrods vanish from my mind as I watch the infamous Sir Richard Brocklebank working his magic on the actors who are involved in the scene that they're rehearsing this morning. It's a love scene that's an integral part of the plot and, I have to say, Caroline plays it superbly. She's changed into her Missoni kaftan to rehearse and floating around even this shabby room, with the lines of the stage marked out on the floor in masking tape, she appears ethereal and other-worldly, which is precisely how she's supposed to come across, and — let's face it — is quite a stretch from her natural persona. I have to admit to experiencing the odd pang of envy — how wonderful it must be to be so well known and so good at your craft that you can tackle parts like this. Jeremy, who plays her love interest, is not even in the same league, but is improving all the time under Richard Brocklebank's painstaking direction. Still, despite the guidance he's being given, I can't see him ever being a match for Caroline Mason and it's not a great piece of casting. You are supposed to believe that the two of them are madly and passionately in love and that she only feels protected when he is around. As it is, it's plainly obvious that she could have him for breakfast any day of the week and compared to her strong yet subtle performance he comes across as brash and rather pedestrian. I suspect that if I can sense this then Richard Brocklebank must be more than aware, but you'd never know and, apart from a couple of instances when I notice him scratching his goatee beard anxiously, he exudes calm and control. After each big section of dialogue he stops and gives them extensive notes, but skilfully manages to criticize without offending their fragile egos. The rest of the cast are encouraged to chip in with their thoughts and suggestions and when a younger cast member dares to make a constructive comment about one of Caroline's lines he receives a glacial look from her.

All the actors are very luvvie when they discuss anything, particularly Caroline, who'll take Richard into a corner now and again and have impassioned, whispered discussions with him while the others stand around waiting and drinking more coffee. I would wager money that poor old Jeremy, who is entirely unaware of his shortcomings and who has no idea quite how much he is irritating Caroline, is probably the main topic of her conversation. To be honest, I can see her point and now, having watched her act in the flesh, I certainly have newfound respect for her. During her breaks she snaps out of character in seconds though. One minute she'll be on the floor crying and wailing, wringing her hands in despair, and the next she'll stalk over to me and say, "My iPod needs looking at. It's not working properly," or "Where's this bloody journalist? She's late. Call Kenneth immediately because I still need you to go off and do everything else for me and I don't want you to go until after the interview."

Personally, I couldn't be more delighted by Linda Myles's tardiness but I scuttle out of the room and make the call to Caroline's poor beleaguered publicist, Kenneth, who permanently sounds as if he's about to have a heart attack from stress.

"Is she not there?" he asks as soon as he knows it's me.

"No, not yet."

"Shit, OK. I'll call you back. How is she? Is she cross?" he asks, sounding terrified.

"She's fine. Don't worry, it's not your fault," I reply, not wanting to be responsible for a cardiac arrest. The truth is, of course, that if the journalist doesn't turn up soon Caroline will be seething. Even I know that it's supposed to be the actress who keeps the journalist waiting. Kenneth calls me back.

"Her bloody child was taken ill at school. She had to pick her up so she's going to be there in twenty minutes," he splutters. "What should I do?"

"I'll explain," I say reasonably. "If this poor woman's child is ill, I'm sure she'll understand."

Caroline doesn't understand at all.

"What do you mean, her child's ill? That's not my fucking problem," she hisses at me in a quiet corner of the room so that Richard Brocklebank can't hear her. "Where's Kenneth? Get him on the phone for me."

I wipe her spittle off my face and with a heavy heart tap in Kenneth's number, but at the last moment he gets a reprieve he's not even aware of because just then a very harassed-looking Linda Myles, features editor from the *Evening Standard,* arrives. She races in panting and my heart goes out to her.

"Hello, Miss Mason. I'm so sorry I'm late. I've had childcare nightmares. You'll know what it's like, being a mother yourself."

I grin. Nicely played; there are no flies on Linda Myles.

Miss Mason's not stupid either and she knows when to play the game and when to turn on the charm offensive.

"Absolutely," she drawls. "You poor, poor thing. Is your child OK?"

"Yes. It's her tonsils, but she's with Granny now so hopefully we can get an appointment for . . ." She trails off, realizing quite rightly that Caroline couldn't care less.

"So, anyway, where would you like to do this?"

"Follow me," barks Caroline, striding out of the room without so much as a backward glance in Linda's direction to check that she's following.

Linda turns to me briefly and smiles sympathetically. Then, with the air of someone resigned to a life of interviewing divas, she allows herself a quick roll of the eyes before the two of us trot obediently off in Caroline's wake.

CHAPTER
TWELVE

One Saturday morning, a few days later, I'm sitting at home in my kitchen happily writing away in my diary.

3rd May
I've started writing something called "The Diary of a Personal Assistant" on the computer. Obviously it's based on what I'm going through at the moment but I'm embellishing everything to make it really juicy. I must say that, after a long day of being ordered around, writing it is rather therapeutic and the first chapter is all about the PA trying to chase her tail in order to get everything done, just like I have been. I've learnt from my mistakes though, so for the sake of discretion, the actress in it is called Miss M. Come to think of it, maybe from now on it would be wise to refer to "her" as Miss M in my personal diary too.

Anyway, with this new project I'm not interested in stitching Miss M up and if I'm going to base a fictional character around her I'm aware that I need to be ultra discreet. So for the purposes of my story Miss M will have a daughter, not a son, and a partner called Mr X whom she is married to.

I'm already excited about having a project to really get my teeth stuck into and with first-hand experience of what it's like to work for a famous actress I don't think I'm going to be short of inspiration. Besides, due to a practically non-existent social life at the moment I don't really have anything else to write about, although that's probably for the best seeing as I'm usually so exhausted at the end of the day that all I do feel like doing is a bit of writing. I often can't even face speaking on the phone to my friends, having had it glued to my ear all day long. As a result, I think Ella and Sabina might be a bit put out about not seeing me for so long and I'm well aware that today's lunch is not before time.

I put my pen down, yawn and contemplate whether or not I want another cup of tea. I feel really lethargic today and I think all the excitement and stress of the last few weeks have finally caught up. Still, a month into the job and things are going pretty well. I'm becoming quite adept at anticipating Caroline's needs and wants, and now that I've managed to work out that being overly efficient actually works against me I feel like I've had a minor breakthrough.

For the first few weeks of the job I busted a gut every day to achieve all the items on my "To Do" list, but every time I reported back to Caroline that I'd done everything she'd asked me to, rather than seem pleased she just seemed mildly put out and instead of giving me a pat on the back proceeded to act as if I'd issued her with some kind of challenge. The more I got done, the more she'd give me to do, until in order to achieve it all I had no choice but to work flat out till ten, eleven o'clock at night, every night. A few days ago I eventually got to the point where I felt completely and utterly done in and thoroughly fed up that I still hadn't won even the tiniest bit of appreciation. Finally I decided to stop running myself into the ground and, for the first time in a long time, spent a day functioning at a normal pace and finished work at a decent hour with a few items left pending on my list.

The next morning, feeling terribly nervous, I told Caroline politely but firmly that I simply hadn't been able to get everything done, and her expression told me that I'd done the right thing. The victorious glint in her eye told me that she had been playing a very odd game and now she'd won. Since then she's eased up a little and even though she hasn't praised me out loud I suspect that deep down she probably thinks I'm doing an OK job. After all, she hasn't fired me yet and, according to Jodie, firing useless PAs is a blood sport she has always been quite keen on. Still, with only a short while till rehearsals are over, the status quo is about to change and soon we're going to be seeing an awful lot more of each other, but there's no point in dwelling on this now.

I make myself some toast and Marmite and, as I eat it, I take a moment to appreciate the heavenly peace and quiet. That's the thing about working, it makes being at home a fantastic novelty. The last few weeks may have been tricky at times but it doesn't matter and I shouldn't moan; it's still brilliant just to be doing something so exciting. There's a lovely fragrant breeze wafting through the window indicating that spring will segue into summer at some point in the not too distant future and I am looking forward to the prospect of

114

lunch with the girls who I've really, really missed, so all is well.

I flick the kettle on for a second cup of tea. As it bubbles away I can hear the post landing on the mat, so I venture into the hallway, pick it up and bring it back into the kitchen. I thumb idly through it. Pizza flyers, electric bill, water bill . . . then I notice that there is one more envelope. It's cream, it's very expensive-looking and it's addressed to me. I rip it open and read the contents, read them again and then collapse on to the nearest chair.

Like a baffled fish I gape in sheer disbelief at the stiff cream card with the silver embossed writing. The penny finally drops with a resounding clunk. What the hell?

I hold the card between two fingers as though it is a dirty nappy and relocate to the sitting room. I flop on to the sofa to digest what I've just found out. I feel completely outraged and have to scan the card for a third and final time just to make sure I've got it right.

There's no mistaking it. Harry is getting married.

At the top of the card, written in Harry's handwriting, it says "Miss Francesca Massi and Miss Abbie McCrew" and underneath in silver italics it reads:

The pleasure of your company is requested
at the marriage of
Miss Sandy Reed
to
Mr Harry Robinson

Blah blah blah. I'm not interested in the details of when, and where, just who. I'm absolutely flabbergasted. How the hell has he had time to find a bride since we split up? I've only just about managed to find a job. The bastard! What was all that "no commitment" bollocks about? I kick the table and stub my toe, although I don't know why I'm injuring myself when the person I really want to inflict pain upon is the groom-to-be. I could kill him. I try to scrunch the invite up in disgust, but it doesn't happen — it's very good quality card.

The phone rings. It's Abbie.

"Hi, Fran. Listen, I'm not coming home to get changed, so I'm on my way to the pub now," she pants.

"What happened to you last night?" I ask lamely.

"I'll tell you all about it later."

"I've got something to tell you too, but it'll also keep, so I'll see you in a bit," I say in a grim voice. We ring off.

I glance at the clock. I can't face the tube on my day off and I'd like to have a drink. I need to get dressed and phone a minicab.

When I arrive at the pub, Abbie, Ella and Sabina are already seated at our favourite table. It's lovely to see them and as I regard them affectionately I feel myself relax after a slightly stressful time in getting there.

"I'm so sorry I'm late," I say, kissing them all and sitting down. Sabina is already filling up my glass with wine before replenishing her own. "I've had the journey from hell. My driver had no idea about anything, so I had to direct while trying not to inhale his incredible

B.O. Then I got charged seventeen quid for the pleasure. Daylight bloody robbery. But, hey, that's illegal minicabs for you. Anyway, how are you all? It's so nice to see you."

"You too, Fran. It's been far too bloody long," replies Ella. "I would have a go at you for being a crap friend but I'm not going to because I don't care. Just being in your proximity makes me feel in some small way closer to Carson Adams."

"We've ordered, by the way," interrupts Sabina. "Go on, Abs, quickly finish the story and then I want to hear all the latest Caroline Mason gossip."

It's funny, but when I'm with people I've known a long time I tend to feel the age I was when I first met them. So when I'm with the girls I revert to being about twelve years old. I guess it's something of a leveller when you know that someone witnessed you going through your luminous sweatbands and jazz shoes stage, or that they can remember you having an enormous crush on Michael J. Fox. Abbie, Sabina, Ella and I have done everything together — bunked off school, first package holidays, Saturday jobs. We've seen each other through those teenage years, when your biggest worry in life is whether Justin Brookes is going to ring you or not, and we've been there for each other every time life has thrown something not so great at us. When Abbie's dad died, for instance, we were the ones who held her hand at the funeral, and it was us who were still there to listen six months later when everyone else assumed she was now fine. We may not see each other quite as often as we used to — Ella's married

117

now and obviously we all have other close friends — but I know that I'll know them forever. Abbie, Sabina and Ella are more like family than friends.

Sabina is looking good today; her long, strawberry blonde hair looks clean and shiny and, as ever, she is groomed and immaculate. She works in advertising as a producer and earns an excellent wage. This, combined with the fact that she firmly believes in quality over quantity, means her wardrobe, although slightly too conservative for my tastes, is enviable. Today she's wearing 7 For All Mankind jeans with Tod's loafers, a light cashmere sweater and what looks suspiciously like a Cartier bracelet on her wrist. Sabina thrives on gossip and is obviously relishing the tale of Abbie's latest exploits.

"Well, in the end he said I didn't have to pay for the damage, so I just passed out fully clothed next to him while he banged on about what an amazing team player he is. God, he was boring. Islington's answer to David Brent. Anyway, I got the shock of my life this morning when I woke up. Then it all came flooding back, so I legged it before he woke up," Abbie finishes triumphantly, clearly proud of her antics.

In direct contrast to Sabina, Abbie is one of the scruffiest people I have ever met. She couldn't care less if her nails aren't done or her hair's not coiffed, but is still very attractive with her straight, dark-brown bob and pale complexion. She is the trendiest out of all of us and today she's wearing a T-shirt, a pair of black tuxedo trousers and Converse trainers.

118

"You're such a freak," says Sabina, laughing. "I could never crash out at someone's house like that. If I stay somewhere, I have to have my cleansers and make-up and a spare pair of pants for the next day."

"Yeah, well, when I'm that pissed it doesn't occur to me to get my nice little washbag out and start giving myself a mini facial. Splash of water on my face maybe and that's about it," grins Abbie.

Ella leans back in her chair as she speaks. "I'm with Sabs on this one. I feel far too old now to pass out just anywhere. It wouldn't matter how drunk I was, I'd find a cab number somehow and get home. Not that I'll probably ever be in that sort of a situation again anyway."

Ella's looking really beautiful today, as always, but she looks tired too. I notice that she's not on the wine either. She must be hungover.

"Yeah, I don't think Paul would exactly appreciate you staying out at some random guy's house," says Abbie, laughing at her. "Why aren't you drinking anyway?"

"Feeling rough," replies Ella quickly. "Overdid it last night."

Thought as much. Sabina changes the subject.

"Fran, you're very quiet. Are you OK?"

"Yeah, I'm fine . . . Well, I'm sort of fine," I start. "Actually, if I'm totally honest, I'm pretty shit but I'd forgotten for a minute because I was too busy thinking how we're slowly turning into some sort of pastiche of a crap drama. Anyway, the point is, I've got some news. Good news and bad news. What do you want first?"

I had their attention.

"Good news first, please," says Ella.

"OK. The good news is that Abbie and I have been invited to a wedding." I leave a pause for dramatic tension. "The bad news is that it's Harry's wedding."

"What?" they all say in unison.

"Harry, Harry? Harry as in your ex-boyfriend Harry Robinson?" asks Abbie, wrinkling her nose.

"The one and only. Unless you know any others, that is?" I say weakly, almost wanting to laugh at my friends' shocked faces.

"But hang on a minute," Sabina says slowly. "When he dump — I mean, when you guys split up, didn't he say he didn't want to be in a relationship and that . . ."

"And that the only reason he was ending it was because he couldn't make a commitment to anybody? Yes, that was it pretty much in a nutshell," I offer, not really wishing to be reminded of the exact dialogue.

"Bloody hell," says Sabina, digesting this information.

"Well, that was obviously a load of old crap," says Abbie. "Oh, Fran, you poor thing. The soap opera continues, eh?"

I shrug weakly.

"Hang on a minute," Ella interjects. "How long ago did you guys split up?"

"Um, two and a half months ago or so," I say, trying to give the impression of vagueness, although in reality that monstrous destiny day in February will probably be imprinted in my mind forever and has been

120

recorded for posterity in my diary in unbelievable detail.

"Yeah, that sounds right. And when's the wedding?" Ella continues.

"I'll show you," I say, rummaging in my handbag and producing the invitation with a dramatic flourish. Three pairs of hands grab for it.

Abbie gets there first. "Saturday sixth of June, so not long away at all."

Ella looks thoughtful. "Oh, babe, I'm so sorry. Are you all right?"

"Yeah, I'm fine," I say, trying to analyse how I really do feel. "It's just a big shock, I suppose. I haven't burst into tears or anything, but then I think we all know that Harry and I were never that serious. I just feel like such a twat. I mean, at the time, I believed all his bullshit. The 'I don't want to get into anything heavy right now' line. And now he's getting married. I mean you don't get much bloody heavier than that, do you?"

Just then the waitress deposits four plates of fishcakes, chips and salad at the table. As we all tuck in, Sabina is the first to speak. "Well, I hate to be the one to say it, but it's obvious that Harry must have met this Sandy Reed while he was seeing you. I mean, I've heard of whirlwind engagements but this is crazy."

"I know, although I did ask Harry if he was seeing someone else at the time and he said no. I've also spoken to him a couple of times since we broke up and he hasn't mentioned anything about anyone new."

By way of reply Sabina simply arches one eyebrow to amazing effect.

"OK, obviously now I realize he was bullshitting, but I was thinking about it on the way here and getting hitched so quickly just doesn't make any sense," I say quickly.

"Maybe Sandy Reed is Australian and desperate for a visa?" suggests Ella.

"Maybe," I say, sounding doubtful. "It's either something like that or he's been secretly seeing her for years. Other than that, I just don't get the rush, and the other thing I really don't get is why on earth he's invited me to the wedding?"

Abbie pipes up with her mouth full of chips. "Well, one way to look at it is that he must have really meant it when he said that he wanted to stay friends. Let's face it, there's no way he would have invited you to his wedding otherwise. In a weird way, it's a compliment and I think we should go."

Sabina puts her knife and fork down. "Do you know what? She's right. OK, so clearly he didn't love you, was two-timing you and lied when he finished it . . ."

I stop mid bite. "Do you want to just rub some salt and lemon into the wound while you're at it?"

"Not great, admittedly," Sabina continues, "but you always had such a laugh with him, and Abbie's right, he must hold you in very high regard to invite you to his wedding. I mean, he obviously hasn't considered the possibility that you might sabotage it."

"I can't really go, can I?" I say. "I mean, that possibility hadn't even crossed my mind."

Sabina is on a roll. "You've got to go. It'll be so much cooler than declining, which will mean he'll know you care. Besides, you've told us that you weren't in love with him so you should go and be gracious, and drink as much free booze as you possibly can."

I'm so confused. Shouldn't I be angry with Harry? By rights his invitation should feel like a huge insult and I should probably tell him where to stick it. Yet the girls are right, there is something quite touching about the fact that he's invited me. That piece of card spoke volumes. It said that he regarded me far more highly than just an ex-shag. It said that although we failed as lovers we could succeed as friends.

"Well, I suppose I wouldn't mind checking out this Sandy Reed, Randy Seed, Bandy Weed character," I say.

"And I've been invited too," says Abbie. "And I think we should definitely go. Apart from anything else, we'll have a laugh and you'll die of curiosity if we don't."

Sabina laughs. "Abbie's right and you'll know lots of people there, so there's no excuse really."

"Ella?" I look at my sanest friend.

"Go. No question about it."

"Well, it looks like you lot have made the decision for me. Abbie, you're on. We'll go to this goddamn wedding. But if I get upset when I see Harry, just promise you'll stop me from saying or doing anything I'll regret." I push my plate away. "Oh my God!"

"What?" the three of them chorus.

"What the hell am I going to wear?"

CHAPTER
THIRTEEN

A couple of weeks later and I'm on my way to work. After a great deal of debate with Abbie I decided to RSVP Harry by phone so that the ice would be broken before the big day. It didn't go too badly. At first when he realized it was me he'd sounded terrified, but he relaxed once it became clear that I wasn't phoning just to chew his ear off, although I'm not sure that when I offered my congratulations they sounded entirely heartfelt. Still, for whatever reason, Harry seemed genuinely pleased and excited that Abbie and I were coming and I even managed to ignore my natural instinct which was to interrogate him in the manner of a frenzied policeman about his wife-to-be. We said goodbye politely.

No matter how much they try to pretend they don't, men gossip just as much as women in their own monosyllabic way, and within minutes of me speaking to Harry, Briggsy phoned to insist that he would drive Abbie and me to the wedding. I agreed, mainly due to the fact that the thought of driving back the day after with a stonking hangover doesn't appeal at all.

Anyway, part of me thinks I must be mad for going, but at least I have a couple more weeks to get my head round the whole idea. And now it's Monday morning and the time has come to move Caroline into the theatre, deep in the heart of the West End. With only two weeks to go until opening night, all rehearsals will now take place on stage and in costume. Caroline has asked me to meet her at the theatre at nine o'clock so we can go through what we need to get for her dressing room. I can't believe I've started to use the royal "we" now too. What I mean is, what she needs and what I will get for her dressing room.

With opening night looming, Caroline is being even more neurotic and bad-tempered than usual and, just to add to my woes, her mobile phone is playing up, so I've spent more time hanging on for customer services recently than is really healthy. Also, not a day has gone by when she hasn't nagged me about her flaming iPod, which doesn't seem to be working, but I honestly don't know what's wrong with it and nor does anybody in any of the shops I've taken it to. I even phoned Jodie to see if she could shed any light all the way from America.

"Have you checked that it's charged?" was her suggestion.

"No, but that would have been the first thing Caroline would have checked before handing it to me," I said.

"Oh, you'd be surprised," sighed Jodie. "That woman doesn't know what she's doing half the time and she wouldn't want to waste her precious time doing something as mundane as plugging something in."

125

I laughed. "Jodie, do I detect a note of bitterness in your voice?"

"I guess you do. Hey, I tell you what though, I am having the nicest time just looking after Carson. My life is so easy when *she's* not around. I don't even know what to do with all the time I have for myself."

"Make the most of it," was my advice. "After all, she'll be back before you know it."

"Yeah, I know, don't remind me. Oh, by the way, is there any news on her movie?"

"Not yet. It's all gone a bit quiet," I said.

"Hey, that sounds worrying. I'm praying it comes through so I have more quiet time here. Also, just to let you know, Carson will probably be coming over for opening night. He has a gap in his schedule and he's still debating about whether to sign for that romantic comedy that his agent is gagging for him to do. Anyway, I'll keep you posted on that one."

Now, as I rush through a rather putrid-smelling part of Chinatown, I think about how exciting it will be to finally meet Carson Adams.

I arrive at the theatre and announce myself at the stage door. Then I race up the narrow stairs and locate the dressing rooms, which are all still locked. I decide to go back down and wait in the main auditorium, where lots of crew, who are dressed in black trousers and T-shirts, are rigging scenery and lights. I choose a seat and check to make sure I have reception on my phone for when Caroline arrives. I watch people busying around, all engrossed in what they're doing, and at one point a lady with four earrings in one ear and dyed red hair catches my eye. She approaches me, clearly wondering who on earth I am.

"Hi, can I help?"

"Oh hi, I'm Francesca, Caroline Mason's assistant. I'm just waiting for her to arrive."

"Oh, Francesca, hi," she says warmly, extending her hand. "I'm Janice, stage manager. Pleased to meet you. You've got a bit of a wait, I'm afraid. Her call time isn't till eleven today, but I can show you her dressing room if you want and you can wait in there."

Thanks, Caroline. Good of you to let me know, I think, feeling irritated.

When Caroline finally shows up two and a half hours later, she enters the dressing room, which is large and the best the theatre has to offer, and groans.

"God, is this it?" she says, hands on hips.

"It's the best dressing room there is," I say.

She looks as if she's trying to come up with something to challenge this but seems stumped.

"Right, Francesca, I hope you've got a pen handy."

One hour later I emerge from the theatre, dazed and blinking in the strong sunshine, with a list the length of my inner thigh. It starts off simply enough — earbuds, cotton wool, throat pastilles, etc. — and gets more complicated as it goes along until number forty-eight is a special wine fridge and number fifty-two is an air filter. I don't know whether to laugh or cry.

CHAPTER
FOURTEEN

Later on that evening, having purchased roughly a quarter of the items on my list and having spent in the proximity of a thousand pounds already, I find myself on my way to meet Caroline once more, with a new SIM card in my clutches for her mobile. I'm meeting her at a catering company where we are having a tasting of sample canapés for her birthday party.

I'm early so, as instructed, I wait for Caroline outside so that we can go in together. I can only presume that she wants me with her to act as the human equivalent of a comfort blanket. While I'm waiting, I get a call and for once it's one that I'm sure Caroline will actually be pleased about. I'm just finishing it when she arrives a mere fifteen minutes late and breezes straight past me and into the building.

Inside, the caterer has laid out the most amazing array of foods for us to taste. I can't help but notice that Caroline bypasses all the fattening and carbohydratey-type canapés and passes them all my way to taste. Now I understand why I'm here. Never mind *my* cellulite or that *I* might have my ex-boyfriend's wedding coming up. Not that I'm complaining, because they are all absolutely delicious and it will save me from having to stop at Tesco on the way home.

Once the tasting is over and Caroline has finished discussing outrageous prices with the caterer, we leave. Outside, she immediately lights a cigarette and signals for me to get in the car. As soon as we're both in she barks, "Let's have the day's debrief on the way home, shall we, and have you sorted out my phone?" before signalling to Terry to drive on.

I install the new SIM card in the back of her phone and pray to the Lord above that it works. Someone must be listening because it looks like it does, although she grabs it before I've had a proper chance to check.

"Now, what do I need to know?" she snaps.

For the next ten minutes I run through the usual list of who's called and what errands I've run, and I'm just getting to the end of my list as we reach her house.

"From tomorrow I want all this typed up into a daily report and left on the desk at home. Right, let's finish off in the car and then you can both go on," says Caroline.

Terry lives in the same direction as me, so it looks like I might be getting a lift home. What a joy.

I carry on. "So the tuna in olive oil is in the fridge with the rest of your groceries." I wonder if she wants me to write stuff like that down on my report? "I've picked up the scarf from Burberry and your lawyer is talking to *Now* magazine about the . . . um . . . unflattering photograph."

I decide not to mention that the photograph of her with the merest suggestion of cellulite on her thighs is stuck on my fridge at home.

"And guess what?" I continue, keen to move on as I see her face start to thunder at the mere mention of the picture. "Prada want to dress you for the party on the opening night of the play."

It was Prada's PR, a girl called Amanda, who had called me earlier to say that Prada would be no less than honoured to dress Miss Mason.

I wait for her response.

"Really?" she says, her face lighting up for a fraction of a second. Or, at least, it would if only her Botox would let it. "Oh good. Phone them back and tell them I want some of their make-up and see what other freebies you can get out of them."

God, she's unbelievable. I sigh and I think she hears.

"When do they want to do the fitting?" she asks sulkily, narrowing her eyes. She definitely heard.

I consult my scribblings. "Well, they'd like to do it soon, what with the show being so close. They've suggested the twenty-eighth of May and they've offered to fly the head of women's wear over from Milan so that he can do the fitting personally. He's called Paulo."

Even she can't help but sound mildly impressed by this, even though she does her best not to show it.

"Really? Great . . . Well, just make sure that they plan the appointment round my schedule, won't you?" she says, lighting up another cigarette.

I slide down the window in an attempt to preserve my lungs. I had thought she'd want to show a bit more cooperation to her kind clothing benefactors. Personally, I think it's a bit of a coup that they've even offered to dress her just for a poxy party, although I suspect it has a large amount to do with the fact that Carson Adams is rumoured to be flying over for it. Amanda, the PR, asked me at least ten times on the phone whether Carson was going to be there, but since I genuinely don't know yet I've just given her suitably vague answers. I feel like telling Caroline that the real reason Prada are so keen to dress her is to cash in on Carson's popularity, and then maybe she might stop pretending that this is as ordinary an event for her as going to Sainsbury's is for normal people.

"Fittings will have to work round me," she says. "I mean, I'm far too frantic with things like . . . um . . . maybe trying to remember my lines, for a start." She laughs loudly and somewhat menacingly. I am taken aback. I don't think I have ever heard her laugh before and she sounds like Doctor Evil. I stare at her with my mouth open until I realize with a start that she has cracked a joke and that I am expected to laugh too.

I join in feebly.

She is still going ten seconds later as we pull up outside her house. It's all rather alarming and then she stops just as suddenly as she started.

"Ha ha haaaaa . . . Got to go."

And with that, she gets out of the car and slams the door.

Terry catches my eye in the mirror and winks.

She has got the strangest sense of humour, I think as I dial the number for the Prada press office.

22nd May
This might sound faintly slanderous but I do sometimes

genuinely wonder if Miss M is entirely right in the head. She has the weirdest way of expressing everything — humour, emotion, day-to-day social niceties — and sometimes I wonder if she actually functions in the same way as the rest of us. For example, she speaks to her son, who's at school in LA, every night before she goes to bed, but when her housekeeper bought him up in conversation today Miss M was so dismissive. Maybe she couldn't handle talking about him for fear of getting upset and displaying some sort of emotional weakness in front of me? Little does she know how much stronger, warmer and likeable this would in fact make her appear.

I put my pen down for a second and chew thoughtfully on a nail before going to switch my computer on. I open up the file marked "Miss M" and pretty much copy word for word what I've just written in my personal diary, simply changing the sex of the child.

Caroline's dress-fitting takes place a few days later at the Prada headquarters in Sloane Street, straight after rehearsals have finished at six o'clock. Since our initial chat, I have spoken to Amanda at least three times a day and I think she has been somewhat taken aback by the number of requests that have come from our end. There have been demands for free make-up, any handbags that are going and a pair of boots from the new winter collection. Caroline has also insisted that there be champagne available and that it must be Dom Pérignon and that Prada must pick up the bill for her car and driver on that day. To be honest, it's all been excruciatingly embarrassing and I blatantly disobeyed her for the first time this morning when she asked me to ring Amanda and ask her if there might be a spare set of luggage that could come her way.

Terry drops me and Caroline off at Sloane Street and agrees to return in an hour. We enter the building and are met by a very gushy Amanda.

"Hi, Miss Mason, come in. This is such an honour. May I just say on behalf of Prada that we are thrilled you've chosen to wear Prada on your opening night."

Of course she did — it's going free. They chose her. I catch myself — gosh, I'm getting cynical in my old age.

Caroline smiles graciously. "Hello, Amanda. How lovely to meet you. On the contrary, it's me that's delighted. I wouldn't have wanted to wear anything else on my big night. What lovely offices you have here."

"And you must be Francesca?"

I jump as I realize Amanda is talking to me. I was miles away, trying to reconcile the polite, charming woman in front of me with the rude old moo that I usually work for. I have to hand it to Caroline, she can certainly lay on the charm when she feels like it.

"Hi, Amanda," I say finally. "Nice to meet you."

We walk through the offices to the other side of the building, where there is a special fitting room that is specifically used for these sorts of occasions. Inside, the room is luxurious, with the thickest carpet and the most flattering lighting, and a small army of people are lined up waiting for us. It isn't hard to work out which one is Paulo, for he embodies all the stereotypical

133

features you would expect from an Italian designer. If I just say hair, leather and crucifixes, I think you can imagine. He throws wide his arms by way of greeting.

"What a pleasure, Miss Mason. I have always admired you," he says, kissing her hand.

"Oh, you're too kind and I'm so grateful that you've come all the way over from Milan just for little old me. You're all so sweet," she simpers.

I've never seen Caroline in action like this before and as she works her way round the room on full charm offensive I realize that Amanda and the five assistants are all completely taken in. In fact, I suspect that the only one who's really got her sussed is Paulo. I reckon he's seen right through her and is probably a kindred spirit, proving the old adage — it takes one to know one.

Eventually we all run out of small talk, drinks have been fetched (tea for me, Dom Pérignon for her), and it's time to get on with the business in hand.

"If you wouldn't mind slipping out of your clothes, Miss Mason?" asks Paulo, motioning to a curtained partition.

Miss Mason clearly doesn't mind at all because she stays exactly where she is and strips off without a shred of self-consciousness, apparently delighted to have the opportunity to show off her what can only be surgically enhanced breasts to all and sundry. Amanda looks terribly embarrassed, coughs and averts her eyes. Paulo smoulders at her with a look that tells her she's ravishing, his assistants just stare blatantly at her nipples and I sip my tea.

The fitting finally begins and Paulo's team of five all fuss around Caroline in a manner that would probably have me swatting them away like flies, but that she obviously loves. It's an amazing thing to spectate. One is holding bags and shoes up to the frock, one is playing with her hair, one is pinning and two are complimenting and "oohing" and "aahing". Caroline looks absolutely stunning in the gown, which is a sheath of the finest pale peach satin. She remains impervious to all the fuss for quite a while and takes the opportunity to give me more instructions to add to my ever-increasing list and — to Amanda and Paulo's obvious fear and paranoia — to smoke throughout the proceedings.

Once she reaches her boredom threshold though, her instructions become more clipped and a faintly ratty tone starts to creep in. I almost feel glad. Her sweetness and light act was making me uneasy.

"Have you fixed my iPod?"

"Not yet, I haven't had a chance."

"Hmm. We need to send flowers to Pierce Brosnan. Fifty pounds' worth and use Jane Packer."

"No problem. What will the note say?" I ask, scribbling away like fury.

No reply. She closes her eyes, exhaling smoke through her capped teeth. A vision in peach.

"Sorry, what will the . . ."

"I'm thinking."

I wait. My wrist throbs gently. One of Paulo's assistants pokes Caroline with a pin by mistake.

"Ouch, be careful," she snaps.

That mask is slipping, I note gleefully.

She closes her eyes again. "Say this: 'My darling Pierce . . . Let these brighten up what has been . . . a bleak time for us all . . . Let these remind you that we too are like flowers — delicate, in need of food and water . . . in order to survive . . . but in need of love and care to truly live, love always, C.'"

Amanda turns away and I notice that her shoulders are shaking.

Caroline opens her eyes and looks to me for reassurance and general praise for her writing talents. "What do you think?"

What I think is that she sounds stark raving mad and that I hope she's joking, but I find myself saying, "Really lovely."

God, I hate myself.

Half an hour later and Paulo is finally happy with his creation. Caroline gets dressed, making sure everyone gets one last eyeful of her unnaturally perky boobs (I suppose she's got to get her money's worth) and thanks everybody in the room.

Before we leave, Amanda approaches her. "Miss Mason, as a token of Prada's appreciation, we'd like you to have these gifts."

Caroline bestows her with her with the gracious smile she used earlier and grabs the enormous bag of goodies that is given to her. "Oh, Amanda, you are a darling. You're so kind, you really shouldn't have. I mean, I specifically said to Francesca, make sure you don't ask for anything because the dress is such a treat in itself, so I really appreciate it."

136

Amanda raises her eyebrows and looks at me quizzically. I decide it's probably not worth trying to defend myself and my reputation. If nothing else, at least Caroline will be in a good mood now, having got her presents, and at this stage in the day that's all I'm bothered about. Anything for an easy life.

We leave the building with Caroline smiling, waving and blowing kisses at everybody. However, the minute we hit the pavement the smile disappears and gets put back in its play box along with her manners.

"Right, let's see what we've got here then," she says, practically diving into the car. Inside, she rummages feverishly through the vast bag.

"Suede boots, fantastic. Make-up, good. Ooh, a crocodile handbag."

It's like a very expensive version of the *Generation Game*.

"Sandals, though it's a bit late for stuff from this season. Cashmere sweater, very nice. A watch . . . No bloody coat or any luggage then."

I tut.

"Francesca, did you just tut?"

"No." God, did I do that out loud?

"You did. You bloody tutted," she says petulantly. She sits back and regards me crossly for a second, her presents forgotten. I studiously gaze out of the window.

"Aah, I know what's wrong with you," she says.

"Nothing's wrong, Caroline, I really didn't mean to tut."

"No, I know what's wrong. You want a present, don't you?"

I turn round to face her. "Honestly. Caroline. I don't. Really."

"Mmm . . . Well, you can have this lip gloss if you like," she says doubtfully, offering me a gloss from the Prada goodies.

"It's all right, honestly." I can feel myself wanting to laugh for some reason.

"No, take it. I want you to have it," she mumbles, her nose in the air and looking away from me.

Her awkward gesture of generosity is so out of character that I actually feel quite touched and I reach out to accept it graciously.

"OK, thanks. That's really kind."

"I don't like the colour anyway," she adds, ruining the effect slightly.

Traffic is terrible and we don't move far over the course of the next five minutes. Caroline is on her way to Bibendum for dinner with her friend Leticia, who for some reason seems to think that I'm employed to tend to her every whim too. Occasionally I get phone calls saying, "Darling, it's Leticia here and I really want to go for drinks at Century. Can you sort out the guest list for me? I want Caroline Mason plus three." Quite extraordinary. Even more extraordinary is that I always do as I'm told.

I'm glad we're heading in the right direction for me to get home back to Clapham. We come to a complete standstill on the King's Road and Caroline breaks the silence first.

"I've been meaning to say, Francesca, my phone is not working brilliantly again, so I need you to sort it."

My heart sinks.

"If they give you any shit, just tell them who the phone belongs to for Christ's sake. I mean, you know me, I hate using my name to get stuff, but sometimes it's the only language these people understand."

Terry catches my eye in the mirror and we both smirk. She beggars belief. Another gem that I must remember to write down.

"Also, Carson is coming over for my opening night and we'll be staying at the Dorchester for a long weekend. I don't suppose you could work on the Saturday, could you, just to make sure Carson settles in OK?"

I don't believe it. My first opportunity to meet Carson Adams and I can't do it.

"I'm really sorry, Caroline, I can't. I've got a wedding to go to that weekend and it's in the country. Do you remember I told you?"

"Oh right," she says, looking distinctly irritated. "Well, you'll just have to make sure that everything is in place for the weekend then."

"Of course I will," I reassure her, wondering how long Carson Adams is going to be in town for.

Later on that evening, I'm in bed scribbling away in my diary, venting some of the stresses of the day.

28th May
I have now gone right off the idea of meeting Miss M's other half because if the arrangements for his visit are anything to go by then he must be more of a pain in the butt than she is.

139

I don't think travel arrangements for the Prime Minister or the Pope could be more complicated, and if she makes me call Special Services at Heathrow once more to check that he's definitely going to be met from the plane I'll scream.

Jodie, who I've been speaking with on a day-to-day basis, assures me that he's actually really nice and that if it wasn't for Miss M he'd be happy with no fuss, but I don't believe her. After all, when I initially questioned her about the multitude of doctors that Miss M has, her response was, "Well, I just thought you should have everything in case, God forbid, one of her veneers should get damaged or something."

She had a point, but it was the "God forbid" bit that got me and now I question her judgement.

Already I feel better. For me, writing works as a wonderful stress-buster, but now I'm torn between having an early night and doing some more work on my latest chapter of *The Diary of a Personal Assistant*. Despite being exhausted, I think writing is going to win. I've pretty much got the next bit planned out in my head and it would probably be wise to get it all down while it's still fresh in my mind. I suddenly grin as I contemplate how ludicrous my job is at times. Caroline may as well be serving me up chapters on a silver platter.

Earlier on today, for instance, I was walking down the street when my phone went and this is the exact conversation that followed:

"Hi, Caroline."

"Where are you?"

"I'm just about to walk into La Perla to pick up your underwear."

"Don't shout about it on the street," she hissed.

I looked around, trying to locate one person amongst the crowds who was interested in my phone conversation.

"Sorry."

"Listen, once you've picked up the you-know-what, I want you to phone Special Services and — what?"

"I didn't say anything."

"I'm not talking to you. Got to go."

The line went dead. This type of phone call happens quite regularly. She sneaks out of rehearsals to give me urgent instructions and then gets called back in and has to go. It amuses me to think of her performing her lines when her mind is actually concentrating on finding jobs for me. I'm sure the playwright would be delighted to know that, while performing his work, Caroline's mind is firmly focused on British Airways Special Services and buying some new g-strings.

I was at the cash desk paying for her negligee and lace thongs, which were more like cheese wires, when she called back.

"Got to be quick. Call Special Services and tell them that Carson will want escorting to his car."

"I've told them that already."

"Tell them again and then phone the Dorchester and make sure that we're going to get the upgrade on the suite and I want a copy of his itinerary, three hundred pounds for Carson, five hundred for myself and . . ."

"Whose itinerary?" I asked.

"Carson's, of course. Got to go."

Anyway, I shouldn't grumble. As I said, at least she keeps on giving me new ideas for my project and, as a result, it's going rather well . . .

CHAPTER
FIFTEEN

Saturday 6th June dawns dry and sunny and I actually find myself feeling grateful to Harry for choosing this day to get married because it means I have an excuse not to have to see Caroline all weekend. Yesterday I left work for the night having triple-checked all of the weekend's arrangements, and having left out pocket money for Caroline and Carson in envelopes in their suite at the Dorchester. (Seemingly they are incapable of going to a cashpoint themselves.) My initial disappointment about not meeting Carson has evaporated completely and I'm just ecstatic to be having a weekend off and that everything is under control — although I will, of course, be taking my mobile just in case.

For now, though, I turn my attention to what lies ahead.

Today I will be seeing Harry Robinson for the first time since we split up. Today Harry Robinson is getting married.

Abbie's in the sitting room, singing along to the radio as she puts her make-up on in the mirror above the fireplace. She catches my eye.

"You look stunning," she says.

Stunning is probably a bit strong, but even I have to admit that I'm pretty chuffed with what I can see in the mirror. I'm wearing a lovely blue-and-white silk wrap dress that I've had for ages, having managed to resist the temptation to spend money that I should really be saving on something new. How mature am I these days? Having said that, I have splashed out and had a manicure and a pedicure and I can't stop looking at my feet. I'm wearing dainty silver sandals and the pretty pale pink polish on my toes sets them off perfectly. It's nice to think about getting myself ready for a change.

"Cheers, babe. You look gorgeous too. Are you nearly ready? Briggsy will be here in a minute."

I laugh as she turns to give me a look. Abbie knows only too well that Briggsy will try to grope her at some stage this weekend, and she wasn't exactly overjoyed when I mentioned that he was driving. Still, it suits me fine. We'll have a laugh in the car and I know without a shadow of a doubt that driving tomorrow would be a very bad idea, for I will have an almighty hangover. That, I'm afraid, is a given.

Turns out, though, that there's no such thing as a free lift with Briggsy and since he first made his seemingly kind no-strings offer to drive us, he's phoned back a couple of times to negotiate what he'll be getting out of it, apart from the opportunity to ogle Abbie, that is. As a result, I got lumbered with finding and booking a room for us all to stay in, plus paying the deposit.

Having to feel like he's got the best deal or the upper hand in everything is only one of Briggsy's many annoying habits. Others include popping round unannounced, which admittedly he's stopped doing quite so much since Harry dumped me, eating everything that's in the fridge and using our phone to make transatlantic calls to one of his "chicks" in Florida without asking. Briggsy is a DJ and leads a pretty carefree existence.

The wedding is taking place in a small village called Todpuddle at three o'clock and Briggsy has promised us that it won't take more than two and a half hours to get there, but I know full well that he wouldn't exactly be distraught should we happen to miss the service, so I'm a bit suspicious of his calculations. I myself would feel mortified and very rude if we were late, so we've compromised and he's agreed to pick us up at twelve. It's five to now.

"I am ready," says Abbie, applying a last bit of blusher.

"You really do look fab," I say.

She's wearing a cream trouser suit with a lilac camisole underneath, high heels and a big floppy hat.

"Thanks, babe. I'm just a bit worried about where I'm going to keep my fags."

Twenty minutes later and this is the least of our worries. There's still no sign of Briggsy and we have both started to pace around the flat muttering curses. A horn beeps outside.

"Thank God for that," I say, grabbing my clutch bag and pashmina. Precariously, we totter out of the flat as quickly as our heels will allow us to, and into the drive.

"Where the bloody hell have you been?" demands Abbie.

"All right, darlings? I had one or two things to sort out this morning," says Briggsy by way of explanation.

I don't believe for a moment that whatever it is he's been doing this morning couldn't have waited. I get in the front seat.

"Oh, by the way," says Briggsy gleefully, "I saw you on that dodgy advert again the other night. If you've had a prang or . . . what was it? . . . If you've had a prang or a major bang, just call up Claims for . . ."

I'm not in the mood. Besides, I've been choosing to ignore the fact that I've been starting to get one or two looks in the street again recently, which could only mean one thing — the dreaded ad had returned.

"Briggsy, what the fuck are you wearing?" is my not-so-friendly riposte. What Briggsy is in fact wearing is jeans, a T-shirt and a pair of flip-flops that show off his revolting hairy toes.

"Oi oi, Abs, you look a bit tasty, darling," he says, totally ignoring me. So annoying. "Actually, so do you, Fran. Your tits look great in that dress."

I start to get the anxious feeling that I always have when I think I'm going to be late, and then something that's been niggling me for a while suddenly rears its resentful head.

"Actually, I've been meaning to say for ages, Briggsy — I've got a very large bone to pick with you. Why the hell didn't you tell me at any stage that Harry was seeing someone and that marriage might be on the cards? I mean, you must have known and if you'd warned me then it might not have come as quite such a shock when an invite suddenly turned up."

Briggsy looks sheepish, but only faintly.

"Look," he blusters, "if you lot are going to make everything so bloody complicated then I'm afraid that Briggsy just isn't going to get involved."

Briggsy often refers to himself in the first person.

"I mean, would it have really made any difference if I'd told you?"

I don't answer and Briggsy chooses to take my silence as "No, probably not."

"Well, there you are then," he continues. "Besides, I knew if I did say something that I'd just get it in the ear. You've heard the expression 'Don't shoot the messenger', haven't you?" he finishes, giving me a little wink, which for Briggsy is about as close as one is ever going to get to an apology. I decide to forget about it.

"Tell you what though, Fran."

"Yes?" I say, mistakenly anticipating a rare pearl of wisdom.

"I like the sound of you picking my very large bone. You can do that any time you like, don't even have to ask." And with that, Briggsy lets out his trademark very juvenile but incredibly infectious laugh, before reversing out of the drive.

"Right," he says, his arm hanging out of the window boy-racer style. "Where's good for men's suits?"

"Briggsy, you shit," barks Abbie from the back. "We don't have time for this."

I'm glad she's dealing with the situation because I no longer trust myself to speak.

"Chill out. Honestly, look at you both. Have you got your periods or something? Trust me, we've got plenty of time."

I think I hate him. I really do. I also know that if I rise to the bait he'll love it, so I stare fixedly out of the window. Abbie sulks in the back. Oblivious to the hernias he's causing, Briggsy simply pumps the stereo up and drives to Jigsaw for Men on the King's Road. When we get there, he begs us to go in with him and help him choose a suit. Knowing that this will only slow things down even more, I tell him to "Piss off and hurry up."

The sun beats down on to the black roof of the car and Abbie and I start to cook slowly, but still stubbornly refuse to get out. Instead, I verbally annihilate Briggsy while Abbie chain-smokes out of the window. Then we both realize at exactly the same time that in all the hurry we've left our overnight bags at home, sitting by the front door. This does nothing to improve our mood. Bugger it.

Briggsy finally emerges on to the street and, despite everything, I have to bite the side of my mouth to stop myself from laughing. He's wearing a powder-blue suit, which Carson Adams might just about pull off. Briggsy, however, looks ridiculous. His old clothes are stuffed into a carrier bag and he's still wearing the offensive flip-flops.

"Who do you think you are? You look like a pimp," I laugh as he gets into the car.

Abbie snorts. "You're far too much of a lager lout for that suit."

Briggsy's ego is such that you can say things like this and he honestly believes you're joking. He looks at us both, turns up the stereo, winks and swerves out on to the King's Road.

"I'm Briggsy, I look super cool and don't you forget it," he shouts over the beginning of an Ibiza anthem.

Now that we are finally on our way, the mood in the car improves drastically. The sun is shining, the music is loud and Abbie and I relax, mainly because the traffic is unbelievably clear. Briggsy drives all the way to Wiltshire in the manner of someone who has passed their advanced driving test — very fast, but very safely. I am navigating, so it is a small miracle when we only get lost once and I can hardly believe it when we arrive at the church with twenty minutes to spare.

"Was I right, or was I right, ladies?" asks our pimp as he switches off the stereo and then the engine.

"You were right," we concede as we get out of the car, eager to stretch our legs.

I gulp down a lungful of country air. How lovely to be out of London. After the noise of the car, it's nice just to drink in the comparative silence. It's very calming and I can feel all the tension in my shoulders ebbing away as I survey my surroundings. Most of the guests have already arrived and people are chatting away in small groups. The men look handsome in their traditional morning suits and the women look beautiful in their finery. It isn't hard to hazard a guess at which of the female guests are from London and which ones are country folk. I reckon that the townies are the ones who have obviously spent a fortune at the hairdresser's especially for the occasion and who are wearing six-inch heels and rock-star shades, whereas the country girls are wearing dresses that aren't quite so revealing, no shades and big hats.

The church itself is beautiful. Around the entrance, an arch of cream and purple flowers intertwined with green foliage has been created and is giving off a wonderful scent. The ancient grey stone looks stunning against its backdrop of a cornflower blue sky and there's a lovely gentle breeze. It's the perfect day for an English summer wedding and it's blissful to hear only the odd bee buzzing past my ear, birds tweeting in the branches, the gentle murmur of conversation and . . . my mobile.

I scrabble around frantically in my clutch bag.

"Hello?"

"My computer's not working."

"Caroline, hi. What computer?" I ask in a loud whisper.

"My laptop. It's not working," she snarls.

"I didn't know you were planning on taking it to the Dorchester," I say, walking away from the church to avoid the stares that I'm getting from some of the wedding guests. Safely round the corner, away from disapproving looks, I continue. "I doubt it will work there because it's American and the wireless was set up especially at your house."

"Well, what the hell am I supposed to do all bloody weekend?"

I can think of a few suggestions, but they're not ones I should say out loud. I can hear her blowing smoke.

"I need to check my emails."

"Well, just call the concierge and I'm sure they'll be able to find a computer that you can do that on."

I hear a noise that is halfway between a sigh and a snort and then the dialling tone. The woman is unbelievable.

I walk back round the church and spot Briggsy talking to some people who I don't recognize. Abbie sidles up next to me and grabs my hand.

"Are you OK?"

"Yeah, why shouldn't I be?" I ask, putting on my own dark Christian Dior sunglasses.

Abbie resists the temptation to reply "Because you're about to watch your ex-boyfriend get married", and simply says, "You just suddenly looked a bit tense, that's all."

"I'm fine," I reply. And I am, or at least I was until she reminded me that I shouldn't be. I suddenly start to feel a bit nervous about being here. After all, people might find it rather odd and I don't really know how I'm going to feel watching the ceremony unfold before my very eyes. Right this second, though, my overriding emotion is anticipation. I feel a huge lurch in my stomach as I remember that any minute now I am bound to see Harry. I'm glad — I suddenly realize that I've missed him.

My mobile rings. For God's sake.

"Hello," I snap.

"Next week I want you to make sure that my computer works everywhere so that I can take it to hotels. Otherwise there's no point in me having it,"

Caroline hisses, clearly having been stewing since our last conversation.

"Caroline —" I try to remain patient — "can we please talk about this next week? I'm just about to walk into church for a wedding."

"Fine." She puts the phone down.

Thank God Carson will be there soon. Maybe she'll stop ringing me for five minutes. I roll my eyes at Abbie, who by now has grown immune to Caroline's daily barrage of phone calls.

"Look who it is," says Abbie delightedly. She gallops across the grass as fast as her heels will allow her. "Wayne! How are you?"

I follow her at a slower pace, feeling a bit apprehensive. I haven't just missed Harry, I've missed his best friend too. Wayne is wearing full morning dress, which doesn't suit him at all and has very obviously been hired for the day. The trousers are just a couple of inches too short for his six-foot-five frame. He looks pleased to see us.

"Abbie, you old troll, how lovely to see you. And Fran, I almost fancy you in that dress. How are you both?"

"We're great, thanks," says Abbie. "Despite getting a lift with Briggsy, we're actually fine."

"Good." He kisses Abbie on the cheek and then turns his attention to me. "And how about you, my angel? Are you going to be standing up in church to halt the wedding or will you be forever holding your peace?" He looks me straight in the eye.

"Don't be such an idiot. I couldn't care less. I only came for the free booze anyway." I decide to brazen my way through the entire day.

Wayne gives my arm a little squeeze. "That's my girl."

I swallow. "Right, well, we'll see you later. Good luck with your speech. I'm presuming you are best man?"

"Oh yes. Although I think Harry's going to be regretting that," says Wayne.

Abbie laughs. "This is one speech I'm really looking forward to."

"Yes, I'm going to be quite evil," says Wayne seriously. "I intend to lose him any inheritance his parents were planning on leaving him and to have the rest of his family disown him by the end of the day. I've started well because I've already given him a black eye, I'm pleased to say."

"Yeah, right," I giggle. "See you later. Come on, Abs. Let's go and get a seat, shall we?"

It's at least thirty degrees in the sun, so it's pleasant to retreat into the cool of the church. Our eyes take a while to adjust and I wrap my shoulders up in my pashmina. The organ is playing softly and it looks like we're amongst the last to take our seats.

"Bride or groom?" asks an usher, whom I recognize as one of Harry's drinking buddies.

"Groom, please," Abbie replies, taking an order of service. Most of the pews are full, so we squeeze on to the end of one halfway along. Briggsy is two pews down from us and has managed to sandwich himself between two attractive-looking blondes.

I tentatively look down the aisle.

There he is, Mr Harry Robinson. To my dismay, as I study the back of his head, I feel a pang of hurt pride and then something that feels surprisingly like a quick shot of lust. Then again, I suppose when you're the one that's been dumped there's no reason why you would necessarily have stopped fancying someone altogether.

Abbie nudges me in the ribs.

"Ow, what did you do that for?" I whisper agitatedly.

"Because you're staring," says Abbie from out of the corner of her mouth.

I avert my gaze and try to look as if I'm studying the flower arrangements. I sigh. It's all so surreal.

Harry, the man who didn't want any commitment, is waiting to get married. Despite having his back to us, I can tell he's nervous. He is shifting from one foot to the other and staring fixedly ahead.

Just then Wayne walks past us and down towards where his friend is standing. The arrival of the best man seems to indicate that something is about to happen and the congregation all start to shuffle about in their seats. There is a feeling of excited anticipation in the air. Normally this is my favourite bit at a wedding: waiting to see the bride, watching the proud father and the look on the groom's face.

The organist suddenly springs into action and I jump out of my skin. The "Wedding March" echoes around the church and, realizing that his bride is on her way, Harry turns round.

There is a collective murmur as everyone looks at him. Not, I hasten to add, because he looks so devastatingly handsome, although I have to admit he does look good, but because he's sporting a huge black eye. Wayne had been deadly serious.

I turn to Abbie to see if she's noticed too, only to find that she has her sleeve in her mouth and is obviously doing her best not to laugh out loud. I start to grin. Somehow it makes it much easier for me to watch my ex-boyfriend marry someone else when he looks like he's done three rounds with Tyson. Abbie and I nudge each other.

"Nice one, Wayne," I whisper.

Then, like at a tennis match, everyone simultaneously turns the other way round in their seats. This is it. I'm about to see the girl who has managed to tame Harry Robinson enough to make him want to settle down for the rest of his life. The girl who I'm unbelievably curious about and not particularly predisposed to liking very much.

Any second now.

And there she is. Miss Sandy Reed.

As the bride appears in the doorway on the arm of her father, there is a collective gasp from about half of the guests. Again, this has nothing to do with her beauty, although I have to say Sandy Reed is undeniably very beautiful. In fact, she reminds me of a pre-Raphaelite painting, with her tumbling dark-blonde hair. Her dress is stunning (empire line, very romantic and covered in tiny beads and pearls) and her flowers are beautiful. But I digress.

The reason there are gasps is nothing to do with what she looks like or what she's wearing, but everything to do with the fact that Sandy Reed is pregnant. Very pregnant. In fact, she has one of the most enormous bumps I've ever seen.

I suppress a yelp and bite my lip.

My head is spinning as I absorb this new discovery. Sandy Reed is pregnant. There's no mistaking the fact. She definitely isn't just fat. I know because I check over and over again as she makes her way past us and down the aisle. She is unmistakably well and truly up the spout and not just by a few months either. In fact, she looks as if she's about to drop any minute. Another fact that everybody seems to have mysteriously forgotten to bloody mention.

Now I am experiencing a whole range of different emotions: shock, humiliation and amazement, to name but a few.

No wonder Harry got rid of me so sharpish. Not only was he seeing the two of us at the same time, but he must have found out that Sandy was pregnant pretty quickly too. It's a shotgun wedding. The man who claimed to be commitment phobic was not only getting married but was also soon to be a father. It was so farcical it was almost funny.

I look at Abbie. Her arm is still stuffed in her mouth, her shoulders are heaving and tears are falling down her face.

"This is brilliant," she snorts.

Sandy Reed reaches her groom. The organ stops and the vicar begins.

"We are gathered here today . . ."

My mobile rings.

156

CHAPTER
SIXTEEN

I'm sure you already know that one of the most common nightmares is the one where you find yourself naked in a public place. Well, try being at your ex-boyfriend's wedding and having your insane boss call you on your mobile (I just know it's her) during the ceremony and suddenly that scenario doesn't seem so bad any more.

At first, as the lively ringtone echoes into every corner of the building, I have exactly the same thought as the rest of the congregation: "Which stupid pillock has forgotten to switch off their phone?" Then, in one hideous moment, I realize that, of course, the stupid pillock is me and I nearly die on the spot. Two hundred people turn round to stare at me with varying degrees of anger, irritation or pity, and momentarily I consider trying to "style things out" by pretending that it isn't my phone that's ruining proceedings. However, I quickly have to accept that this will never wash as it's blindingly obvious the noise is coming from my bag. The fact that everyone sitting directly around me is slightly edging away certainly doesn't help matters.

"Sorry, sorry, I'm so sorry," I mouth at as many people as I can at once, not quite daring to look in the direction of the bride and groom. My shaking hands finally locate my wretched phone, which by now I am having murderous thoughts about, and switch it firmly off.

One hour later, Harry and Sandy are officially man and wife and I'm still getting over the trauma.

"You two look a bit freaked out. Didn't anyone tell you that the bride had a bun in the oven?" enquires Briggsy, subtle as ever, as he bowls over to where Abbie and I are standing in the church grounds.

"No, *they* didn't," I snap. "And I know that for the first time in God knows how many years you've discovered the art of discretion but, frankly, you could have given us the heads up in the car so we didn't appear quite as shocked."

Briggsy looks a bit taken aback by my tone.

"Don't worry, Briggsy," says Abbie. "Fran's just stressing about her phone going off in the church."

I stand blinking in the bright sunshine. She's right. At this moment, the discovery that Harry not only managed to meet his future wife while dating me, but also managed to get her pregnant, is the least of my worries. For now I need to concentrate more on worrying about the fact that people must think I'm so terribly rude. Bloody Caroline. Even more annoying is the knowledge that at some point I'll have to phone her back and that when I do she'll berate me for putting the phone down on her.

"Oh, don't worry about the phone thing, Fran. It was classic," says Briggsy, doing nothing to ease my pain. Somehow I don't think he'll ever be my barometer for what is and what isn't socially acceptable.

"And maybe I should have filled you in about the bride being up the duff but, you know, I didn't want to upset you. I mean, look how moody you're being now. Though, personally speaking, I think you've had a narrow escape, babe. I mean, Harry's a dark horse, isn't he?" Briggsy continues gleefully. "Married and a kid on the way. Could be you and me one day, Abs, if you play your cards right."

Abbie laughs at his sheer outrageousness and Briggsy chuckles before slapping her on the bum.

Calming down, I glance over to where the family photos are taking place. I don't think the photographer has ever seen such a motley bunch. The groom is grinning from ear to ear but looks like a total hooligan with his black eye on display, and the bride looks as if her going-away car should be an ambulance. I notice with some satisfaction that Harry is at least a couple of inches shorter than his bride, but have to admit that they both seem very happy and certainly don't look as if the act of marriage has been thrust upon them. Thinking about it seriously, the whole notion of a shotgun wedding is rather an outdated one these days, and probably not something that Harry would ever feel compelled to do. Being brave about it all isn't coming totally naturally, if I'm honest.

Just then I feel a large arm round my neck. I don't need to turn round to know who it is.

"Why didn't you tell me, Wayne?"

He comes round to face me.

"What was I supposed to say? By the way, I just thought I'd ring and let you know that not only has Harry done the dirty on you but he's also expecting a baby."

"Something along those lines would have been better than nothing, yes," I say crossly. "Look, it doesn't matter. I've got to go and check my messages now."

"Was that your phone that went off?" asks Wayne, laughing.

"Yes. I was so embarrassed. I'm working for an actress at the moment and she phones me every two minutes."

"Anyone I'd know?"

"Yeah, probably. Caroline Mason?"

"Oh yeah. She was the fit one in *The Love Story*."

"That wasn't her. That was her arch bloody rival, Marina Madson."

I leave Wayne and stalk round to the back of the church where I am out of view, then turn my phone on. There are two new messages.

Message One: "Francesca . . . Francesca . . . Are you there? Francesca . . . Hello — ah, my drinks, at last. You can put them over there . . . Francesca, Francesca . . . Darn it, where is she . . . ?"

Message Two: "Francesca, it's me. I don't know why you're not picking up. Maybe there's no reception? Anyway, on your list for next week can you add a reminder for me that I've seen a T-shirt that I want in Matches. I said that my assistant would pick it up. Got to go now. I'm off to meet Carson at the hotel. Oh, one other thing I need to know: what time does Harrods shut?"

I press delete, make a decision and switch my phone off for the remainder of the weekend.

A couple of hours later and the reception is in full swing. We dine on melon medley, followed by rubbery chicken, all washed down with copious amounts of alcohol. Abbie and I have been seated at the same table, and with the phone incident becoming a distant memory thanks to the contagiously happy atmosphere and all the wine, I start to have a really good time. When the plates are cleared, it's time for the speeches and the crowd, who are all well oiled by now, cheer loudly.

First up, it's the father of the bride, who delivers a sweet but fairly predictable speech. There's no mention of the fact that the happy couple seem to have rather rushed into parenthood or that his new son-in-law ought to have taken better precautions, but he does at least crack a couple of funnies about his daughter's condition. Then it's Harry's turn and as he stands up to a huge cheer I find myself telling my table that I need to go to the loo. Accompanied by plenty of "Oh, what dreadful timing" and "I can't believe you're going to miss the groom", I manage to extricate myself from the table and head for the portaloos. Of course, the truth is, listening to Harry wax lyrical about the girl he was two-timing me for was always going to feel a bit weird and suddenly the prospect of listening to his speech also feels oddly invasive, so I escape and return to my seat ten minutes later under the cover of the thunderous applause that Harry is getting for what must have been his romantic words. As I sit back down, Abbie squeezes my hand, knowing full well that my bladder could never really have timed things quite so aptly.

It's Wayne's turn. He gets to his feet, tings the side of his glass with a spoon and the marquee explodes. This, on the other hand, is one speech I'm really looking forward to. This was going to be good.

"Ladies and gentlemen. I had a few lines prepared but it seems that Harry's sniffed them all . . ."

Later on, when the dancing is in full swing, I leave the marquee for some fresh air. I've already had a lot to drink and I'm aware that I need to try to pace myself slightly. I decide to sit down on the grass for a while. Abbie, however, has other ideas.

"Fran, what are you doing out here on your own?"

"Just having a bit of time out."

"Come on. Let's go and find some nice men. There are quite a few here, you know."

I laugh. "I'm all right, Abs, honest."

"No you're not," she says, plonking herself down next to me and getting grass stains on her cream suit in the process. "You haven't even had a date since Harry and you're always getting bogged down with worrying about work and stuff. Quite frankly, it's time you had a bit of fun. Look, what about him?"

Abbie points towards a man who has just staggered out of the marquee and who also looks in need of a bit of air. I had actually noticed him earlier, but only because he's the only man at the wedding who's wearing black tie. Abbie takes my silence as an invitation to call him over and I cringe as she yells.

"Hey, you. Come over here and meet my friend."

The man looks round, trying to figure out who Abbie's talking to, and when he realizes it's him, he stumbles a few paces nearer. He's quite drunk. He's also tall, I'd say six footish, slim and, from what I can make out, not unattractive.

"Are you talking to me?" he asks, adjusting the black-framed glasses on his nose. He's got nice colouring. His face is quite tanned but his hair is light brown, almost sandy.

"I certainly am," says Abbie. "I want you to meet my friend, Francesca."

"Shut up, Abbie," I mutter, embarrassed beyond belief.

He doesn't seem to share my embarrassment, however, and comes over.

"Hello, Francesca. I'm Tom. It's a pleasure to meet you."

I shake the hand that he has proffered and look up. Now that he's closer I can confirm that he definitely is nice-looking, his shoulders are broad and his face is handsome, albeit in a rather British, dashing type of way. He also has a slight air of eccentricity about him, but that could have more to do with the incongruous tuxedo and the black-rimmed glasses that he's wearing. Still, there's something about him that's making me smile and on first impressions I'd say he's definitely worth investigating.

"Why are you wearing black tie?" I ask.

"Bit of a long-running joke with the lads, I'm afraid. They seem to find it hilarious to ensure as often as they can that I get the dress code completely wrong. Been going on for years and this time they did a bit of a double bluff. Wayne told me it was morning suit, so I assumed it was black tie. Feel a bit stupid, to be honest."

Abbie and I both laugh. At least he wasn't arrogant.

We all grin at each other foolishly for a while and then Abbie gets to her feet.

"Where are you going?" I call after her.

"To the bar," she says, disappearing back into the tent, leaving the two of us alone and suddenly awkward.

Tom eventually clears his throat. "Would you like to dance, Francesca?"

"Why not?" I say shyly.

Four hours later and I am drunk. Drunk and happy. I have spent the entire time with Tom and we have had a riot. We have danced non-stop, drunk countless glasses of wine, champagne and beer, and we've talked and talked and talked.

We are currently taking a break from our exertions on the dance floor and doing some more talking.

"Do you know the wonderful thing about tonight, Francesca?"

"What's that?" I ask.

"Well, we've talked all night and still haven't had to discuss what it is we 'do'. I take this to be a very good sign."

"So do I," I agree. "Except that now you've just made the question inevitable."

"I suppose I have, haven't I? Well, I'm a vet."

I start to laugh.

He looks slightly offended. "There's no need to laugh. It's not that funny."

I recover and grin at him. "I know it's not. It is surprising somehow, but it's not funny at all. It's just that when I was a kid, I was desperate to be an actress and the idea of me being permanently skint and unemployed absolutely petrified my father, so he always used to go on about me becoming a vet when he was trying to give me an example of a stress-free and solid career."

"So he wasn't exactly a pushy dad then?"

"No, quite the opposite. It wasn't that he didn't encourage me, it's just that he was fairly realistic about how much most actresses or presenters work."

"And was he right?"

"Well, sort of, I suppose. Actually, that's a lie. He was entirely right seeing as I've never actually earned enough from acting to be able to call it my main income. Ironically, I'm working for an actress at the moment as her personal assistant. Caroline Mason, actually."

"Should I know who she is?" asks Tom.

"Well, she's Carson Adams's girlfriend," I offer as way of explanation. The more I get to know Caroline, the funnier I am finding it when people don't have a clue who she is. She's obviously not quite as A-list as she likes to think she is.

"Oh, right. Well, I know who he is," says Tom. "Though I can't say I'm a major fan of his films. I'm more of an old movie buff myself."

I giggle again. I'm not laughing at him; it's just that it's so unusual to meet a guy who uses words like "movie buff". Not only is he quite gorgeous, but he also has more character than anybody I've met in ages.

"So what's it like then, working as a PA?" asks Tom.

I mull the question over. Where to begin?

"It has its moments. Caroline is a bit of a taskmaster and can be rather rude and out of touch with normality at times, but then nothing about the world she inhabits is quite real so it's not altogether surprising. On the whole, though, I like it. It's fascinating to see how the other half live and to some degree be a part of such an exciting and glamorous world. The money's pretty decent and most of the time I find Caroline hilarious to be around. In fact, I do quite a bit of writing as a hobby and at the moment I seem to find myself desperate to write about what's happened pretty much on a daily basis, so it definitely isn't dull."

There's a comfortable silence. I glance at Tom. He's regarding me with a smile on his face. Then, from out of nowhere, he strokes my cheek and surprises me by saying, "Sounds like you've got stars in your eyes, Francesca."

It's such a strange thing to come out with, having only just met me, that I have to check to make sure he's

166

not teasing me. He looks perfectly serious though and I realize that he wasn't being judgemental. He was just making a statement. I look down at his hands. They're nice and brown and smooth, but in a manly way. Unsure of how to react to what he's just said, I swerve having to do so.

"What's your favourite film then?" I ask.

The answer to this question is crucial. It could mean the difference between me deciding that I definitely fancy him or going off him altogether.

"My favourite film is a film you probably haven't seen. It's called *It's a Wonderful Life*."

By the time Tom asks me if I want to step outside for a breath of fresh air, I have decided that I want him to kiss me.

We sit on the damp grass and talk for a further ten minutes before finally he looks me in the eye. I notice through his glasses that his eyes are a lovely grey-green colour and then we kiss. It's a great kiss — very passionate and very long. It's a while until we come up for air and when we do it's obvious that we're both aroused. Tom is out of breath and I think his glasses have actually steamed up a bit.

I tell him this to break the ice.

"I'm not surprised." He grins. "That was quite a kiss. Come on, you, let's go back for some more dancing."

Just as he says this, the DJ puts on "Sex Bomb" by Tom Jones and Tom grabs my hand. Then we do that awful thing that everyone does at weddings, where we half dance to the dance floor, neither of us being entirely sure whether to start freaking out now while on our way to the dance floor in a half-dance, half-run manner, or whether to wait until we reach the appropriate place for dancing, that being the black-and-white floor, and then begin. Anyway, we get there one way or another and, when we do, we dance for ages and I can't wipe the huge beam off my face that seems to have appeared. I feel as if I'm dancing really well, with a good variety of moves — a sure sign I've drunk too much. At some point Abbie joins us, clearly delighted that for once her matchmaking seems to have worked. I yell to Tom over the sound of the Nolans' "I'm in the Mood for Dancing" that I'm going to the bar and he gives me a thumbs-up.

I weave my way through the crowd and walk slap bang into Harry.

We stare at each other for what seems like ages and then both speak at the same time.

"You first," I say.

"It's good to see you, Fran. I'm really glad you came. Come to the bar with me?"

At the bar, armed with a fresh drink, I come out with the question I've wanted answered for weeks.

"So come on then, when did you meet Sandy?"

Harry looks pained. "Fran, don't. I'm so sorry that I mucked you around, but when I met Sandy I was just bowled over and I didn't know how to tell you. I know I took the coward's way out but . . ."

I come to his rescue. He's suffered enough and, besides, it doesn't matter any more.

"Harry, don't worry. It's fine. I didn't spend too many nights crying into my pillow, to be honest. I've just missed you and I hope I can finally take you up on your offer of being friends."

Harry grins and raises his glass. "To friendship. If it makes you feel any better, Wayne gave me a really hard time for ages."

"Did he?" I'm touched. "Yeah, I have to admit that does help. So when's Harry or Harriet Junior due?"

"Only a few weeks left to go, actually," says Harry, looking really proud. "It's been a bit of a race against time to get the wedding organized so quickly, what with everything happening so fast and . . ." He trails off, looking sheepish.

"Harry, don't worry. It's fine, really. I can see how happy you are and I'm glad. Sandy's obviously an amazing girl." To my delight and surprise as I'm saying this I realize that I actually mean it. Today has been a confusing mixed bag of emotion, but it's all good really. "I'm also touched that you invited me and Abs today."

Harry gives me a look I can't work out.

"What?"

"You're a great girl, Fran, which is why I wanted you here today. And maybe it'll be me feeling happy for you soon — I saw you with Tom earlier and you looked like you were getting on really well."

I wish I didn't blush so easily.

"Oh, you know what it's like at weddings — everyone gets on with everyone. Anyway, shouldn't you be getting back to your wife?"

"Yes, I suppose I should. I'm so glad we had this chat, Fran."

Harry walks away.

"Harry?" I call after him.

"Yes, Fran?"

"There's something I never asked you."

"What's that?"

"What's your favourite film?"

"What a funny question," he says, looking baffled. "Um, I don't know . . . probably the *Die Hard* movies, I suppose."

I laugh and go to walk away but, as ever, Harry has to have the last word.

"Thanks for the wedding present, by the way."

What does he mean by that? I haven't got him a wedding present yet. Shit, how embarrassing.

"Um, I was going to get you something and give it to you when you get back from your honeymoon," I say, not having forgotten the art of improvisation.

"Honestly, don't bother, Fran. My present came gift-wrapped and delivered courtesy of my TV only last night, when your truly incredible advert came on and your dulcet tones started screeching round my room: 'If you've had a prang or a major bang . . .'"

I don't answer because there's no point, but as I walk away I'm grinning.

CHAPTER
SEVENTEEN

My hangover is so bad it actually wakes me up. My head is throbbing and I can't work out where the funny aroma is coming from. I gingerly open one eye and then the other. I've got a half-eaten tuna sandwich on my face, which explains the smell, and I am lying fully clothed on the floor of my hotel room.

There are three mounds lying in the bed that I organized, booked and paid for and yet seem to have missed out on. I stand up, brushing flakes of dry tuna off my face and trying not to retch. I take the kettle to the bathroom, fill it up at the sink and then plug it in. The mounds in the bed stir and I go to inspect. Briggsy is in the middle and, on either side of him, are two blonde girls. I am grateful to see that they, too, are fully clothed.

"Morning," says Briggsy, with his eyes still shut.

"Thanks for taking up the whole of the bloody bed last night, Briggsy. I woke up on the floor," I say, battling with how much my head is thumping.

Briggsy chuckles.

"What?" I say as I rip open a sachet of coffee and a little tub of Coffee-Mate.

"You could have got in if you wanted, but you were so hammered you just passed out after room service arrived with your sarnie."

Bits and pieces start coming back to me.

"Shit."

"Keep it down, Fran. I've got a terrible headache."

I rush over to Briggsy.

"Briggsy, I don't want any joke answers or I'll have to kill you. Did I or did I not have a conversation with my boss last night?"

"Hee hee," Briggsy chuckles again. "Yes."

"Yes I did, or yes I didn't?" I ask in vain, knowing full well what the truth is but willing it to be wrong.

"You did. You switched your phone on when we got back here and she rang, and she was banging on and on and on and on. You were laughing so hard you couldn't talk, so you passed the phone to me."

I sit on the floor with my head in my hands.

"She was well stressed and said she needed to speak to you because she couldn't find something you were supposed to have packed. Anyway, I had a chat with her and she was fine."

"What was I doing?" I ask weakly.

"Your sandwich turned up and you were more interested in that than speaking to her."

"Oh God," I moan. "What did you tell her?"

"I just gave her a bit of the famous Briggsy charm. I said that you couldn't come to the phone because you were in the middle of something and that you'd call her another time. Then I thought I'd butter her up a bit, so I told her I thought she was great in *The Love Story*."

172

I can't bear it.

"Who's in bed with you?" I mumble, my head still resting in my hands.

"I'm Tricia and that's my sister, Claire. We're Harry's cousins," says one of the girls sleepily, her head still buried in the pillow. "Was that *the* Caroline Mason you were talking to last night?

"Yes." I nod weakly.

Just then someone hammers on the door. I go to open it, half expecting to see a furious Caroline on the other side. Luckily, it's Abbie, whose hangover hasn't kicked in yet. She's in very high spirits and has obviously enjoyed a night of lust with some unsuspecting soul. She tells us that everyone is meeting in a pub down the road for lunch and we decide to go there. I spend a good ten minutes looking for my overnight bag before remembering that, of course, I've left it at home. God, I'm horrifically hungover. I peel off my once beautiful dress that is now creased and covered in grass stains and bits of dried tuna, have a quick shower and then have to put it back on again, which feels and smells pretty gross.

As we march to the pub, I wonder if Tom will be there and despite my anxiety about Caroline I feel really excited about seeing him again — not that I'd ever admit this in front of Briggsy.

As soon as we walk in the door, I spot him. He's standing at the bar, still wearing his black tie, and I realize I've got that silly butterfly feeling in the pit of my stomach. Even in the sober light of day he still looks really fanciable, which is a relief, and I give him my most winning smile. However, to my crushing disappointment he turns away and hardly even looks at me.

"Do you think he's ignoring me because I look such a state?" I ask Abbie, who I've just noticed has a footprint on the back of her cream jacket. I won't ask.

"No, you look fine. Maybe he's shy?" says Abbie unconvincingly.

We find a table and Briggsy goes to the bar to get some drinks. I look towards Tom again and, when I'm positive he's looking my way, I tentatively wave, but he just looks straight through me as if I don't even exist. It's the height of rudeness and the sort of behaviour I would only expect from a lad of seventeen or below, and even then I would class it as pathetic. "I can't quite believe I'm having to say this, but I think I've just been 'blanked'," I say incredulously to Abbie, trying to mask how bitterly disappointed I feel.

Abbie doesn't reply, which means she must agree, and she proceeds to shoot filthy looks in Tom's direction.

Briggsy returns to the table with our drinks. I glug back my Diet Coke and tell him and Abbie that if it's all right with them I'd really like to leave. Due to the fact that their hangovers are just starting to really kick in, thankfully they feel the same way. They drain their glasses and we gather our stuff together. It's only as I'm walking out of the door that Tom calls my name.

I turn round.

"I'll call you?" he says, making phone gestures.

I give him a look that I hope is suitably evil and walk out of the door. Maybe it was just the booze that made everything feel so wonderful last night.

I can't face phoning Caroline. I'm too hungover and too morose, so I keep my phone switched off. I decide that I'll arrive at work promptly in the morning and face the music then.

CHAPTER
EIGHTEEN

I don't officially start work until ten o'clock, but this morning I arrive at the house at nine on the dot and let myself in. I pick up the post and then go straight to the study, where I ring Caroline's mobile knowing full well that she will still be at the Dorchester. I decide that the best tactic is to pretend nothing out of the ordinary has happened in the hope that she will have forgotten our drunken chat. Doubtful.

Thankfully, I get her voicemail — anything to postpone actually having to speak to her.

"Morning, Caroline. It's Francesca here. I'm glad your phone's off because hopefully that means you're having a good rest before your big night tonight. Everything's under control and I'll speak to you when you wake up. Bye."

Good, I've got that over and done with. I start to wade my way through the faxes that have come through in the course of the weekend.

"Hi, you must be Francesca."

I jump out of my skin and gasp as I spin round and come face to face with Carson Adams, who's wearing nothing but a small white towel.

Jesus Christ. He is gorgeous. Nothing could have prepared me for the effect of being in the presence of arguably the best-looking man in the world. Pictures don't do him justice. I have literally gone weak at the knees and I feel like I did when Mum took me to a Curiosity Killed the Cat concert when I was twelve and I screamed throughout it. I want to squeal and yelp and just generally lose control. Obviously I can't, though, because I'm twenty-nine and I work for him, so I make every effort to get a grip. Still, I am positively grinning as I take in his tanned biceps, smooth chest and the first six-pack I've ever actually seen in real life. And that's all before you take into account his tousled dark-blond hair, piercing blue eyes and chiselled features. This must be how women are supposed to feel when they're watching male strippers, but never really do. Marvellous.

He must be used to his devastating impact upon women because he doesn't seem at all fazed by the fact that I am staring with my mouth open, and he crosses the room to shake my hand.

"I'm Carson Adams. Pleased to meet you."

His near-nakedness is now only inches away from me. It's all a bit overwhelming and I'm struggling to cope. However, feeling very odd, I manage to shake his gorgeous hand and finally find my voice.

"Hello, Carson, pleased to meet you. I'm Francesca. I thought you were staying at the Dorchester." I suddenly realize that I have backed up against the desk and am clutching my files to my bosom, which is actually heaving. I readjust my stance into something less wanton, smooth down my skirt and wish I'd washed my hair this morning. Suddenly I love my job.

"Oh, yeah . . . we were, but I woke up really early and thought I'd give Cas a bit of space today, it being her first night tonight and all. Besides, I hate hotels. I'd much rather be at home, you know?"

"Oh yeah, sure," I say as if I casually book suites at the Dorchester and then don't use them all the time. I flick my hair over my shoulder, an entirely reflex action.

Carson marches out of the room. "I'd better go get dressed, I guess."

It takes all my strength not to yell, "Nooooo, I don't want you to," run after him and just hug him. I have never been affected so strongly by a man's physical presence in my life. Lucky, lucky Caroline. No wonder she's prepared to wear cheese-wire thongs.

I pull myself together. This won't do. I can't start lusting after my boss's boyfriend, even if it *is* Carson Adams. I can't wait to phone the girls.

My mobile rings.

"Hello?"

"Francesca, it's me."

"Oh hi, Caroline. Are you OK?" I answer brightly, still flushed with excitement.

"Yes, I'm fine. Why shouldn't I be? Now, I'm not particularly happy with your conduct at the weekend but I'm prepared to overlook it because I've got far more important things to worry about today."

"Yes, I'm very sorry about that. I was a bit . . ."

"Yes, well, we don't need to go into all of that. Just make sure that I have your full attention this week and that you have your wits about you because there's a lot to do. Now, what time are Prada arriving at the theatre to dress me?"

"Prada, Jimmy Choo and De Beers are arriving at five o'clock to make sure you're all sorted out and happy before the show starts. Your car is organized to take yourself and Carson to the party and your three pairs of house tickets have all been sorted out."

"Right. Well, I think the best plan is if you meet me here at the Dorchester at two o'clock and you can travel with me to the theatre and we'll go from there. Are my waxer, hairdresser and make-up artist all set?"

"Yes," I confirm, still feeling post-coital and silly from my encounter with Carson and smothering an impulse to shout "sir" and salute.

"Good. Make sure that Carson's haircut is still happening at three o'clock too. Also, I need you to organize four bottles of Cristal, another four bottles of Chablis and a case of mineral water for my dressing room."

Careful, all that liquid and you'll be needing the loo all night, I think. Stop it, Francesca.

"Will do, and I can tell Carson about the arrangements for his haircut now."

"Why, have you got his number?"

I'm confused. "No, he's here."

There is a long pause. "Of course. See you at two."

Something occurs to me. I think they might have had a row and that Carson probably ended up staying here last night, which would explain the general air of confusion and why Caroline doesn't sound sure of his whereabouts at all. Maybe he had to get away from her neuroses, which are on red alert with tonight looming. This wouldn't surprise me in the least bit. I think if I were Carson I would rather keep away too. Anyway, I feel as if I've got off lightly for my behaviour at the wedding.

Lorna pokes her head round the door. "Morning, Fran. How are you? Did you have a lovely wedding?"

"Yes thanks, Lorna. Carson's here, by the way," I say, rushing over to her excitedly to impart this delicious piece of information.

"Oh great," squeals the older lady in obvious delight, running out of the room to find him without so much as a backward glance. I don't blame her. Her voice travels up the hall.

"Carson, my darlin'. Where are you? . . . Ooh, look at you now. Don't you look well?"

I agree. I agree. I get up and follow the sound of the noise to the kitchen. Carson seems equally pleased to see Lorna and they hug and then chatter away nineteen to the dozen. For an odd moment I feel quite jealous of her ability to be so normal around him and of their obvious mutual affection for each other. This is highly irrational though, and I silently admonish myself. Pushing away such silly thoughts, I concentrate on being grateful for the fact that he is clearly a nice guy and not going to be too much of an added nightmare. He's definitely not cut from the same cloth as his girlfriend, I can tell that much already. Caroline never really talks to Lorna unless it's to bark orders at her, which is criminal considering how many years Lorna's been looking after her when she's in London, whereas

180

Lorna and Carson, on the other hand, seem to have a much stronger bond than your average cleaner — employer relationship.

Carson, who sadly has now put on a T-shirt, spots me standing in the doorway.

"Come in, Francesca. Lorna and I are just going to have a cup of tea — do you want one?

"Oh, er, lovely, thanks," I simper, before realizing with a jolt that it was probably less of an offer and more of a request. I stop leaning on the doorway and fiddling with my hair and straighten up. "But of course I'll make the tea."

"No, don't be silly," he says, flashing me his megawatt smile that alone justifies his twenty million dollars a movie fee. "I'll make it."

And he does. Carson Adams is making me a cup of tea. "Um, Carson," I begin hesitantly. "Caroline asked me to make sure that you know about your haircut this afternoon. It's at three o'clock and Daniel Galvin's coming here."

"Oh, great. Thanks for that."

He just said "thank you". I think I'm in love. I accept a cup of tea but don't feel comfortable enough to sit down and join in. I would hate for him to start questioning what I was doing in his house other than standing around gawping at him, so I busy myself with checking the contents of the fridge, as I have to do on a daily basis anyway. While I do so I listen to Carson and Lorna's easy banter. He tells her about his latest movie and how "Julia" was really nice to work with. She regales him with tales of how her niece is currently going through IVF, which is a terrible business, and how her bunions are playing up. Their lifestyles may be light years apart but they chatter away, clearly relishing each other's company, and it turns out that there is one subject they're both united on. When Lorna asks, "How's the little lad?" Carson's face really lights up. He's clearly a besotted father.

"Did you know that Lorna's daughter, Steph, looks after my son?" asks Carson.

I'm just finishing my shopping list and it takes me a second to register that he's talking to me.

"Oh no, I didn't realize Steph was your daughter, Lorna," I say, wondering if I've got any make-up in my bag that I can hastily slap on. "I guess that explains why you two know each other so well then."

Lorna reaches out for another Rich Tea. "That's right. I've been working for Carson here for years, haven't I, Carson? And my daughter, Steph, has been little Cameron's nanny since he was born."

"Oh, that's lovely," I say. "Is there anything either of you need from the shops because I'm going out now?"

"No, I'm fine, thank you," says Carson.

"You couldn't get us a free-range, organic chicken, could you, love?" asks Lorna. "Her Highness phoned from the hotel and she wants me to roast another for her to have cold for lunch tomorrow, although why I don't know, when she never eats any of it," she finishes, rolling her eyes and shrugging her shoulders.

Shocked, I look from Lorna to Carson to gauge his reaction, but he doesn't seem to mind the fact that Lorna has just been fairly rude about his woman.

182

"No worries," I tell Lorna. I'm always happy to help her out and hate the fact that Caroline expects her to trek for miles to buy her stuff when she knows full well that Lorna's arthritis is playing up.

"She's a good girl is our Francesca," says Lorna, who I could kiss.

As I cruise the supermarket aisles looking for, amongst other things, wheat-free bread, organic salmon, organic pineapple chunks and the chicken, I digest the fact that I have just met one of the biggest stars in the world. I wish he was staying in town longer, but sadly he's going straight to the airport after the party. It's not surprising so many celebrity relationships hit the rocks. Their schedules simply don't allow them to spend any time together.

It intrigues me that Jodie was right. Carson really does seem like a nice guy, so what the hell is he doing with a freak like Caroline?

My mobile rings.

"Hello."

"Hi, is that Francesca?"

"Speaking." Oh great, they've got the brand of honey she wants. That saves me from having to make a separate trip to Harrods food hall.

"Francesca, it's Tom. We met at Harry's wedding."

Oh.

"Francesca?"

"Hi, I'm here. How are you?" I ask politely. He was the last person I was expecting to be on the line.

"Fine, thank you. How are you?"

"Fine."

"I'm sorry I didn't get a chance to speak to you at the pub yesterday."

"Don't worry about it," I say, determined to sound as offhand as is humanly possible, though secretly I'm surprised that he's bothered to phone at all.

"Right. Well, I was just wondering if you'd like to have dinner on Friday?"

"Um, I can't do Friday," I lie.

"Oh, that's a shame. What about Saturday?"

"No, can't make Saturday either," I say primly, still smarting from the humiliation of being ignored in the pub.

"I see. OK, well, maybe I'll call you another time then?"

"Yeah. Why don't you . . . If you want."

"Right."

"Right."

"Bye then."

He sounds genuinely disappointed, but I'm pleased with myself for standing my ground. It was so rude of him to ignore me.

Still, I feel a bit mean as I load up the trolley with bottle upon bottle of mineral water and, if I'm honest, a touch regretful as we had got on so well at the wedding. Had I been slightly more prepared for his call I doubt I would have been quite so rude. In fact, if I think about it, I suppose the very fact that he called must mean he can't be that bad. Oh well, hopefully he'll call again. I try to ignore the growing sense of regret that I'm feeling. Right, puy lentils and then I'm done.

At the cash desk I forage around in my bag for the washbag that doubles up as a purse that I use for all Caroline's purchases. It has to be this size to fit in not only all the banknotes, but also the mounds of receipts that I acquire on a daily basis. When I eventually stagger out of the supermarket, weighed down by bags, I try to hail a cab to my next shopping destination, which is Dixons to buy her a new adaptor for her iPod to see if that works. I also need to find somewhere that hasn't run out of wretched free-range, organic flipping chickens.

Caroline is fine about me getting cabs when I need to; only problem is, no cab appears, so I realize that I'll have to struggle back to the house to dump this lot off before buying anything else from my other lists. If only I'd known on that fateful day when I first met Caroline what qualities I'd really need in order to do this job well — arms like a navvy and biceps like Popeye. In case you're interested in what other qualities are needed to be a first-class celebrity PA, I'll tell you. It is imperative that you have an obsession with lists, a head like a Yellow Pages and a degree in fashion. Incredible skills in diplomacy are a must, as is a built-in bullshit radar. Due to my obsession with lists, let me also say that, should you be thinking of becoming a personal assistant to someone like Caroline, make sure you've done "The Knowledge", that you have close relations working at the airlines and all the local councils and that you have a degree in the inner workings of a mobile phone and computers. Much of this is what one would expect a top PA's life to involve, but what I didn't anticipate was the fact that all of the above would have to be carried out with a sense of disproportionate urgency and that my insides would feel permanently wound up like a coiled spring. Also, that I'd be constantly stressing not about what I'm doing, but what I need to be doing next.

I stop for a minute to give my arms a break and to readjust the bag handles so they're not cutting into my hands quite so painfully.

Recently I have come to strongly suspect that Caroline is preparing for an apocalypse. She stockpiles everything and I have become completely used to buying in bulk. Why buy one Diptyque candle when you can buy five? Two bottles of Evian? Don't be so ridiculous. Buy three cases and make sure that at least ten bottles are in the fridge at any given time. (She also seems to think her fame elevates her above having to consider issues like recycling or chancing her life by drinking water from — shock, horror — her tap.)

Twenty minutes later and I've made it back to the house, but have to sit on the bottom step for a minute before even attempting to climb the rest of them. Once I've finally got my breath back, I relay the bags up the steps one by one till they're all gathered on the porch. I still remember to run my hands through my hair though, before letting myself in, so Carson doesn't catch me looking a total mess.

I can hear his voice. He must be on the phone in the study and from the sound of it he must be talking to Caroline.

"Hey, baby . . . I love you too, so much it hurts. I can't wait to be with you again, you know that."

I grin to myself as I hurry quietly down the corridor. They've obviously made up then. It's quite sweet really.

I'm just putting the Evian away in the fridge when my mobile goes.

"Hello?"

"Francesca, it's me. I need you to bring my silver Manolos with you to the Dorchester in case I don't like the Choos, OK?"

She didn't waste any time savouring her sweet nothings, I think ruefully.

"No problem."

I wander into the hall to get the last of the shopping bags while she launches into a lecture about who I am allowed to give house tickets to and who I should avoid at all costs should they ring. I'm not listening, however, as I've been distracted by the fact that Carson is still on the phone in the study.

"It won't be long before I'm back with you and you'll have my full support. God, I miss you, honey. OK . . . love you too, so much, bye."

I scuttle back into the kitchen with Caroline still droning on in my ear.

"So, Francesca, have you got that? Anna Wintour's a 'yes'. Anybody from any other magazine who claims to be my best friend is a 'check with me'."

"OK, fine. I'll see you later and I'll bring the shoes," I say, but there's no time for feeling shell-shocked as I have a call waiting.

I'm just fielding a call from a man who claims to "go back a long way" with Caroline and who wants house tickets for next Thursday week, when Carson cheerfully breezes into the kitchen with a shopping bag in his hand.

"You left this in the hall," he mouths at me.

"Thanks," I mouth back, grabbing it. I turn round so I don't have to meet his eye. As much as Caroline annoys me, I feel really sad for her that her long-term lover is clearly cheating on her. I must be so naive, and I hate the fact that I feel let down and disappointed. They are supposed to be one of the strongest couples in Hollywood and yet, despite his easy charm and down-to-earth persona, Carson is a walking cliche. For God's sake, is nothing sacred?

"Look, I'm sorry, all right?" I snap, interrupting the person on the other end of the line. "I haven't got my file in front of me and, to be honest, most of the tickets have gone. Who did you say you were again? . . . Oh . . . Sir Ian McKellen. Right. Um, why don't I take your number and get back to you? I'm sure I can sort something out."

I put the phone down sheepishly on Sir Ian, amazed that he has the ability to actually use his initiative and pick up a phone at all. Everybody else always gets their assistants to ring.

"Are you all right, Francesca? You look really pissed," enquires Carson, looking slightly alarmed. I suppose I have been crashing around the kitchen a bit; still, there's no need to accuse me of drinking.

"I haven't had a drop actually and doubt I will until after Caroline's performance, when I shall have some champagne to celebrate her brave return to the stage."

Carson looks baffled. "Great. I didn't realize she'd got you a ticket."

"She hasn't," I answer hotly. "I shall be at home by then but, you know, loyalty and all that."

"Right, good. OK, well, have a good time."

Suddenly I hope I haven't overstepped the mark. I do want to make a point but at the same time, seeing as I hardly know the man, I don't want to be rude.

Carson is staring at me, his expression quizzical.

"Well, let me know if you need me to get you anything, or anything else . . ." I mumble as I scurry out of the room, cheeks flaming.

CHAPTER
NINETEEN

8th June

All is not as it seems at first glance into the world of Miss M. Maybe having a partner who is so ridiculously handsome that on a good day he even makes George Clooney look a bit plain isn't such a great thing after all. I don't know why, but I've been really affected by Mr X's betrayal and feel terribly let down. I must be a total sucker to believe what the stars' big PR machines feed us. Anyway, it's also got me thinking more than ever that, when it comes to my book, I must be awfully careful as the feelings of real people are at stake.

There's a very fine line between making a comment on the life of a famous actress and the professional equivalent of a kiss and tell. So I'm not going to include anything that could possibly flag up the true identity of Miss M and Mr X or that sounds like their relationship. Therefore in the book Mr X is average-looking with pock-marked skin that he covers up with camouflage make-up. Miss M will still be beautiful, but the whole thing will now be based in Hollywood and will centre on Miss M preparing for a film role as well as the relationship between her and the beleaguered PA.

On the way into work the next morning, I check some of the papers in the newsagent's and I'm relieved to see that Caroline's reviews seem to be pretty good. As usual, I walk the extra ten minutes to Starbucks to get her coffee and arrive at the house at ten on the dot. Lorna opens the door to me just as I'm putting the key in the lock.

"Fran," she says, looking both ways down the street and then beckoning me in.

"Morning, Lorna. How are you? Is everything OK?" I ask.

"She's acting very strange this morning," Lorna confides to me in a stage whisper, tapping one side of her head with her finger. "She hasn't even been to her gym lesson."

"Really?" I say. This is unusual. Caroline never misses a training session.

I take off my jacket and hang it on the coat-stand and it's only when I turn round that I notice what it says on Lorna's T-shirt. The "Shit Happens" slogan looks completely at odds with the rest of her M&S ensemble. Lorna definitely dresses to live and not the other way round.

"She got in at four o'clock in the morning," she tells me, leaning on the vacuum and placing her other hand on her hip. Lorna's obviously been pretending to clean the hall for ages so that she could lie in wait for me as I arrived.

I am just about to respond to this gossip when Caroline flings open the kitchen doors and half runs towards me. She's still in her silk pyjamas and dressing gown and seems to be in a state of high excitement, and possibly still a bit drunk. Carson may have had to leave the party early last night, but that obviously didn't prevent her from having a good time.

"Good morning, Francesca darling," she says, beaming at me beatifically.

Darling? Definitely still drunk.

"Morning, Caroline. Congratulations, your reviews are amazing.

"They are, aren't they?" she says, hugging her gown around herself. I notice she hasn't taken her make-up off yet.

"I've done it. I was amazing!" she yells, flinging her hands in the air and then skipping back to the kitchen for further examination of the papers, which have all been couriered round by good old Kenneth.

Nobody over the age of fifteen should ever skip.

Lorna and I follow her, exchanging looks all the way and nudging each other. I've never seen such a huge mound of papers as the one that's on the table.

"Here's your coffee, Caroline."

"Thank you, Francesca," she says, reaching out for it.

I nearly drop it in shock. Caroline Mason just said "thank you"; this is an historic occasion. Lorna and I raise our eyebrows at each other simultaneously. We watch as she picks up another review and contentedly drinks in every word of praise for her performance.

Just then, her publicist rings me on my mobile.

"Hi, Kenneth," I answer merrily.

"Ssh. Don't say it's me if you're with her," he hisses.

"Oh right. OK, um . . . well, I am," I say, unsure of how I should answer.

"Don't let her see the *Independent*. Whatever you do, just hide it. Get rid of it," he pleads desperately.

His timing is bad. She's just picked it up and her good mood evaporates in a cloud of disgust. "Bastards!" she screams.

The phone goes dead.

Lorna looks at me, clearly petrified, and starts to wash the same dish and cup that she just finished washing.

"Um, I tell you what, Caroline. Don't bother with that one, eh?" I offer nervously.

"Why? What are you trying to protect me from?" she says, scanning it furiously.

I'm not trying to protect her from anything. It's me and Lorna I'm worried about. It's too late though. Caroline's good mood dissolves before our very eyes and a black cloud descends upon the kitchen. If this was a movie, thunder and lightning bolts would suddenly appear outside.

"It cuts like a knife, let me tell you," she thunders.

"I know," I try. "But I guess one 'not so good' review is inevitable. This critic probably doesn't know his arse from his elbow. I really wouldn't worry about it." I sit down next to her at the table. I'm exhausted and it's only 10.30.

"It's not just the review. I had an awful night last night," she says and, with no further explanation, she's on her feet and sweeping out of the room, her dressing gown billowing behind her like Dracula's cape. We hear her stomping upstairs, presumably to her bedroom.

193

I shrug at Lorna and tiptoe to the table to read what has distressed her so much. It's certainly not a great review, for it accuses her of severe over-acting, but it's not that bad. God, if they want to see her over-acting they should bypass the theatre altogether and come round here. Ten minutes pass and Lorna and I finish our cups of tea.

"Do you think we should check on her?" Lorna asks.

"I suppose so," I agree. "Especially after that last leading comment. She's probably in position and waiting for us."

Giggling, we transfer her Starbucks into a mug, heat it up in the microwave, grab a pile of papers (not the *Independent*) and then both wander into the hall and up the stairs towards her bedroom. We stand outside her door like nervous schoolgirls, until eventually I have the nerve to knock on the door. I have to try something or she'll be late for her Botox.

"Caroline?"

"What?"

"I've got your coffee for you."

"Come in," she whimpers.

I tentatively pop my head round the corner. She's lying prostrate on the bed.

"Are you all right?" I enquire, never sure of the reaction I'm going to get.

"Yes, I'm fine. If you can call someone who's been abused fine."

Here we go. I perch on the end of the bed and put the papers on the floor.

"Honestly, one bad review out of all of all of those is an amazing achievement," I venture.

"I know." She frowns. There's an uncomfortable pause. "But it's not just the review."

Now I'm confused.

"Yes, you mentioned that you didn't have a good night, but if it's not the review then what is it, because you seemed pretty happy before?" I speak to her in the same kind of tone that my mother used to employ with me when I was a hormonal teenager — and therefore totally irrational and borderline insane.

"How do you know I was happy?" she says accusingly. "You have no idea what I've been through. It was my big night last night and it was awful."

"Why?"

Caroline frowns as she tries to think of a reason. "Well, my bloody friend Leticia came to see the play and I gave the performance of a lifetime and what could she say by way of praise? Nothing."

"Really?" I say doubtfully.

She looks up and pouts like a little girl who's been told that she can't have another pony. "Yes, really."

"Well, I'm sure she did love it."

"No, she didn't."

She stretches her toes out and examines her pedicure dolefully. "I mean, I am in a very vulnerable place right now and I need reassurance, you know."

I survey the room. Judging by the state of it, she didn't let Leticia ruin her night that much. Her couture Prada gown is in a rumpled heap on the floor.

She follows my gaze petulantly. "Can you tidy for me in here later?"

I nod. Now would probably not be a good time to point out that tidying up her bedroom isn't exactly part of my job description. Anything for an easy life.

Caroline lies back, props herself up on one elbow and tosses back her dark mane. Even with dried mascara down her face, she still manages to look beautiful in a haughty kind of way.

"Anyway, I acted my bloody socks off and all Leticia could say was that I looked nice and that my performance was different. Different? I'll give her different," she spat.

Then, as if she's heard the vitriol in her own voice, she changes her tone.

"I mean, darling Geoffrey, my agent, came backstage and he was crying, my performance moved him so much. The man actually physically wept."

"Did he?" I reply, desperately trying not to laugh as I picture the scene.

"Yes. Wept in my arms like a baby and said that I gave a definitive performance."

I'd weep for twenty per cent of what you're earning too, I think, while bending down to pick her undies up off the floor.

Caroline reclines back on the bed and reaches out for her eye mask. "Read me some of the reviews, Francesca."

I put her knickers in the wash basket and sift through the pile of papers, looking for the best headline.

"Did Carson enjoy it?"

196

Caroline takes off her eye mask.

"Carson thought I was amazing. He certainly acted like he thought I was afterwards, that's for sure."

Slightly too much information. Two-timing bastard.

There is an angry snort from behind the door. Maybe Lorna knows what I know?

"Lorna, will you stop listening at the door and do something useful. Roast me a chicken."

Later on, once I've packed Caroline off in the car with Terry to go to her Botox, Lorna and I sit at the kitchen table and drink tea and eat HobNobs together. We regurgitate the morning's dramas and Lorna laughs so hard the tears fall down her cheeks and her accent becomes even more Irish than usual.

"That stupid man crying in her dressing room. It's not right," she gasps.

"I know," I agree. "But even more surprising is the fact that she actually thanked me for her coffee this morning."

"And so she should too, Francesca. I mean, you're like her fairy bloody godmother," says Lorna, full of indignation. "Here's your coffee, Caroline. I'll sort it out for you, Caroline. Three bags full, Caroline."

I laugh. It was true in a way. I suppose Caroline really did pay me to be her full-time fairy godmother — only difference being that Cinderella always remembered to say thank you.

"Lorna?" I ask tentatively.

"Yes, love?"

"Do you think Carson ever . . . ever, you know? I mean, do you think that him and Caroline are very strong together?"

"I don't know what you mean," replies Lorna swiftly and more than a little defensively. She definitely knows something.

I am so pleased when the end of the day comes round. Caroline left for the theatre at four, but only after I'd had to tell her that Great British Films had been on the phone wanting to set up a meeting, which sounded rather ominous. She didn't look remotely concerned, but that was only down to the latest lot of jabs in her face. She now seems incapable of expressing anything stronger than mild bemusement. How this will affect her acting I don't know, but that's her problem. I leave work and collapse on to the sofa the minute I get home, and then it dawns upon me. The time has now come: Caroline's play has started and rehearsals are officially over. With only a couple of matinees a week and with one of those being on a Saturday, she's going to be around constantly to plague me. I feel shattered just thinking about it. Still, at least I'll have even more new material than usual for my story. Speaking of which, I heave myself up to fetch my laptop. I switch it on and I'm already starting to giggle as I think about what fun I'll have writing the next chapter.

I flex my fingers and begin to type.

CHAPTER
TWENTY

With work and my writing taking up so much of my time and headspace, it's brilliantly refreshing when something happens in my much-neglected personal life. Something that has nothing to do with Caroline or her crazy life whatsoever. Something nice, something normal — and I mean that in the best possible sense of the word.

Yesterday we were all invited to Ella's house for dinner and I couldn't wait, especially since I knew that Caroline would be ensconced in the theatre by six, so I could actually guarantee leaving at a sensible time for once. After work I met up with Abbie and we got the tube to Ella's house in Tooting, where she lives with her husband Paul. The minute Paul came to the door, I suspected that something was up. He seemed edgy, not quite himself, and he and Ella kept talking over each other and blushing a lot. This went on until Sabina arrived, at which point they finally told us their news.

They stood formally in front of the fireplace, Paul with an arm proprietarily round his wife and . . .

"I'm pregnant," Ella announced, beaming from ear to ear. "Thirteen and a bit weeks. We had a scan yesterday and I'm due in December."

All hell broke loose. Abbie practically shattered my eardrum with her scream, Sabina burst into tears and I just yelled "Oh my God, oh my God" over and over again. Then we all hugged Ella and stroked her tummy, and Paul shook our hands really vigorously and looked very pleased with himself and his sperm. It was a wonderful evening and one I shall never forget.

Now it's the day after and I'm trying desperately to recall the happy feeling I had at that moment in order to hang on to it — a technique I once learnt in one of my acting classes many moons ago.

Madam is bored.

As ever, I have a very long list of things to plough through and she keeps distracting me.

Her mobile rings.

She doesn't answer.

Neither do I.

She wins. I put my pen down huffily and reach over for it, my happy bubble very much burst.

"Hello, Caroline Mason's phone," I say. "Hi, Mr Devine. Yes, she's here. I'll just pass you over."

Caroline flaps her hands at me and shakes her head violently.

"Oh, hang on, Mr Devine . . . Oh, I think I'm going mad — she's not here after all. She's gone to the gym for her workout . . . I know, very disciplined . . . OK, well, I'll . . . oh, hang on."

Caroline is mouthing something at me from across the room, but I can't make it out. She tries again and again, her mouth growing wider and wider until the veins in her neck are sticking out. Eventually, frustrated by my unbelievable stupidity, she gives up and flaps at me to get off the phone.

"Hi, Mr Devine . . . so sorry about that. Why don't I ask her to call you back when she gets home from the gym?"

I put the phone down.

Caroline rolls her eyeballs. "I was trying to find out what he wanted."

"To speak to you, I suppose," I say, unable to conceal my irritation.

"Well, I'll just have to bloody ring him now, won't I?" she says, reaching for her phone.

"Hi, Mr Devine," she drawls, all sweetness and light. "How are you? I'm so sorry about my assistant. Apparently she thought I was at the gym but I'm right here."

I turn my attentions back to the FedEx form that I have to complete in the next five minutes.

"OK. So if your lawyer wants to speak to mine about it, that's fine. Listen, will you give my assistant all the details?" She passes the phone back to me and I reach for a pen and a Post-it pad. I scribble down the info, put the phone down and carry on with what I was doing before.

She crosses the room and stares at me.

I ignore her, too engrossed in what I am doing to pay her the attention she is so obviously after.

She drums her fingers on the desk.

Still I ignore her.

"Francesca."

"Yes, Caroline?" I sigh.

"Why are you being so stingy with the Post-its?"

I am very grateful that just then the doorbell rings, which means that her trainer is here and that it is indeed time for her training session.

While she is out I make the most of the quiet time and start to make a small dent in my workload. There are plenty of calls to make and things to organize, plus all the usual extra stuff like sending this FedEx to Jodie, which has in it a diamond earring, would you believe? Caroline managed to lose the other one on a night out to Claridge's after the theatre and she wants the insurance rushed through ASAP. The jewellers, who are in LA, need to see the remaining earring in order to make one exactly the same, and to make the whole process even quicker Caroline won't let me declare it, so I've had to wrap it up in a scarf. Jodie is beside herself with worry in case it gets held up at Customs or lost. It probably will, because everything that Caroline has anything to do with generally seems to go wrong. She's permanently losing things, messing up arrangements and complicating life, but I'm learning to get used to it. Just for the record, you know the whole iPod drama? Jodie was right all along — it just needed charging. Honestly, sometimes I think if it wasn't for the money I'd be very tempted to tell Madam where to stick it.

It's amazing how much I can actually get done when Caroline isn't breathing down my neck. An hour later I'm feeling pretty pleased with myself and like it might be time for a coffee with Lorna. Then my mobile rings for the hundredth time that day.

202

"Hello."

"Hi, it's Tom here. Tom Worthington, who you met at the wedding."

Well, I was not expecting that. "Oh, hi, Tom. How are you doing?"

"Great thanks."

All the easy, comfortable banter we experienced at the wedding is missing completely, but I'm pleased he's called again. I was a bit hard on him the first time he rang, but this is the trouble when you've been let down by men in the past: when a decent one comes along you make them pay for the crimes of past boyfriends.

"Look, I'll come straight out with it. Francesca, would you . . ."

Damn, I'm going to have to interrupt. I've got a call waiting and I can see that it's her. Oh, annoying, what should I do? I don't want to sound uninterested and put him off again, but if I don't answer she'll kill me.

"Tom, I'm so sorry, but would you mind calling back later? It's just I've got my boss on the other line and . . ."

It's obviously his turn to interrupt me now. "No problem, I'll leave you to it. Bye."

And with that, he's gone. Bugger it. I press green.

"Yes, Caroline?"

"Get out the Donna Karan look book will you? I'm on my way back and I need to pick an outfit for my birthday party."

Well, thank God I got off the phone for that pressing need, I think drily as I head towards the kitchen and Lorna. Damn it. Why am I so pathetic? I should have dropped her call and explained later. I hope he tries again.

"She's on her way," I warn Lorna, who's reading a magazine at the table.

She springs into action. "Oh thanks, Fran. I didn't realize it had got that late." She brushes the crumbs off her top and puts her plate and cup in the sink just as we hear a key in the lock.

Caroline comes in, clearly still buzzing from her workout and looking irritatingly glamorous in today's baby-pink ensemble.

"Organic apple juice, please, Lorna darling," she says, sweeping in, flinging open the French windows and lighting a cigarette. "Fran, anything important I should know?"

I must be losing it as I get a huge sense of satisfaction watching Lorna pour out her juice knowing that I couldn't find any organic apple juice and that it's plain old Safeways. I launch into my PA patter, still feeling rather irked that I missed out on talking to Tom properly. Still, he knows what I do and therefore how busy I am, so hopefully he won't take it personally.

"Next week is all sorted in terms of tickets and all your dinner reservations. Leticia will meet you at the theatre tonight before going to the Ivy, where your table is booked for 10.30, which should give you time to get changed after the show. I spoke to Julia Roberts's manager and sadly she can't make your birthday party but sends her love. All the bits from Joseph have come in, so I can pick those up later. Graham Norton has come back with some dates for his show, as has

Jonathan Ross, but Kenneth thinks you should choose between the two, and your housekeeper in Bermuda has received the reference you sent her and the new one starts on Monday."

Caroline gulps down the apple juice and stays upright, despite the fact that it is non-organic.

"Which chat show do you think I should do, Fran?"

I ponder the question. Gosh, how wonderful to be in a position where you were asked to do either.

"To be honest, that's a tricky one. You see, if you go on Graham Norton you'll be very much superfluous to the show in a way because much of it centres round the games that he plays and funny calls to fans, etc. I'm not sure that's really up your street. And Jonathan Ross is great, but again it's all quite light-hearted and the guests usually rely on humorous anecdotes and I'm not entirely sure that's you either."

I finish my musings only to discover that Caroline is staring at me, open-mouthed, clearly trying to assess whether I'm being cheeky or helpful. Actually giving an opinion is not expected from a mere assistant. When asked a question you're really only ever required to say "You'll be brilliant whichever you do" or "You look amazing" or "I think what you think".

Lorna is frozen to the spot, looking petrified and waiting for an outburst of hysterical proportions. However, one doesn't come. Instead Caroline finishes her cigarette and fixes me with a stare.

"So seeing as you've suddenly transformed into an expert on both publicity and my personality, what do you suggest I do, Francesca? Go on nothing at all and do fuck all to promote my play?"

I recoil slightly, but only slightly.

"No, actually I was just wondering, have you given any thought to going on that new show that's starting soon. You know, the one that's going to be hosted by the clever chap from Radio Four, who's being hailed as the new Parkinson. It's being advertised as the show that will concentrate on the interview without any frippery, allowing the subject to come across more seriously. Apparently they've got some really big-name stars lined up, including John Travolta and Meg Ryan."

While Caroline thinks this over, I realize that I might be on the verge of being sacked. I also wonder how much of the bad behaviour of celebrities happens precisely because they are allowed to get away with it, with nobody daring to question anything for fear of losing their job? I mean, I have just been fairly frank with her but, let's face it, if I was being really honest I would have said, "Listen, Caroline, let's cut the crap for a minute. If you go on Graham Norton or Jonathan Ross you're going to come across really badly because you don't understand either sarcasm or irony and, to top it all, you have little or no sense of humour. However, you're a reasonably intelligent actress, so go on a proper talk show where you don't have to be funny and you'll be fine."

Lorna is still rooted to the spot, hardly daring to breathe.

Caroline looks at me. "Mmm, Kenneth did mumble something about that one to me last week." She pauses for a minute, weighing up her options, and then seems to make a decision.

"OK, call Kenneth and tell him to get me on that show. I did the Parkinson show a few times over the years and I do remember feeling more at ease on that kind of programme."

I smile. Lorna exhales.

"Right, where's the Donna Karan look book?"

Like an obedient puppy, I scamper to fetch it and bring it to my master. Caroline flicks through it, sticking Post-it notes on the pages she likes. What a way to shop.

"What do you think I should wear to my party?" she asks.

This is unheard of. It seems that my little bout of honesty has inspired some trust in me and my opinions.

"Well, I think that dress is amazing," I say, pointing at my favourite.

"So do I," says Caroline excitedly. "Will you organize it for me to borrow?"

"I will indeed. I'll get on to it later, but now I think I should head over to Joseph and pick up your stuff."

"OK, good plan. Now, also for your notes, Carson is coming over for the party and this time Steph and Cameron are coming too."

"Oh great," whoops Lorna at the thought of seeing her daughter.

"Yes, that'll be nice for you, Lorna, won't it?" she says in one of her rare attempts to be friendly, sounding totally patronizing.

I'm delighted to see Lorna looking so excited, but I'm dreading Carson coming over and having to maintain polite conversation with him after my discovery the other day. I get up to go to Joseph.

"Don't forget to stock up on Post-its, Fran," Caroline calls after me.

Later that day I'm at the stationer's purchasing said Post-its when it occurs to me that Tom still hasn't called back. In a pathetic attempt at rebellion, I purchase eighty packs.

CHAPTER
TWENTY-ONE

That evening when I arrive home, I'm delighted to find Sabina and Ella both sitting at the kitchen table. Abbie has made a delicious chicken salad and it's great to have a glass of wine and a good catch-up.

Now that she's told us she's pregnant, it's as if Ella finally feels like she can let go and her tummy is already beginning to look like a proper little belly. It's incredibly exciting and we all make a huge fuss of her. I probably go a bit overboard, but then I feel bad about having seen so little of her over these last few months.

"I hope I'm not out of the running for Godmummy due to being such an absent friend lately?" I enquire, only half jokingly.

"Don't worry, Fran," says Ella. "Seriously, we know how hard you're working and, besides, you can make it up to me by telling me lots of showbiz gossip to brighten up my humdrum existence."

I laugh. "Oh God, if only you could see me struggling round various supermarkets most days you wouldn't think it was quite so glamorous, I promise."

Abbie cuts in. "Come on, there must be some more gossip. Have you told them about seeing Carson Adams in a towel?"

Sabina screams. "Noooo! Oh my God, you lucky bitch. What did he look like? What did you say?"

I laugh again. "Listen. I promise I'll tell you everything, but first I'd really rather hear about all of you before we even mention anybody whose name begins with C."

So I sit back and my friends regale me with all their tales and I find out what's going on in their lives and it's so nice just to listen to normal people. People who don't need constant attention and ego-bolstering. People who have normal relationships and who aren't two-timing each other. People who wouldn't send someone halfway round London to find one brand of bread because it's wheat free and Gwyneth likes it, and who know the value of money.

A lot of the shine on Caroline Mason has tarnished for me recently and, although I can't help but like Carson, I now feel a bit let down by him too. When I started working for Caroline, I wouldn't exactly have described myself as a major, paid-up-to-the-fan-club type of fan, but then that's partly because she hadn't done anything for such a long time. I certainly admired her though. I thought she had the perfect, happy life, that she came across as a lovely person and that she also happened to be stunningly beautiful. One out of three isn't bad, I suppose.

It has shocked me that, despite not being a celebrity who I ever particularly thought about a great deal, I did have a fully formed opinion about what Caroline Mason would be like none the less. Then, when my impression didn't reconcile with the reality, I guess I

210

felt a bit cheated. It just goes to show that subconsciously we all consider ourselves to be experts on celebrities, thanks to the Internet and ever-increasing media interest. We are exposed on a daily basis to countless images and constant titbits of information about the lives of stars, so we feel fully entitled to make bald statements about them. We have all at some time or other offered up an opinion like "I can't stand her — she's such a diva and she's too skinny" or "She's so lovely, I really rate her", when we haven't even met these people ever before. What are our opinions actually based on?

Abbie gets my attention. "So my news is that Adam and I are now going out officially."

"Oh, Abbie, that's great. He's such a lovely bloke," I say, feeling delighted for my friend.

Abbie must really like this one to be making announcements like that to us, and so she should. Having met him quite a few times at the flat now, he seems like a really nice guy.

"So that's just you and me single at the moment then, Fran," points out Sabina.

"Yeah, well, that's all right," I say, shrugging. "Actually, Abs, I meant to tell you — that guy Tom we met at the wedding rang me the other day again and asked me to go to dinner with him."

"Brilliant," yelps Abbie. "I'm so pleased. I thought you'd blown that one. When are you going?"

Now I wish I'd never mentioned it.

"Well, I'm not because I had call waiting on my phone so I had to go."

Three disappointed faces stare back at me.

"What?" demand Abbie and Sabina.

"You're a bloody nightmare, you are," interjects Ella. "Why?"

"Because you never give anyone a chance and you don't give yourself a break either. You should have gone. Abbie told us how well you clicked at the wedding and that doesn't happen every day. The poor guy's gone to the effort of ringing you twice now and has really put himself on the line and all he gets back is the ice queen."

I'm shocked. "That's a bit bloody harsh, isn't it?" I ask the others, knowing full well that if it's coming from Ella it's probably a pretty spot-on assessment. Damn them. The most annoying thing is that I know they're absolutely right and secretly I'd already managed to reach the same conclusion on my own.

Sensing that they may have hurt my feelings, the subject is changed and we spend the rest of the night discussing names for Ella's baby, which get gradually more and more ridiculous as the evening progresses. By the time Ella leaves at 10.30, if it's a girl it's going to be Fransabbella, a mixture of all our names, or Holly. If it's a boy it'll be Benmignicju, after all the members of Curiosity Killed the Cat, or Rudolph. When Sabina eventually leaves I go straight to bed, trying desperately to ignore the nagging feeling of regret that keeps creeping in whenever I think of Tom. Which is quite often.

CHAPTER
TWENTY-TWO

It's Monday and Caroline's birthday arrangements are nearly all set for the weekend. I will spend the rest of this week finalizing everything and making sure that Cameron, Steph and Carson are looked after and have everything they need. (Caroline's words, not theirs.)

The party is going to be a late one as Caroline doesn't finish her play till ten, so she won't even be arriving at Brown's till eleven. Then on Sunday she is also hosting an intimate lunch for forty at the Sanderson. No expense has been spared and it makes me feel faintly ill to think what she is spending on food alone. Especially since she probably won't eat much of it.

I'm in the study talking on the phone to the manager of the Sanderson about décor for the room when I hear Carson and the others arrive from the airport.

"So that's no scented candles on the food table, please, and Dom Pérignon to be served after the main course before speeches. Also, Orlando Hamilton will be in touch with you directly as he's doing the flowers himself. Is that OK?"

Just as I'm finishing up, a cute, apple-faced little boy comes charging into the study yelling, "Jaaaaanet!"

He's got a brilliant bowl haircut and very chubby cheeks, making it easy to picture how gorgeous he must have been as a baby. His build, however, is very much that of a six-year-old. He looks strong and full of energy, and his skin is lightly tanned from the Californian sun. He's a very handsome little boy with his blond hair and blue eyes, but then I wouldn't expect anything less from the spawn of Carson Adams.

Cameron stops in his tracks when he sees me. "Hey, who are you?"

His accent is adorable — a strange hybrid of Irish and American. I know I'm not a mother myself, but it must be weird when your child spends so much time with its nanny that it speaks like her, and not you.

"Hi, you must be Cameron. I'm Fran. I work for your mum and dad."

"Cool," is his response, before he charges off again.

Lorna's been making all the beds upstairs and she's obviously only just become aware of the arrivals for she suddenly screeches and heads downstairs as quickly as her arthritis will allow her.

Meanwhile, Carson pops his magnificently gorgeous head round the door.

"Hi, Fran. How are you today?"

"Good, thanks," I murmur, unable for a moment to do anything but bask in the rays of his dazzling smile. I still catch myself in this job sometimes. I mean, I, Francesca Massi, am on first-name terms with Carson Adams. "I have a few messages for you here and also can you call your agent as soon as, please? She wants a response to the script. She said you'd know which one she meant."

"Sure thing," he says in a manner that tells me he's probably not that fussed about the script at all. His agent has called me four times about it already, but it looks like I'll be taking a few more calls before she gets an answer.

"Is Cas here?"

"No, she's having her legs waxed," I say, embarrassed beyond belief that, despite not having seen her son for months on end, her stubble comes first. I'm actually blushing and feel strangely hateful towards Caroline for not being here. Carson doesn't seem particularly surprised however.

"Steph!" he calls before turning back to me. "You should meet Steph."

"Coming," calls a quieter, lilting voice, followed by another head poking round the door. "Hi, Francesca. It's great to meet you."

Steph's photo doesn't do her justice. She's really pretty and very natural-looking, without a scrap of make-up on her delicate face. I can see the resemblance to Lorna about the eyes, which are warm and friendly.

"Hello," I say, standing up. "It's really nice to meet you too. How was your journey?"

"Oh, fine. I'm not mad keen on flying, but it was OK, thank you. I'd better pop back to Mum — she's beside herself at seeing Cameron. Carson, come and see."

They bounce off together and again I marvel at how different Carson's attitude towards people is compared to that of his partner's.

My mobile rings and I'm astonished to see that it's my long-forgotten agent of all people.

"Hello?"

"Hi, Francesca, how are you?" John says, sounding as adenoidal as ever.

"Um, fine thanks. Long time no speak."

"It has been a while, hasn't it? Still, it seems that Claims for Dames is working its magic. Have you seen it?"

"Yes," I admit, cringing inside. I should be bloody grateful I don't have any time to watch telly at the moment really.

"Fantastic. It really is on every five minutes, isn't it? Anyway, largely thanks to that I've got you an audition next Monday. Now, before you protest, it's not for an acting role, but you need to remember that beggars can't be choosers," he says, sounding a bit huffy merely in anticipation of what my response might be.

"OK," I reply. "What's it for then?"

"Right, well, it's for a new game show on the digital channel FAB and they're looking for a sidekick for the main presenter and they think you'd be great for it. They were even saying that if you got it maybe they'd have you dressed in the Claims for Dames costume, so try to wear something similar, will you?"

"That sounds great, John," I lie. "Though I am in a full-time job at the moment, so it would depend when it was." I suddenly realize that I haven't given my

216

so-called acting career even a minute's thought during the last few months or so. I haven't had the time or the inclination, now I think about it.

"Oh right. Well, I'll email you the details and you can decide whether you want to go or not," says John, sounding really put out.

"OK," I agree distractedly. I've got call waiting.

"And, Francesca — in future let me know when you're not available for work, eh, love?"

I don't have time to dwell on the sheer audacity of this final comment now. I press green.

"It's me," drawls Caroline. "I've finished my waxing and my car's not here. Where is he?"

"Terry dropped everybody off here about five minutes ago, so he should be with you any second now, seeing as you're only round the corner. They're all here, safe and sound," I say, filling her in, quietly dismayed and shocked that her family's safety wasn't her first line of enquiry.

"Great. Look, seeing as I've got you on the line . . ."

My call waiting is going again. I glance briefly and I see that it's the number that Tom called me from before. After last time I saved it . . . just in case. I swiftly evaluate the situation.

"Caroline," I say, cutting her off mid-flow, "I've got to go. This is a call about your party."

I press green, feeling slightly worried about what will become of me in the future. I hope this is worth it. "Hello?"

"Hi, it's Tom here. Tom from the wedding."

"Hi, Tom from the wedding."

"Hi. Right, er . . . now I know you weren't terribly keen the last time I rang, but I thought that I'd just ask one last time and then I'll leave you in peace forever. So would you like to have dinner or not?" This tirade tumbles out of his mouth almost indignantly and my heart goes out to him.

"Yes, I would actually," I reply.

"Oh, would you?" he says, sounding completely surprised. "Great. That's great."

I take a deep breath. "If I'm honest, I did before, but I was a bit annoyed that you ignored me the day after the wedding. It made me feel a real idiot, although having thought about it recently there is a chance I overreacted a bit. I mean, in your defence, you have rung since so . . ." I trail off, not entirely sure what my point is.

"Francesca," he says, "I wouldn't have ignored you if I'd had my glasses on. I'm embarrassed to say that the reason I may not have noticed you at first is because I couldn't see you properly and couldn't be sure it was you until you got nearer, by which time you were leaving and your friend was shooting me venomous looks."

"Oh, right." That's told me then. I feel rather silly.

"So are you free on Saturday?"

A frantic debate takes place in my head. Saturday is the day of Caroline's birthday party and I should probably be standing by in case anything goes wrong. Then again . . . what's the worst that could happen? I mustn't blow this.

"Yes, Saturday would be great."

218

Sounding greatly relieved, Tom says, "OK. Give me your address and I'll pick you up at eight."

I get off the phone feeling flustered and excited and only then do I register the six missed calls sign on my phone. I'd ignored the beeping of call waiting throughout the conversation and there are no prizes for guessing who it was.

I hear a key in the front door and brace myself.

"Fraaaaancesca!"

"In here," I call out meekly.

"Well, come here," she booms imperiously.

I scuttle out of the study. Caroline is standing in the hall with her hands placed ominously on her hips. However, I am saved from certain death for Carson comes crashing down the stairs just at that instance.

"Cas, how you doing?" he says, pecking her on the cheek.

This is the first time I have actually seen them together and it's fascinating to see her face change completely as soon as she sees him. She quickly puts on a smile that doesn't quite reach her eyes and adopts a far more subservient manner. I had wondered how on earth he put up with her and now I know.

"Great, thanks. Good flight?" she enquires pleasantly.

She knows when she's on to a good thing.

"Yeah, fine. Cameron and Steph are upstairs," he says, heading back up there. He takes the stairs three at a time and reminds me of an excited puppy. If he had a tail, it would be wagging.

"I'll go straight up and see them," she says, gliding up the stairs behind him, stopping only to turn and say to me, "Never cut me off again," through gritted teeth. The lack of interest in her son's homecoming sickens me and for the first time since I found out about it I start to feel glad that Carson's straying — or at least more sympathetic anyway. You can hardly blame him. Still, I just don't understand why such a seemingly lovely guy picked her in the first place. It's not as if he would have been short of offers.

The phone's ringing and it's Caroline's trainer, so reluctantly I get back to the business of running her life.

Later on that night at home, I take refuge in the one thing that is keeping me sane at the moment — my book, *The Diary of a Personal Assistant*. (And, yes, I did definitely say book! I can hardly believe it myself, but I think once you reach two hundred pages it really does classify as a book, doesn't it?) Now that I'm not simply writing about my daily struggles, the characters are really starting to develop and a plot is emerging. It still centres around a PA who works for a crazed actress, who is married to an equally famous actor who isn't quite what he seems. Miss M is eaten up with jealousy and goes out of her way to destroy Mr X's career while simultaneously bolstering her own, which by default ends up having the exact opposite effect. There's plenty of comedy (all of which is directly inspired by Caroline) and the other day I got Abbie to read a bit of it and could actually hear her laughing out loud in her room, which completely made my day and was really encouraging. In fact, secretly it made me start thinking that maybe when it's finished I should try to do something with it. Maybe send it to some agents? Anyway, I'm probably getting awfully ahead of myself and carried away but, no matter what, the great thing is that I'm enjoying it. I feel happy now, too, that enough of the finer details and circumstances have been changed for it to all appear purely fictional, just in case, for instance, my computer is stolen. Maybe what happened with Geoff and Stacey back in February was a very crucial destiny day for me. Maybe I needed to learn how potentially cruel writing about someone who really exists can be and how a lot of damage limitation is required. Who knows? But one thing I do know for sure is that when I've had a stressful day at work, writing helps me to keep things in perspective and, once I've finished a chapter or two, I can finally switch off from the day's events and think about the real world once more. It's great to be writing again. I've never written anything this substantial before, even during the days of Diamond PR, and I realize now how much I've missed it.

CHAPTER
TWENTY-THREE

It's the Thursday before Caroline's birthday party and, more importantly, it's the Thursday before my date with Tom. It suddenly dawns upon me that I'd better get Madam a present myself, although what I really don't know. In the meantime, I am delighted that Donna Karan have come through and that her party dress has arrived by courier from the States this morning.

After she'd picked it out last week, many phone calls had ensued to their PR people. There was only one sample of the dress in her size that could be borrowed and it was in New York. I hadn't mentioned to Caroline that Penélope Cruz had first dibs on it as this would have made her apoplectic with rage, but thankfully for me Penélope found something else to wear for her première so the dress was available.

Caroline's out training at the moment so I've hung it up in her room and I can't wait for her to see it. It's absolutely stunning. It's a fifties' style, black satin, strapless dress with a layer of chiffon laid over the top with sparkly black patterns sewn on. It is gorgeous and, though it pains me to say it, she will look fabulous in it. Like a good PA, I lay out a selection of her shoes that will go with it for her and also some accessories, handbags and earrings.

When I hear her returning from her run, I rush to greet her at the top of the stairs.

Today she's in baby-blue Lycra and a white Juicy hoodie.

"Good session, Caroline?"

"Yes, great. Stick the shower on for me, will you? Where is everyone?"

I head for her en suite. "Carson and Steph have taken Cameron to London Zoo. I arranged for it to be closed to the public for two hours so that Carson could go and they said to call them if you want to meet them there."

"Why the hell would I want to do that?" she says, peeling off her leotard and seeming genuinely baffled.

My brow furrows. She hasn't spent five minutes with Cameron since he got here as far as I can tell. Still, I get the impression they have a better time without her anyway. I decide her question must be rhetorical.

"Have you seen what I've hung up for you?"

"No, what is it?" she asks from the shower.

"Your dress."

"Oh, great," she says.

Minutes later she appears in the bedroom wearing a towel. She has got incredible legs.

"Are you going to try it on?" I enquire.

"Yes, I will," she says, slipping out of her towel. I avert my eyes from her totally bald beaver, which I can't help but notice looks like an economy chicken fillet.

As I expected, the dress does look fantastic on her and I'm not just being sycophantic when I tell her this. A debate ensues about which shoes to wear.

"I think the black satin Guccis look best."

"Mm, I'm not convinced," she replies, looking disgruntled, having rejected at least a dozen pairs that all look fine. "Where's the look book?"

I retrieve it for her and she flips to the page with the dress to see what the model is wearing.

"I want those shoes," she says, pointing at the black sparkly sandals the beanpole in the picture is sporting.

My heart sinks.

"Are you sure you don't like your black Christian Louboutins better?" I try feebly.

The rest of my afternoon is taken up with phone calls to New York, pleading and bargaining with the PR girl who, by now, is less than enthusiastic. Still, after some proper begging she promises to let someone else down and to FedEx the shoes over.

However, I decide not to leave anything to chance and spend the next day running round the West End like a nutcase. Summer has arrived with a vengeance, it's a boiling hot day and I can think of at least a hundred things I'd rather be doing than traipsing round every single Donna Karan outlet, begging for shoes that haven't come in yet (sticking needles in my eyes being one of them). Sure enough, there isn't one pair in London, so I am left praying that FedEx will come through. This also means that I will now have to come into work tomorrow, on my day off, and personally wait for FedEx and then take the shoes over to the theatre.

It's at this stage that I decide not to bother getting Caroline a present myself. Oh well, it's all material for my book I suppose, which at this rate is well on its way to becoming a bloody epic.

On Saturday I wake up feeling chuffed to bits that I'm being taken out for dinner tonight. I'm really excited about seeing Tom and hope that we get on even half as well as we did at Harry's wedding. I feel less chuffed when I realize that I have to heave myself out of bed and go into work to wait for a pair of shoes, but even that doesn't ruin my mood.

The tube ride is twice as quick as it is normally during the week and it's another gorgeous day. When I'm not having to race around, I love the sun and I walk through the streets of South Kensington feeling cheerful. As I approach No. 47, I'm full of anticipation for the day ahead. I climb the steps and let myself into the house, listening out for the beep of the alarm. It's not on so someone must be in.

"Hello?" I call out in the hall.

Nothing. The hall is completely quiet and I can even hear the grandfather clock ticking in the study. The sun is pouring through the stained glass of the window above the stairs and dust is swirling in the shafts of light. Everything else is still. Caroline must have forgotten to set the alarm again.

I head for the kitchen, where I plan to wait until FedEx arrive, and then I think again and decide to go up to the bedroom first, so that I can get everything else ready that I need to take over to the theatre.

Caroline decided that as I was coming over to the theatre anyway I might as well bring everything that she'll be wearing for the party as well as her weekend bag for the Sanderson, where she'll be staying — hopefully — through till Monday. The bag was one less thing for her to think about. I smile ruefully as I remember how she made out that she was doing me a favour by thinking of this brainwave for me.

I head upstairs, taking them two at a time, and make for the second door off the wide landing, which leads to her bedroom. I push open the door, stand rooted to the spot in silence for what feels like an age and then scream with shock and slam it shut again.

Oh my God. My heart hammers in my chest and all the blood in my body races to my face. Fuck fuck fuck fuck.

"Francesca!" calls Carson.

Fuck fuck fuck fuck.

"Yes?" I whimper timidly, rooted to the spot with embarrassment.

"Francesca, it's not what you think."

"Don't worry about it," I offer to the shut door, at a complete loss as to what to say. I gather my thoughts and scuttle down the stairs, wishing I could leave and forget about what I've just seen forever.

I'm sitting in the kitchen cringing and trying to figure out what to do when I hear footsteps coming down the stairs.

"Francesca," says Carson, standing at the door looking really sheepish and crestfallen. "Honestly, I

226

know it looks bad, but you mustn't say anything about this to anyone. If this got to the press . . ."

At this point he's not so famous that I can't give him a filthy look.

"Carson, it's none of my business. I won't say anything to anyone, especially not the press," I say quietly. "It's probably for the best if I resign on Monday though, I guess."

Carson has at least now put on a pair of trousers and a shirt, which is buttoned up wrong, but his feet are bare and he looks rumpled and guilty as sin.

I gulp. It's not every day you catch an A-list movie star stark bollock naked and shagging his son's nanny as if his life depends upon it.

The man must be having affairs left, right and centre, and bedding the nanny just confirms my new impression that he's a walking cliché. That being said, I am surprised at Steph.

"OK, Francesca. I am going to level with you like I haven't levelled with anyone before. Not my family, not my agent or even Robert and Brad."

His best friends, De Niro and Pitt, in case you're wondering.

"OK," I say, still having trouble breathing and very doubtful about whether or not I actually want to hear this.

"I'm going to tell you the truth because you seem like a good person and I'd rather you knew the truth than went away and invented it, based on what you just saw." At this point Carson runs his hands through his hair and looks genuinely stressed and absolutely sexy as hell. I don't blame Steph for shagging him, really. I don't think I'd be able to say no myself, if I'm honest.

I check myself and dismiss these wanton thoughts, then concentrate on looking traumatized and disapproving again.

"Listen, Carson, you don't have to tell me anything. I think it's plainly obvious what's going on and I don't want to hear you telling me that Caroline doesn't understand you any more. Honestly, I'm not judging you," I fib. "And I'll sign a piece of paper saying I won't go to the press if that's what you want."

Just then, Steph joins us in the kitchen.

"Hi, Fran," she says, looking sheepish. "Sweetheart, are you all right?" she says to Carson.

So it's "sweetheart" now, is it, I think, feeling outraged by her temerity. Who does she think she is after a quick fumble under the sheets?

"I'm going to tell Fran the truth," Carson tells Steph, who is blinking furiously.

"Are you sure? What about Cameron?" she pleads quietly.

"That's a point. Where is Cameron?" I ask, feeling thoroughly confused and rather annoyed at all this cloak and dagger behaviour, when the doorbell goes.

"He's out with Lorna," whispers Steph.

"That'll be FedEx," I say, as I get up to answer the door.

When I return to the kitchen with Caroline's shoes under my arm, Carson and Steph are in the middle of a heated debate. I interrupt, feeling much less inclined to be polite to my boss now that I've seen his genitals.

228

"Look, I've got to go upstairs now and get Caroline's stuff for the weekend. Is that OK?" I say sullenly.

"Yeah, sure," says Carson, having the grace to look fairly shamefaced.

I plod wearily up the stairs, still amazed by what I've just seen and quite shocked by Steph. She was really going for it like the clappers and the image of them bouncing around in that extraordinary position keeps popping back into my head. If I wasn't so disturbed, I might even feel aroused. I wouldn't have thought she had it in her. I'm annoyed with myself for letting their display of sexual gymnastics make me feel so prudish. I'm also experiencing a feeling of real inadequacy in the bedroom department compared to them. I had thought I'd covered pretty much everything, but clearly not. Still, that's hardly the point.

I enter the den of iniquity, noting the rumpled sheets, the smell of hormones and the trail of clothes on the floor. I hope they're going to change the sheets by the time Caroline gets home on Monday, that's all I can say. I suppose they must have been only too aware of the fact that she was going to be at the Sanderson all day and, indeed, all night.

I open Caroline's vast cupboards and grab her Mulberry weekend bag. Then I think again and take out a larger Vuitton case. I've just realized something. Later on today Carson will be joining Caroline to celebrate her birthday at her dinner. Some birthday present.

Feeling thoroughly disillusioned, I start to pack. I have to cover every eventuality so that Caroline can't find fault and will therefore stay away longer, giving me a much needed break and some headspace. While I pack I feel quietly satisfied that I can hear raised voices downstairs. Good, they should be rowing too.

Twenty minutes later and I've finally finished packing Caroline's lotions, potions, vitamins and all the other stuff that is apparently so vital. I lug the bulging case on to the landing and down the stairs. Then I leave the case in the hall and stick my head round the kitchen door.

"I'm going to the theatre now to give Caroline's stuff to her," I say, looking pointedly at Steph when mentioning the woman she has just cuckolded. Her eyes are red and she's obviously been crying.

"Francesca, please don't leave like this," begs a very stressed-looking Carson. He turns to look at Steph questioningly. She gives an almost imperceptible nod of the head before looking down at the floor mournfully.

"Please, Fran. Hear us out?"

"OK," I shrug.

"We're going to fill you in properly. Take a seat," says Carson manfully.

Reluctantly, I draw up a chair and sit at the table, waiting to hear his pitiful excuses. Steph doesn't move a muscle and the tension in the air is palpable.

Carson sits opposite me and fixes me with a very beautiful stare. He's all the more beautiful because he really isn't aware of his looks. I don't mean that when he looks in the mirror in the morning he doesn't acknowledge that his reflection is an attractive one. I mean, he must do — after all, he can see. But he's not arrogant. He doesn't use his looks as a tool to gain control or to get the upper hand in a situation and if he is passing a mirror he doesn't feel the need to check that he's still looking gorgeous, as so many handsome men do. As a result, his looks are all the more powerful.

"Francesca, you see, the thing is, Caroline and I have a relationship of convenience . . ." he says falteringly.

I'm disappointed with his line of defence. I realize that I really don't want to not like Carson.

He clears his throat. "You see, we have never been in love and it was our managers who engineered the entire . . . the entire thing."

"I beg your pardon?" I manage gormlessly.

Carson sighs heavily before launching into a proper explanation, while Steph remains transfixed by the floor.

"Back in the nineties, Caroline had just finished making *Baby Don't Leave Me*. She was huge, the hottest property in Hollywood at the time, but she wasn't choosing love matches whom the studios considered to be good for her romantic image."

I can't believe what I'm hearing. "Go on."

"I was a new kid in town and at that time pretty much nobody had heard of me. However, I had been cast in a movie that was tipped to do pretty well, so my manager and Caroline's manager decided it would be fabulous for both of us to be together. Actually, to be perfectly honest, they wanted us married within a couple of months, but I refused. There was no way I was going to make solemn vows to someone I didn't even care about. Or particularly like."

I gulp. I'm not sure quite how to deal with these revelations so, thinking of Sabina, I go with my instincts and say what any sane person would in this situation.

"Carry on. Then what happened?"

"Well, that's it really. I guess we've got used to the weirdness of the situation and it has been useful for our careers, especially hers as fate would have it. My film took off in more of a way than anyone could have predicted. I've thought about getting out hundreds of times, but other factors have prevented me from doing so."

"Like what?" I say. "Cameron?"

Carson runs a hand through his hair again and Steph comes over and reaches out to hold the other one for comfort.

"I fell in love with someone," says Carson.

"Right," I say, confused beyond belief.

"I fell in love with Steph."

"Oh," I say, turning pink.

"And I fell in love with him," says Steph quietly.

"We fell in love seven years ago and have been together ever since," adds Carson, putting an arm round her shoulder to cement his point.

"I see. Except, actually, I don't really. I mean, call me old-fashioned, but why don't you just come clean and be with Steph and leave Caroline?"

Steph picks up where Carson left off. "It's mostly because of me. I mean, part of the reason is because being with Caroline is undoubtedly better for Carson's career than being with me would be, but mostly it's me. I hate attention of any kind. I hate Hollywood parties and all the bullshit that goes with them and, as things are now, I enjoy a comparatively quiet, peaceful existence. Carson is one of the most famous men on the planet and whoever is connected to him is destined to become just as well known and to be photographed constantly wherever they go. I just don't think I could handle it." She fiddles nervously with her hair. "In fact, it makes me feel agoraphobic just thinking about it. As it is, I live with Carson pretty much all of the time and I go unnoticed, which is exactly how I like it."

I feel rather sorry for her, having to talk about these intensely private matters. It clearly isn't easy for her.

"Does Lorna know?"

"Yes," says Steph fervently.

"Does Caroline know?"

"Yes," the lovers reply in unison.

"Doesn't she mind your relationship going on under her very nose? And what about Cameron? Isn't it all a bit confusing for him?" I have so many questions.

Carson and Steph both look a trace guilty at the mention of Cameron.

Carson clears his throat before speaking. "Sadly, any child who has famous parents is subject to a slightly strange upbringing, but we protect him as much as we can. We want to tell Cameron the whole truth fairly soon . . . and that is . . ." He trails off. This is obviously all terribly difficult to talk about.

I can't take the suspense any longer. "Carson, what is it?"

". . . Steph is his real mommy." Carson finally fires this cannonball of truth at me. Bloody hell.

It all starts to make sense: Lorna being so close to Carson and Cameron; Carson not staying at the Dorchester with Caroline when he came over for her opening night. That had struck me as strange at the time, but I'd presumed they'd had a row or something. Then, of course, there was the glaringly obvious clue that Caroline clearly doesn't give even the smallest of shits about Cameron, and Steph is so besotted by him. Plus, Cameron is a lovely little boy, which I'm certain he wouldn't be if he really was Caroline's offspring and had inherited any of her genes at all.

My mobile rings.

In a daze, I answer it, and Steph and Carson both stare at me, nervously awaiting my reaction to their bombshell.

"Caroline, hi. Yeah, I've got everything here. Don't worry, I'll be there shortly."

The couple look uncomfortable and I get off the phone as quickly as I can.

"So how do you and Caroline cope with all of this? Do you get on as friends?" I direct this last bit at Carson.

Without batting an eyelid he replies, "She's the rudest, most selfish, horrendous individual I've ever had the displeasure of sharing a fifteen-year sham relationship with."

I can hardly believe what I'm hearing. It's all so bizarre.

"Listen," I reassure them, "I've got to go to the theatre now to deliver this stuff, but I want you to know that I won't breathe a word of this to another living

soul. I really won't, and I meant what I said, Carson —
if you want me to sign something legal saying exactly
that, I will."

Steph has tears in her eyes and looks so pleased she
could burst. "I don't think you should have to do that,
Fran. I trust you. Besides, my mum's always raving
about you and saying how lovely you are. To be honest,
it just feels so nice to tell someone else the truth for
once. I hope you don't think I'm an awful mother,
letting someone else take credit for my baby, do you?
It's just we couldn't face what the scandal and the
publicity would do to us and to him at the time."

Now the tears come and all the strain and tension of
the past seven years seems to erupt. It can't have been
easy living a lie for so long.

I go to rub her back, not unaware of how surreal the
situation is. Everything seems to have turned on its
head and in a very short space of time I have been
elevated from assistant to confidante and keeper of
secrets that the whole world would love to be privy to.

Carson still looks churned up with worry, so I
attempt to placate him.

"Listen, I don't judge you both for any of this. I
mean, I did at first when I thought you were being
unfaithful and that you, Steph, were just shagging a
married man who you worked for, but now that I know
he was your man to begin with, not to mention the
father of your child, and that you . . . well . . . I'll shut
up, shall I?"

Steph laughs and gives me a grateful hug and then
puts her arms round Carson, who is also looking happy

to get their secret off his sexy chest, but slightly less assured about the fact that his girlfriend has dismissed the idea of a legal document quite so readily. After all, he is the one worth hundreds of millions of dollars in terms of box office and the one who has the power to sell millions of papers just by changing his hairstyle. Let alone the mother of his child.

"Thanks so much, Fran, for not making this harder than it could have been, and we'll talk again at some point when you've got more time. Um . . . just one thing though. I'd really appreciate you not mentioning that you know to Caroline."

"Don't worry," I agree vehemently. "I won't be saying a word."

It really is time for me to go.

"Just one last thing . . ." I can't resist asking. "Is Caroline seeing anyone at all?"

"Er, yeah." Carson and Steph both look a bit shifty.

"You know her friend Leticia?" says Carson.

"Yes?" I prompt.

Carson just looks at me and raises an eyebrow.

"Oh my word. Right. Got you. OK, bye."

CHAPTER
TWENTY-FOUR

I feel absolutely drained and exhausted, and thoughts are whirling round my head in no particular order as my brain tries to make sense of this muddle. I realize there's still so much I'd like to know. How can they possibly think it's for the best that Cameron thinks he has Caroline for a mother? Do their current agents know the truth of their situation? Are they planning on living like this forever? Where did they learn how to have sex like that?

Outside, as arranged, Terry is waiting with the car to take me to the theatre. I should be grateful that most of the time I only do a five-day week. Poor Terry does six days, week in and week out. If he's not needed by Caroline for a few hours he will always help me out, so as a result we spend quite a bit of time together. Terry says he'd rather be driving than sitting around, and we get to have a bit of a chinwag and compare notes about Caroline's latest dreadful behaviour.

"All right, Fran?"

"Yeah, not bad, thanks, Terry," I say, still dazed and confused and trying to digest the mornings' revelations. We stick the bags in the boot, the dress hangs up in its special bag in the back and I keep the shoes on my lap in the front where I always sit — though I pray Terry doesn't feel like chatting too much today.

"It's your date tonight, isn't it?" says Terry.

"Yeah," I mutter distractedly. "Yeah, it is."

"Everything set for the big birthday bash then?"

"Sorry? Oh, um, yeah."

With one final stab at conversation, Terry tries, "So, I hope you haven't forgotten, Fran, I'm booked in to have my veins done next week and I really can't miss it because I've been waiting such a long time for it."

"Oh yes, Terry," I say distractedly. "Don't worry, I haven't forgotten. I've already sorted out Caroline's cars for the week and I've made sure she can smoke in all of them, which took a bit of doing actually."

"I know," says Terry. "There aren't many mugs like me who don't mind having the interior valeted every other week. Thanks, Fran — you're a star, love. Also, just so you know, I've booked a bit of a holiday too. Not till November because, what with having time off for my veins, I thought we'd better wait a bit, so we're going to have a week in the Canaries then and hopefully get a bit of winter sun. I have cleared it with the boss woman, although I'm not sure she was listening. It'll be lovely though: bit of golf, the missus can do a bit of shopping. Wonderful."

But I'm miles away and for a rare change not in the mood to chat. "What's that? Mmm, great. Sorry, Terry, ignore me. I've had such a hectic week. The Canaries sounds great."

Poor old Terry eventually gets the hint and we travel along in companionable silence.

238

Upon arriving at the theatre, I rush in laden with all Caroline's party gear and Terry carries in her case. I spot Janice, the stage manager, who — seeing my look of intent — doesn't bother with small talk and just punches in the security code that lets us through to the backstage area. I rush through the crew room, where various people clad in black are drinking tea, and down the corridor towards Caroline's dressing room. They are all used to the sight of me arriving laden down like a veritable packhorse and they all smirk and raise their eyebrows at me. How much stuff Caroline has crammed into her dressing room has become a bit of a standing joke and they've nicknamed it Room 101.

When they see Terry bringing up the rear with a stuffed case, there are a lot of wisecracks. Today, however, I don't stop for a banter and just rush through to find Caroline, struggling not to drop everything as I knock.

"Who is it?" calls Caroline imperiously.

"It's me."

She opens the door.

"There you are. I was beginning to think you'd forgotten all about me and that I'd be turning up to my party in my freaking costume," says Caroline, who is currently still sporting her kaftan and a cigarette. Upon entering the room, I realize that Leticia is ensconced in the corner in the armchair and I feel relieved not to have caught them at it too. That really would be too much to take in one day.

"Ah, Terry, hello. Stick the case in the corner, would you?"

Terry does as he's told then. Puffing and panting, he produces a handkerchief from his pocket to wipe away the beads of perspiration from his brow. I'm busy hanging Caroline's party gear up and from the depths of her cupboard I call, "Good luck with your operation next week, Terry, and thanks so much for all your help."

After all, someone's got to thank him.

"Ah yes," says Caroline, looking up. "Your varicose veins. How could I possibly forget about those?"

Leticia covers her mouth with her hand in a feeble attempt to disguise the fact that she's laughing.

"It'll be good to get it over and done with, that's for sure," says Terry. "Oh, just one other thing before I go, Miss Mason?"

"Yes?"

"Did you get the dates for my holiday? I just wanted to double-check that they're OK."

Caroline smiles at him. "Oh yes, fine — whatever. Francesca can take care of all the necessary arrangements for cars again that week and you must have a holiday. You deserve one. Where are you going?"

I'm glad she's being nice and not playing up to her audience for once. She shouldn't give Terry any grief because, she's right, he does deserve a break.

"A lovely little resort in Lanzarote."

Leticia actually shivers.

Caroline's smile remains fixed. "Oh, well. I'm sure that'll be charming."

"Thanks, and happy birthday. I got you a card from me and the missus," he says, taking a crumpled envelope from his pocket.

"Wonderful, I'll open that later," she says, sounding sincere but turning to wink at Leticia behind his back. I suddenly feel a rush of pure hatred. I should have known she couldn't find it within herself to actually be genuine. She can be such a loathsome snob.

Terry says his goodbyes and tells me he'll wait outside for me and give me a lift back, if that's OK with Miss Mason, of course.

"He's a funny little man, Cas, isn't he?" says Leticia, who is sitting in the corner sipping champagne. She can bloody talk, I think.

Leticia is an extraordinary-looking creature with hair that is coiffed to within an inch of its life and a whippet-thin, almost bony figure. She is also the proud owner of a very pongy little dog called — wait for it — Froo Froo, who always seems to be about her person and who is currently making Caroline's dressing room smell like a guinea-pig hutch, which may explain all the Diptyque candles, come to think of it. Leticia wears clothes that I imagine she thinks are quite bohemian, from places like Nicole Farhi, but can never quite disguise the fact that underneath the beads and crochet cardigans she is, in fact, a roaring Sloane. I glance at her and spontaneously blush. It's time for me to get out of here.

"Right, everything's here, including the shoes. They're the only pair literally in the world," I say, desperate for Caroline to acknowledge my achievement.

She grabs the box excitedly and greedily scrabbles to open it. She pulls out the desired sparkly black sandals that are a perfect match to the dress.

"What do you think, Ticia?" gushes Caroline.

"Gorgeous, darling. Wonderful," enthuses "Ticia", who I have just realized reminds me more than a little of an Afghan hound, with her dangly earrings and long, thin face. "They'd go really well with my Balenciaga pants, actually. Fran, can you get me a pair in size thirty-nine?"

I squash a desire to tell her to fuck right off and simply say, "I'll have a go," obviously fully intending not to. She may be sleeping with Caroline, but that doesn't mean I work for her.

Sensing that the gruesome twosome are happy, and eager to leave before Caroline dreams up any more tasks for me on my day off, I turn to go.

"Francesca, before you go. I'm running a bit short of Chablis. I've only got four bottles left, so will you organize some more?"

Irrationally, but not surprisingly, I very nearly burst into tears. I have had more than my fill of being Caroline Mason's slave for one week. I have had enough of her demands, of not ever being thanked and of her weird, strange life. I gulp and roll my eyes upwards to prevent any tears from escaping.

"Um, it's supposed to be my day off, so I'm actually going now and I'll get you some more wine on Monday. In the meantime, Threshers is just down the road, so if four bottles isn't enough and you're desperate, I'm sure someone from the theatre can go for you."

Caroline stares at me and I can see her trying to decide how to respond. In the end, Leticia decides for her.

242

"Sweetheart, let her go. I only want champagne tonight anyway, and there's loads of Cristal left and some Dom," she says nonchalantly, wafting her hand as if to indicate that she'd rather I just got out of their hair anyway.

Caroline narrows her eyes. "All right," she splutters. "Go then and I'll see you at some point next week." She crosses the room to shut the door behind me.

Having regained some composure, I manage to shout through the shut door, "Have a great party and happy birthday."

Later on at home I find myself doing some serious soul-searching. When I took this job, I never could have imagined what I'd be getting myself into, and now I find myself doubting whether or not I should even stay any more. I feel very uncomfortable with all the deceit and I'm not certain I can pull off pretending not to know anything to Caroline, who I am starting to dislike more and more on a daily basis. However, by the same token, I genuinely like Carson and would love to prove to him and Steph that they can trust me. Plus, on a less altruistic note, if I finish now I don't have anything else lined up, so I'd be out of work. Frankly, I'm getting a huge amount of satisfaction from paying my cheque in every week, always silting some away into a savings account, and I am thoroughly enjoying earning sufficient to keep me in the black for once, so it would be great if I could just stick things out for a bit longer.

I make a decision: I'm not done yet.

For my own personal sense of satisfaction I shall try to stay until the end of the play, at which point it will feel as if I've seen this thing through to some sort of natural end. If Caroline's film does go ahead, then I'll have to assess how I feel then, but I'll probably say that I'm not going with her. I may not have reached my limit yet, but I suspect that there's only so much more of Caroline and her mad world that I'll be able to handle.

That's it then — I'm staying.

I'm glad because, for some perverse reason, I know that if I left now I would feel as if I had thrown in the towel — given up without a fight — and that's just not in my nature. Being completely honest, there's also a big part of me that is finding events intriguing as they unfold. The level of scandal is beyond comprehension and I need to know what happens next.

I decide to do some work on my writing, which always seems to calm me down, and forty minutes later I sit back feeling sated, having written a scene that's even surprised me. In it the PA catches Mr X having sex with Miss M's Mexican gardener José, which finally explains his penchant for fajitas and huge collection of Enrique Iglesias CDs.

Thank goodness I have my writing, I muse. At least in some obscure way it makes me feel as I've offloaded and got things out of my system, making it far easier to keep any secrets. Feeling better, I go to my room. There's just time to have a quick nap before getting ready.

★   ★   ★

Later, I'm perched on the edge of the sofa, washed and groomed, and wearing a pretty summer dress with a denim jacket and flat, jewelled sandals, waiting for Tom to pick me up. I'm nervous as anything, but I'm also excited and looking forward to being taken out and having some nice dinner. If he turns up, that is.

The buzzer goes. My stomach lurches.

I grab my handbag and call down on the intercom, "I'm coming."

And there he is, standing in the hall, and I'm suddenly overcome with shyness.

"Hi," I say, studying the ground with all the social ineptitude of a three-year-old.

"Hello, Francesca. You look lovely," he says, looking pretty lovely himself. He's wearing a really beautiful suit in dark blue with an open-necked shirt. The style is very Paul Smith. He looks great.

"Thanks," I say.

One hour later and I'm sitting opposite Tom in a lovely, intimate Italian restaurant in Pimlico. I've finished my tagliolini with crab and I'm waiting for my fish. A whole fish cooked in salt — it looks delicious. What a treat.

We are having the nicest evening, conversation is flowing and my mobile, for once, is switched off. I can't help but worry occasionally that everything's set for the party, but I did ring before I left and it all seemed to be under control. I wonder if Carson will turn up . . .?

"So would your father approve of this restaurant?" Tom asks, once the waiter has sprinkled Parmesan over his ravioli, bringing me back to the here and now. "I feel rather foolish for bringing you here, now that I know you were practically raised in an Italian restaurant by an Italian chef. This probably doesn't measure up at all," he says, tucking in.

I shake my head vigorously. "Oh God, no. My father would really approve of this place. His bugbears are great service, fresh ingredients and that the menu is the right size, and this place covers all three. Dad's restaurant is obviously my favourite restaurant in the world, but it's much more modest than this, to be honest. It's more of a trattoria really and it's usually full of families. Mmm, this fish is delicious."

"It sounds great," smiles Tom, who is better looking than I remembered.

"Well, maybe I'll take you there one day. My dad loves playing the host to my friends, has done ever since he bought the place twelve years ago," I say, wishing even as the words come out that I wasn't saying it. Too forward for a first date. Far too forward.

"I'd like that," comes the answer, however, and — even better — he shows no signs of shoving aside his ravioli and running away.

I sigh contentedly.

"What's that sigh for?"

"Oh, nothing, really. I suppose I'm just starting to relax. I've had a bit of a day of it at work, as usual."

"I must say, you've always sounded a bit under pressure whenever I've rung," says Tom. "They say never work with animals or children, don't they? But I tell you, I'd rather work with animals than a mad actress any day of the week."

"Still," I say ruefully, "it's all good material."

"Material for what?"

"Well, I can't remember whether or not I mentioned at the wedding that I do a bit of writing, but I've been writing a story based on what I do and the ridiculous relationship that I have with my boss. It started out purely as a bit of fun and a form of therapy for me in many ways, but it's developed into a bit of a project. Well, a book actually. Anyway, I've always loved writing, but it's been a while since I've been so 'in the flow'."

Tom looks interested. "What's it called?"

"*The Diary of a Personal Assistant* and the main character is a neurotic actress called Miss M. She's devastatingly beautiful, but cruel and with no sense of humour."

Tom chuckles. "I wonder who that could be?"

"I know, it is ridiculous. If Caroline only knew what I'd written, she'd implode with fury, but thankfully she never will."

"So, an actress, a PA to the stars and a writer? I'm starting to wonder what other secret talents you've got hidden," says Tom casually, before looking mortified as it suddenly dawns upon him that what he's said sounds loaded with creepy innuendo.

If neither of us reference it, then this could easily be the first awkward moment of the evening.

"I'm so sorry. That came out a bit wrong. I really didn't mean to sound like Peter Stringfellow. I mean, I was genuinely wondering if you had any other talents, but in the professional sense of the word."

Tom spots that I am grinning and visibly relaxes.

We munch contentedly. The food is delicious and the Rioja is slipping down very easily too. We move on to other subjects and I concentrate for the next ten minutes or so on finding out about this man who I'm having dinner with. I discover that his parents are separated and both living near Leicester, that he's travelled a lot and that he loves animals passionately. He has a sister and a brother and he once went to see U2 in concert when he was sixteen. He and his best friend had cheered and rocked to the band, only to discover that they'd wasted all their energies on the support act. He tells the story really well and I find myself laughing out loud and trying not to spit wine all over the table, which, let's face it, would not be a good look.

In turn I tell him about growing up in the suburbs of Teddington and how I miss my brother, who I hardly ever see any more because he's moved to Brighton, and about how incredibly important my friends are to me. Then I tell him some more Caroline stories.

"Is she actually a good actress?" asks Tom.

"Do you know, I think she probably is if the reviews are anything to go by. I'd like to go and see her in the play at some point, although obviously I shall have to wait in line for weeks to become worthy enough of a ticket. I'm very much her last priority." I take a big gulp of wine. "If I do ever get a ticket, I would ask you to come and see it with me, but it's probably not a good idea."

"Why's that?" asks Tom, looking intrigued.

"Well, we'd have to go backstage afterwards and no matter what we really thought of the play we'd be expected to lavish Caroline with compliments. You'd see me in a terrible light as I fawned and went completely over the top. It would make you feel quite sick and yet, as my guest, you would be fully expected to do the same."

"I could handle that," Tom says, grinning and wiping a bit of sauce off his chin.

I think he thinks I'm joking.

"So, Francesca, how long are you going to be working for her then? When I met you in June you gave me the impression that you wouldn't be sticking at it for much longer, but weeks later and you're still there."

"I know. Well, I'm supposed to be there till the play finishes, which is in December, and then go on to her next movie with her, although I'm not entirely sure that's going to go ahead at the moment, so we'll see. I've been too busy to give it that much thought really, but it's just great to have a regular wage coming in. Besides, I don't really have anything else lined up. The acting side of things seems to have dried up completely and I'm still not sure what else I want to do."

Tom gives me a look that makes my heart beat faster and then he says, "Francesca Massi, I'm pretty sure a girl like you could do anything she set her sights on."

The evening goes as well as you could ever hope a date to go. There's never a gap in the conversation. He doesn't drop any horrendous clangers that would imply he might be a closet homophobe, racist, right-wing bigot or mummy's boy. His taste in music is good, but not too pretentiously cool, and he is intelligent, funny and attentive. Plus, at no point is he creepy or lecherous. He's just quietly sexy and, by the end of the meal, I am realizing that I would really quite like to snog his face off. We even have a filmic moment just to frame the evening perfectly and to make sure I never forget it, and it's so romantic. You see, we are talking and talking, and I realize that I didn't just imagine how well we'd got on at the wedding and that we genuinely do get on famously, even without three litres of alcohol inside us, and we are toying with our coffees when a waiter taps Tom on the shoulder.

"Excuse me, sir. Your bill."

We hadn't got round to asking for the bill, so both of us look up, surprised, and then realize that the restaurant is entirely empty and all the waiters are standing around waiting for us to finish so that they can go home. We'd been so absorbed in what each other was saying that we hadn't even noticed, which is incredibly romantic for us and rather a pain in the arse for them.

"I'm so sorry. Let me pay right away so you can get off home," says Tom, which makes me like him even more as I can't stand people who are impolite to waiters.

"No, let's do half each," I insist, as I scrabble in my bag for my credit card.

"I hope this isn't construed as me being sexist or old-fashioned, but I really would like to pay for dinner, Francesca," says Tom, handing only his card to the waiter.

250

He pays and I notice that he leaves a hefty tip for the patient waiting staff. It's fair to say it's been a great date and later, when we're snogging outside my flat like a couple of teenagers, it takes all my powers of restraint to say goodnight. Eventually I do, although, alarmingly, the kiss is so potent it seems to propel me back into the 1950s. I suddenly feel as fey as Sandy in *Grease* and, after cooing "Bye, Tom. Thanks so much again for a lovely dinner," and fluttering my eyelashes, I demurely shut the door only to find myself doing that incredibly Doris Day-type thing where I turn round, lean my back against the door and squeal with girlish delight and giddiness. Somebody slap me.

CHAPTER
TWENTY-FIVE

It's Monday morning, I'm at work and the house is in absolute chaos. Fortunately for me, it looks like my bag-packing was acceptable because Caroline is still languishing in her suite at the Sanderson, where I'm praying she'll stay all day — although of course this could change according to a whim at any point. It also appears that her birthday celebrations have gone without a hitch due to the distinct lack of phone calls from her. No news is good news, although it goes without saying that a thank you would be nice. I know it's pathetic, but I would also quite like to hear how her outfit went down, after spending so much time arranging it.

Having said that, it would still be better not to see her today. Apart from not having to look at her petulant face, I think the shit is going to be hitting the fan any time soon. Carrie Anne phoned an hour ago and things are looking very bad with regard to Caroline's film going ahead. Great British Films have decided that they want to concentrate on other projects before hers and are making noises about cost and sweeping statements about a resurgence in the market for feel-good romantic comedies. Caroline's film is about a mental woman and her delusional episodes, which is clearly neither funny nor romantic subject matter, unless you have a very twisted sense of humour. The trouble is, Thomas Anderson, the director attached to the project, has decided that he no longer likes the script and Great British Films can't bear the thought of further rewrites. They, of course, own the rights, so they can do what they like and, essentially, Caroline can't do anything about it if they start to backtrack now. Besides, they've already started considering different projects for Thomas Anderson to work on.

Anyway, the bottom line is that I'm to expect a call or email from Mr Devine and it's unlikely to bring news that I shall enjoy conveying. On a more selfish note, if the film doesn't get made, then Caroline will go back to the States and I'll be free and won't have to think of any excuses not to work on the film with her. I've still got five whole months left as Miss Mason's PA, which actually feels like plenty, and having an end in sight is beginning to appeal enormously. Part of me is incredibly anxious about the prospect of unemployment and part of me is just not sure how much more of her I can stand.

Other reasons to be cheerful about the fact she's not around this morning are that I can daydream about Tom and not worry about her noticing I have a daffy smile on my face, and also I don't have to try to act naturally whenever she and Carson are in the same room at the same time.

There's a loud thump from above and the room seems to shake. Carson, Cameron and Steph are upstairs and I don't know what they're doing but, whatever it is, it's very noisy and involves a lot of jumping off the bed. Once or twice I've half expected a pair of legs to come crashing through the ceiling. Lorna is going about her business, seemingly oblivious to the chaos, for she is too engrossed in stuffing vases full of hundreds and hundreds of flowers.

When I'd walked in the door this morning, my nostrils had immediately been assailed by the perfume of beautiful blooms and I'd wondered briefly who had died, before realizing that, fortunately, their presence had nothing to do with death and everything to do with birth — the birth of Caroline Mason forty years ago, to be precise.

In the hall there are at least four huge arrangements, mainly in Caroline's favourite shades of cream and pink. Lorna has managed to fit three on the bureau and one huge one on the round Italian antique table at the foot of the stairs. In the study are yet more floral tributes, on the desk, on the shelves and even on top of the fax machine. The colours are amazing. I'm surrounded by yellow roses, pink lilies, white orchids, magenta gerberas and vanilla-coloured begonias, to name but a few. In the kitchen you can tell that Lorna's enthusiasm for arranging has started to wane and many of the flowers haven't even been taken out of their cellophane before being plonked in vases. When I'd walked in earlier, I'd only just been able to make out the top of Lorna's head in amongst some foliage at the far side of the island.

"Morning, Lorna. It looks like a florist in here," I'd exclaimed.

"I know and I tell you what," she'd panted, coming round to see me. "You and me will be taking some of these home with us. I've already bagged the pink roses and the long purple things. What do you want?"

So I chose some stunning white roses with lots of green foliage and some beautiful irises, and I can't wait to take them home. I don't feel guilty in the slightest as Caroline will never notice they're gone and at least they'll be appreciated before they wilt and die. I'd just been about to fill Lorna in on my date when my phone started to go ballistic, as usual, and I haven't had a minute's peace from it since. As a result, I still haven't had a chance to clear things up and let Lorna know that I know about Steph and Carson. I've grown extremely fond of Lorna and it doesn't feel right continuing the charade with her. Still, I suppose I should check with Carson and make sure he doesn't mind me telling her I know.

One of my many phone calls had been from Carrie Anne, who was ringing to update me on the movie situation.

"It doesn't look good," she'd said. "Between you and me, it's not going to be happening and I suspect that part of the reason is that Thomas Anderson has not only gone off the script, but also thinks Caroline may be too old for the lead."

"But the main part is for a woman in her prime. Someone who's lived through enough shit to make her at least forty," I exclaimed, having read the script myself.

"Yeah, and if they can get a twenty-year-old to play old, they will. But it's not even an issue. Thomas Anderson has changed his mind completely. It's all political bullshit," Carrie Anne said resignedly, obviously hardened to the industry she works in. Although the news was bad there was one advantage to having Carrie Anne on the phone, which was that I could pin her down on a date to come over for dinner.

"Come over next week and I'll get the girls over too. We'll have a bit of dinner and a catch-up."

"Do you know what, I'd love that," she said. "And I've got so many days owing to me, I may even leave work early."

"Shock horror," I said jokingly, and we arranged to see each other at mine next Thursday.

Now I sort through all the gifts, cards and faxes that have arrived over the weekend and start writing "thank you" cards. I know Caroline will want them sent out today, despite the fact that she hasn't even set eyes on any of the gifts yet.

Apart from the flowers, her agent, Geoffrey, her publicist, Kenneth, and various friends have also sent her some very generous presents. There's perfume, a voucher for a day at Bliss spa, a giant tub of Crème de la Mer and a cashmere sweater. I can't help but think that some of the stuff has been sent to Miss M in order to suck up vicariously through her to Carson. For example, I notice that the director who is attached to *Save All Your Kisses*, the film that Carson's agent is desperate for him to sign up for, has sent her a scarf from Hermès and a Fendi bag. As far as I know, she's never even met him, and unless I tell Carson I can't imagine he'll ever know or care about this rather blatant ploy.

I scan my emails and ignore my phone, which is merrily ringing away. I can see that it's Leticia and I'm not in the mood for any of her demands. There are house-seat changes and requests to sort out first, and it's all rather frantic.

I can hear Lorna muttering to herself in the hall about where to put yet another vase. I'm surprised she hasn't run out yet. I guess this is where Caroline's stockpiling comes in handy. Nobody else I know owns more than about three vases. Meanwhile, Cameron's upstairs screaming and pleading for mercy and it sounds like he's being tickled to death. The whole atmosphere isn't really conducive to working and I don't think I can ignore Lorna's huffing in the hall for much longer.

"Are you all right?" I call, frowning at my emails. I've totally forgotten about the audition that I'm supposed to be going to today. John's emailed me to say that he's gone ahead and organized it and that they are expecting to see me this afternoon. Bugger. Still, with it looking more and more likely that by Christmas I'll be out of work again, it would probably be a good idea for me to try to make it somehow. I need to keep my hand in, plus doing something different would be a good reminder that I won't be working as Caroline's assistant forever.

At a loss to know where to put it, Lorna simply gives up looking for any more free surfaces and deposits a vase on the hall floor. Then she pads in to see me. Today she's wearing a pair of tartan trousers that look suspiciously like golf slacks and a Mickey Mouse T-shirt.

"Why do you think they all send her such lovely flowers? It's such a terrible waste," she stage whispers indignantly.

"I don't know. As far as I can make out, they all just love sending each other things, these film people. Especially flowers. Caroline will send a bouquet to someone if they've had her round for a cup of coffee." I stick my biro behind my ear, wondering what I should do about this audition.

"I'm going to have a break from them though," says Lorna. "They're starting to give me hay fever. I've only three lots left and I've just plonked them in the sink for now. I want a cuppa and a nice biscuit. How about you, Fran? Then you can tell me all about your date."

I love the fact that although it's thirty-odd degrees outside Lorna will still drink boiling hot tea all day long.

"Um, yeah, I might come and grab some water or something in a minute. Oh my word."

Through the door I see Cameron and Carson suddenly come hurtling down the stairs in a very alarming manner.

"Cameron, stop it. You'll break your leg. Carson, stop this nonsense now. Enough is enough," Lorna bellows. They ignore her though and a miraculously unscathed Cameron charges past her, heading for the kitchen and ultimately the garden, panting and whooping all the way. Carson stops for a second to give a shrug and ruffle Lorna's hair, and then he's off, doing nothing to discourage his son by running after him like a lunatic.

Steph appears at a slightly more dignified pace with a face wreathed in smiles, and I'm not surprised really. She's got a lot to smile about. I turn my attention back to the screen in front of me and with a heavy heart I notice that an email has popped up from Mr Devine's PA. Mr Devine is the Managing Director of Great British Films and he wants a meeting with Caroline to discuss some unforeseen difficulties with the film. Looks like my decision about when to leave is definitely going to be made for me after all. I think I'm pleased and I really must try to get to that audition.

I am engrossed in replying and setting up a mutually agreeable time for a meeting when Cameron comes hurtling into the study.

"Hi, Fran," he says, panting from all his exertion.

"Hi, Cam. What are you doing, charging around like a mad thing?"

Cameron giggles delightedly by way of reply. "Fran, will you arm wrestle with me? I bet I can beat you."

"Sure," I say, grateful for the distraction. My chair is on wheels, so I roll towards him and place my elbow on the desk. He places his grubby little hand in mine and starts making loud grunting noises as he tries to force my hand back.

"Look at my muscles," he says between gritted teeth, going red in the face. I let him win after a bit of a battle, although I have to admit he wasn't far off beating me, and he sticks both arms in the air.

"I am the champion. I am the champion. I am the champion. I am the champion."

Realizing that he could repeat this forever, in that annoying way that young children can repeat things forever, I decide to interrupt.

"You may have big muscles, Buster, but I reckon you were just lucky. I've got bigger muscles than you," I say, flexing my biceps.

"No you haven't," he chuckles. "I've got bigger muscles than you."

"No you haven't," I say. "I've got bigger muscles than you."

"No, I have bigger muscles than you and my daddy's got even bigger muscles. Wait there," says Cameron, running to the door.

I wheel back to the computer and turn my attention back to my emails.

"Daddy!" shouts Cameron. "Daaaaaddy!"

"Yes, Cam?" I hear Carson reply from the kitchen, where he's got Lorna and Steph giggling away like schoolgirls.

"Daddy, Francesca wants to see your muscles."

At this, I look up. "Cameron, don't say that . . ."

"Daddy, come and show Francesca your muscles."

I'm up and on my feet, ready to rugby tackle Cameron to the ground if that's what it takes to shut him up.

Too late — Carson's here and he's heard.

"I'm sorry, Fran, did Cameron say that you wanted to see my muscles? What have you been saying?" he asks, enjoying watching me squirm.

"I really don't want to see your muscles, Carson. I absolutely did not even mention them, did I, Cameron?" My cheeks are flaming.

"Don't worry about it," Carson says, looking amused. He's clearly terribly used to women making random declarations about how much they want to see his body, so is very blasé about my apparent request.

"Actually, I was wondering — have you got a min, Francesca?" he says, still slightly breathless. I can't help but smile. He has the same amount of energy as his son. It's bizarre.

"Sure."

"OK, Cam, scram for a minute and go see Steph. I'll be out in a sec and we can shoot some hoops."

"Cool," says Cameron, charging off.

Carson glances furtively behind him and comes in.

"About the other day, Fran. I just wanted to check that you were OK. You looked a bit freaked when you left."

Inwardly I marvel to myself how, back in the days of working at Diamond PR, never in my wildest dreams could I ever have imagined having this sort of intimate conversation with Carson Adams.

"Oh, right. Well, er, it was a lot to take in and, you know, it was a bit of an embarrassing way to find out and everything," I say, referring to the fact that I have

261

seen him, and Steph for that matter, entirely naked and in a somewhat un-everyday position.

Carson has the grace to look away, though I can tell he's not as embarrassed as any normal person would be. But then he's got absolutely nothing to be embarrassed about. I smile at the memory, which is stored in my memory bank forever to be relished and enjoyed in the future.

"But you're not leaving us, are you?" he asks, in a way that indicates he truly likes having me around, which is nice. It makes a change to feel appreciated.

"Not yet, no. Um . . . I would like to ask you something though — a favour."

Carson looks concerned for a second, probably worried that I'm about to extort huge amounts of money out of him. It's quite odd for a fleeting moment to consider that if I did have the morals of an alley cat then I do actually have the power to do this.

"Firstly, if it's OK with you, I'd like to be honest with Lorna about the fact that I know. I feel a bit uncomfortable lying to her."

Carson looks visibly relieved and perches on the edge of the desk, nearly knocking a vase over in the process.

"That's cool. Steph will be happy about that, I'm sure."

"Well, the other thing is — and this has nothing to do with what happened the other day and I don't want it to affect your decision — I could really do with a couple of hours off this afternoon. I would be really quick — it's just that something's come up and . . ."

262

"Take the rest of the day off, Fran. It's a beautiful sunny day and I've noticed that sometimes you help us out at weekends, so go." Then, seeing my face, he reads my mind. "Look, don't worry, I'll square it with Caroline. If you want I could always say you're ill."

I suppress a giggle.

"What?"

"No, nothing. It's a bit cheeky."

"Go on, I like cheeky."

"Well, it's just you're as scared of her as I am."

"Too right I am." He grins.

"Look, thank you, and I really hope you don't think I'm taking liberties or trying to take advantage in any way," I add.

"Not at all. I appreciate your honesty." He turns to go, then stops and adds, with a twinkle in his eye, "Are you sure you don't want to see my muscles again? Only I think you've seen more than enough of me for a while, don't you?"

I haven't a clue how to reply and blush to my roots, but fortunately I'm saved from having to respond to the sexiest man in the world by the instigator of my embarrassment — Cameron comes bounding in. "Daddy, Daddy, Steph's made some lemonade in the kitchen and she says to come and get some."

CHAPTER
TWENTY-SIX

And so it is that I find myself on the tube heading for the offices of a small production company who are based in Chiswick. Only now that I've taken the time to actually read the email from my agent I sincerely wish I hadn't bothered.

All auditionees for new light entertainment show *The Family Win Zone* will be required to talk about themselves for a minute and then to perform a piece of dance or a song. We are not looking for brilliant dancers or singers, but we do want people who aren't afraid of performing and looking silly. *The Family Win Zone* is looking for a female sidekick who is sassy, self-deprecating and ballsy. We do not want a run-of-the-mill game-show hostess.

Why hadn't I read this properly before? I haven't done an audition for months and now this? I haven't prepared anything. I can't sing and I can't dance, but that doesn't mean I can sing and dance badly well either. Whatever happened to getting a sensible audition? The tube is like a furnace and my growing sense of alarm only contributes towards the large sweat patches that are forming under my arms.

When I get off the train, I have absolutely no idea where I'm supposed to be going and I'm just in the middle of a consultation with my *A to Z* when Tom calls. It's lovely to hear a friendly voice and for a blissful minute he manages to take my mind off what I am about to do.

"I had such a great time on Saturday," he says.

"Me too," I say, remembering the long kiss we'd had when he dropped me off at home. I feel tingly just thinking about it.

"When can I see you again?" he asks. "Are you free tonight or Thursday?"

"Well, I'm going to see my parents for dinner tonight, but Thursday sounds great."

"Thursday it is then."

"Oh damn, hang on a minute. Carrie Anne, Ella and Sabina are coming round that night, but you could come too. I'm sure they'd love to meet you!" I say hopefully.

Tom pauses. "Um, if it's all girls then I think I'll leave you to it, to be honest."

"Well, actually, I think Ella's husband, Paul, is coming too and Abbie's boyfriend, Adam, so you wouldn't be totally outnumbered," I say casually, chewing my bottom lip.

There's another pause and then, "OK. If you're sure it's all right, then I'd love to meet your friends."

"Great. Listen, Tom, honest to God I'm not cutting you off, it's just I'm on my way to an audition and I've got to get a shift on, but how about I call you after and we can talk properly then?"

"Audition, eh? Sounds intriguing. Well, good luck and ring me when you're done. I'm off to see to a poorly duck now."

"OK, great. Well, good luck with the duck. Speak to you later."

One hour later I'm sitting on a plastic chair outside the room where the auditions are being conducted, feeling like I might actually be sick. I ended up finding the building quite quickly, but forgot that at auditions they always like to keep you waiting just long enough for it to totally mess up your day. Despite Carson giving me the whole afternoon off, I had been planning on popping back to demonstrate my seriousness about not wishing to take the piss, but that won't be possible now. Why on earth do I let myself be put into these situations?

The door eventually opens, another dazed and confused auditionee emerges and a bearded man sticks his head round the door.

"Hello, Francesca is it? I almost didn't recognize you without the beret."

I smile weakly and follow him into the rather shabby, bare room.

The bearded man, who's tall and lanky, shakes my hand and says, "I'm Roger, the director, that's Jan, who's casting, and David, the producer."

"Hi," I say, trying to appear sassy, but failing miserably when I catch sight of the ominous CD player that is on the table in front of them. It doesn't bode well.

I won't bore you with the details of what happens over the course of the next few minutes. Suffice to say that I talk about myself for a minute and manage to make myself sound vaguely interesting and then feel nauseous as the full realization hits me that I am about to have to sing and — worse still — dance in public.

At this point, Roger, Jan and David may as well be Roman emperors watching a poor slave girl in the coliseum who's about to face the lions and certain death.

"OK," says Roger, who is wearing a crumpled, grubby linen suit and has a mullet. "What dance have you prepared for us?"

"Well, the thing is, Roger," I begin, "if I'm honest, I didn't receive the information from my agent until today, I'm afraid, so I'm really sorry, but I haven't had a chance to prepare anything."

Roger doesn't look impressed. "I see."

"But seeing as you're not looking for professional dancers, then maybe I could make something up now?"

Roger looks slightly mollified; everyone else just looks blank.

"Right. OK then. I'll choose a CD and you can improvise for us," he says.

I feel sick. "Can I just warn you, though, I'm a pretty horrific dancer. But hey, I'll have a go!" I say, giving them self-deprecating, sassy and ballsy all at once.

Roger ignores me and I see him take out *NOW 63* from the pile in front of him. As he slides the disc into the player and presses play, I wonder what on earth he's chosen. I quickly recognize the beat of "Biology" by Girls Aloud. Could be a lot worse.

OK, there's nothing for it — I may as well just give it my best shot. After all, what the hell have I got to lose?

I turn round so my back is facing the panel and jig one knee tentatively, then spin round to face the panel in what I hope is an impressive display of ballsiness. Then I launch into the sort of routine my mum does at Christmas after one too many sherries. This painful ordeal lasts much longer than is reasonable and after forty seconds or so I am really scraping the barrel for moves. I'm also, to my concern, already quite out of breath. I grimace in what I hope is a self-deprecating manner as I go through my ridiculous paces, taking in the bemused expressions of my audience. Suddenly my situation triggers a memory I haven't thought of for a long time. I think about Stacey at Diamond PR and how desperate she was to be famous and how much I loathed her for it. Truthfully, I know now that part of the reason she made me feel so uncomfortable was because I was probably just as sad and desperate as her. I think how much Stacey would relish seeing me suffer in this ridiculous situation and for some reason this thought strikes me as funny rather than sad and I start to grin. I recall all the auditions I've ever been to, all the acting classes I've taken, the plays that nobody came to see in tiny run-down theatres and, of course, Claims for Dames. And now, jigging around in this grotty room in the middle of the day for no apparent reason, it all just seems like the funniest thing in the world, which can only mean one thing — I no longer bloody care, which is the best and most liberating thing to happen to me in a very long time. The tune picks up speed and I almost forget why I'm there and even start to enjoy prancing around the room. It's rather freeing.

Then I think how funny it would be if Caroline could see me now. I picture her face wrinkled in disgust and it makes me want to laugh out loud. What would Tom say? What the hell would Tom say if he could see me clapping my hands and spinning around in this undignified show of madness? Because it is madness. Carson, Caroline Mason, desperadoes like me and Stacey who don't even really understand what it is we're lusting after in the first place, auditions, the whole ridiculous business of show. Putting yourself on the firing line in order to be told that you're good or bad, that you look wrong or right, in a completely subjective way is absolutely nuts and for that reason more than anything I love it. I love it, but I now get how silly it all really is and I'm certainly not prepared to look a total and utter penis for it any more. With this last thought I decide that I've had enough and I dance towards the door and, without bothering to explain to the bewildered panel, I leg it down the corridor and Girls Aloud grow quieter and quieter until I can't hear them at all.

CHAPTER
TWENTY-SEVEN

It's Tuesday and it's fair to say that Caroline's not a happy bunny. She was perfectly fine until I'd been obliged to fill her in on the situation with Great British Films and things have been a bit tricky ever since.

When I first arrived this morning at 10.00 precisely with the usual venti quattro decaff skinny latte with hazelnut shot in tow, No.47 had seemed a happy ship. Steph and Carson were upstairs somewhere, probably gazing into each other's eyes, Cameron was finishing his third bowl of Coco Pops and Lorna was bustling around the kitchen, singing along to Capital FM and clearing up the debris from breakfast. Caroline was in her usual seat at the table by the French doors, smoking and idly flicking through a copy of *Hello*.

"Morning, Caroline," I said brightly, sensing that today she might be in one of her rare good moods.

"Morning, Fran. Oh great, my coffee. Look at this," she said, licking her finger before searching for a certain page. "Here we are."

I'd taken the magazine from her and found myself staring at some grainy pictures of her and Cameron outside the house on the pavement. I recognized it as being a day when Caroline was leaving for work and

Steph and Cameron were leaving at the same time to go for a walk. The photographer had managed to cut out Steph completely and, if you looked very closely, you could just about make out my elbow. I guess the photographer was after a nice picture of "mother" and son outside their house. I looked at Caroline to gauge her reaction to this invasion of privacy and exploitation of her "son". It wasn't the one I was expecting.

"It's rather good of me, isn't it?"

It seems she still has the power to render me stunned by her awfulness.

Just then I realized that I hadn't seen her since her birthday celebrations.

"Caroline, how was the party and your lunch? Did it all go well?" I enquired.

"Yes. Though my lamb was slightly overdone on Sunday, but apart from that it was fine," she said, without even looking up or taking a break from studying herself.

"And . . . did everyone love the dress and the black glittery shoes?"

"Oh, I didn't wear them in the end. There was so much going on I decided to just go more casual."

I could honestly have throttled her and at that precise moment decided it would be a good time to tell her that the brakes were about to be put on her career. As I explained the latest developments, her good mood vanished and, over the course of the day, she's grown increasingly livid until now her bad temper has managed to infect the entire household. For the last hour we've all been keeping out of her way. Caroline has locked herself in her study so that she can speak in

271

private to Geoffrey, Kenneth and her lawyer, and I have taken the phone into the formal living room to get on with some work. Steph is hiding upstairs and packing bags for herself and Cameron, who are leaving for the States tonight. They're going to New York for a while and then when it's time for Cameron to go back to school they'll be returning to Los Angeles. Carson tends to give Caroline a wide berth at the best of times, so when she's in a mood like this he keeps well away. Now he's upstairs with Steph and Cameron, pretending to help with the packing. Lorna's hiding in the bathroom, where she's supposedly cleaning, although the last time I looked in she was sitting on the edge of the bath squinting at the infamous copy of *Hello*.

The minute Caroline gets off the phone from talking to "her people", I'm summoned back to the kitchen, where I have to deal with Cruella de Vil on my own. It's not pleasant.

I try my best to pacify her. "Look, you won't know anything for sure until the meeting next week, so try not to worry about it until you know exactly what they're intending to do."

She looks me straight in the eye and I swear I can feel my blood cool.

She's wearing her favourite lounging kaftan, her hair is loose and tumbling round her shoulders and the ever-present cigarette is burning away in her fingers. Without any warning, she flings her head back and lets out the most primeval, guttural roar, which makes me jump out of my skin and — if I'm honest — question her sanity.

She stomps to the island and smacks the surface, her hands bunched into fists.

"Fucking bastards. Fucking, fucking, fucking bastards."

At this point I don't care if she's the Queen of Sheba. She is behaving like a spoilt brat and I interrupt her tirade firmly:

"Caroline, Cameron is upstairs."

This at least shuts her up as she remembers that, more importantly as far as she's concerned, so is Carson and that therefore she should moderate her behaviour. She slumps on to a chair, defeated. Then she narrows her eyes and I can see her mind racing: *How can I make life difficult for Francesca?*

"My phone still doesn't work properly. The reception's crap and you said you'd fix it."

"I said I'd look into it, yes," I acquiesce.

"Well?" she challenges.

"Well, you're never going to have crystal-clear reception with any mobile all of the time, but if you're really that worried then there is one handset you could upgrade to, if you pay an extra eighty pounds."

"Well, why haven't you done that then?" she positively snarls.

"I told you the other day," I begin, trying to control the reflex desire to roll my eyes. "Because you have to be present in the shop to sign the new contract and I won't forge your signature — it's illegal," I explain patiently for the hundred and fourteenth time.

"You're so provincial," she snaps, just as Carson comes in.

"What's going on in here, Cas? I do wish you wouldn't wail like that when Cameron's around. It scares him. He thinks you're in pain," he says, flinging open the fridge door and examining the contents.

Caroline obviously doesn't think this comment is even worthy of a reply and she gives him a look behind his back that is pure Kevin the Teenager, then diverts her energy back to annoying me.

"So you're saying I would actually have to go to the shop if I want to change my phone?" she says in a tone that suggests that going to the shops is on a par with sticking needles in her eyes.

"Yes," I say calmly, going to perch on one of the bar stools and watching Carson gulp a pint of milk in one go.

She considers this while frowning in Carson's direction, who's wiping his milk moustache off his mouth with the back of his hand.

"When are you going back to the States?" she asks him sulkily.

"Not till next week now," he says, replacing the milk back in the fridge. "I've got to meet this damn director. My agent's insisting on it and he's going to be in London from next Wednesday, so there's not much point going back till after then."

I can't help but notice how thoroughly uninterested Carson sounds in the whole thing.

"Mm," sniffs Caroline, and I just know that she's quietly seething with envy. If only directors were queuing up to meet with her.

"Francesca, what do you suggest we do about this phone then?"

274

I don't know whether Carson being in the room makes me feel braver or if it's because I'm just so sick to death of her nagging me about her bloody phone, but my answer comes without a moment's hesitation: "Chuck it out the window?"

Carson laughs out loud. Caroline looks like she's sucked on a salty lemon.

"Francesca, we're going to go to this wretched shop now. Get Terry to bring the car round."

"Terry's having his operation this week," I remind her. Sometimes I wonder if she ever listens to a word anyone says or, for that matter, ever reads a word I write. "Remember? I told you and you said to only book drivers to take you to the theatre who will allow you to smoke in the car, which I've done. It's all written on the daily reports that you asked me to do."

Carson catches my eye before leaving the room and rolls his eyeballs in mock exasperation while shrugging his broad shoulders.

"Fine, but how the hell do you suggest I get to this bloody shop if I want to change my phone?"

I slide off the stool, careful not to knock over any of the flower vases. "Come on, we can walk there. It's literally five minutes up the road."

She looks at me, aghast. "Walk?"

"Yes, walk," I reply simply.

"OK, fine, we'll walk," she says mutinously. She heaves herself melodramatically out of her chair and follows me out of the kitchen and into the hall, where she slips on a pair of Gina flats. "What do I need to bring?" she asks, suddenly sounding strangely excited about our impromptu trip.

"Nothing. I've got your cards, your phone and house keys. Steph, Carson — we're just popping out for five minutes," I yell up the stairs.

I open the front door and it feels lovely to be out in the fresh air. It's damp September day.

"Francesca?"

"Yes, Caroline?"

"I've got Botox next week. I don't want anyone except Terry driving me there," she says, walking in such a way that it looks like her legs aren't used to such a strange sensation. Maybe her feet have never felt pavement underneath them before.

"That's fine. Terry will be back by then, as long as his leg isn't too sore, so he should be able to take you. I told you that on my daily report and I also wrote that as a back-up plan, if the very worst came to the worst, I could drive you in my little car."

"Well, hopefully it won't come to that but I suppose it's best to have a plan in place," she says, and she bestows a smile upon me. Honestly, she's more changeable than the weather in the Caribbean.

We're nearly at the end of the road now and I can see that someone has clocked Caroline. It's a young lad of about fifteen and he seems to be making his way over for an autograph. It would be physically impossible to walk the streets with Carson, who does literally get mobbed in quite a disturbing way, but Caroline doesn't usually get too much bother as far as I can make out whenever I've been in clothes shops or restaurants with her, although she always turns heads just because she is so striking that people can't help but notice her. I look at Caroline and I can see that she too has spotted this rather shy-looking boy and she's trying terribly hard to look as though she's not bothered, but she's far too transparent and I know that secretly she's chuffed to bits.

"Hello," says the boy, holding out a scrap of paper and a biro towards me for some reason. "Are you that girl off Claims for Dames and, if you are, can I have your autograph?"

Caroline's face drops and I want the ground to open up and swallow me. Doesn't this boy realize that I'm standing next to a bona fide movie star? Obviously not. I scribble my name as fast as I can, thank the boy and he slopes off, looking very pleased with himself.

"Well, that hasn't ever happened before," I bluster, trying to make amends, but Caroline isn't listening and she stalks ahead, unamused and clearly determined not to ask me what "Claims for Dames" might be, even though I can tell she's secretly gagging to.

The whole situation is hysterical, but she mustn't catch me laughing, so I bite the inside of my mouth so hard I can feel the metallic taste of blood and trot along quickly behind her.

I think a lot of my friends wonder why I've stuck at this job for so long, putting up with Caroline's bad behaviour and being taken for granted on pretty much a day-to-day basis. And apart from the money, which is obviously a legitimate reason, it's hard to explain. The thing is, as much as Caroline can be a nightmare and as much as I may not like her, I honestly don't hate her. In fact, I have to admit that in some sick way I feel a weird sense of belonging in her strange world and feel quite comfortable in the little niche that I've carved out for myself as part of her household. Of course, there are times when I could quite happily wring her scrawny neck, but on the whole I find her more fascinatingly awful than anything else and, I mean, what just happened with the boy asking me for my autograph in front of her is such a classic bit for my book. Ever since I started writing the book, it's put an entirely different slant on the whole experience of working for Caroline and sometimes I find myself positively willing her to be dreadful so that I have more material.

"Caroline!" I call, realizing she's gone past the shop.

We enter the phone shop, where she looks ridiculously out of place in her multicoloured Missoni kaftan. In this mundane environment it suddenly makes her appear less movie star and more Joseph and his technicolour dreamcoat; but to my relief the manager recognizes her, which immediately acts as damage limitation for the autograph fiasco. She proceeds to bat her eyelids half-heartedly, but I know she's not that fussed about making an impression and I see none of the megawatt charm I know she is so capable of. We sort out her new phone — sorry, *I* sort out her phone — and then all Caroline has to do is to sign her name and I can pay for the upgrade.

"Francesca," she drawls, wafting her hand around vaguely. "I'll leave you to it then, and I'll see you back at the house."

278

"Well, I'm only going to be a second," I say.

"No, I'll go ahead and leave you to deal with everything," she says, sidling out into the street and waving regally back at the shop manager, who according to his name badge is called Nigel and who has taken the cash and is just about to hand me a receipt.

"She'll just be a second . . ." he tries, but she's gone.

It's as if she can't quite allow me to think that we've actually done something together. For some unfathomable reason she has to feel that I have sorted out the phone for her. Of course, now I'm ready to go and she's only a few feet ahead of me, which means I end up following her back to the house, unsure whether I should jog and catch up with her or just carry on stalking her, like Cato to her Inspector Clouseau.

At my parents' house in Teddington that evening, I act out this ridiculous scenario, but it's slightly lost on Mum and Dad as they can't understand what's so funny about her coming out to a shop with me in the first place.

CHAPTER
TWENTY-EIGHT

You can always tell if you really like someone because you want your friends to really like them too, and it matters enormously that you get their seal of approval. Tonight Tom is going to meet everyone and I'm desperate for it to go well and for them to think that he's as amazing as I do. I'm well aware that it's only our second date, but the last one went so well I feel confident that he'll be able to handle my friends. So tonight he's coming round to mine, where he'll be meeting Sabina, Ella and Paul and Carrie Anne for the first time. He's already met Abbie, of course, and she's invited her new boyfriend, Adam, too, so hopefully it should be a good evening.

Dad gave me a lasagne to take home yesterday, which is warming up in the oven now, and I bought a crusty loaf and some salad stuff on the way home from work. It's 7.30 and I've asked Tom to come round for 8.00 so that I can get myself organized and catch up with everyone else before he arrives. Everybody's in the sitting room, except me and Carrie Anne, who has left work early for probably the first time ever, an unexpected treat. It's great to catch up with her. I've been filling her in on some of my favourite Caroline anecdotes and the tears are rolling down her cheeks.

"Oh my God," she splutters. "I'm so sorry I got you into all of this. You must curse me most days."

"Hardly," I say, searching in a cupboard for the oil and vinegar. "If it wasn't for this job, I'd probably still be temping, on the verge of dying from boredom and in serious financial ruin. You offered me an escape route from all of that so I'm nothing but grateful to you."

"Oh gosh, well, you're very welcome, and as long as you're not going crazy, that's all right."

"Not at all," I say, making a dressing for the salad. "In fact, I would go so far as to say that it's been a really interesting experience and one that's certainly opened my eyes up to a few things."

"Like what?" asks Carrie Anne.

I pause before answering. "Well, for instance — and this is quite embarrassing to admit — but I've always been a bit obsessed with the notion that being famous would be completely fantastic. And now that I've seen firsthand the doors that fame can open, the privilege it brings and how much fun there is to be had, well, I still think it to some extent. But what I'm finally coming to understand is that unless you're a very secure and happy person to start off with, then fame is only ever going to mess you up."

Carrie Anne smiles and I can tell that neither my obsession with fame nor my profound thoughts on it have left her feeling particularly enlightened. She's obviously had all this worked out for a while.

"I suppose realizing that fame doesn't automatically make people happy or provide them with absolute freedom has been quite an education for me, really," I say, thinking of Carson. "God, Carrie Anne, you must think I'm so naive."

"I don't think you're naive," says Carrie Anne. "Although sometimes I do think you're a bit idealistic."

"Probably," I say, adding a clove of garlic to the dressing I've just made and stirring madly. "Anyway, it's all good and I've been feeling quite inspired of late. In fact, I've really got back into my writing again."

"Have you? What are you writing?" asks Carrie Anne, picking at the big hunk of Parmesan that I've just taken out of the fridge to grate.

"Well, it's called *The Diary of a Personal Assistant* and hopefully it's quite funny. I've probably got a bit carried away with it, but it's actually developed into a bit more than just a short story and has turned into something resembling a book," I say, feeling a bit shy about saying this out loud.

"A book!" exclaims Carrie Anne. "Oh my God, Fran, that's such an incredible achievement. I'm so proud of you."

"Thanks," I say, suddenly feeling quite proud. "I've been really enjoying it, actually, and I know after having pursued acting for so long it would be foolish to pick an even harder and more competitive profession, but somehow I feel with this that I really might be on to something. So when all this is over, I might see where it leads me."

282

"You've got to let me read it, Fran. It sounds really intriguing. Then if it's any good, which I bet it will be, I can help steer you in the right direction. I could even show it to some of the readers at Great British Films and they could give you a critique, if you like," offers Carrie Anne kindly.

Despite the fact that Carrie Anne has read many of the short stories and articles that I've written in the past, for some reason I feel incredibly protective about this particular project. It just feels much more important to me and crucial that I get it absolutely right. Somehow with this one, the mere thought of a professional like Carrie Anne reading my attempt turns my stomach with nerves. It also crosses my mind that she may find it a tad disloyal to be exposing my boss's worst foibles when I am supposed to be her loyal and devoted servant. Especially since she was the one who got me the job in the first place.

"That's really kind, but I'm afraid it's nowhere near a ready state at the moment," I say, swiftly changing the subject. "More wine?"

The doorbell rings and I suddenly feel all flustered.

"Door, Fran!" yells Abbie from the sitting room.

"OK," I say with my heart in my mouth.

I take a deep breath and race to the intercom in the hall, which takes all of three seconds — the flat's not that big.

"Come on up, it's the second floor," I say breathily to my new man through the intercom. I wait for him at the door.

As soon as I see him I realize that, of course, he's one hundred times more nervous than I am.

"Hi, Fran," he says, kissing my cheek and handing me a bottle of Merlot.

"Oh, thanks for that. Right, come on in."

I lead Tom through to the living room where I introduce him to everybody and I am so proud of my friends because they all really make an effort to make him feel at home. As he shakes hands with Paul and Adam I can see him visibly relaxing.

"And my powers of deduction tell me that you must be Ella," he says warmly to my now obviously pregnant friend. "Abbie I know already. Or, at least, we've done the 'YMCA' together at a wedding so . . ."

And I just stand there with a ridiculous grin on my face until Carrie Anne kicks me and tells me to go and get him a drink.

One hour later and there's not one bit of lasagne left in the tray. Everybody's slumping away from the table one by one and I'm the only one who's not too stuffed to contemplate clearing up and that is purely because Tom is here. Otherwise I would have happily fought to the death with Sabina for the last bit and overeaten as usual.

"Oh my God," groans Ella. "I shouldn't have eaten so much. There is no way I'm going to sleep tonight now." Her tummy is looking uncomfortably stretched.

"How long have you got to go?" asks Tom.

"Three months," replies Paul proudly.

"Bloody hell," says Abbie, lighting a cigarette, but moving to the window so she can hang herself out of it, making sure that no smoke blows Ella's way. "I just can't believe I've got a friend who's going to be a mummy. Do you think it'll come on time?"

"No," says Ella. "Everyone says that first babies almost always come late, so it could in actual fact not arrive for another three and a half months or so, which is a terrible, terrible thought. Apart from anything else, baby would end up having a birthday awfully close to Christmas. Like you, Fran." She rubs her tummy affectionately and I nod sagely as someone who does indeed appreciate the annoyance of a December birthday. "It's funny, I never thought I'd be willing the birth bit to come along so fast, but I think God must have planned it so that pregnant women get so uncomfortable they don't feel fear any more at the thought of shoving a watermelon out of their vaginas."

We all reflect on this last lovely thought until Ella suddenly looks up and says hastily, "Sorry, Tom."

"Don't mind me," he says, fortunately looking more amused than disgusted.

Ella heaves a big sigh while trying to shift into a more comfortable position and failing miserably. "Paul, I'm so sorry to be a killjoy, but could we go now? It's just I've got heartburn and I really need to be naked and to lie down — sorry again, Tom."

"I know how you feel," he says, unabashed and patting his stomach.

Paul and Ella say their goodbyes and leave, which frees up a lot more space on the sofa. I spot an opening next to Tom and dive in.

Carrie Anne, who has been chatting away to Adam at the table, looks up and interjects. "Fran, now that we've had dinner and there are a few less people here, can I see a bit of your book?"

"No."

"Oh, come on, please?" insists Carrie Anne.

"No, I don't want to show it to you yet. It's not ready," I try.

"Oh, go on," says Tom, joining in. "I'd love to see it too."

"Don't you start," I say, putting a cushion over my face. There's no way in the world I'd let Tom see it. I couldn't stand the humiliation if he thought it was a load of old dross.

"Oh, go on, Fran. I mean, fair enough you don't want Tom to see it, but how long have you and I known each other? Plus I already know you can write, so what's the big deal?" persists Carrie Anne.

I know full well that the only way to shut Carrie Anne up once she's got an idea in her head is to give in, so reluctantly I go to the computer. I figure if I acquiesce straight away then there is less chance that all the others will jump on the bandwagon and start pestering me about it.

I'd forgotten how bossy Carrie Anne can be sometimes, but as I watch the fresh white pages pouring off the printer I realize that it might in fact be quite a good idea to get an opinion at this stage. I suppose there's not much point writing if I'm never going to allow anyone to read it. I just wouldn't be happy if one of those people were Tom, who — let's face it — could go off me completely if he found it to be terrible clichéd tripe. Someone being deluded about being good at something is a major turn-off as far as I'm concerned. Fortunately he seems to have sensed my discomfort, taken the hint and has started chatting to Abbie about something else entirely. I discreetly hand the first few pages to Carrie Anne as it'll be a long time, and much A4, before it's all printed out. She settles into a chair and starts reading immediately. Oh well, at least she's had a couple of glasses of wine to take the edge off her judgement.

I strike up conversation with Tom and Abbie in order to divert their attention further and try not to think about the fact that Carrie Anne is currently reading my words. It's at least ten minutes before she looks up again.

"This is great, Francesca, but I can't believe how much of it there is. You actually have written a flipping book — it's amazing. You must be so proud of yourself."

"Um, yeah," I admit, blushing furiously.

"Give me some more pages," demands Carrie Anne and, encouraged by her interest, I happily obey and go to fetch some more.

With Carrie Anne ensconced in my book, the rest of us have a fantastic time chatting away and I'm sad when it's finally time for everyone to head home. The evening has been a total success. Tom's goodbye kiss is heaven and it takes all my willpower not to drag him into my bedroom and give him a right good seeing to, but I stop myself because with this one I'd like to wait just a bit longer. Maybe a couple of weeks, or a week, or at least till next time I see him. I mean, what am I, a nun?

CHAPTER
TWENTY-NINE

12th October

I know I haven't written for absolutely ages, but writing my book seems to be taking up all my spare time and energy lately. Well, that and a certain Tom Worthington.

Yes, since I last checked in Tom has officially become my boyfriend and these days we are pretty much inseparable.

Actually, technically speaking, that last bit is a lie as, sadly, I can't take Tom to work and at the moment I seem to be stuck there for anything between ten and twelve hours a day. Still, even if I could take him with me I probably wouldn't for a couple of very good reasons: firstly, when we're together I can't keep my hands off him and I'm not sure how Caroline would feel about that as she likes to have my undiluted attention while she's nagging me to death; secondly, I'm not sure how Tom would feel about watching his girlfriend being bossed around and generally treated like a second-class citizen, as he can hardly even stand to be in the same room when I'm merely on the phone to her. Honestly, Caroline really is getting worse as the days go by. Anyway, I digress — enough of her and back to happier things.

When I'm not at work, Tom and I are together all the time and I feel so irritatingly happy that even the onset of cold, dark autumnal evenings, the reappearance of tights and bobbly jumpers in my wardrobe and the desire to eat my body weight in mashed potato isn't depressing me too much.

To be honest, I'm quite overwhelmed by my own cleverness at having snagged such a lovely bloke whom I honestly don't think even my parents could find fault with. Being in a proper, fully functional, grown-up relationship feels quite the novelty and for the first time ever I'm really enjoying being someone's girlfriend. Going out with Tom doesn't feel like the usual angst-ridden, completely confusing, diet-inducing nightmare that going out with someone usually feels like. I don't have to worry about how to be, or when to ring, if I'm seeing him too much or "playing it right", to the point where the other day I found myself wondering why this was. After much reflection I have eventually managed to work out the answer: he likes me. That's it — it really is that simple.

He fancies me too, of course, but much more importantly Tom just seems to like me for who I am, so I don't have to put a load of effort into being anything but myself. The fact that the feeling is mutual is, frankly, a bit of a joy and I really can't think of anything I don't like about him. I'm even having the best sex I've ever had in my life, which I shall now attempt to describe. Although really to do it justice would involve me getting all Jilly Cooper about it, and having to use verbs like "caressed", "entered" and "stroked", along with adjectives like "gently", "manfully" and "passionately", none of which I can employ without feeling utterly self-conscious, even if it is only in my diary. (All power to anybody who can write a successful sex scene.) What I will say is that, although on our first attempt the world didn't exactly spin off its axis, we must

290

have been just finding our feet, because the second time was something of an eye-opener, the third was a downright revelation and it's got continually better and better every single time. Suffice to say that, while it took us a little bit of time to find our groove, we have now definitely located it and are really making the most of it. God, I can't wait to see him later.

Of course, I can't be totally smug and puke-inducing because truthfully there have been a few blustery patches while we've been navigating the "getting to know someone" and "testing all the boundaries" stage. In fact, a few weeks ago I discovered during our first official row that, despite Tom's calm demeanour, he's certainly no pushover.

I put my pen and diary down and think back to that night. With hindsight I would say that it definitely marked the point when our relationship shifted up a gear, as it became clear that we both had strong feelings for each other.

It was a Saturday night back in September and we'd gone out for a few drinks with Harry, Briggsy, Abbie and Adam, Wayne and a few others. It was one of those nights that had started as it meant to go on, in this case badly, and we'd only been at the bar for about ten minutes before I started wondering what I might be missing on telly. Never a good sign.

On reflection, there were two major flaws in the evening's planning, the first one being that the venue was awful. At Briggsy's suggestion we'd met in a small, claustrophobic bar in Richmond that, for starters, was really inconvenient for us all to get to and certainly not worth the struggle. The minute we walked in, I'd felt tired. It was absolutely heaving with people, there was nowhere to sit and the queue for the bar was four people deep. By way of compensation for our stressful wait for an overpriced double vodka, they were blasting unbelievably loud R & B directly into our inner ears. (I know I sound like my mum, but I don't care.) Loud music is what you want when you're at a gig, a party or a club, not when you're at a bar where you've met up with friends to chat, or for that matter in a clothes shop when you're trying to make important sartorial decisions — but that's another story. Anyway, the music was without question too loud, although at least this meant that nobody could hear us tutting, sighing or asking each other what the hell we were all doing there in the first place.

The second problem was within our group. Briggsy had arrived at the bar very early with Harry and, as a result, the two of them were on a completely different plane to the rest of us. They'd already reached the shouty, insulting stage of being drunk, whereas we were all still at the "how are you, shall I buy a round, I can't hear myself think" part of the evening.

With Sandy at home looking after baby Max, Harry was determined to make the most of his night out and was very thoughtfully drinking enough for the whole family, aided and abetted by Briggsy, of course, who seemed to have taken it upon himself to assist Harry with forgetting all about his responsibilities and to ensure that when he got home later that night Sandy would have two babies to look after.

Briggsy had already started making desperately inappropriate jokes so, in a bid to avoid them, Tom and I tried to chat more with Abbie and Adam. Still, by the time I'd yelled pardon to Adam a record eleven times in a row I was losing the will to live so I gave up and listened to Briggsy's foghorn voice instead, which was the only thing capable of penetrating the din. I wish I hadn't bothered. For my benefit he proceeded to crack a lot of Claims for Dames jokes, then moved on to a hilarious anecdote about a girl that Tom had dated, before finishing with a trip down memory lane to the time when Harry and I got caught having sex on his sofa by Wayne. How my ribs ached. Tom made a show of laughing, but it was very unconvincing and the set of his jaw was so tight I thought his teeth might smash.

Needless to say, I was more than a little relieved when it was time to scream our goodbyes and leave. Ears ringing, Tom and I slumped into a taxi and out of habit I checked my messages. There were a couple from Caroline, so I phoned her back. At first she hadn't believed it was me because my voice was so hoarse from all the shouting, so she'd made me answer some strange security questions that she made up on the spot. Anyway, eventually I got off the phone and when I did I could sense that Tom was slightly nettled, so I told him that it was entirely natural to feel jealous of the fact that I had gone out with Harry. However, he refused to admit that this was why he was grumpy, preferring instead to blame his bad mood on the fact that I'd phoned Caroline on my night off.

Not surprisingly after such an unbelievably shit night, Tom and I had ended up having a bit of a debate, and by the time we got home neither of us were in the mood for any bedroom antics, so instead we sat perched on either end of the sofa, sulking. The atmosphere was so strained that I switched on the telly, thinking it might help us to avoid having our first proper, full-blown argument. How wrong could I have been?

"Do you want a drink?" I asked. "I'm just going to get a glass of water."

"Yes, please," Tom said.

As I ran the tap, waiting for the water to turn icy cold, I heard a horribly familiar sound coming from the TV, which took a while for me to place. When I did, though, I blushed to my very core and my entire body felt clammy with sick anticipation.

I heard the inevitable first splutter from Tom, but knowing it was coming did nothing to ease the pain. In fact, it made it worse.

"If you've had a prang or a major bang, then be a doll, get on the phone and call up Claims for Daaaames . . ." trilled my voice around my living room.

"Oh my God," Tom said.

Hesitantly, I poked my head round the door.

"That is hilarious. What the hell is that beret you're wearing? You look like Frank Spencer." At this point, Tom, having cracked himself up, stuffed his fist into his mouth in an attempt to stop laughing, but to no avail. As the advert ended he clutched his sides, clearly powerless to avoid being swamped by the mirth that seemed to have miraculously washed away his bad mood. My embarrassment started giving way to anger. How dare he ridicule me in this way?

"Briggsy said it was hilarious," Tom panted, "but, oh my God, if I'd known it was that funny I would have made sure I'd kept the TV on more. It's one of the funniest things I've ever seen . . . I . . . I . . ." He gasped for breath, unable to continue as another attack of the giggles threatened to take over. "Oh my God, my ribs hurt. The way you looked down the lens like that . . . it's priceless . . ."

Only now did it finally dawn on Tom that I wasn't laughing with him. Quite the opposite, in fact. My anger had completely dissipated, along with the urge to shout at him, and had been replaced instead by acute self-pity. To my horror, I found myself weeping with embarrassment, feeling more humiliated than I ever had before.

"How could you?" I asked through my tears.

"How could I what?" said Tom, his face falling as he realized that something had gone seriously awry.

"How could you laugh at me like that?" I wailed. "Have you got any bloody idea how shit that makes me feel?"

Tom looked at me aghast and for a second I assumed that, due to the fact he'd never been anything but totally soppy with me, the next sentence he uttered would incorporate an abject apology, a plea for a pardon. I was wrong.

"Why on earth are you crying, Fran? Can't you take a joke? I'm sorry if I've upset you, but you seemed all

295

right when Briggsy was taking the piss tonight, so why does it suddenly become an act of cruelty when I do it?"

"Because maybe I actually care about what you think," I suggested sheepishly, stunned that he wasn't begging for my forgiveness. "And maybe it's a bit humiliating for me that that advert happens to be the pinnacle of my acting career so far. So, in fact, what you are laughing at is not just the advert but all the years I've wasted in trying to follow my dream," I added, less sheepishly.

Tom sat down, gave me a pitying look and put his head in his hands.

"What?" I asked, feeling rather wrong-footed. He wouldn't answer though and just looked into the middle distance.

"What?" I raged. Nothing winds me up more than someone who won't argue back. It must be the Italian in me, but I like to get things out in the open and off my chest. I like a good shout. Tom, however, seemed to have shut up shop, both physically and verbally, and I just couldn't read his expression.

"Don't look at me with such disgust," I squawked like an old fishwife, knowing that he was experiencing a side of me that he'd never encountered before; we both were. At this point I remember knowing that I was letting my temper get the better of me, but of course it had been rather unhelpfully offset by six double vodka lime and sodas. Shaking his head, Tom finally spoke.

"I just can't work you out sometimes, Francesca. I mean, I meet this wonderfully intelligent, kind, gorgeous, sweet girl who I think I'm falling for, but then you say something that displaces everything I think about you and I realize that maybe I haven't got you worked out at all."

I felt completely thrown.

"Things like what?" I asked hesitantly.

"Look, it's probably not for me to say, Fran. I mean, who am I to sit here psychoanalysing you, anyway?"

I sort of agreed but was too curious to let him take the easy option.

"You're my boyfriend, Tom, and if you don't tell me how it is then no one else will."

"OK, well, if you're sure?"

"I'm sure," I said firmly, not feeling it in the least bit.

"Well, I just don't understand why you take yourself as an actress so seriously. I mean, I appreciate that you really wanted to be a serious actress, but you've had a good stab at it and it hasn't happened. Now, I'm not completely naive and I do understand that as a profession an incredible amount of luck is needed in order to get off the ground, but I would imagine that talent is a pretty necessary tool as well and it strikes me that whenever I've heard you lamenting your lost acting career, you never seem to consider the possibility that maybe . . . it just wasn't meant to be?"

At this point Tom gulped nervously and I realized simultaneously that he really wasn't trying to hurt my feelings. But he had.

The truth hurts and, although he hadn't spelt it out in black and white, I knew exactly what he was skirting round, and he was right. I had never considered the possibility that maybe I hadn't made it as an actress simply because I wasn't very good.

Sadly, at this point, rather than calmly say, "Wow, thanks, Tom, you're absolutely right. I am not only untalented but deluded too. Thank goodness you pointed that out," I said something along the lines of: "You bastard. How can you sit there and tell me I'm a shit actress? What gives you the fucking right . . ." etc., etc.

The row had escalated and it wasn't pretty.

Tom accused me of being obsessed with unimportant crap and for being a doormat around Caroline. I told him that he couldn't possibly understand what made me tick, seeing as he didn't possess even the tiniest amount of healthy ambition, to which he replied that what he did understand quite clearly was that I was a bright girl who wasted her efforts on dreams that were totally unrealistic when I should in fact be focusing on more tangible things like my writing. I told him that I was writing a fucking book, so how much more could I do, and then Caroline rang and Tom told me that he would leave if I took the call and I took her call.

When I got off the phone, Tom was livid and, true to his word, he stormed out, but only for about ten minutes because once I realized that he had actually left and wasn't just lurking in the communal hallway, I phoned him on his mobile and begged and pleaded with him to come back.

To my immense relief he did, but then he asked me what had been so important that it couldn't have waited till Monday, and when I told him that Caroline had needed to know where her clean tights were, he became incandescent with rage.

Never having seen Tom so angry before, I felt rather taken aback and more than a little defensiveness had started to creep in, so I unadvisedly mentioned, for good measure, that as a vet he couldn't possibly appreciate that some people, particularly creative ones, have different temperaments and that me taking her calls really wasn't such a big deal.

At this point Tom said calmly that I was right, that he would never be able to appreciate people whose temperament was stark staring nuts.

The row rattled on again for ages, but eventually we did both manage to calm down and rowing gradually turned back into heated debate, which ultimately morphed into a "kiss and make up" chat, in bed.

So that, in a very large nutshell, was our first row and the moment I found out that Tom is a force to be reckoned with and not someone who'll be pushed around, which has ended up making me like him even more.

Horrid though it was at the time, the row quickly ended up seeming worth it when later that night Tom held me in his arms and told me that he loved me for the first time. I told him that I loved him too and then we had sex and he gave me the biggest orgasm I've ever had. Thinking about it now, it's probably very lucky that he can do that to me or I'd have to use my acting skills and fake them, which according to him probably wouldn't work as I'd do it really badly and he wouldn't believe me.

CHAPTER
THIRTY

It's late November and Terry is in Tenerife. I can't wait
for him to get back as somehow I've managed to end
up as designated driver for most of the day today,
leaving me no time for anything else.

"Is that your car, Francesca?" Carson enquired when
he spotted me going to feed the meter this morning.

Carson's been backwards and forwards across the
pond these last few weeks and now he's in London to
sign the contracts for the movie that his agent has
coerced him into doing after weeks of emotional
blackmail and bullying.

"Yes," I replied, shutting the door behind me and
hoping that Caroline would be ready to leave on time
so I didn't have to worry about finding any more
twenty-pence pieces for a short while.

"Wow, it's so great. I love your little cars with their
big, bold number plates. It's so full of character," he
enthused, gazing out of the window.

I looked from him to my rusty green Fiat Uno that
was sitting outside and wondered if he was being
sarcastic.

"Are you driving Cas today?"

"Yes, I'm taking her to Harley Street," I replied.

"I don't suppose you could give me a lift to my meeting in town later, could you? It's just that I'd prefer to go with you and also I'd just love to ride in a regular car for a change," he said.

"Sure," I replied cautiously, still searching for any hint of sarcasm, but not detecting any. "Your meeting is at twelve thirty, isn't it? I can come and pick you up for about twelve," I said, wondering how on earth I was supposed to get any work done at all today.

"Thanks, Fran, you're a star," he said, bounding up the stairs.

I retreated to the study, feeling slightly perturbed. Recently I'd heard Carson extolling the virtues of many seemingly ordinary pursuits. He'd dreamily spoken of hanging one's washing out to dry on a line, being able to pop out for a pint of milk and now of having a distinctly average car like mine.

I'd realized that it was starting to grate a little. I mean, what was stopping him from buying a Fiat Uno if he wanted one so much? He could have mine for six hundred quid. He could afford to buy the factory if he wanted to. Nobody was forcing him to travel around in luxurious, air-conditioned cars with leather interiors. His other flights of fancy I have more sympathy for, as he genuinely is a prisoner in his own house at the moment. The paparazzi have been stationed outside for so long now that over time I have become immune to their presence, and I know that if Carson was to go to the local shop to buy a pint of milk there would be a riot. Still, he's the one who chose to be an actor and if he hates it that much then why is he going to meet someone about another starring role this afternoon that will merely fuel his fame further? If he hates it all so much, why doesn't he retire to the hills where he can drive around in a Fiat Uno, buying pints of milk and hanging out his washing to his heart's content and taking photographs for a living? Or is it just that, when it comes down to it, twenty million dollars is far too big a carrot?

I forgot to mention the photos to you. Carson confided to Lorna and me the other day that his dream job would be a professional portrait photographer. I hadn't taken much notice until he'd shown us his portfolio, which contained some of the most stunning black-and-white photographs I've ever seen. The fact that many of them were of very famous people in everyday situations certainly helped make them so great. There was Robert De Niro behind a barbecue with some tongs in his hand, Brad Pitt fishing on a riverbank with Angelina sitting next to him, dangling her bare toes in the water, and Julia Roberts drinking coffee at a breakfast table to name but a few. With subject matter like that it would be difficult to go wrong, but I could tell that these pictures were still very special. Lorna had studied the one of Julia Roberts with her steaming cup of coffee in her hand and had remarked, "It doesn't look like she's using a coaster."

I'd told Carson that I thought they were fabulous and he'd looked wistfully into the middle distance as if pained to think that he couldn't pursue his interest more whole-heartedly. To be honest, this also irritated me a little. I guess I just can't feel that sorry for someone who has everything that most people can only ever dream about and who doesn't use it more to their advantage.

Still, there's no more time for reflection as I have to take Caroline for her injections.

I go to the formal living room, where she's reclining on the settee listening to her iPod.

"Is it time to go?" she asks wearily.

"Yes it is. I'll wait in the car for you."

She's feeling very sorry for herself today and for once I don't blame her. Her film has been on and off more times than a whore's drawers. At one point in October they were almost at the point of signing on the dotted line and then something happened and it was all hanging in the balance again. Now, as of yesterday, the film is officially off, which means I've only got a matter of weeks left as Caroline's personal assistant. Despite being glad of the reprieve, I'm starting to feel a bit panicky about what on earth I'm going to do when she's finished the play, jetted back to the States and out of my life, and it's all over. As much as I'm enthused about my writing at the moment, it's not going to pay the rent, certainly not in the short term anyway, so I must save every penny I can over the next few weeks. Needless to say, Jodie is most unhappy about this recent turn of events and she sounded as if she was actually crying the last time I spoke to her to tell her that Caroline wanted every item in her US winter wardrobe laundered before she returned.

Life after Caroline Mason is certainly going to be strange for a while. Being a personal assistant has meant that my life has really been Caroline's life for a long time now and there are aspects of the job I think I'll definitely miss. I'm just grateful that I won't have to say goodbye forever to Lorna, who says that I can always pop in to No.47 to see her when she's there twice a week to clean the house.

Outside, Caroline circles my car, regarding it with a faint air of disgust. She walks tentatively round to the passenger side of my two-door car and, looking thoroughly confused, searches for a way to get into the back seat. Eventually, unable to find a door, she gives up and clambers resignedly into the front passenger seat. Pulling the front seat down by way of a lever was always going to be way beyond her. Of course, there is only one reason Caroline would ever consider being seen sitting in a car like mine, and that is vanity. The only driver in the UK she trusts not to leak stuff to the press is Terry, and a trip to a cosmetic surgeon on Harley Street is just the sort of information and pictures they would love.

Despite the fact that I've cleaned out all the mouldy sweet wrappers and been to the car wash, Caroline still spends the entire journey looking mildly surprised to find herself in such an unworthy vehicle. Still, at least she's quiet. It seems that her film being cancelled has really taken the wind out of her sails and my "To Do" list is relatively tiny today. The only time she speaks is to tell me to switch off my phone, which is ringing incessantly and which I can't answer because I'm driving.

As we draw nearer the clinic, she dons a Pucci headscarf and a pair of sunglasses, which immediately makes her look like a celebrity who doesn't want to be recognized. I don't know why she bothers going to such cloak-and-dagger extremes to keep her facial injections under wraps. Why celebrities seem to think they can keep these things private when, quite frankly, any fool can see that their faces are so taut they're totally devoid of any natural expression, I don't know. For the record, as well as her boob job Caroline has also had work done to her eyes and Jodie told me she's pretty sure she's had lipo too.

Anyway, I drop Caroline off and now I'm rid of her for the rest of the day because Leticia is picking her up from the clinic, presumably so that she can play nursemaid, and then she's going to the theatre. Before heading back to South Ken to pick up Carson, I switch on my phone to check my messages. There are fourteen, but only one is of any real interest and that is the one from Tom asking if he can see me tonight. I immediately leave a message back saying that I'd love to and to call me later. I tentatively add a "love you" at the end, still somewhat self-conscious about saying it out loud, and for a second I feel completely gooey. God, I love him.

Right, it's time to go and pick up one of the most famous men in the world and take him to a meeting. Again, I'm not sure why he's bothering to go at all. He seems so miserable and unenthusiastic about the entire project, so why do it?

Don't get me wrong, I really am quite fond of Carson and I understand that fame and fortune presents its own set of problems such as lack of privacy and other pressures that us mere mortals can't begin to relate to. But, without wishing to sound cynical, if he's so dissatisfied with his situation, then why does he do nothing to rectify it? It seems to me that Steph, Carson and Cameron could all potentially be much happier with a few adjustments to their lives. But maybe, despite all his protestations about wanting to be a normal guy, Carson doesn't really want to give it all up? After all, let's face it, Carson's wealth could buy him his freedom if he *really* wanted it. Maybe he's been pampered for so long he doesn't know what it is he really wants.

Anyway, I hope he doesn't complain about his lot today because I'm not in the mood to hear it. Frankly, if I had a fraction of what he has, I wouldn't be wasting any of my precious time doing anything I didn't want to do. Still, once he's got this meeting over and done with he can go back to Los Angeles where, by all accounts, he's left alone much more and — more importantly — he'll be reunited with Steph and Cameron. I suddenly realize that with the end of the job on the horizon, today could be the last time I ever see him and, despite everything I've just said, that makes me feel rather sad.

Outside No.47 I toot the horn and giggle as I note the bewildered paparazzi snapping pictures of Carson Adams bounding down the steps and climbing into a rusty Fiat Uno. They must be wondering what on earth's going on today.

"Hi, Fran, thanks for coming to get me," he says, flashing his megawatt smile in my direction.

I melt. "That's a pleasure."

He smells of citrusy, expensive cologne and is wearing a very stylish coat that would definitely be worth more than my car. A scarf is hanging round his lovely neck and the overall effect is pretty heart-stopping. His beauty doesn't diminish over the course of time spent with him. Quite the opposite.

"Hey, this car is so neat," Carson exclaims. "It reminds me of a toy one that I bought in LA for Cameron when he was really little. It had a real engine and everything and he used to drive it round the garden for hours. This is practically the same size. What a gas."

I look at Carson and at that moment he looks so pleased by the memory that he's just evoked that I know he has no idea how unbelievably patronizing he's just been.

"So I bet you're looking forward to getting home to the States?" I say.

"Yeah, I am actually. It's going to be great. I can't wait to see my boy."

"He's great. He's a real credit to you," I say, turning on to Brompton Road.

"Yeah? I'm glad you think so. Steph and I have done our best, given the circumstances, and I must say I'm very proud."

He starts fiddling with the stereo. "Have you got CDs in here?"

"No," I giggle. "Here, I'll put Heart on."

I tune the radio in and we end up singing along to an old ABC track. Carson seems to really enjoy our impromptu karaoke session and sings with gusto. As the track ends, he says, "So, Francesca, is there anyone special in your life? If you don't mind me asking."

"Actually, there is someone. I met him at a wedding nearly six months ago now," I say.

"At a wedding, eh? That's romantic. Well, Fran, he's a lucky guy."

If Sabina could see me now, I think, and I grin broadly.

My mobile rings.

"Would you mind answering it?" I ask shyly. "It's just, it's illegal if I do. If it's someone work-related who you don't want to speak to, you could just say you're a friend of mine so you don't have to talk to them."

"Francesca, I'm not Caroline — I am capable of answering a phone, you know."

I didn't meant to patronize him, it's just I'm so used to treating Caroline like a dense child.

"Hello . . . Yes, she is, but she's driving. Can I help you? . . . No, OK, no worries. Jeez, Fran, it's for you and it sounds important," he says, pointing at the side of his head as if to indicate that the person on the other end is a bit loopy.

I keep my eyes on the road as we sail past Harrods. "Damn. Look, would you mind pressing the green button again and it should go on to loudspeaker and I'll talk to them. Thanks. Hello?"

"Fran, it's Ella. My waters have broken and I'm three weeks early, Fran, and I can't find Paul." She's crying and she sounds really panicky. This is not what I was expecting to hear and my heart almost skips a beat.

Sitting next to me and holding the phone gingerly aloft, Carson looks startled.

I brake suddenly at some red lights. "Shit, Ella, what do you mean you can't find him? Isn't he at work?"

"Oh, Fran," cries Ella. "He had a really important meeting today and I told him to go."

I try to remain calm. "Well, where's the meeting? Let's get a message to him and get him back."

"It's in Cardiff and his phone keeps going to voicemail," whimpers Ella. "Ooooh, wait a minute . . . oooooooh, ooooooh, moooooooooooh."

I hear the phone clatter to the floor and Ella puffs, pants and groans for at least a minute, sounding not dissimilar to a mooing cow, while Carson and I exchange stunned looks. Finally she picks up the phone again.

"Shit, that was a strong one," she says weakly. "What the hell am I going to do, Fran?"

"Um, right . . . well, things could be worse, Cardiff's not too far," I say over-cheerfully, privately thinking that things could be a lot better too. "I'm sure we can get Paul back in time," I try hopefully, sounding much more convinced than I really am.

"Fran, I don't know why it's coming now. I don't want to have it now. I haven't bought a buggy yet," she moans.

"Look, Ella, just hold on. I'm coming over. Just hold on till I get there, for God's sake, and keep ringing Paul. He might be under a tunnel or something."

"OK," she sniffs.

By now we're approaching the top of Knightsbridge and I swerve dangerously into the right-hand lane so that instead of going straight on to the West End I can do a right down Sloane Avenue and head for Sloane Square. Shit, shit, shit, I can't believe this is happening and Paul's not here. And then I remember the A-lister sitting next to me.

"Oh, Carson, I'm so sorry — what about your meeting? Listen, I'm going to have to find you a cab, if that's OK, of course. We're not that far away now anyway, but obviously if you'd rather I didn't . . ."

"It's fine," he says, looking genuinely concerned.

I head down Sloane Avenue and decide that the best place to drop Carson will probably be Sloane Square. Typically, the traffic seems to be slower than ever and it feels like an age has passed until we finally get there.

"Let me out here, it's fine," insists Carson, eyeing up the crowded streets more than a little warily. Despite the fact it's not even December yet, terribly organized Christmas shoppers are out in force.

"Are you sure?" I ask, silently praying that he'll say yes and having nightmare visions of Ella giving birth in her living room on her own. "It's just that Tooting is still quite a drive away."

"Yeah, I'm sure," Carson says bravely.

With that, I swerve to the left and mount the kerb by the bank, where I screech to a halt, nearly causing an almighty crash in the process, and deposit Carson on the pavement. However, just as I'm crunching into first gear and about to drive away, I hear the first whoop: "Carson Adams, it's Carson Adams, everyone."

Not wanting to notice the riot that is about to ensue, I consider leaving Carson to his fate, but when I spot in my mirror outside Peter Jones three young girls and their determined-looking mother charging across the road to get a glimpse of their movie idol without even a thought for the oncoming traffic, I realize that I can't . . . and so does he.

"Francescaaaaaaa!" he yells, sounding really freaked out and already trying to shake people off like annoying insects.

I reverse back and lean across to open the passenger door.

"Get in," I say grimly.

People's noses are squashed against the glass in seconds and I have to rev the engine as if I really mean business in order to lose them. I can't believe people behave like this.

"Shit. What now?" I say, feeling more and more unravelled and worried about Ella.

"Francesca, your friend is, by the sound of it, in labour, so I wouldn't waste time putting me in a cab. Put your foot down and let's go get her, for Chrissakes."

Relieved beyond belief, I bark instructions at him to go into my phone and find her number. She picks up immediately. "Where are you? The contractions are coming every two or three minutes now and they really hurt."

"Darling, I'm on my way. Any luck with Paul?"

"Yes," she says, sounding distraught beyond belief. "He's getting off the train at the next stop and he's coming on the first one back to London. But what if he misses it, Fran? He'll never forgive himse — ooooooh!"

We can hear her panting for all she's worth.

"Breathe?" I instruct helplessly as I charge down the bus lane towards the Embankment and the nearest available bridge. "Don't worry, Ella, I'm sure first babies are supposed to take forever to come, aren't they?"

"I don't fucking know . . . moooooooooh. It doesn't feel like it's going to be forever . . ."

Shit, this is horrendous. I speed up even more. If the police stop me, it'll be an interesting one. And where are you and the most famous actor in Hollywood going in your Fiat Uno, madam? Oh, your friend's having a baby in Tooting, jolly good.

"I'm coming, Ella," I yell at my distressed friend.

Minutes later I charge through the lights, which have just turned red, and make it on to the bridge. I turn to glance at Carson and to my surprise he's rather glassyeyed. "What? Is it my driving? I'm sorry, but don't worry — I'm perfectly safe," I say, ignoring another red light and being beeped at by a furious-looking man in a Range Rover.

"Oh, I'm fine," Carson says dreamily. "I'm just remembering the day Cameron was born. It was the best day of my life. Steph was so brave. With her the labour lasted almost three days but she went for thirty-six hours before she had an epidural. Before that she did it all with gas and air. Then poor thing needed stitches — five, I think it was."

Slightly too much information.

"And I shall never forget this little bundle and the realization that I was a father, which to this day is the one single thing I am most proud of. Forget the Oscar nominations, the movies and having a place in history. None of it matters. All that matters is that my boy is healthy and happy. Although I think I've stuffed that one up."

"Nonsense," I say, swerving round a roundabout and thinking that now is a strange time to pick for a deep and meaningful. "Cameron is one of the happiest little kids I've ever met. The only thing that must be weird for him and that might affect him later on in life . . . if you don't mind me speaking plainly, that is?"

"Look out, Francesca . . . no, go on."

"Well, it must be very weird for him to think that his mother doesn't love him. He's obviously given up trying to get any affection or reassurance from her. But in his little head it must occur to him that it's a bit strange that his nanny loves him so much more than his own mother does." I'm too stressed out to mince my words.

Carson nods gravely. "I know and I hate it. You know what, Francesca? This script that I'm supposed to be signing up for today is such a pile of uninspiring crap. Driving now to go and help your friend who's about to have a baby, I mean, this is what life is all about. I haven't felt this energized in a long time."

I don't answer. I'm too busy trying to negotiate driving up on to the pavement to get past this jam.

"I mean, don't get me wrong, I adore the craft of acting and I'd love to make some art house films or something more creative than my usual genre, but apparently I don't have the right look and directors are always so narrow-minded when it comes to casting."

"Oh well, never mind," I say, not in the mood to indulge him.

Carson obviously detects the scepticism in my voice. "It's not about the money, you know. It's true — I'd love to make smaller scale movies."

"Well, here's a thought, Carson," I say bluntly, while driving like a total lunatic. "If it's not about the money, then don't do it. Don't do this next movie that you hate the thought of so much and yet you're about to sign up for. Who the hell says you have to? You're your own man, Carson, and you don't *have* to do anything you don't want to do. What you get paid for one picture, most people won't make in a lifetime. No . . . in twenty lifetimes. So if you really want to do something creative, then why not write a film? Take a year off and . . . rent a villa in Tuscany and write something you really want to do. Or buy a theatre and put on some plays. Or . . . Get out of my way, you moron . . . Not you, Carson . . . Or just don't do anything. You see, you can't moan about your situation because you have precisely nothing to moan about and if your biggest problem in life is being too good-looking, well, quite frankly, my heart bleeds. Obviously not wanting to be rude or anything," I quickly add as an afterthought.

314

"Francesca, I didn't mean to upset you. It's just that my agent and a lot of people all depend on me, including Caroline, and I do know how lucky I am. I guess I just never bargained on being so famous."

"Well then, duck out," I say frustratedly. "Shun the limelight — it can be done, you know. Sack your publicist for a start and stop making films. I know I'm probably speaking out of turn, but you've got enough money to live on for the rest of your life. You could sell a couple of your properties and take up your photography. Give it a few years without any exposure and I'm sorry to say that people will have forgotten about you and you won't be mobbed any more and someone else will have taken your mantle. Of course, your manager and your agent and Caroline have always encouraged you to keep working because it's in their best interests, but what about the important people?" I say, stopping reluctantly at some lights and turning to face him. "I'm sure Steph would leap at the chance of having a 'normal' life and you can't tell me Cameron wouldn't benefit. So I'm afraid, Carson, that I'm not wholly convinced that you wouldn't miss all the trappings, the attention, the money and the life-style that fame brings with it . . . Not meaning to be rude, obviously."

I realize rather late that I have completely overstepped the mark. Too much adrenaline is surging through my veins to care, although I am relieved when my phone rings and interrupts my tirade before I say something I'll really regret. Carson, who is looking extremely taken aback, answers the phone as if on autopilot and puts it straight on to loudspeaker.

"Hello?" I yell.

"Francesca, it's Tom. Are you OK?"

There's no time for pleasantries.

"Tom, Ella's in labour and she's early and Paul's not here and her contractions are coming every two to three minutes."

"Shit. She's quite advanced then. She should definitely be in hospital by now. Have you called an ambulance?"

"No. Should I have?" I shout.

"She should be all right. First babies usually take a while. Look, I know I only specialize in delivering dogs and cats, but why don't I meet you? Where is Ella?"

"Tooting, and I'm in Clapham now," I reply into the handset that Carson, who has somehow become my assistant, is holding aloft.

"OK, I'm going to ring an ambulance in case you don't get there quickly enough, so give me her address and I'll see you at the hospital."

"17A Pleshey Road," I reply.

"You may as well still head there in case the ambulance takes a while, OK?"

"OK," I say, thoroughly grateful that he's taken charge of the situation and is thinking clearly. The line goes dead and I bark at Carson: "OK, call Ella back."

Carson does as he's told as I bomb past Clapham Common.

"Ella, I'm coming and there's an ambulance on the way."

"I just want Paul," she moans.

"I know, honey. I know."

"I'm sorry, Francesca," says Carson in a small voice once we've rung off.

"That's OK. You don't need to apologize to me. It's just that ever since I was a little girl my biggest dream was to be a movie star and to act in movies and to attend events like the Oscars. I know that anyone with an iota of sense knows that these are not the most important or meaningful things in life, but they'd still be a dream come true." Then, more gently, I add, "Things really aren't that bad, Carson, and anything that is you can change."

By the time Carson and I have arrived at Pleshey Road, the ambulance is already there and I just have time to yell at Ella through the window that we'll follow her to the hospital, before they close the doors.

CHAPTER
THIRTY-ONE

The nurses at Tooting General are more than a little surprised to see Carson Adams appearing through the swing doors of the maternity ward and, of course, the usual pandemonium breaks out. Suddenly, delivering babies drops way down the nursing staff's list of priorities and getting a picture with Carson Adams or indeed an autograph becomes a far more pressing matter. Rather than feeling put out by this shift in the focus of the nurses, many of the patients who had previously been concentrating on their contractions seem to be in agreement that getting a glimpse of the gorgeous Carson Adams is far more urgent than having an epidural, and a potent form of pain relief in itself.

One woman actually struggles out of bed and makes it down the corridor, despite the fact that she only gave birth a couple of hours ago and can barely walk, leaving her brand-new baby doing his best to suckle his dismayed father's man boobs.

It's clear that Carson's presence has thrown the entire department into disarray and eventually I have to insist very loudly to the star-struck matron that no, Carson can't sign her uniform and that instead we need to see Ella now.

At last, batting her eyes at Carson all the way and with a small crowd following, Matron shows us to the delivery room where Ella is now in quite an advanced state of labour. When we get there, I have no choice but to leave Carson outside with Matron to the mercy of his ardent fans.

"Fran," says a sweaty Ella as I enter the room. "Thank God you're here. It's all happening so quickly. I'm nearly ten centimetres already. I don't want to do this on my own."

"You won't have to," I soothe, wondering what on earth she's talking about and averting my eyes from her downstairs area. I go to her side to hold her hand. "Besides, if you can just hold on a while longer, Paul will be here really soon. He's in a cab now and he was at Paddington last time I spoke to him. Thank goodness he hadn't got that far on the train when you rang."

"Ooooooooh," says Ella, grimacing with pain. "I want to push."

"Not yet," says the midwife. "It won't be long though — you're nearly fully dilated."

Just then we hear a huge commotion outside in the corridor. I realize that news of Carson Adams's surprise visit must have trickled round the whole building. It sounds as if the crowd has grown considerably and that the entire female population of South London has descended upon him.

"What the hell is all that noise?" demands Ella.

A worried-looking doctor barges into the room. "Excuse me — oh, sorry," he says, shielding his eyes to protect Ella's modesty. "We're going to have to do something about this situation. The gentleman outside is causing quite a stir and I'd say that things could get nasty. He's asking for a Francesca?"

"Who's asking for you? Don't leave me," pleads Ella.

"Look, can you just bring him in here?" I ask the doctor, feeling at a total loss to know what to do. "I know it's a bit unorthodox, but he's going to cause so much mayhem otherwise."

The doctor scratches his head. "Look, it's not hospital policy, but I actually think we might have to . . . if it's all right with the patient," he adds.

I explain quickly and apologetically. "Ella. Carson's outside and they're baying for his blood. Would you mind awfully if he came in?"

Ella, who is trying to deal with a rather large wave of pain, looks flummoxed and very sweaty. "Whatever. I don't give a shit."

"Francescaaaaa!" I hear Carson yell from just outside the doors, sounding as if he's being torn to bits.

"Please bring him in!" I appeal to the doctor.

And so it is that seconds later a ridiculously handsome but dishevelled-looking film star bursts into the delivery room, looking relieved beyond belief and not at all perturbed to be confronted by the sight of Ella, who is now on all fours, biting a pillow. Predictably, it's the turn of Ella's large West Indian midwife, Connie, to be temporarily distracted.

"You're not him, are you? Carson Adams? Are you the father?" she says, looking stunned and retrieving her hands from Ella's nether regions mid-examination.

320

You can't blame her — it's not every day you see celebs in Tooting General, after all.

However, at this point Ella decides that enough is enough.

"Will you please concentrate on me for just a bloody second . . . Oooooo, aaaaaaaaaaaaaaaaaah," she screeches, a wild look in her eye. "Oooooooooooh, aaaaaaah . . . it hurts. I want to push and if it's not too much to ask I would like a bit of your fucking attention, you bastards . . ."

Carson and I must look a bit shocked because Connie turns round and says matter-of-factly, "Totally normal language at this stage. Hormones are changing."

Then, as fast as it started, the contraction seems to stop and, despite the oddness of the situation, Ella and her hormones remember their manners:

"Hello, Carson, nice to meet you, by the way."

After that, everything seems to happen rather quickly.

Mercifully Paul finally arrives, breathless and stressed beyond belief, which means that I can at last take a back seat in the proceedings, which I'm really pleased about, to be perfectly honest, as I'm starting to feel a bit faint. Carson keeps well out of the way, but remains in the room, obviously terrified about what would happen to him if he were to leave. In fact, it takes a while for Paul to even register that he's there because the minute he arrives he races to Ella's side saying, "Darling, I'm here. I'm here. I'm so sorry you've been on your own."

Ella yells at him for a few minutes and then Paul checks with the midwife that everything's OK with the baby, despite it being three weeks early, and it's only then that he clocks Carson Adams of all people, standing in the corner opposite his wife's spread-eagled legs. He jumps out of his skin and then looks terribly confused but quite chuffed at the same time, so I introduce them and the two men end up shaking hands furiously. But there's no time for any proper explanation because then it's as if the baby knows that finally both its parents are present and decides this is the moment to make his or her entrance. It isn't long before Ella's pushing with all her might and one hour later I can see the head crowning, which is both the most amazing and the most gory thing I've ever seen in my life, and then the head is followed by a tiny little body that's covered in blood and gunk, but is beautiful none the less, and then there's a second when everything seems to stop.

And then it comes. A roar of indignation. A cry that says: what is this cold, bright place I've come to with its harsh lights and loud noises?

Now an exhausted, tearful Ella and an elated Paul are hugging and kissing and crying and desperate to hold their little bundle, who is swiftly being cleaned up, checked, weighed and handed to them.

Their little girl. Their daughter.

And I'm weeping with happiness and emotion and so is Carson, who hugs me tight, tears rolling down his face. Then I hug Ella, who is suddenly beyond shattered, pale and rather puffy, but happy, and Paul hugs Carson, who is then grabbed by Connie, who's clearly decided it's time to get in on the action and presses herself right up against him until he feels moved to prise her off. Then it's time to leave the new parents to it and Carson and I exit the room only to find Tom sitting in the waiting room.

"It's a girl," I say, falling into his outstretched arms.

Half an hour later and Carson, Tom and I are all squashed into my car, which has got a parking ticket on it probably due to the fact that I left it carelessly on a single yellow line and about four foot away from the kerb. Carson is next to me in the front, Tom is wedged in the back and we're all in a jubilant mood.

"We have to all go and celebrate," suggests Carson.

"What about your meeting though?" I ask. "You can probably still catch your director before he leaves for the airport if we hurry."

"Francesca, that won't be necessary because I'm not going to be doing the movie. In fact, I'll be phoning my agent later on to tell her exactly that, and if she doesn't like it she can go jump. Tom, how are you fixed?" he says, turning round and tapping Tom on the knee.

"I told the surgery I was taking the afternoon off the minute I got Francesca's call," he replies excitedly.

"Great."

I stare at Carson, shocked. "Did I just hear right? You're not doing the movie?"

"No, I'm not doing it. Today, what with one thing and another, I've started to see clearly about a lot of things and that is just one of them. So are you on for lunch?"

"I can't," I say, still amazed by what I've just heard. "I've got so much work to get on with. There's Caroline's flights to sort out and stuff, so I really should get back."

"Francesca, I am insisting that you take the rest of the day off and spend it celebrating the arrival of little Rosie, seven pounds three ounces, and if Cas doesn't like it I promise you I will make sure she knows that it was my idea."

"OK," I giggle, happy to be persuaded as the last thing I want to be doing right now is anything as mundane as sorting out Caroline's travel arrangements for her return to the States. I scrabble in my bag, looking for my mobile, and wonder where we should go.

"Shit, I've just realized — you guys probably want to be alone, don't you? Listen, I'm sorry, I'm thoughtless, just drop me off at home, Fran," Carson says magnanimously.

I'm embarrassed and I don't know what to say without offending someone, but thankfully, as ever, Tom steps into the breach.

"Carson, we wouldn't hear of it, not after what we've all just been through. It would be a pleasure to have a celebration lunch together and then, if I'm lucky, I might get to see the gorgeous Francesca on my own tonight."

Carson grins at me like a schoolboy and then turns in his seat, straining against his seatbelt to face Tom in the back, and shakes his hand awkwardly through the gap.

I'm very touched by what Tom's just said and I'm also amused to note that, although Tom is about as unstarry a person as you can get, he's obviously quite taken with Carson and is rather relishing the prospect of hanging out with a movie star for the afternoon. Good — maybe Tom will start understanding why I'm so fascinated with the world that Caroline inhabits and by Carson himself, for he really does make a huge impact on everyone he meets. He certainly left the hospital having gained a few more fans in the shape of most of the nursing staff, the doctors, many of the patients and Paul and Ella who, despite the unconventional circumstances surrounding their meeting, were utterly charmed by him. Even little Rosie stopped crying when Carson held her.

"I know exactly where we should go for lunch," I say, smiling at Tom in my mirror. "It's a bit of a drive, but it's high time Tom went there, we'll get a great table and Carson should be able to eat his lunch in peace."

So after quickly ringing Sabina and Abbie to tell them that we're all aunties, I switch the engine on and head for the suburbs of Teddington, feeling utterly content and listening to the two men chatting away about Tom's work, Cameron, football and the government.

By the time we arrive at Massi's, the lunchtime customers have mostly left, although one or two are still lingering over their coffees. When Angelo (who has worked as Dad's head waiter for as long as I can remember) spots us, we are all greeted like superstars — just as every single other customer who eats here is.

Angelo, seemingly the only person on the planet oblivious to Carson's fame, kisses us all on both cheeks before rushing to the kitchen to fetch my father, who is ridiculously happy to see me. He greets Tom and Carson warmly and insists that we don't order and that instead he'll just send plate after plate of delicious food over to our table. He doesn't hide the fact that he's "incredibly delighted and honoured" to have Carson dining at his restaurant, and asks if he can take a picture so that he can frame it and add it to the ones of Keith Barron from *Duty Free* and Valerie Singleton. Carson happily obliges and then my father turns his attentions to Tom.

"You're looking after my girl, eh?"

"Dad," I protest, feeling about twelve years old.

Tom and Carson laugh, and my father grins and pats Tom on the back. "You seem like a very nice boy. Right, are you still hungry? What would you like now? A little more pasta, some fish or some more meat? Tell me what you want."

"Dad, you choose, but can we get some more wine?"

"Of course, I've got a wonderful red that you will love."

He's right, we do, and I'm just refusing a second glass when Carson says, "Francesca, drink. I'll pay for cabs for us all to get home."

"No, we couldn't," mutter both Tom and I.

Carson looks at us both and says, deadpan, "Please let me. I promise it's not that big a deal. As you pointed out earlier, Fran, I do earn twenty million a picture, which means that last year I earned at least sixty

326

million and that's before you've taken into account my share of the box office, so I reckon I can shout a couple of cabs."

Tom and I roar with laughter at the sheer outrageousness of what he's saying and then we accept, saying thanks very much and that we would love to take him up on his offer of a cab.

Lunch is a really happy affair and a fairly drunken one too. The birth of my friend's little girl has touched us all, but it seems that Carson is the one who has been most deeply affected by the afternoon's events. It's as if he has experienced some kind of an epiphany for, once the antipasti, the pasta dishes and the meat and salad have all been served, eaten and cleared, Carson changes the mood at the table from uproarious to solemn.

"Francesca, Tom. If you don't mind, I'd like to say a few words."

"Go ahead," says Tom, who has put away an impressive amount of food, which has not gone unnoticed by my proud father.

I move my glass away, aware that Carson is about to say something important and faintly amused to note that he is definitely what one might describe as "a bit squiffy".

"Over the last seven years," begins Carson earnestly, "there has only really been one sensible influence in my life. One person who has always wanted what's best for me and who has only ever had my best interests at heart."

"Who's that then?" asks Tom.

"That person is, of course, my lovely Steph who I love so much," Carson replies, prompting Tom to look rather baffled, but not stopping to explain. "There have been times in the past when we've discussed what it would be like to start over, for me to stop acting and to essentially retire from Hollywood. We've discussed what it would be like to live together as man and wife with our son and for us to be able to tell the world that we're in love. Trouble is, I don't think she's ever tried to really persuade me that what she wants isn't necessarily what I want and that I'd be giving up an awful lot for her. In some ways she's right, I would."

With a start, I realize that I'm staring at Carson rather gormlessly. I can't help it. He really is mesmerizing and the way he's delivering this speech is Ocscar-worthy in itself. I look at Tom. He mainly looks confused.

"Sorry, guys," says Carson. "I'm getting a bit carried away. Jeez, why is it I only ever feel this drunk when I'm with you Brits?"

"So you don't want to give it all up?" I ask, not wanting him to lose the thread.

"What I'm saying is that we do have a fabulous lifestyle and it's always been the far easier option to carry on as we are," answers Carson non-commitally. "I've always earned a fortune and maybe a few years ago I did still get a bit of a kick out of the whole glamorous side of the business. But not any more. Now I've got more money than I know what to do with and Caroline spends it as fast as I can make it anyway."

I nod in agreement. I really can vouch for that.

328

Carson drains the rest of his glass and goes straight in for a refill. "A huge chunk of the money I earn goes towards paying my agent, my manager, my publicist and all the other people who play a part in deciding my life for me, and I guess I've always felt a certain amount of responsibility to these people, a sort of loyalty to the guys who have shaped my career all these years. But maybe that loyalty is somewhat misguided."

I glance at Tom, who's still looking baffled but intrigued. I can tell he's trying to decipher what Carson's talking about with regard to Steph.

Carson takes a deep breath.

"Today, Francesca, when we were driving to the hospital, you told me a few home truths and maybe you were saying things that Steph has already hinted at in the past. You weren't as subtle as Steph — you were a bit more brutally honest, a bit more direct in your approach — and I didn't necessarily like what I was hearing at first. But maybe that's exactly what I needed."

I blush.

"For the first time in years I felt like here was someone with absolutely no agenda, giving it to me straight. Telling me how it really is ... I mean, me ducking out and giving everything up doesn't affect you in any way. You don't have a vested interest in me and you're not directly wrapped up in the complicated mess that is my life. You're also not so sycophantic that you agree with everything I say and you won't let me forget how lucky I am and how much choice I have. You see, you're right, Fran, it is a wonderful business I'm in and

I didn't mean to sound so churlish earlier. Showbusiness is the most privileged business anyone can work in, if you're lucky enough to have some degree of success. You get paid vast amounts of money to act, to dress up and pretend, which is hugely fun and, let's face it, the most self-indulgent profession anyone can choose. The perks are endless, you're driven around, catered for and showered with gifts. You are lauded and applauded for entertaining people, for people loving you. Yet it's all utterly unimportant if you don't have the right foundations, the right platform from which to enjoy your success. And that's the point. All the people whom I regularly pay twenty per cent to have never let me acknowledge that, because they've always been too busy reminding me that I have an obligation to my fans, to them, to myself, to my talent to keep making movies at no matter what expense to my private life. And why are they saying this? Because they care? Because they love my movies? No, because they're getting twenty per cent and because they have no interest in what is really right for me, Cameron or Steph."

The penny, it seems, has finally dropped. I realize that Carson, although he's unaware of it at the moment, is having the most spectacular destiny day. Tom takes my hand under the table and gives it a gentle squeeze. Carson continues:

"At the hospital today I watched those doctors and nurses working their asses off and you know it was quite a different environment to the hospitals I'm used to, like Cedars-Sinai. Anyway, what these people do is so important and yet goes largely unnoticed. When I

330

sounded ungrateful earlier, it's because too much of a good thing can really spoil your appreciation of things. If fame is a cake, well, I've had one slice too many. I feel sick and from now on I'd like to eat more plainly. In short, I've overdosed on Hollywood and I want to do something a bit more worthwhile with my time now. I want to put something back and, Fran, you've made me realize that I can. You've made me think, what's stopping me? Am I being honest with myself?"

I can sense that we're nearly at the climax and Tom and I don't interrupt his flow. We just listen intently, both utterly transfixed.

"I have properties all over the world that are worth millions of dollars and enough money in the bank to live on forever. I don't even know what to do with it all any more. I live with a woman who I detest, who I don't think cares about me in the slightest."

"Steph?" asks a confused Tom, desperately trying to keep up.

"No, Caroline. I mean, I watched that birth today and I just thought, how can we do this to Cameron? Steph is his mother and he has a right to know that. So it's time I did what I should have done a long time ago. I'm going to leave Caroline and I'm going to ask the mother of my child to marry me. Then I'm going to sit down with Cameron and have a long, long talk with him and pray that he can forgive us. After that I'll take things from there, but things are going to change and I'm not going to waste any more time doing things for people who mean nothing to me. So thank you, Francesca. Thank you so much for making me see what

I should have seen a long time ago. It's about time I did something with my life, something worthwhile, and I'm going to start right now by writing out a cheque for one million dollars to the hospital where Rosie was just born."

Tom and I are both far too stunned to speak and we stare open-mouthed as Carson produces his chequebook and scribbles out a cheque with a ridiculous amount of noughts on the end. Just as I'm realizing that I may have underestimated Carson Adams, my father comes over and asks if we'd like some tiramisu.

CHAPTER
THIRTY-TWO

As our cabs arrive at the restaurant, I feel really sad about having to say goodbye to Carson. Tearfully, I wish him all the best and give him a big hug, silently willing him to be brave enough to go through with his intentions and promising to make sure that his cheque gets to Tooting General. He's due to fly out tonight to LA and I know that, despite his promises to keep in touch, our worlds are so far removed from one another's that realistically it is unlikely that he will. Tom and Carson share a moment of manly affection which involves patting each other on the back really hard, and with that our famous friend is gone.

Tom and I take the other cab back to mine. By now the events of the day and the lunchtime drinking have all caught up with me and I'm feeling soporific and in need of at least a pint of water, yet also strangely frisky. During the journey back to Clapham, I sit snuggled into Tom, hoping he'll get the hint that I'm feeling affectionate, and I fill in all the gaps in Carson's story for him and answer all of his questions. By the time we are home he has definitely got the hint and his hands have been all over me for the last fifteen minutes of the journey. Neither of us has to spell out how impatient we are to make it to my bedroom and I have to stop myself from telling the driver to "forget the bloody receipt" when he takes an age to write it out, even spelling out the amount in longhand.

All in all it has been a highly emotional day and when we do eventually tumble into bed all our last reserves of energy are called upon. What goes on between the sheets is highly charged and incredibly passionate and for a while my jumbled mind empties and I just concentrate on the wonderful delights of this rampant early-evening romp. At one point I even feel brave enough to try to incorporate what I saw Carson and Steph doing all those months ago, but Tom seems slightly shocked so I give up. Apart from that, it all goes very well.

Cuddled up in bed afterwards, Tom tells me that he's proud of me.

"Why?" I ask dreamily, wondering for a moment if he's referring to my bedroom skills.

"Well, you obviously made a huge impact on Carson with whatever it was you said and as a result I think he will sort his life out."

"Do you?"

"Yes I do."

I giggle.

"What?" asks Tom.

"I just can't believe how well you two got on. There were a few moments over lunch when I thought I should leave the table and let you both get on with it. Three's a crowd and all that."

Tom grins. "Yes, I think my mates will be quite impressed to know that I am now Carson Adams's official football correspondent. When you were chatting with your dad, he asked me if I'll text him footy scores and updates when he's back in the States and he's given me his email address too. I'd better not let the girls at work know that or they'll extract it out of me with torture, I should imagine."

He's right and for a brief moment I worry for his safety.

"On a more serious note, do you really think he'll finish with Caroline?" I ask.

"Yes, I think so."

I hope he does and I fall asleep playing out the scene in my head of what would happen if he did.

The next day I arrive at work punctual as usual, with a serious spring in my step and bursting to talk to Lorna about yesterday's events. However, unbelievably, I don't get the chance, for just as I'm putting the key in the lock I get a phone call that totally rains on my parade and then urinates on it to boot.

Ever since I got this job, it's never ceased to amaze me how circumstances can switch from normal to alarming so rapidly and so often. It gets rather exhausting and, to be honest, after yesterday's dramas I could really do with a few days of dull, a portion of normal, a taste of ordinary. Still, for as long as I'm working for Caroline I'm clearly not going to get it.

I check my caller ID and am not entirely surprised to see that it's Leticia who is ringing. Upon answering, however, it becomes clear very quickly that all is not well and now I am entirely surprised and quite freaked out.

"Francesca, you have to help me. There's something wrong. Her breathing's all funny."

"Oh my God," I reply. "Is she conscious?"

"Yes, but she just doesn't seem right and I'm worried it might be serious. I mean, we were lying on the sofa, cuddling up and sharing some wonderful kisses, and I was just stroking her tummy —"

What is it with these people? Always too much information.

"— when I noticed that her breathing was rather irregular and now I've put her to bed, but she's gone very quiet . . ."

"Shit. OK, well, keep calm and I'll get a doctor to you. Are you at your place?"

"Yes, but please do hurry, Fran. I'll never forgive myself if anything happens to her."

Oh God. Although Leticia sounds relatively calm, which is a good sign, she also said "please", which is a very bad sign. I feel rather panicked and can't believe that I'm having to be the responsible one in a crisis yet again. It all seems so sudden. Caroline was fine yesterday. Maybe the bad news from Great British Films has prompted a funny turn? I hurry to the study, where I discard my bag and coat and begin feverishly leafing through files, trying to locate the long list of doctors that I'd always hoped would never come in handy. Ah, here it is.

"OK, Leticia, I've found the list of doctors, so I'll ring them now, try and find one that's appropriate and who can come and see her ASAP. First, though, tell me exactly what her symptoms are again so I can tell them."

"Right. Well, as I said, her breathing seems a little irregular."

"Irregular breathing," I scribble, while balancing the phone under my chin. "What else, Leticia?"

"She's got hot feet."

"Hot feet?"

"Yes, hot feet."

"Is it just her feet that are hot? Or is there anything else?" I enquire, wishing to God that Leticia had phoned a doctor herself so that she could speak to them directly. It seems ludicrous that even in a potentially very serious situation she still deems it too menial to address a problem herself.

"Actually, there is something else — her breath is unusually smelly."

"Smelly breath . . .?" I am at a loss to know what that might mean. Poor Caroline.

"Right, I'm going to find a doctor straight away and I'll meet them at your place. Should I bring anything for her? Does she need a clean nightie or anything?"

"A nightie? Why on earth would Froo Froo need a nightie?" says a flabbergasted-sounding Leticia. "No. What you can do though is let Caroline know what's going on as soon as possible, as I'm sure she'll want to come straight round."

Oh my God.

"Leticia," I say slowly and deliberately, "I thought you were talking about Caroline. Why didn't you say it was Froo Froo who was ill? I nearly had a heart attack."

There's a pause and then Leticia, clearly sick of being stoic, lets forth what can only be described as a tirade of hysteria.

"Don't be such a bitch, Fran. What are you saying? That you don't care that Froo Froo is ill? Uuurgh, I can't stand this. I don't care what you thought. My doggy is ill and you need to get someone over here right now. Just SORT IT OUT!"

Her dog is ill so I must allow special dispensation for vile behaviour. With a heavy heart, I pick up the landline.

And so it is that all the usual dating etiquette — that is to say, letting your boyfriend recover from dealing with one emergency situation before ringing him with another — goes flying out of the window and it's Tom who's next in line to receive a neurotic phone call. Fortunately he's not at the surgery yet, but is on his way there from a home visit.

"Hi, Tom, it's me, Francesca," I begin, feeling a trifle nervous.

"Oh, hello, I was just thinking about you. Everything all right? Have you heard from Ella?"

I can hear his smile in his voice. Unlike me, he's obviously been able to hang on to the lovely afterglow of our romantic night and is in a great mood. Still, I'll soon put a stop to that.

"Not yet, no. Shit, Tom, I'm so sorry to do this to you when you're working, and I know you must be sick

338

to death of helping me out in really surreal situations but . . ." I gabble.

"What now? Surely not another birth?"

"No. It's a dog. Much more your department this time. It's Leticia's dog, Froo Froo, and by all accounts she's not very well at all and I have to fix it and quick . . . or I'm stuffed. Obviously you're the only vet I know, so I was wondering if there was even the smallest chance you might be able to help me out and meet me at her flat in Notting Hill?"

"She must have a vet she already uses," says Tom flatly. "It makes much more sense for her to ring the person who will have all of — Froo Froo, was it?"

"Yes."

"Right, well, the most sensible course of action would be to ring the person who'll have all of Froo Froo's notes and . . ."

As Tom carries on talking perfect sense, I'm distracted by a very strange sight and find myself tuning out. Through the study window I've spied Caroline jogging up the pavement towards the house with her personal trainer in tow. While there's nothing odd in that per se, what is weird is that today she is running like an absolute mad woman. Her arms and legs are flailing about wildly and her head is wobbling from side to side so violently it looks like it may snap off altogether. She looks so bizarre that if I wasn't so stressed out I would laugh out loud. I quickly realize that she must, in fact, be jogging to music and I would hazard a guess that whatever she's listening to is very "high energy" and has a frenetic beat. If not, then that woman has some serious rhythm issues.

"I've got a really busy day ahead, plus I don't understand why you sound so worried because it's not really your problem. I mean, why she automatically rings you when . . ." I can't concentrate on anything Tom's saying. Caroline's beefcake of a trainer is looking distinctly embarrassed about being out in public with someone who looks so mentally challenged and is deliberately trailing a few feet behind her with a pained expression on his thickset face. Caroline couldn't care less though; she's far too engrossed in whatever tune is blasting into her ears and it must be reaching its climax because now she's beating some imaginary drums. Oh my word, she's punching the air. Where are the paparazzi when you actually want them?

Everybody gets carried away by music sometimes, but in the privacy of their own kitchen, not out in the street in broad daylight. Admittedly, we're all susceptible to getting caught out in the car. When a great tune comes on the radio it's easy to forget that, although technically you're on your own, the windows actually afford you a 360-degree audience. But jogging? No.

As Caroline reaches No. 47, she nudges a bewildered-looking passer-by out of her way, takes the steps two at a time and bursts into the hall.

Tom's still calmly trying to convince me that Leticia should be on the phone to her local vet as Caroline comes crashing in.

340

"Ba ba ba ba ba ba ba. What a fucking tune, Francesca. I'm SO glad I've caught you. I've been listening to Carl's iPod all morning and . . ." mid-sentence she proceeds to carry out an amazing star jump. "Fuck, I am so energized and PUMPED this morning."

"Yeah . . . um, Caroline, I've just got someone on the phone at the moment . . ."

"Oh, shut up, Francesca. You do witter on sometimes. Try not to be drab today, will you? Now, Carl has got some simply fabulous Ibiza anthems on his iPod and you need to download them for me. Make sure you put that on your list as top priority. I don't have any house music on mine," she finishes angrily, as if this is all my fault and something that I should feel really bad about.

Carl, who has finally caught up with his freaky mistress, hovers awkwardly in the background hoping to retrieve his iPod.

"Caroline," I begin, feeling dismayed as I take in what the clock is telling me. I feel ready for dinner, a glass of wine and an early night already and it's only ten fifteen in the morning. "Caroline, listen, it's Froo Froo. She's not well."

"What do you mean, she's not well?" Caroline demands, as she stops doing star jumps and tries and fails to frown.

I can just make out a few small purple marks on her forehead, the tell-tale signs from yesterday's injections. Judging by her demeanour, I would say that when they injected the botulism they must have added something else too, for clearly her moping around phase is a thing of the past and the old Caroline is back and very much on the warpath.

"Damn it, Ticia's going to be off the chart with worry," she sighs, less with concern for the state of her girlfriend's emotional health and more with annoyance because it might mean that some sympathy will be required from her. "Do you know, it's unreal? Just for once I'm having a tiny bit of 'me time' and you have to go and spoil it by giving me bad news," she huffs, hands firmly on hips. "So what are you doing about Froo Froo?"

"Tom," I beg quietly into my mobile, which I've been holding to my ear throughout. "Please?"

Tom lets out a long sigh. "I can probably put my next patient off, but I must be back in an hour and a half."

"Oh, thank you, thank you so, so much," I gush.

"Give me the address. I'm leaving now," he says tightly.

Forty minutes later, myself, Tom, Caroline and Leticia are gathered round Froo Froo's sickbed in Leticia's palatial Notting Hill apartment. When I say sickbed, I'm not joking. The small, fluffy, unassuming creature that is Froo Froo is actually queening it up in the middle of a huge four-poster bed, on some of the best linen Cologne and Cotton has to sell, propped up and surrounded by at least eight large square pillows. Brilliant.

The gruesome twosome have done nothing but bark orders at me, squawk at each other and issue instructions to Tom since we got here and throughout it all Froo Froo has simply stared back at us balefully with her perpetual expression that, roughly translated, says "Whatever."

I understand completely. You would have to have a lot of "whatever" about you to be Leticia's pet. Come to think of it, you have to have a lot of "whatever" about you to be Caroline's assistant. Anyway, despite the odd circumstances, I'm delighted to be seeing Tom so soon again, but the feeling doesn't seem to be entirely mutual. Seemingly impervious to the circus around him, he's been quietly getting on with his job, only stopping to give Caroline disapproving looks whenever she says something rude. That being said, he's pretty much giving her disapproving looks the whole time and as a result has hardly had time to so much as glance my way. Through a combination of defensive body language (he's permanently had his back to me while tending to Froo Froo) and some choice brooding looks, he's making it very clear that he's not at all impressed at having had to leave work yet again to do me a favour. This is totally understandable and I know I've probably overstepped the mark by expecting him to "jump" just because I'm in a predicament, but it would be nice to get a glimpse of the happy Tom I left in bed this morning. I guess he'll stay angry with me until he feels happy that his point has been made.

I can't believe I actually feel jealous of a dog, but I do. Froo Froo has been the focus of all Tom's attention and tender loving care and that's despite her revolting breath. Leticia was not exaggerating.

"So she's going to be absolutely fine," says Tom, giving Froo Froo one final little pat. "She's just got a common cold. She's also getting on a bit and could probably do with quite a lot more exercise. How often do you walk her?"

Leticia glares at Tom, then flushes and looks mutinous.

Caroline butts in: "Ticia walks her as much as she is able to, given her full-on lifestyle. Don't you, babe?"

"Yah. Exactly."

"Right, well, that's not good enough, I'm afraid," says Tom plainly. "Once Froo Froo has recovered from this cold, she needs to be walked for at least an hour every day until she's lost the extra weight and got a bit fitter." He puts his veterinary instruments back into his battered black leather bag and starts to put his coat on.

This businesslike and rather moody side to Tom is one I've never seen before and it's actually quite sexy. Despite the fact that amends need to be made, because essentially I am the instigator of his bad mood, part of me is enjoying seeing him take charge of the situation in such a no-nonsense manner. In a very British, anally retentive, unable to do proper displays of emotion kind of way, he's positively smouldering. I think I might quite like to bear his children one day.

"Walk for an hour a day?" Leticia gasps, as if Tom's just asked her to gouge her own eyeballs out with a rusty nail.

"Yes, walk for an hour a day," reiterates Tom firmly and a tad impatiently. With that, he buttons up his coat and stiffly bids us all goodbye, barely acknowledging me as he does so. I have a quick surge of irritation. Suddenly he's in grave danger of taking this whole moody thing too far. There's a very thin line between making your point and being a bit of a bastard. By not saying goodbye to me, he's most definitely crossed it. While he has every right to be fed up, I don't like being given the cold shoulder or being made to feel as though I've been told off. Honestly, I mean if my father was English and had a poker up his bum, then Tom would be reminding me of my father right now. Plus, although the circumstances are hardly ideal, he is after all still meeting my boss for the first time and he's not exactly making much of an effort to be polite, even if just for my sake.

I notice that Caroline is regarding Tom through slanted eyes. I'd recognize that expression anywhere. He has displeased her.

"What's your name?" she asks his retreating back.

"Tom Worthington," he says, at least having the good grace to turn round.

"Well, Tom," she spits, "I'm not sure where Francesca found you, but just so you know, people like us don't have hours and hours of free time to go walking around in muddy parks for no good reason. People like us have diaries and schedules to keep. So Froo Froo will be walked, but it will have to be by my assistant, which is why people like me have people like Francesca."

Bloody great, I think dolefully.

Tom looks furious. "Well, that's up to people like Francesca, isn't it?"

For a moment he fixes Caroline with a formidable stare and his eyes are positively steely. Even Caroline is momentarily taken aback.

"Yes . . . it is . . . Well, goodbye and send an invoice."

Tom doesn't even bother to reply and is already heading for the door without so much as a backward glance. His leaving finally spurs me into some sort of action. I'm not letting him leave like this. I'm going after him.

"Caroline, I'm just going to give him the address to send the invoice to," I inform my boss, without waiting for an answer.

"Fine, and tell him from me that actually it is up to me, not you," she fights back, having missed the moment completely.

Outside, the air is cold and damp. I do a quick scan up and down the road only to spot Tom across the street, already climbing into his car. I'm disappointed and thoroughly confused. I had half assumed he'd be waiting for me, having guessed that I'd come after him.

"Tom!" I yell.

He looks up, but instead of coming over he just shakes his head and puts on his seatbelt.

I'm not having this. How dare he ignore me? What the hell has got into him?

"Tom!" I yell again, much more forcibly, and — quickly checking for cars — I sprint across the road to demand an explanation.

"Tom, what on earth is wrong with you? Why are you ignoring me? I know you've done me a massive favour, but if it was going to put you in this much of a bad mood then you really shouldn't have bothered. I mean, I don't think I've done anything to deserve you treating me like this. You're making me feel like complete shit, especially after last night." I pause to catch my breath and I'm met by a horrible, tense wall of silence.

After what feels like an age, I finally get a response, but he keeps his hand on the key that's in the ignition, making it only too clear how desperate he is to escape.

"You really don't get it, do you, Francesca?"

"Get what, Tom? What the hell have I done to piss you off so much?"

Tom sighs and no longer looks angry, just completely miserable. He's starting to do my head in now.

"What?" I demand. "I fucking hate it when you do this 'I'm pissed off but I'm not going to tell you why' act. It drives me mad and I don't know why you can't just spit it out."

"Fine," shouts Tom, taking me rather by surprise by doing exactly what I asked. "I'll tell you exactly what this is about, although I can't believe you think it's about me being 'pissed off' about doing you a favour."

I shrug.

"You read things so wrong sometimes, Francesca. To be honest, I wasn't going to help you at first, but when I heard Caroline talking to you like dirt I changed my mind because I knew that if I didn't you'd be in trouble. That was my decision and not something therefore that I would be cross with you about. But what I hadn't expected was to find that what I heard this morning on the phone was only the half of it and now I'm left wondering if maybe I've misjudged you completely."

"What do you mean?" I say, feeling panicked. "What can possibly have changed your mind about me so dramatically in the space of one morning?"

Tom looks at me with something that looks horribly like regret. "Francesca, I have loved being with you these last six months, but just as I think I have a very good idea about what kind of person you are, I suddenly find myself filled with doubt again. You know, it's always bothered me how you jump to attention whenever Caroline clicks her fingers, but I've never actually witnessed your relationship with her. Then today for the first time I see you with these people, these dreadful, hideous, stupid people, and I see that I had every reason to feel uneasy."

"Oh, so wait a minute, you're judging me because they're awful. Oh, that makes a lot of sense," I say heatedly, turning away so he can't see the tears that are starting to freefall down my face. I can't stand this — why is he being such a pig?

Tom clicks his seatbelt off and clambers out of the car. He holds my elbows and forces me to look at him.

"Francesca, you've described Caroline to me as being dreadful before, but you've always made out that really she's quite funny. Today, though, I heard with my own ears how that woman talks to you. She is so unbelievably rude and the way she treats you is terrible and you just take it."

I can't stop crying now. I'm so upset.

"But the worst thing about all of this is that you don't stick up for yourself at all and you've let her get away with treating you like shit on her shoe for all this time. You don't even flinch. It's like you've got so used to someone treating you badly that it's started to feel normal."

"Oh, for God's sake," I snap furiously. "Will you get off your high horse? She's not *that* bad. I mean, I know more than anyone that she can say some horrific things, but it's not that much of a big deal. Caroline's an idiot, but her bark is much worse than her bite and at the end of the day I would stick up for myself if she hurt my feelings, but she doesn't. It's water off a duck's back and, if I'm really honest, most of the time I do find it quite amusing."

"Yes, so you've said before, Fran. But, hey, guess what? It's not funny. Being that loathsome to anybody is simply not funny. It just isn't, and for the life of me I can't understand why you put up with it. I can only guess that it's something to do with your inexplicable obsession with fame."

Now it's my turn to feel livid.

"How dare you be so bloody patronizing? Firstly, I'm not obsessed with fame, and secondly, if I were — which I'm not — then it wouldn't be inexplicable, as fame and everything that goes with it happens to be a damn sight more interesting than many other things, like bloody football for instance. And, all right, I know Caroline can be an utter cow at times, but at least no one can ever say my job isn't interesting."

I realize that my nose is running and I don't have a tissue. It's cold and I left my coat inside. I sniff hard before continuing.

"Do you know how many people would love to be in my shoes right now, Tom? I get paid to hang out with movie stars and actually, to be perfectly honest, the money is a consideration. I'm hardly going to look a gift horse in the mouth just because you can't handle somebody who's a bit out of the ordinary. Before I started working for Caroline I was skint and now I'm finally in the black again, so I don't mind taking the odd bit of stick for that."

Tom regards me incredulously. "I'm more than aware that you need to earn a living, but do you really expect me to believe that you couldn't find anything else to do? I don't believe for one minute that skivvying for Caroline is your only option. What about your writing, for example? You clearly have a talent for it and you enjoy it, so I just don't get why you haven't explored making that work for you as a career."

Great. Suddenly Tom appears to have transformed into my own personal careers advisor, which is a shame as I can't recall asking for his opinion.

"Have you got any idea how competitive writing is? Getting something published is nigh on impossible," I splutter.

"Look, Francesca, don't get so defensive. I'm merely pointing out that you do have other options and you also have lots of great contacts — like Carrie Anne, for instance, who would like nothing better than for you to exploit her. What I've only just this second worked out though is that the reason your friends don't bother saying anything to you any more is because, unlike me, they know how intoxicated you are by fame and celebrity."

Ouch. Bastard. How dare he bring my friends into it?

"Just because you think what I do is totally worthless, Tom, doesn't mean that other people do and for your information my friends have always been incredibly supportive of what I want to do. In fact, the truth is that most normal people are probably a bit jealous of my job."

At this, Tom looks disgusted and once again he makes for his getaway car.

"Stop it. Stop trying to leave before we've sorted things out," I say and now I am really crying, but he no longer seems to care.

"Do you know how pathetic you sound?" he says frustratedly. "How on earth can you think that anybody would be jealous of your job if they really knew what it entailed? Only a total moron would be jealous of you right now because there really isn't anything to be jealous of. Fran, you need to have some self-respect and realize how special you are, and that the real measure of whether a person is worth knowing in this life is how they are to others and how they make other people feel. Now, Carson Adams I can understand people getting excited about. He's a really great bloke and that makes him a proper star, but that creature in there, she's just a horrible —" he visibly struggles to find the right word — "a horrible — twat." He yanks his seatbelt on and this time he's clearly determined to go.

"And don't think I didn't notice the thinly veiled dig at my own job. Being a vet may seem totally boring to you, Francesca, but what bores me is seeing a girl who I thought had real backbone transform into a weak, shallow coward before my very eyes."

"Hang on," I say, sobbing my heart out. "Yesterday you said you were proud of me. It seems to me that maybe you're the shallow one if your feelings can change so dramatically in the space of a day."

"I was proud. Prouder than I've ever been in my life and really excited that maybe I'd finally met someone special, and now I am so, so disappointed."

And with that he drives off, leaving me on the pavement feeling absolutely desolate and sensing that this was one destiny day I could have done without.

CHAPTER
THIRTY-THREE

As Tom's car disappears into the distance, I stand rooted to the pavement, paralysed by shock and sadness and trying to make some sense of what just happened. I'm so upset I don't even worry or care about what Caroline might be thinking, although unsurprisingly she soon fills me in.

"Fraaaaancescaaaaaaaa!" she screams from the other side of the street.

With a start, I spin round and am met by the sight of Caroline hot-footing it across the road towards me, propelled by a stream of outrage.

"What the hell can possibly be taking so fucking long? I've got a list as long as my arm of things that need to be discussed and I don't pay you so that you can wander off and flirt with Mr "shit for brains" Vet, so I would appreciate it if . . ."

As she finally catches up with me, she stops spouting long enough to notice what sort of state I'm in. My face is so ravaged by my sobbing, it warrants, on her part, an intake of breath, followed by a look of horror as it crosses her mind that for the second time in one day some kindness may be required.

She clearly has no idea how on earth to handle the situation and seems faintly repelled by my upset, but I don't throw her a lifeline. I can't. I simply don't have the wherewithal and seem to have stopped functioning normally. So we just stand there, awkwardly gawping at each other. Caroline keeps trying and failing to start a sentence, but nothing comes to her, not even, "Are you OK?" so in the end she plumps for another tack.

"Um, something's obviously up, so why don't you just go home?" she eventually mutters, trying her best to resemble someone who cares but failing miserably.

"Thanks," I blub, too drained even for the most feeble of protests. I think we both know that for today at least I'd be no use to anyone.

So off I go, which means that Caroline doesn't have to feign concern or spend the day feeling repulsed by my snot-stained face and I can be a useless teary person at home. Everyone's a winner.

That night as I lie in bed, desperate but unable to take sleep up on its offer of comfort, I replay what was said during the argument over and over again. I oscillate from feeling utterly self-righteous and that Tom is a pompous idiot who needs to get a life, to feeling like the smallest, most stupid person on the planet who, in letting Tom go, has made the most monstrous mistake. I'm also horribly embarrassed. Being accused of basically being a doormat, shallow and cowardly, doesn't do a great deal for one's ego. I feel as though I've been tried and convicted as a loser and it's all come as a bit of a shock.

Deep down I know that in some ways Tom does have a point. I mean, I've been working for Caroline for quite a while now and if I think about it I'm pretty sure her level of rudeness has grown stealthily, almost by osmosis, like a stain. Now it's a stain that's been left for far too long and is impossible to get out.

Caroline has constantly pushed the boundaries to see how much I am willing to take and at no point have I suggested to her that there are limits. Like a toddler, she has chosen to interpret the lack of boundaries as a green light for foul behaviour. For this I only have myself to blame and yet somehow I can't help but blame Caroline. It may be irrational, but I feel like her poison infects everything she comes into contact with and I deeply regret having let Tom anywhere near her.

On the flipside, I still think he overreacted and that if he had genuine feelings for me he would try harder to understand where I was coming from. Surely if I feel capable of handling Caroline, and if her shoddy treatment of me hasn't bothered me, then why should anybody else have a problem with it? As long as I can handle working for her and as long as I don't start emulating my boss, does it really matter? The only question I avoid dwelling on is the one I need to know the answer to most: are Tom and I over for good?

When I wake up in the morning after not nearly enough sleep, nothing is much clearer, but at least my tear ducts are empty. The first thing I do once I've dragged myself out of bed is check my phone. There are no messages, not even one lousy text. My heart plummets and I can almost taste the disappointment.

355

On autopilot, I start getting ready for work, knowing that Caroline will expect me in early seeing as I absconded yesterday. At least she was decent enough to let me go home, I think, still feeling incredibly defensive after Tom's verbal attack.

I pull on some clothes. I've had my day to wallow and now I need to get myself together and get used to the fact that Tom and I might well be no more. Even before this thought is fully formed though, I can feel my bottom lip wobbling dangerously. Maybe it's a tad early to be attempting brave, so I try depressed back on for size and it's a much easier fit.

I stare at my miserable reflection. I look so ugly. My skin is blotchy and doughy, my eyes are spectacularly puffy, my hair is matted and I have no desire to have a shower to rectify the situation. Shit, so much for feeling better in the morning. I have to acknowledge that the only thing that has become staggeringly clear out of all this is that I have fallen for Tom in rather a big way. Pulling myself together is going to take all the strength and resolve that I can muster, but I am prepared to put in the effort as anything's got to be better than feeling like this. Plus, deep deep down, I feel like surely Tom won't want to lose what we have just because I didn't stick up for myself. Maybe, after a couple of days to simmer down and cool off, he'll ring or text at the very least. I clutch on to this thought. Of course, I could always phone him, but I need to keep reminding myself that although I may have let Caroline take advantage at times, Tom has been incredibly quick to judge and somewhat unfair. So I see no reason why I should be the one to call begging for forgiveness. I just pray that he can swallow his pride and be the one to pick up the phone.

I arrive at work and for once am incredibly grateful to find a huge pile of paperwork in my in-tray. Having something mind-numbingly dull to concentrate on is a great distraction from the swirl of conflicting thoughts and emotions that are invading my head.

At nine thirty I hear a key in the door.

"Hi, Lorna," I call from the study.

Her surprised face peers round the door. "You're in early, love. What are you up to?"

"Oh, just catching up on some filing and doing Caroline's expenses," I reply. It takes a couple of seconds for me to realize that Lorna hasn't bustled off to the kitchen and that she's still scrutinizing me from the doorway.

"Francesca, is everything OK?" she asks suspiciously.

"Yes, everything's fine, thanks."

I look down. The last thing I want right now is any sympathy. However, Lorna's not being put off the scent that easily. She's sensed that something's up and the next thing I know she's in full-on mother-hen mode. In many ways she is the polar opposite to Caroline. She is so maternal and can't stand to see anyone looking sad.

"Come on now, love, tell Lorna everything. What are you doing here so early, pet? Have you been crying? What's she done now then?"

"Caroline hasn't done anything, Lorna. Honestly, please don't worry."

I don't think she's ever known me be anything other than relatively cheery and it obviously pains her to see me looking down, but she's sensitive enough to realize that I'm feeling too fragile to talk about it, so she makes do instead with shuffling round to my side of the desk and, with a look of intent, lunges towards me for a hug.

In terms of affection we've never shared more than a peck on the cheek before, so I'm slightly taken aback as I find my head travelling towards her ample chest, but I resign myself to it and actually a hug is just what the doctor ordered. She pulls me in close and strokes my hair. It's rather soothing and we stay like this for a short while. Her T-shirt smells of washing powder. Then, as suddenly as our embrace started, we simultaneously realize that it's time to pull away before we enter the realms of self-consciousness.

She clears her throat. "Right . . . Well, you know I'm here if you need a little chat, and now I'll go and make us a nice cup of tea."

Released from Lorna's grip, I return to my receipts, definitely feeling a little bit better.

A peaceful hour passes and then Caroline arrives back from an early training session. She jogs through the front door and past the study door, which is still open. She does a double take as she spots me and then jogs backwards so that she can yell in my general direction.

"I'm glad you're here early, Fran."

And then she's off again.

Knowing that Caroline's arrival signifies the end of getting anything really useful done, I close down the computer. I meet her in the hall just as she's jogging back out of the kitchen where she's grabbed herself a banana. Now she's headed for the staircase, and ultimately the shower one would assume, seeing as she's just peeled off her green Juicy hooded top and thrown it behind her.

"Yes, I'm sorry about yesterday, Caroline, and thanks for being so understanding," I say.

"Mmm. Well, just thank your lucky stars you've got a boss who's so compassionate. Many assistants aren't so fortunate," she says, leaning over the banisters and striking a pose, her hair tumbling down.

Lorna appears and chuckles to herself before bending down to pick up the abandoned hooded top and Caroline's banana skin from off the floor. Caroline silences Lorna with a look and then returns her attention to me.

"Anyway, try not to let it happen again." She hesitates and then adds as an afterthought, "Though if it's menstrually related, I do have a man I can recommend."

"Um, no, it wasn't . . . um . . . menstrually related . . . it was —"

"Well, you've bucked up now, so that's the main thing, OK? Just take a day's money off your next invoice and we'll forget all about it," she says, flapping her hand about in a dismissive manner.

"Oh . . . right," I say, feeling pretty astounded seeing as I've never once invoiced her for all the hours and hours and hours of overtime I've put in.

"Follow me upstairs so we can talk while I shower," she orders, peeling off her Nike vest and throwing that behind her too. As ever, she's not wearing a bra.

With a sigh I follow Caroline's toned Juicy-encased buttocks and bare back up the stairs, hating the fact that today, after only a few minutes in her presence, Tom's analysis seems more accurate than it did yesterday. Why am I so incapable of sticking up for myself? Why haven't I ever invoiced for all the extra hours, indeed days, I've done? I hate to admit it, but in the cold light of day Caroline's behaviour suddenly doesn't seem even remotely funny to me.

I follow her and Lorna follows me, picking up Caroline's trail of sweaty clothes as she goes and tutting under her breath. It's a very strange conga, if you like. I feel tired and fed up.

As we reach the landing my mobile goes and I fish it out of my bag, hoping for a giveaway second that it might be Tom. Stop it, Francesca.

It isn't Tom. It's Great British Films calling.

"I'll be with you in a moment, Caroline. I'll just take this call. Hello?" I say, doing an about turn that nearly causes a collision with Lorna.

"Hello, is that Francesca Massi?"

"Yes, speaking," I say, heading back downstairs for the study.

"Hi, my name's Scott James. I'm calling from Great British Films, where I work closely with Mr Devine."

"Oh, hi. One second, I'm just going to the office to grab her diary. Do you want to put in a meeting?"

"Oh, has someone already called?"

"Hang on one moment," I say, moving some files on the desk and retrieving Caroline's diary. "Sorry about that. OK, called about what?"

"About *The Diary of a Personal Assistant*."

"I'm sorry?" I put the diary back on the desk slowly. There's a long pause.

"Is this Francesca Massi, author of *The Diary of a Personal Assistant*?"

It doesn't take Einstein to hazard a guess as to what might be going on here, but I still have to think terribly quickly none the less.

"Er, that sort of depends," I say, trying to buy more thinking time. Carrie Anne must have taken what I printed out for her that night at my flat. Has she pinched my writing and given it to her work without telling me? "Um, sorry to be vague, but can I just ask — did Carrie Anne give that to you by any chance?"

"Yes, didn't you know?"

"Um . . . yes," I lie nervously. My mind's racing. What the hell has Carrie Anne been up to? Either I am about to be pleasantly surprised or I'm about to be sued. Which is it to be?

From upstairs I hear Caroline bellow, "Fraaaaaaaaaaaaaaancesca. What are you doing?"

"One moment. I'm on the phone," I yell back.

"Look," begins the voice on the other end of my mobile, who sounds as if he's beginning to regret ringing me, "our readers here have passed on your manuscript and Carrie Anne has told us a bit about you too. I understand that this is your first stab at writing?"

"Yes, that's right, and it's not actually finished. What you've seen is really just a first draft," I say, feeling a bit defensive.

"Well, for a first draft it's really pretty good. In our opinion, and I hope you don't mind me saying this, it is a bit rough round the edges in parts and might need a few rewrites, but the basic idea is fantastic."

"Really?"

"Yes, really. So the long and the short of it is, would you or would you not be interested in coming in to discuss it? You see, we feel that it has real movie potential, that the material is fresh and that the subject matter is fertile new territory."

"You do?"

"Yeah, we do. Speaking personally, I just love the way you've turned everything on its head. Making the hero, that is to say the star, the anti-hero. It's modern-day Cinderella, it really is. In fact, we want to know if you'd be interested in selling the rights. It has the potential to be a very original movie and one of our directors here has already expressed an interest."

"Right . . . Well, yes. I think so."

I've got to speak with Carrie Anne. I am in way over my head here.

"Shall I come in then?"

"Yes, great. Can you do ten o'clock tomorrow? You'll be meeting myself, Mr Devine and the director I spoke of."

"OK, that sounds great. I'll see you then," I say, too stunned to even consider the fact that I should be here at ten o'clock tomorrow. I sink into a chair, trying to

362

digest what I've just been told. My overwhelming reaction to this incredible and surreal turn of events is worry. Does Mr Devine know that the manuscript came from Caroline Mason's assistant? After all, I've exchanged enough emails with his assistant. But then again, I doubt he does. In fact, I'd bet good money on the fact that Caroline probably couldn't name one of her friend's assistants. I imagine Mr Devine would be the same but, then again, you never know.

What am I going to say in the meeting? How am I going to get the morning off without telling Caroline what's going on? Great British Films might want to make my idea into a film.

The sheer enormity of this fact finally sinks in and worry is shoved into the back seat by excitement. Bloody hell! Great British Films like my writing. I must tell Tom. I can't tell Tom. Tom would be so pleased for me . . .

Things like this don't happen to me — except it just has.

I spring to my feet, determined not to fret about anything any longer and to just be excited and to go with the flow. I grab my pad and some files and sprint up the stairs, taking them two at a time and squashing a strong desire to scream. My sadness about Tom will have to go on hold. It will be revisited, of course, but right now I have to enjoy this feeling and I refuse to let him spoil it.

Caroline is just getting out of the shower and she eyes me warily as I burst into her bedroom, where

Lorna is busily tidying up the clothes that are strewn all over the room.

"Hello," I say breezily.

She looks at me suspiciously as she takes in my sparkling eyes, my flushed cheeks and my total change in mood. Lorna also looks surprised.

"Francesca, we've got a lot to do, so do try to keep up and don't get distracted."

"OK," I say, beaming recklessly and perching on the end of her bed. Lorna looks at me questioningly, but for now I avoid eye contact.

Caroline stalks up to her dressing table, drops her towel and starts to apply moisturizer to her legs. Her nudity is something I hardly even register these days, but Lorna looks disgusted and gives one of her little snorts. I let out a small giggle, which Caroline hears.

"Francesca, please try to stop looking quite so pleased with yourself — it doesn't suit you. Now grab a pen."

I dutifully open up my notebook, but I'm finding it extremely difficult to concentrate on what she's saying. I'm too desperate to phone Carrie Anne.

"Now, flights. To be perfectly honest, I can't believe you haven't organized them already. I thought you would have definitely done that by now. I want first class and I want to fly in the morning and I want Special Services to check in all the luggage and see if you can just pay a business-class fare and get an upgrade . . ."

She drones on for the next ten minutes or so and almost every sentence is prefixed with "I want".

"I want Kenneth to know that I'm very annoyed with him. He left me to cope with a photo shoot for the *Telegraph* at the theatre the other day on my own. My US publicist would never let me do any shoot on my own. Tell him I'm waiving his fee for November. Lorna?" she says abruptly, having finished moisturizing every inch of her honed body.

"Yes?" Lorna mutters apprehensively, while folding up T-shirts on the bed.

"Have you done my whites wash? I need my little camisole for tonight."

"The cycle should be almost finished by now so I'll just go and wait for it so I can put it in the dryer," she says obediently, leaving the room but turning to give me one of our conspiratorial looks before she does. She's understandably very curious to know what has changed my mood so dramatically.

Gosh, I'd love to tell Tom that my writing was going to amount to something. I know he'd be so pleased and, given some of the things he said yesterday, the timing would be perfect. Maybe this would be a good excuse to ring him? It would be awful if he didn't take my call though. Even worse would be if he took my call but was totally indifferent to my news. I also mustn't forget how downright insulting he was yesterday. I silently remonstrate myself for allowing him back into the forefront of my mind at all. Summoning up all my best efforts, I determinedly shove him to the back again.

"Are you listening, Francesca? I said you need to get my membership for Soho House extended . . ."

I nod and make a show of scribbling on my pad, but I'm a million miles away. Maybe I should start believing what I've suspected for a long time: that while I'm not necessarily destined to have the perfect love life, I might just be destined for success. I suppose it's not such a terrible thing to have to start accepting. I would love to have a relationship with Tom while pursuing an exciting, fulfilling career but, being realistic, I doubt there are many people who really do "have it all". This turn of events couldn't have come at a better time and I shall find a way somehow of letting Tom know that this "shallow coward" may be on the brink of a new and exciting career. It'll be one in the judgemental eye for him. This vengeful thought doesn't feel as satisfying as I'd hoped it might though. I think I may be teetering on the edge of hysteria.

I glance at my notepad. It says *Sort out Soho House*. Oh God, what on earth do I mean by that?

Caroline gets up and starts pulling out items from her vast wardrobe and then discarding them on the floor, despite the fact that Lorna has only just finished clearing up her last lot of mess. She eventually settles on a tiny Miu Miu miniskirt with patterned designer tights for her bottom half and, as she climbs into them, she turns to me and says in a loud whisper, "Bless Lorna. She's very sweet and everything but she's not really very capable, is she? I want you to phone Carson in the States and recommend to him that we need a new cleaner. He adores her for some weird reason, so just say that you think it would be in her best interest and that you don't think she can cope any more."

I am absolutely flabbergasted.

"But Lorna's a star," I protest weakly.

"Is she? Well, that depends on what your definition of a star is, doesn't it? I mean, she is very dear, don't get me wrong, but I certainly wouldn't use the word star to describe a woman who doesn't clean thoroughly and who has the dress sense of a hobbit." She flings back her head and laughs long and hard at her evil idea of a joke. Her laughter is hollow and the opposite of contagious. It actually makes me upset.

And in that instance I detest her and wonder how on earth I can possibly put up with her for another three long weeks.

I go very quiet and quit writing down any more of her instructions, letting her boring drone wash over my head as she pulls on a cashmere sweater that hangs off her St Tropezed shoulders and adds a pair of Gucci boots to complete her outfit for the day.

"So make sure you buy wild organic salmon in future, not farmed salmon, and I'd like you to go to a place called Borough Market if you wouldn't mind on Saturday. I know it's your day off, but I guess you kind of owe me a day after yesterday anyway. It's just that Ticia said you can get the most wonderful smoked almonds that go beautifully with a glass of champers. Now, stop looking so glum — I almost prefer that silly smile you were sporting earlier — and let's go and see if Lorna has managed to at least get this washing sorted out, shall we?"

I am seething inside and on the stairs I have a strong urge to stick my leg out so that she trips on her ridiculously high boots and tumbles down the stairs like a broken Barbie. If she says anything nasty to Lorna, I'm going to have to say something.

"Lorna?" barks Caroline as we enter the kitchen. I am dismayed to realize that there has been a problem with the washing, probably for the first time ever, which is typical. Lorna is cowering by the washing machine with a pile of washing in her hands, almost in tears.

"Caroline, you must have given me a black vest in the pile because it's all gone slightly grey," she says, looking really panicked.

"AAAAAH!" screams Caroline, as if she's just learned that her entire family has been wiped out as opposed to the fact that her white jeans have the *slightest* grey tinge to them, which can obviously easily be remedied.

"My favourite jeans and my camisole. Oh my God," she moans, sinking into the nearest chair.

To get this into perspective, I should tell you that upstairs she has at least five pairs of white jeans and about fifteen pairs of jeans in other colours. She also has camisoles in every colour known to man and when I say that the wash has been slightly tinged with grey, I mean it is the colour of most normal people's whites. Normal people who actually wear their clothes for a few years and not for a few months. Plus, if Lorna didn't notice one small black vest it's probably because she has to do about three loads of washing per day, as Caroline refuses point blank to ever wear anything more than once. Add to the fact that she swaps her outfits more times a day than a puking baby has its babygro changed and you can see what hard work it all is for poor Lorna. As for her point about Lorna not being the most efficient cleaner, maybe there is a grain of truth in that and if I were being totally honest I'd have to say that sometimes her cleaning can be a bit superficial, but she's loyal, sweet and has worked at No. 47 for years. She is an integral part of the house, so who cares?

"How could you?" Caroline demands.

Seeing that Lorna is positively quivering with fear, I decide to take charge of the situation and simultaneously I come to understand that Tom was right. About everything.

"OK," I announce. "Lorna, don't worry, I'll sort this out. It's fine. Caroline, I'm just popping to the shops to get something to fix this and I won't be long."

"But I don't want new jeans," she hisses petulantly.

The woman is demented.

"I'm not getting new jeans. Now just sit tight and don't worry."

I stomp out of the house, eager to get out and to gulp some air that I don't have to share with that poisonous witch. I really have had enough. I'm so angry that it takes a while before I remember the phone call that I received from Great British Films. As soon as I do, though, I dial Carrie Anne's direct line. Miraculously, for once, it's not engaged and she picks up.

"Hello?"

"Oh my God, Carrie Anne, what the hell have you done?" I squeal.

"Hi, babe. It's amazing, isn't it? Well done you — they're genuinely excited about you as a writer and your idea."

"Are they?"

"Absolutely."

"God, Carrie Anne, I can't believe you nicked my book, but I'm so grateful that you did."

"You will be when they pay you, babe."

"Really?" I say delightedly, having not even thought about the question of money. "What do they pay for ideas like this then? Will it mean that I won't have to worry about getting a job immediately after I finish working for Caroline?"

"I would say so, yeah," muses Carrie Anne.

"This is so exciting, fuck me," I screech.

"No thanks, I've just eaten. Listen, I've got to take this call, but I think I should be at the meeting with you tomorrow. Meet me in my office at twenty to ten and I'll talk you through a few things."

With that she's gone, leaving me with my jaw dangling on the pavement. I pull myself together and scamper into the shop, grab what I'm looking for and race back to the house, looking forward to revisiting Carrie Anne's bombshell later when I've got time to digest it.

Caroline is alone in the kitchen, looking very sulky.

"Where's Lorna?" I demand.

"I don't know. She's gone to dust something, I think. She's probably turning furniture grey as we speak. Where've you been? You've been ages."

I ignore her and go to the washing machine, where I deposit all the damp light grey washing back into the drum and add to it the contents of the packet that I bought in the shop.

"What are you doing?" asks Caroline, sounding genuinely fascinated.

"It's Glo White. It's washing powder with a bit of bleach in it. Your clothes will come out sparkling again."

"Really?" she says, looking at me with newfound respect. "That's incredible. Where the hell did you learn to do that?"

I switch the machine on and don't bother answering this silly question.

"I'm going to go and check on Lorna."

I find the old lady in the sitting room with a duster in her hand, looking rather red and watery round the eyes.

"Oh shit. What's she done?"

Lorna looks straight at me and it's only then that I realize she doesn't look sad; instead she has what can only be described as a triumphant look in her tearful eyes.

"She said I was past it and that the reason I didn't spot the black vest was because I probably couldn't see it. Then she said that I should think long and hard about whether or not I want this job."

"And do you?"

"Well, you see, Francesca, that's all a bit beside the point now because I've just had my Steph on the phone and none of this will probably make much sense to you now but it seems that when Carson got home last night he proposed to her and . . . my little girl's getting married."

"Oh my God," I whoop, and Lorna and I link hands and dance around the room, hugging and weeping. Then we both collapse on the sofa with Lorna shushing me.

"Ssh, Fran, because she doesn't know yet and Carson's going to phone her any minute."

We huddle on the sofa together, giggling nervously, unwilling to leave the room because we both know that Caroline is about to go utterly ballistic any minute now.

CHAPTER
THIRTY-FOUR

"You said you wouldn't do this to me, you bastard. How the fuck could you?" is Caroline's initial response to Carson's announcement. I would imagine that the chance of any congratulations being offered is now very remote.

Lorna and I continue to hide in the sitting room while all hell breaks loose in the kitchen.

"But what about me? This wasn't the deal!" we hear Caroline yelling at the top of her lungs.

When screaming doesn't work, she changes tactics and we are forced to listen to her working her way through the whole gamut of emotional blackmailing tactics — pleading, ranting and finally sobbing. The only time she sounds vaguely mollified is when she says, "I know the split hasn't done Marina Madson and James Reddington any harm, but do you really think it will work for me?"

Then the sobbing starts again and when it seems obvious that Carson is clearly immoveable she resorts to smashing plates and throwing pans around. With every crash and new threat of revenge, Lorna and I wince and shiver, but the most frightening part of the whole experience is when it all goes deathly quiet.

It would be fair to say that she hasn't taken the news very well.

"What should we do?" I whisper to Lorna. "Do you think I should go and check on her?"

"You do what you like. I'm not moving," she whispers back, clutching a cushion to her chest for protection. So we sit for what feels like an age, but what is really probably only about ten minutes, and dread fills our hearts when eventually we hear the kitchen door opening and the sound of Caroline's footsteps outside on the wooden floor. My heart is in my mouth as her French-manicured talons slowly appear round the sitting-room door and then the rest of her follows.

Her pallor is deathly, her hair is dishevelled and from where I'm sitting she looks utterly deranged.

"Did you know about this?" she demands in a low voice to a trembling Lorna.

"Know about what?" asks Lorna.

"Don't give me that," she replies slowly, her hands by her sides and her gaze unflinching. "Did you know that Carson was going to mess things up by asking your fucking pathetic daughter to marry him?"

"Please don't swear or say things like that about Steph. She's not done anything wrong," manages Lorna bravely.

Caroline's eyes widen and a vein in her forehead twitches ominously. She turns her icy glare to me. "Francesca, let me warn you that if you dare to breathe a word of any of this to anyone, I will not hesitate to sue you."

"I won't," I say sullenly.

"Get Leticia on the phone and tell her to come round now. And you," she says, pointing a bony finger in Lorna's face. "Get out of my house, you silly old bag. I don't want to see you here ever again."

Hearing her be so revolting to Lorna makes me feel physically sick and I suddenly realize that I have absolutely nothing to gain except self-loathing by putting up with her hideous behaviour any longer. The fact that she is so unhinged only makes me feel even more in control. I have this sudden snapshot of the entire situation and it's almost as if I am seeing everything through Tom's eyes. No wonder it made his skin crawl to see me allowing her to walk all over me. Enough is enough.

"Don't talk to Lorna like that," I say, quietly but firmly.

"I beg your pardon?" Caroline asks, thoroughly aghast at my lack of subservience.

"I said, don't talk to Lorna like that."

"It's all right, Francesca," placates Lorna, but it's too late. I've past the point of no return and I realize now that after the argument with Tom it was only a matter of time before this moment happened. It's almost as if I've been silently willing her to cross the line and now she has.

"No, the thing is, it's not all right," I say. "It's not all right at all to shout and swear at people. In fact, it's downright rude."

"How dare you speak to me like that?" screeches Caroline, thundering towards me until she's a mere three feet away from my face.

375

I stand my ground. "I might ask you the same question because you've been speaking to me like shit for months now. Not one pleasant word, not one measly thank you have I had for all my hard work and that's fine, but I won't have you speak to Lorna like that."

From here I can see all the little hairs on Caroline's face. Her eyes are bulging and there's spittle gathering at the sides of her mouth. Not only do I feel angry with her, but I also feel something resembling pity. Standing there in her silly miniskirt that is far too young for her, she just looks a bit sad and I suddenly feel really glad that I am lucky enough to be me and not her, for she is possibly the most miserable, self-absorbed person I have ever had the misfortune of meeting and, as a result, she is lonely, unloved and unappreciative of all the wonderful things in her life.

My bravery must be contagious because Lorna moves away from the corner where she's been hiding and crosses the room to join me in her polyester trousers and her "Frankie Says Relax" T-shirt.

"Francesca's right, Caroline, you have been a bit of a one and I think you need to stop shouting and think about what you've done."

There was never any way that Caroline was going to take that lying down. "Shut up, both of you!" she screeches indignantly. "What the fuck has got into you? Have you completely forgotten who you're talking to or something? Have you taken leave of your senses? I mean, God forbid I've offended Miss Boring-high-street-clothes, I'm-so-smug-because-I-know-a-thing-or-two-about-washing or Old Mother "can't clean for shit"

Hubbard here. Now I don't want to hear any more of this crap and I don't think either of you can honestly expect to be paid for this week."

But this time it's me who edges threateningly towards her, and Caroline struggles to maintain her composure as I back her into a corner of the room.

"How dare you judge us? And, more to the point, how dare you judge us on such materialistic and meaningless criteria? The only reason you're permanently decked out in designer clothing is because Carson pays for it, but it looks as if that gravy train has just left for good, doesn't it? So if I were you, Caroline, I would stop judging other people and take a long hard look at yourself instead because, trust me, there's a lot of room for improvement."

Caroline is beyond furious and I can see her summoning up all her rage to launch into another verbal attack, but then she seems to think better of it. I realize it is because she knows full well that she no longer has the upper hand and that it no longer matters what she says because neither of us will care. She makes one last feeble attempt to regain control and to make an impact. "You're both fired."

"Good," I say, laughing. "I was hoping you'd say that because I wouldn't stay working for you for another second if you paid me with all the tea in China. So good luck without an assistant to run your life. In fact, good luck with coping with anything yourself, especially the housework. I'll leave all your bank cards and stuff in the study, although you probably have no idea how to use them, do you? Never mind, I'll leave Jodie's notes

377

out for you. They make great reading if you feel like being bored rigid for an hour or three. Of course, as ever, there's loads of food in the fridge, but when you run out there's a place called Safeways down the road," I say, marching past her and heading for the study, where I retrieve my washbag and pour a mountain of receipts and cards all over the desk.

Caroline follows me in. "Francesca, you are fired, but that doesn't mean you can leave me in the lurch. You have to find me a new assistant because I've still got three weeks of the play to go, you know."

"And? Oh, hang on, let me get this right. You've fired me, but you still want me to sort out an assistant for you. Well, while I'm at it I suppose I may as well book your travel arrangements for you too?"

"Yes. That would be the best plan," she says cautiously.

I throw my head back and laugh at the absurdity of the woman. "Yeah, right, good one. You really are a class act, aren't you? Lorna, are you ready to go? I've got to pick my car up from Teddington, so come with me if you like and I'll treat you to lunch at my dad's restaurant."

Lorna looks at me admiringly and takes my lead. "That sounds lovely. Seeing as I'm fired, I suppose I may as well. Ooh, how lovely — I adore Italian food."

"Good, we'll be off then. Good luck, Caroline. Oh, by the way, your car's coming at two o'clock to take you to . . . oh, I don't know why I'm telling you. I'm sure you've read the reports that I write for you every single day. Or maybe you haven't — after all, I'm so boring, aren't I? And one last thing: the milk I've been buying for you is full-fat, not skimmed, and the chicken you had last night — *not* organic. Bye."

Triumphantly, Lorna and I slam the door of No.47 for the last time, leaving Caroline apoplectic with rage, quivering in the hall while calculating how many extra calories I've inadvertently caused her to ingest.

"You were brilliant, Fran," laughs Lorna, as we head towards the tube, both still trembling from adrenaline.

"So were you," I say.

"No, you were the one who really told her. I mean, her face, it was brilliant, and I love the thought of her trying to figure out how to use the iron and the dryer. Let's call Carson and Steph and tell them what's happened."

We stop at a nearby bench and I call the number of the apartment in New York. Thankfully Carson picks up and, I don't know why, but he seems surprisingly shocked at quite how badly Caroline's behaved. I guess he never truly witnessed her in all her terrible glory. He reassures me that I will be paid everything I'm owed and tells Lorna that he's going to send her a ticket so that she can come to New York and discuss wedding plans with Steph. Then he asks to speak me again.

"Fran, listen. We really want to keep our plans secret for the moment because I still have some promotion left to do on my last movie. I've got lots of premières to attend, which I'll go to on my own, and Steph doesn't want the world's press to get this story yet. So my official line will be that Caroline's ill and I'd really appreciate you keeping all this to yourself for a while longer."

"Sure," I agree.

"But after that our lives are going to be very different and I want to thank you so much for being brave enough to make me change things."

"Don't be silly," I say. "You're the one who's been brave. Just one thing though?" I add hesitantly, unsure as to whether or not I have the right to ask it.

"Sure, anything."

"Well, I just wondered — how did Cameron take the news?"

Carson's voice cracks with emotion as he struggles to compose himself. "He was so relieved. He was just so relieved that she wasn't his mom and he said he'd always secretly hoped . . ."

"Oh, that's great. I'm so pleased he's OK. Please send him a big squidge from me," I say, ignoring Lorna, who's making strange faces at me, clearly having figured out that I know a lot more than I've let on so far.

"Carson, I'd love to talk more but I'd better go — I'm taking Lorna to lunch at Massi's so that I can pick up the car."

"Oh, good for you, Francesca. Get a cab there and I'll pay for it — you can stick the receipt in with your invoice."

I grin and don't even pretend to argue. "Thanks, Carson, we might just do that."

"And say hi to Tom, won't you? He's such a great guy, Fran."

My heart aches as I reply. "I know."

380

When I get home much later on that day, having dropped a full and hiccupping Lorna off at home, I curl up on the sofa with the phone in my hand. I'm desperate to tell someone all my news, but I can't decide who to call. There's only one name I keep coming back to and I know that this is the person who I really want to share everything with and who would most appreciate what's happened. It seems ironic that the thing Tom loathed so much, that is to say me working for Caroline, is the very thing that has changed my viewpoint so radically and finally given me a sense of perspective about what's really important. Unable to talk to Tom and missing him dreadfully, I put the phone back in its cradle and find solace in my diary instead.

28th November

When something bad happens, I want to tell Tom. When something great happens, I want to tell Tom. I love him and now he hates me, so I'm going to have to unpick everything I feel for him and I've got a horrible feeling that it might be impossible. Especially seeing as it's the last thing I want to do.

CHAPTER
THIRTY-FIVE

I've had a terrible night's sleep again, although it's probably not that surprising. So much has happened in such a short space of time and I'm feeling a little bit as though events are running away with themselves before I've even had the chance to acknowledge them. Ideally, I would love to have a couple of days before my meeting with Great British Films just to absorb everything, to gather my thoughts and to regroup, as it were. However, I don't have the luxury of this option, so now that I'm awake, having managed about four hours of proper kip, I stand in the shower for ages trying to let the pummelling water cleanse and soothe my weary brain. At least my stand-off with Caroline has eliminated the problem of how to get out of work this morning.

By quarter to ten I'm in Carrie Anne's impressive office at Great British Films in the heart of Soho, discussing how to approach this very important meeting that could change my life.

"Remember, babe, you have the upper hand," Carrie Anne instructs, striding round and round her desk in her black Ugg boots. (She's so good at her job that she's never felt the need to conform to conventional office attire.) "It's your idea and they like your take on it. You're the one with the experience and you're the one who understands how our heroine feels. If you don't understand something they're asking, don't try and guess the answer, just give me a look and I'll help you out. Lastly, have confidence in your idea because, if you don't, no one else will. You are essentially here to sell a product except that you're at an incredible advantage because I know they've already decided that they want to buy it." Carrie Anne stops pacing, takes in my terrified expression, smiles encouragingly and gives my arm a squeeze. "You'll be fine. Come on, let's go."

She pauses at the door and then turns to me, saying, "Just quickly, Fran — we're not friends, we just used to work together, and whatever you do don't tell them who Miss M actually is yet. OK?"

"But what if they guess?" I ask anxiously. "I mean, I've been corresponding with Mr Devine and his assistant for months now."

"Don't worry about that. I've already had a word with his assistant and it's sorted. I promise you, Mr Devine is clueless on that front. Now, come on, let's try and make you some money."

Thanking heaven for Carrie Anne, I take a deep breath and follow my confident friend and ally towards battle.

The meeting is being held in one of the larger boardrooms on the floor above Carrie Anne's and when we arrive I can see through the glass walls that everybody is already present and correct and waiting for us. Mr Devine is there, a stout man in his fifties with a shiny pate and a red, bulbous nose. I'd bet good money on him not being a vegetarian. Then there is a younger man whom I presume to be Scott James, who has strawberry blond hair and a pleasant enough face, scattered with orangey freckles. Lastly, there is a third man, who must be very creative in order to get away with wearing the shabby clothes he's wearing. His brooding expression detracts from the fact that he is actually rather good-looking in a sultry kind of way. He looks the opposite of fragrant.

"Miss Massi," says the clean-cut freckly man. He has a mild Yorkshire accent and he leaps out of his chair and races to shake my hand. "Delighted to meet you. I'm Scott James; we spoke on the phone. Please take a seat. This is Mr Devine and this here is the director Thomas Anderson."

I smile warmly and shake everyone's hand, hoping that mine doesn't feel too clammy.

"So," says Scott, who it seems will be leading the proceedings, "Francesca, where to begin?"

I have no idea, so I say nothing and just smile dumbly.

Carrie Anne interjects: "I think Francesca would probably like to start with our reactions to her work."

I smile gratefully at her and carry on nodding, hoping that they won't start to suspect that I'm a mute.

"Good idea," enthuses Scott. "Well, as you know, we have read your manuscript and we're all in agreement that this would make a fabulous film. It's got black comedy, there's romance with this relationship between the assistant, Abbie, and the Tim character, and, as I've said before, we just love the irony of making a film like this, which essentially is exposing some of the worst aspects of our own industry."

So far, so good. It seems that nodding will get me far.

"Now before we go any further, it's pretty clear that you have had some personal experience of the movie industry, Francesca, so may I ask in what capacity this was?" asks Scott.

I clear my throat and I must look rather apprehensive for Mr Devine winks encouragingly at me in a kind but slightly disturbing manner.

"Right, er . . . well, I worked in production for years, which was when I met Carrie Anne, and then I went on to become an actress and more recently I have worked for someone fairly well known, although at this stage I'd really rather not divulge who that was."

Mr Devine places his elbows on the table, his pudgy hands firmly clasped together, making his fingers resemble uncooked chipolatas, and addresses me in a mellow, deep voice that could easily do the voiceovers in the Odeon. You know, the "coming to a screen near you" ones?

"And that would be because your character Miss M is based on or inspired by this person, is that correct?"
"Yes."

Or he could be the voice in the Mr Kipling ads — he's impressively gravelly at any rate.

Mr Devine cocks his head and gives me another little smile and his eyes twinkle as he mulls over what he's just learnt. Everybody waits for the big man to speak.

"That's fine. I suspected that this character probably wasn't a figment of your imagination and I think the fact that Miss M is based on someone real adds a lot of intrigue if handled in the right way. Now, I'm not going to ask you to tell us who it is here and now, but for professional and legal reasons I will have to find out at some point should we decide to go ahead."

"Fair enough," I agree, wondering if I'm getting in way over my head here, and then I nod (for a change).

Scott picks up where Mr Devine left off.

"Interesting. Now, in terms of casting, you must have a pretty strong idea as to whom you think could handle the part of the mighty Miss M and, indeed, the part of her assistant Abbie. So tell us who you see in those roles."

I look at Carrie Anne, but she just gives the smallest of shrugs. It looks like I'm on my own for this one.

"Well . . . I think the part of Abbie should definitely be a new face, an unknown. Someone who is attractive but in a very unthreatening way. A bit Bridget Jonesey, if you like. But for Miss M I have always thought that someone like Marina Madson would be very good, or . . ." Shit, I've gone blank. Say something. They're all waiting. Say anything . . .

"Caroline Mason?"

Anything except that. I can't believe I just said her name. My cheeks suddenly feel very hot.

There is a long pause and then Mr Devine breaks the silence. "Caroline Mason . . . I think that's inspired. You know, we nearly just worked with her on something else, but I think she'd perfect for this. What do you think, Thomas?"

Thomas fingers his beard thoughtfully and then pronounces, "Yeah. Marina Madson would be good, but I'm pretty sure she's tied up in a three-picture deal with Universal right now and, besides, I'm not sure she could do highly strung as well as Caroline Mason could."

"It's true," gushes Scott. "Caroline Mason is pretty neurotic in real life and if she could just translate that sort of over-anxiousness on to the screen, combined with her looks and her presence, I reckon she could be dynamite. Food for thought indeed."

Thomas Anderson runs his hands through his messy black mop of hair, which looks as if it's been rinsed in chip fat, and adds, "Yeah it would be perfect because she's also just reaching that stage when she's losing her bloom of youth and, although she's still very attractive, basically in Hollywood terms she's done, which would heighten the pathos. Still, if we did use her we'd need A-listers to play Mr X and the assistant because she's not exactly box office."

I look around, interested to see how everyone will react to his rather unfair and highly chauvinistic comments, but nobody else seems to bat an eyelid.

"She'd be great," says Scott authoritatively. "Carrie Anne, if everything goes the way we want it to this week, I think it wouldn't do any harm to start sounding out her agent even without a script. It'll make her feel wanted from the start. I believe she's with Geoffrey

Darnell, over here at any rate, although I'm not sure who she's with in the States."

The meeting seems to be going very well and they're certainly acting as if they mean business. Of course I do know there is one slight snag: Miss M *is* Caroline Mason, which could become apparent to her the minute she reads it. If she doesn't realize then, she certainly will once she sees who's written it, and I'm still struggling to come to terms with the fact that I said her name. Still, I choose not to dwell on this now and erase the niggling doubt from my mind.

Carrie Anne speaks up. "Well, on behalf of all of us here, we believe this project is very timely and that the first step should be for you to get yourself a literary agent, Francesca. Then, if you're still interested in selling your idea, we can come to a financial agreement and the ball can start rolling."

"OK, that sounds great."

Mr Devine fixes me with a steely gaze. "There's one very important aspect that we would have to clear up before we began anything and that is how it all ends, Francesca. Your book stops short and I'm desperate to know how Miss M's denouement is played out."

"To be honest, Mr Devine, I'm not entirely sure yet, although I'm starting to get a pretty good idea," I reply, a secretive smile playing on my lips.

The meeting continues for another hour or so and the long and the short of it is that I need to get myself an agent immediately. There is a lot to be negotiated. You see, they want me to finish my manuscript and then it will be handed over to an experienced

388

screenwriter who will adapt it into a screenplay. Eventually it is time to leave and Carrie Anne and I retreat back to her office, where she equips me with the number of a great agent whom she seems to think will get me the best possible deal.

I feel totally shell-shocked and, by the time we say goodbye, my head is positively swirling. I can't believe how well everything has gone and I've got a fizzing feeling in my stomach like the pressure in a champagne bottle before the cork is popped. I want to scream and shout with excitement and a few funny noises do escape as I half run out of the building with the most ridiculous grin plastered all over my face. The enormity of what could really happen is finally hitting me and I hail a cab to Clapham feeling that, in light of everything, it is a treat that can be more than justified.

When I get home, I can't get to my computer quick enough so that I can get stuck in and start to tackle the ending. There's nothing like a bit of encouragement from the biggest film company in the UK to get the creative juices flowing. This is it. This is my big break, and I now know that the day when Carrie Anne came round to my flat and I showed her my writing was one of the biggest destiny days I am ever likely to experience.

That night I skim read all my writing and feel pretty positive there is nothing I have written that could ever be linked directly back to Caroline. I have changed key factors sufficiently so that the only people alive who would know that it is her are myself, Caroline, Carson, Steph and Lorna, and that's it. As much as I detest the woman, I don't want this to be a hatchet job — even she doesn't deserve that.

Over the next couple of days, with Carrie Anne's help, I secure myself a literary agent who happens to be one of the most impressive, bright and formidable women I've ever met. She's called Lucinda, she's terribly posh and reminds me of a terrier, snapping at people's heels for her clients. I'm still having trouble getting my head round the fact that not only does she genuinely seem to like my book, but that after all these years of getting nowhere on my own I now have this tenacious force to be reckoned with on my side. I know for certain that I'm in experienced and capable hands when she tells me that she's looking to get me not only a book deal but a huge fee for the film rights and also an executive producer's credit and a cut of the back end, which sounds revolting but is in fact a genuine film term for money from box-office revenue.

CHAPTER
THIRTY-SIX

One week later and recent events are still sinking in. I can't believe I'm teetering on the brink of a whole new dream career, and not having to be around Caroline and her nuts behaviour any more is wonderful.

However, on a less positive note, Tom still hasn't rung or even sent a text and, as the days go by, rather than start the healing process I'm hurting even more as it begins to look less and less likely that a reconciliation will happen. I miss him so much and, although outwardly I am genuinely happy and enthused about everything else that is going on, inside I feel positively grief-stricken about the death of our relationship. At the same time, I still can't one hundred per cent believe our relationship is over and part of me is furious at him for not being more careful with something so precious. I may be wrong, but I don't think that what we had comes along every day of the week and it just seems like such a terrible waste.

Of course, all my friends think I should bite the bullet and ring him. Even Raj, who I met up with last week for the first time in ages, thinks I should make the first move and he hasn't even met Tom. But I can't. Deep down I know that if Tom wanted us to be together he would have been in touch by now, so I have no other choice but to lick my wounds and try to get over him.

The one thing that saves me from going officially bonkers is my book, which — thankfully — is going brilliantly. The only bit I'm not entirely happy about is the ending, which still needs a bit of tinkering with, and it even has a name. It is now entitled (after a lot of debate with Great British Films) *Me and Miss M*. It would probably be completely finished already if it wasn't for the fact that I'm still fielding a fair amount of calls from people who don't seem to be able to comprehend that I no longer work for Caroline Mason and therefore no longer care about her eyebrow waxing appointment/her cushions that need picking up/her house seats. I know I should just switch my phone off, but don't — just in case Tom has a change of heart and calls me. Still, I wished I had the other day when out of the blue I heard from Miss Mason herself.

I was busy working away, revising, editing and tidying various sections, when my phone rang.

"Hello," I said, chewing on my finger thoughtfully as I reread a passage that had been bothering me all afternoon.

"Francesca, it's me."

There was no mistaking that voice and, besides, who else would presume that I'd automatically know it was them?

"Caroline, how are you?" I enquired cautiously, hastily saving my work and shutting the computer down, as if she might be able to see it if I didn't.

"How do you think I am, seeing as you've left me up shit creek?"

I said nothing.

"Look, Francesca. This is ridiculous. You've made your point and maybe I was a bit heavy-handed with Lorna, but you need to come back and fulfil your promise and get me through the rest of this freaking play for the next couple of weeks," she said, coming as close to an apology as I'd ever heard her.

"No can do, I'm afraid," I said firmly, relishing the situation.

"I'll give you more money."

"I don't want more money. I don't want to come back. You were very unpleasant and I don't believe for a minute that things would change."

"Francesca, I'm not going to beg," she said warily, her voice faltering slightly, and I could tell she was uncertain of how to proceed.

"Well, even if you did it wouldn't make a jot of difference," I replied, enjoying her discomfort.

"Fine, but at least do this much. Find me a new assistant, just for the next couple of weeks until I go back. I can't do it all on my own. I've got so much Christmas shopping to do."

This wasn't worthy of a response.

"I still . . . haven't even booked my flights back," she whimpered.

Of course she hadn't. God forbid anybody kept her waiting on hold for even a second, I thought, as I recalled all the hours I'd been kept hanging on by the airlines, listening to terrible muzak until I'd almost lost the will to live.

"Caroline, I'm really busy so I'm afraid I haven't got time to find you an assistant."

This was when I knew that she must have been truly frantic because she tried out a word that sounded entirely foreign coming from her.

"Please . . .?"

Then I remembered something that Raj had told me and a most wicked and amusing idea had started to form in my head. In fact, I had to stifle the desire to chuckle just at the mere thought.

"Look, there's one person I can think of who might be available. I'll find out if she's up for it, but if she's not then that's me done, end of story."

"OK," Caroline said, and I knew that she hated feeling so powerless.

And so it was that the same afternoon my old chum Stacey received a call from Raj, who told her how sorry he was that she'd been sacked from Diamond PR for being caught in flagrante with Mike from accounts by a devastated Geoff, and that — should she be interested — he knew of a movie star who was looking for an assistant for a couple of weeks. Of course, it goes without saying that she was interested — who wouldn't be? Stacey had rung Caroline immediately. I know this because Raj told me that Stacey had rung him to say thanks so much and that she'd got the job and was starting immediately. Poor girl won't have a clue, but really I'm delighted for them both and I can't think of two people who are more suited to each other. In fact,

I would pay handsomely to witness the coming together of the two singularly most self-absorbed people I've ever known. They utterly deserve one another.

I have also had "the" chat with Mr Devine and have finally revealed the true identity of Miss M. Thankfully, he was rather tickled and I think secretly impressed by the fact that I'd had the sheer nerve to suggest Caroline should play herself in the film. It appealed to his sense of irony and he took the news much better than he could have done. He also seems to think that in some way Caroline might feel flattered that she is to be the main subject matter of a film. Pretty back-handed compliment if you ask me, but there's no accounting for the warped perspective of a mad actress and, instinctively, I suspect he's right. Caroline may be a lot of things but she isn't thick and I don't think the fact will escape her that by playing this part she would have the opportunity to show the world that she would never really dream of acting like Miss M in a million years, which is precisely why she's been chosen for the part. Confused? You should be.

It would be understandable if you were to question why on earth I'm happy to provide Caroline with such a fantastic opportunity when she really doesn't deserve it, but the truth is she *is* the part and she will play it to perfection. And maybe, just maybe, by playing herself and discovering that "herself" is so horrific, she may reappraise her behaviour. Or maybe not.

Anyway, if I've totally misread the situation and upon reading the script she simply decides to sue me, well, I'll have to cross that bridge when I come to it. Great

British Films have, of course, made sure that their corporate arses are well and truly covered.

Writing feverishly, stopping only for maudlin breaks to reflect on how things have turned out and how things might have been, means that time races by and when my thirtieth birthday turns up on 14 December it takes even me by surprise. I'm not in the mood for a party, so choose to celebrate with a small dinner for my closest friends. Tom and I had talked about taking a trip to Rome, which is something I can't help dwelling on when I'm blowing out my candles.

The worst thing about feeling like this is that I don't even want to be "over him" because that would be so terribly final. So I just let the tap of feeling that I have for him drip, drip away. A highly effective form of torture.

At least one man remembered my birthday. I couldn't believe it when Carson sent me an amazing bouquet of white roses, even though I know sending flowers is much easier when you have a PA to sort it out for you. Still, I also know that he would have asked Jodie nicely and I'm really touched that he bothered. It's very weird because although I haven't seen him for a couple of weeks I still know exactly what he's up to, thanks to the media. Nearly every day there are new pictures of him in the papers or clips of him at press junkets round the world promoting his film, The Reporter, and attending numerous premières for it. The official line from his PR people is that Caroline is still too ill to be by his side.

The week before Christmas I delivered my finished manuscript to my agent and to Great British Films. Pressing the "send" button was bittersweet. I'd never felt such a sense of accomplishment and yet I was sad that writing something I'd enjoyed so much had come to an end. Still, it's very restorative to have a break now and to spend some proper, festive time with my family who are all very wary about saying anything that may upset me. (I think sympathy might be starting to wane though and I've noticed that when it looks like I'm about to start bemoaning the end of mine and Tom's relationship again, people are suddenly finding urgent tasks that need doing in other rooms.) So anything to do with animals, weddings, love, helping out at births or sickly dogs is off limits, which I have to say doesn't seem to hinder conversation too much. At the end of our annual viewing of *It's a Wonderful Life*, Mum, Dad and Daniel all look a bit tense as I cry a bit harder than usual, but apart from that I manage to remain in a relatively stable state of mind and to genuinely relax. We all ride on the usual merry-go-round of eating too much, drinking too much and watching too much telly before the New Year kicks in, bringing with it a diet, a detox and some editorial notes.

My agent thinks that if I knuckle down and get them finished soon, she will be able to get me a book deal in enough time to ensure that the book comes out before the film, which according to her is the correct and sensible order of things. Anyway, I'm right in the middle of it one evening when Abbie calls to me from the front room: "Fran, get in here quick."

I hurry to the sitting room, where Abbie is watching the six o'clock news, and we learn via a special report from Hollywood that Carson Adams has been nominated for an Oscar for his role in *The Reporter*. As I gaze wistfully at his handsome face on the small screen in my sitting room, I realize forlornly that I've really missed him. Of course, the minute I start thinking this, the phone goes and it's him. Life is so weird sometimes.

"Hi, Francesca, how the devil are you?" he drawls, sounding sexy as ever.

"Oh my God, that's the strangest thing — I was just thinking of you and watching you on TV. How are you?"

"I'm fine, although my feet haven't touched the ground much lately."

"I know, I heard. Congratulations."

"Yeah, it's pretty nice actually, especially seeing as it's going to be my last movie and everything."

"So you're really sticking to that plan then?" I say, winking at Abbie and mouthing "It's Carson" at her.

"Yeah, right," she mouths back, then nearly falls off the sofa as she realizes that in fact I'm telling the truth.

I don't blame her.

OK, I know by now I should be really cool and offhand about the fact that I know a gorgeous movie star, but to be truly honest I'm still nowhere near getting over the thrill. Plus, I haven't spoken to Carson for weeks and had half presumed that he'd forget all about me, so to find him on the end of my phone is a lovely surprise.

"I sure am sticking to the plan. In fact, Steph and I have started making wedding arrangements — not that I can tell you when or where it's going to be or anything, only because everything is so secret I doubt even we will know until the day itself. So, anyway, how about you, Francesca? What's going on with Tom?"

Oh.

"Um. Not much actually, Carson. We broke up not long after I last saw you," I say softly, still incapable of masking my true feelings on the subject.

"I know."

"What do you mean, you know? How do you know?" I demand.

"We email about soccer and stuff, and it came up. It seems such a shame and I just don't get what happened. You guys seemed so great for each other."

I'm not sure how I feel about the fact that Tom is still in touch with Carson, but at least now I know he's still alive.

"To be honest, Carson, you've had more contact with him in the last month than me, but as far as I'm aware I turned out not to be the girl he thought I was."

"What do you mean? What happened? Tell me."

"Well, it's all a bit embarrassing really, but basically Tom saw how Caroline treated me and was less than impressed. He seemed to think that I should have stuck up for myself a bit more and I think he had other issues with me too."

"Such as?"

"Oh, I don't know. I think he just thought I had some of my priorities wrong. Anyway, it's over, he doesn't want to know me, so it's all water under the bridge," I say, blushing despite myself.

Abbie has squashed herself right up against me in an attempt to listen in and I try to nudge her away.

"Well, like I said, it seems a real shame. Maybe you should try giving him a ring? You might find that he's really happy to hear from you."

I still find raking the subject of Tom up for examination incredibly hard and when I speak again my voice catches.

"No, Carson. Quite frankly, I really don't see why I should be the one to ring him. He was the one who walked out on me. He hasn't bothered getting in touch and I think it's starting to get to the point where it's too late now anyway."

Carson, who is a thousand times more astute than Caroline ever was, changes the subject but manages to segue from one hot potato to another. "OK, I can tell you don't want to talk about Tom any more . . . So, tell me, what are you doing workwise these days?"

Oh God, I'd almost rather continue talking about my disastrous love life. I swallow.

"Actually, Carson, I've written a book and I've been meaning to get in touch with you because it looks as if it's probably going to be made into a film."

"Wow . . . That is amazing," says Carson, sounding really impressed. "I didn't even know you could write. Good for you."

"Um . . . mm."

"So, what's it about?"

Here we go.

400

"Well, that's the thing. It's kind of about a girl who works for a famous actress."

I listen to the sound of dead air for fifteen seconds or so.

"Carson, I promise you it's not a hatchet job. It is based on my experiences of working for Caroline, but all the names have been changed and there is not one thing that anybody in the universe apart from you, Caroline or Steph could link back to it being about her, I promise."

Finally Carson says slowly, "Francesca, I can't say I'm thrilled about this and if it was anyone else I'd be downright angry and concerned, but I trust you. After all, you've given me plenty of good reason to. So as long as you're telling me it's not vindictive and you can completely assure me that nobody's going to get hurt, then that's fine."

"They won't. I mean, the character isn't particularly pleasant, but I promise nobody knows who it is and the actual plot is a complete figment of my imagination. There's even a possibility that Caroline may end up playing herself, although please don't mention anything about it to her yet."

"Not much chance of that, Francesca. We're only speaking through lawyers at the moment."

"Oh right, of course . . ."

"And I'm not in it, am I?"

"No, absolutely not. There is a Mr X, but he's nothing like you, I swear. He's dark and swarthy with bad skin for a start, has a tendency to be really mean and a penchant for Latin American pool boys . . . It's really nice to hear from you," I say, trying to change the subject and soothe the situation. I guess Carson can't be too overly worried, because he lets me.

"OK, now actually, Francesca, I called you for a reason."

"Did you? Well, if there's anything I can help you with just fire away."

"Basically, Fran, I hadn't counted on being nominated for an Oscar this year. I won the year before last so I wasn't really expecting it, but there you go. Anyway, I wasn't planning on attending this year, what with the wedding to organize and everything. Now, however, I feel I should; otherwise it would be a real snub to the producers and also to the Academy. So it will be my last ever professional engagement as an actor and then I'm done."

"Right, well, if it's advice you're after then I think you should go, absolutely," I advise, while struggling not to laugh at Abbie, who's making obscene gestures with a banana from the fruit bowl.

"It's not advice I need. You see, Steph isn't coming for obvious reasons. We don't want anyone finding out about us in such a public way and even if we did, well, you know Steph — the Oscars would be her idea of hell, especially since the press are really turning up the heat now. They spotted Caroline spending thirty thousand dollars in Gucci on Rodeo Drive last week and they've figured out she's not really ill. I'm really pissed actually because the deal was that she would lie low for a while and in return she'd get a bigger settlement from me."

"Shit, that's a bit out of order," I say, not in the least bit surprised.

"Yeah, ain't it just, but anyway, that's beside the point. The long and the short of it is, I need a date to throw the press off the scent from Steph and I don't want to go to the Oscars on my own. So what I'm trying to say, Francesca, is . . . are you doing anything on February twenty-fourth? And, if not, would you come to the Oscars with me?"

Time stands still. I stop laughing at Abbie's antics and freeze.

Did he say what I think he just said?

I've got a funny feeling he did and, shocked to the core, I clumsily drop the phone, then fling myself on to my hands and knees and scrabble around on the floor until I have the receiver by my mouth again. I'm just getting ready to scream "yes" when I realize, to my dismay, that I've cut him off.

"Shit, shit, shit!" I yell.

"What is it?" demands Abbie. "Is it bad news?"

"No, it's the best fucking news I've ever had in my entire life and I've bloody cut him off!" I shriek, fumbling with the phone and trying 1471 but having no luck, which isn't surprising seeing as Carson was calling from the States.

"Calm down," says Abbie. "He'll realize and call back."

Praying she's right, I stop jumping around and focus on the phone, willing it with all my might to ring. Finally, after an agonizing twenty seconds, it does and I snatch it up.

"Oh my God, I can't believe what happened, I dropped the phone and I'm so sorry. I can't believe it . . ."

"Francesca?"

It isn't Carson, it's Sabina. I recoil and with no explanation to my friend I slam the receiver down. Just as I do, it rings again.

"Oh please, please be him," I whimper. It is.

"Francesca, what are you doing?"

"I'm sorry, I'm just so excited and I can't believe what I've just heard. It's my dream come true. Thank you, thank you, thank you!" I yell, shaking with excitement and suddenly feeling a bit odd. I think a lot of blood has drained away from my head. I may faint.

"OK, calm down," says Carson, sounding like he's trying not to laugh. "You won't be thanking me when your ass is numb from sitting in the same seat for six hours."

But there's nothing he could possibly say that could diminish my excitement and happiness at this point. As far as I'm concerned, once I've been to the Oscars my life will be complete, nothing will ever matter again and my dreams will have become a reality. Feeling light-headed, I sit down.

"I'd gladly sit in the same seat for six weeks," I gush.

Finally Abbie's frustration gets the better of her.

"Tell me what's going on. What's so bloody good that you're crying about it?" she demands loudly.

"Are you crying?" asks Carson, far away on the other side of the globe, now sounding thoroughly amused.

"A bit," I answer and then, turning to Abbie, I scream, "I'm going to the bloody Oscars!"

Her face is incredulous and then as my announcement sinks in she starts screaming too and we jump up and down, hugging and dancing around until I break away, realizing that I'm in danger of cutting Carson off again. I hurriedly compose myself and the onslaught of questions begins: "Are you sure Steph won't mind? When will I come to the States? What the hell am I going to wear? Thank you so much. Shall I book a hotel? I know, I'll book a flight today because they may all go and . . ."

Carson firmly interrupts my inane wittering.

"Francesca, I'm really glad you're so excited — it'll make a change to be there with someone who's so . . . enthusiastic — but you need to calm down for a second."

"I'm calm," I say immediately, sounding anything but. I'm practically foaming at the mouth.

"OK, listen. The thing is, before you so readily agree, there are a couple of things that you should consider."

My heart thumps. I knew it was too good to be true. He's going to change his mind, I know it. Please don't offer me the world and then snatch it away.

"If you appear on my arm at the Oscars it doesn't matter how much I claim that you are a friend or a relative or whatever, the world's press will immediately assume that you are my new girlfriend. Now, in terms of Steph minding, she couldn't be more delighted as it will throw them off the scent of our forthcoming wedding and give her more peace of mind. However, for you it will be a different story. It's highly probable that for a while you'll be hounded wherever you go and you'll feel what it's like to have the eyes of the world scrutinizing you every second of every day."

"That's OK," I gabble. "I can handle it. It'll just be for a while. It'll actually probably be quite fun."

"And you're definitely not seeing anyone at the moment?" asks Carson gently.

"No, Carson, I'm not."

"It's just I have to ask because there aren't many men who would appreciate their girlfriend posing as my love interest. I mean, I doubt Tom will be that happy."

"Couldn't care less," I say, a tad crossly.

I can hear Carson sigh. "Look, I know you've split up, but I wouldn't be surprised if you did get back together and if he's anything like me or like most normal men, then he might not be comfortable with you pretending to be mine."

I decide to spell it out. "What Tom thinks is of no concern to me. We haven't spoken in weeks and because of his sheer pig-headedness we are not going to get back together."

"OK, OK," says Carson, sounding infuriatingly like he doesn't believe me. "Well, it looks like you've got yourself a date and I'm glad. I really want you to come too. Apart from the fact that we'll have a great time, I know I can also rely on you not to sell your story and to keep all my secrets, which counts for such a lot. Francesca, Steph and I are in your debt already and if you help us out with this one, well, I don't know how we'll ever repay you. You see, it would be just as easy for me to take my mother, but hell, she's been three times and she wouldn't provide us with such a perfect smokescreen. We really care about you though and I don't want you to feel like we're using you — that's why I want you to think it over properly before giving me your final answer."

"Right, OK . . . I've thought it over. Yes, yes, yes."

"How about I call you tomorrow to make sure?" says Carson, laughing.

"Yes, fine," I say. "But my answer will still be yes. So don't worry about lining anyone else up."

We say our goodbyes and I fill Abbie in on everything we've just talked about. We laugh at how anybody could construe being mistaken by the world's press as Carson Adams's girlfriend as a problem and, after a careful 0.1 second's deliberation, I conclude that being hounded by the press is a small price to pay for the night of my dreams.

Irrationally, I feel a bit annoyed with Carson for reminding me about Tom again. As ever, I still feel like ringing him with my news. Ooh, that reminds me: I'd better call Sabina back.

CHAPTER
THIRTY-SEVEN

This year the Oscars are being hosted by actor James Reddington (who, since splitting with Marina Madson, is enjoying a bit of a renaissance in his popularity), and Francesca Massi from the suburbs of Middlesex will be sitting in the second row with one of the nominees for best actor. Surreal, isn't it?

Having enjoyed a light meal of chicken royale with wild rice and a glass of bubbly, I sit back, no sorry, lie back, in my very comfortable seat. I've got my free comfy tracksuit bottoms and flight socks on, a movie that isn't even out yet in England is about to start and I am feeling thoroughly pleased with life. And so I should be, for I'm on my way to Los Angeles, on a first-class flight that I haven't paid for, where I'll be staying at a movie star's mansion and going to the Oscars. Carson's flying me out four days before the big event so that I can spend a bit of time with him, Steph, Cameron and, of course, Lorna, get over the jet lag before the day itself and, most importantly, so that I can figure out what to wear.

It's a year of firsts, that's for sure, including first-class air travel, which I'm almost sorry to have experienced for now that I know what lies to the left I'll never want to turn right again. Oh well, I'm not complaining, and now the film's starting so I shall settle down and watch it until the champagne makes me feel all soporific, at which point I shall snooze for the rest of the journey.

I wake up hours later with a dry mouth and slightly gritty eyes, but apart from that feeling relatively fresh. I slug back some water and blearily apply a bit of make-up as the plane prepares to land. By the time the wheels hit the tarmac, I've woken up enough to feel tremors of pure excitement as it hits me that now my adventure is really about to begin. Having flown first class, my luggage is dealt with for me so all I have to do is find Shawn, who Carson promised would be meeting me. And there he is, holding a sign with my name on.

"Hi, Shawn," I say, approaching the huge, friendly-looking driver who's waving at me. He's actually wearing a chauffeur's uniform, complete with peaked cap, and his face is framed by a pair of Ray-Bans.

"Welcome to the city of angels, Francesca."

As I exit the terminal, I have the tiniest taster of Californian sunshine before getting straight into a very air-conditioned car. When I say car I should, in fact, say limousine, especially since there is a minibar in the back that is well stocked with refreshments.

"Help yourself," says Shawn, who has spotted me eyeing up the drinks in his mirror.

"Thanks," I say, pouring myself a Diet Coke and trying to control the grin that is threatening to take over my face completely as we glide away from the kerb.

Palm trees at an airport are always a good indicator that you've arrived somewhere you're going to have a good time, I find.

As he drives, Shawn strikes up conversation and he's soon entertaining me with wonderful stories about what's gone on in the back of his car. It's fortunate that he's so captivating because we get a bit snarled up in some heavy traffic as we hit the freeway, but other than that my entire journey from the UK to Beverley Hills is seamless and it isn't long before we're pulling up outside a spectacular mansion and Shawn is speaking into the intercom. The black gates swing open and we're in. By now I can hardly keep a lid on my excitement and I realize how much I am dying to see everyone. It appears the feeling is mutual for just then I spot Lorna charging out of the front door, followed closely by Cameron and Steph.

"Hello!" I screech, my leg dangling out of the door before Shawn's even had the chance to switch the engine off. A bit of a scrum ensues as everyone jumps about, screams and talks all at once.

It's always weird seeing people you know from home in a different country for some reason. They always look somewhat unfamiliar once they've shed their London skin and literally warmed up. Cameron is really brown, his hair is now incredibly blond and he's lost some of his puppy fat. He's done that thing that children do and over the course of a few months has changed an amazing amount. It's like he's undergone a "SIM update". If possible, he seems even more energized and hyper than usual. Steph is lightly tanned

410

and, seeing her in shorts and a T-shirt, I realize what a truly knockout figure she's been hiding. Lorna — well, Lorna is the only one who is quite clearly a Brit abroad. For a start, she's wearing socks with her sandals and, secondly, her shoulders are sunburned and she has glaring strap marks.

All of a sudden my journey catches up with me and I feel in desperate need of a shower and to take my trainers off and get my flip-flops on.

"You must be shattered, Fran," says Steph, going to help Shawn with the bags. "Come and have a tour of the house and then you must have a nap before dinner."

"Thanks, Steph, that would be great."

An impatient Lorna grabs my hand. "Come on, come in, Francesca. It'll take me till teatime to show you just the bathrooms in this place."

"Where's Carson?" I ask, trying to sound casual but secretly a bit disappointed that he isn't there to greet me.

"He had to go to a lunch for the nominees. He was really sorry he couldn't be here for when you arrived, but he'll be back tonight for your welcome dinner," says Steph, who's bringing up the rear.

"Sounds good," I say, privately feeling a bit silly for my churlish thoughts.

You know a house is big when you're not even sure who's in, so three hours later when I emerge blearily from my room feeling like death warmed up after a nap, I'm surprised to bump into Carson.

"Hi!" I squeal, desperately trying to flatten my hair down. "You're back."

"Yeah, I've been back for hours," says Carson, grinning and looking as full of beans as ever. "We didn't want to wake you before, but you should get up now or you'll never sleep tonight. It's great to see you. You're looking . . . well, you're looking like you've just woken up. Come and have a Margarita, that'll soon get the blood rushing to your head."

For my welcome dinner, Richie (Carson's personal chef) has prepared a delicious Mexican banquet that we eat under the stars and, afterwards, sighing with contentment and enjoying the scent that's wafting from the bougainvillea, I idly comment that I'd better start shopping around for a dress tomorrow. Steph and Lorna giggle and Carson says, "I thought I told you we'd be taking care of that?"

"Yeah," I say doubtfully, not really fancying the idea of entrusting Carson to choose my dress for me. I had secretly thought that by taking care of it he'd been implying that he'd foot the bill, although I'm more than happy, of course, to pay for it with my writing money should I see something really expensive that I love. After all, apart from the day I get married, I'll never have to make such an important sartorial decision ever again.

"Just be ready at eleven tomorrow morning," says Carson, completely deadpan, while Lorna and her daughter, who I think is a tad tipsy, giggle away.

The next morning I wake from a deep jet-lagged sleep to the sound of Lorna banging feverishly on the door. "They're here, Fran. They're here."

I slide out of the very comfortable bed and pad to the door.

"Who's here?" I ask croakily.

"Just get up, bedhead," Lorna says, ruffling my bouffant mane.

Half an hour later, after the best shower I've ever had in my life, I enter the sitting room and my hand flies to my mouth. Rail upon rail upon rail has been wheeled in and hanging on all of them are beautiful, diaphanous, sparkly dresses of every type imaginable and in every different colour. It's like Aladdin's cave, but tasteful.

The rest of the day is definitely a contender for one of the most enjoyable of my entire life. A lovely lady called Rosa helps me in and out of gowns, placing them all one by one in either a "no" pile or a "maybe" pile. In the beginning, as far as I'm concerned, they're all maybes, but after a few hours I grow steadily more discerning. I'm in fashion heaven and at one point, as I float around the room in a sequinned Michael Kors peach number, I find myself checking to see if Steph is really all right with this. Just as I open my mouth to ask her, she catches my eye and seems to sense exactly what I'm thinking.

"Francesca, I am getting more enjoyment out of watching you have so much fun than I ever would if I was going myself," she says reassuringly from where she's perched on the edge of a tan leather sofa, wearing denim cut-offs and a T-shirt and looking stunning in a natural sort of way.

"Promise?" I enquire, finding it difficult to believe.

"Absolutely promise," she says firmly.

In a moment of spontaneous affection, I find myself racing over to give her a big bear hug. "Thank you so, so much for this," I say, squeezing her tight.

Steph just giggles. "You are so funny, Fran. You still think we're doing you a favour when, as far as we're concerned, it really is the other way round entirely."

I just shrug and decide to accept her incredibly skewed way of looking at things and be grateful for it. So I continue to relish my Cinderella moment until much later on in the afternoon when we finally have just three contenders left. There's the vintage Yves Saint Laurent silvery sheath with no sleeves that Rosa suggests I would wear with long white gloves and my hair up. There's a greeny turquoise number by Alberta Ferretti, which is made of floaty chiffon and has a full skirt and is ruched at the top. Then, lastly, there's a classic, vintage, red satin Valentino gown with low back and boning throughout the bodice, which produces a waist that Jessica Rabbit would envy. I don't know how I'm going to decide between the three, but I do, and the next day someone from Jimmy Choo comes round to the house to take a fabric sample from the dress so that they can dye some shoes to match exactly.

The next few days are just as exciting and pass in a heady whirl of being pampered and preened, lazing in the sunshine and catching up with everyone. Clothes aside, just being in this beautiful house is a treat. It's an absolutely gorgeous, sprawling hacienda-style villa with two pools, one indoor and one outdoor. The weather is beautiful every day and it's lovely to see Lorna doing nothing but relax. She's on top form, largely due to the fact that the Californian sunshine is doing wonders for her arthritis. Steph is more relaxed than I have ever seen her too and Cameron is visibly happier. It's not surprising — I would be ecstatic to be given a reprieve from being related to Caroline too.

As for Carson, he's continued to be his usual charming self but has been frantically busy attending Oscar lunches, giving interviews and, of course, making secret wedding preparations. Sadly, he's also having to endure ongoing discussions with Caroline's legal people. Apparently, so far they have thrashed out (via their lawyers) an agreement that states that Carson will pay Caroline off with a lump sum and that he will get full custody of Cameron and keep both this house and the house in London. Bermuda is welcome to her, as is poor old New York.

CHAPTER
THIRTY-EIGHT

On average I usually take about an hour to get ready if I'm going out for the evening. That is inclusive of time needed for showering, washing hair and blow-drying too. However, on Oscars day the whole process of getting ready from start to finish takes a total of five hours. I'm not joking.

On the morning of the big day, an army of beauticians, hairdressers and stylists descend upon the house with the sole intention of making Carson and I look gorgeous. It's utter chaos and the phone is ringing off the hook with well-wishers. To Carson's utmost annoyance, his agent is also phoning him on the hour, every hour, begging him to reconsider doing the romantic comedy, but he's not budging and eventually he takes the phone off the hook.

Cameron is completely over-excited by all the activity in the house and is tearing around the place like a mini tornado. At one point he charges into my room with a glass of juice in his hand, trips up and only narrowly avoids spilling sticky purple liquid down my dress, which is hanging up on the back of the door.

"Time for some swimming races, I think," says Steph, leading her son out to the pool in a bid to wear him out. No wonder she's so slim.

Meanwhile, Carson is wandering around with no shirt on, displaying his perfect torso while some last-minute alterations are being made to his Armani tuxedo, which is somewhat distracting for all the females in the house and all the gay men.

As for Lorna, she's making sandwiches and drinks as if her life depends on it, offering them round on trays and looking distinctly unimpressed when she doesn't get any takers. I don't have the heart to tell her that most of the LA beauty mafia who are here today probably haven't eaten any bread products or indeed any carbohydrate whatsoever for at least five years.

Personally, I'm grateful for all the activity as it's making time go faster. Eduardo, who is really camp and dressed from head to toe in white linen, has been assigned to do my hair. After a summit meeting with Rosa about the critical issue of whether it should be up or down, and once they've thrashed out an agreement (down), he sets to work. He adds a few extra pieces that blend into my own perfectly but give it extra volume, and the overall effect is glossy and rich with just the right amount of curl. He also pins a couple of bits up at the sides so that I have a few wispy tendrils framing my face. Finally, Eduardo pronounces his masterpiece finished and then it's time for Glen to take over and start on my make-up. Glen, who makes Eduardo seem like Sly Stallone, appraises me through narrowed eyes and declares to the room that, on the whole, I have "fabulous skin, darling" but that there are a few open pores to worry about. Everybody nods gravely. Then he takes a sort of small spray gun out and proceeds to apply a fine mist of foundation on to my face.

It's all very exciting and halfway through this most complicated application of make-up, Sabina rings. It's lovely to speak to her and, with a pang, I think affectionately of all my friends. Sabina sounds really excited and I'm pleased to hear that she's going round to mine to watch the event unfold with Abbie and the others. Then I call Mum and Dad, who tell me that they are already in position and that Mum has even had a nap this afternoon so that she can stay awake for the Awards. Hearing that everybody back home will be looking out for me on the telly triggers a strange, gnawing sensation in the pit of my stomach. I find myself wondering if Tom will be watching.

Glen is ready to start on my eyes, so I put my phone (which is coated in foundation) away.

The make-up seems to take hours and at one point during my day-dreaming I think of something that makes me snort out loud with laughter. Glen nearly takes my eye out with his tweezers.

"What?" he snaps.

"Sorry," I say. "I was just thinking about the last time I had my hair and make-up done professionally and what a different sort of experience it was."

An hour later and I am just starting to get really fidgety when Glen stands back with his hands on his hips and announces, "Perfecto."

Eduardo gives him a round of applause and, feeling rather apprehensive, I tentatively make my way towards the mirror.

I hardly recognize myself. I don't know how Glen's done it, but he's made me look flawless and beautiful. I love Glen.

Just then Lorna barges in determinedly with a bowl of crisps and a pot of guacamole. Rather disappointingly, she spots me then looks away. Obviously not that impressed with my transformation, she offers Glen some crisps, which he refuses. Then she does a massive double-take as it finally dawns upon her that the good-looking girl in the corner is me.

"Look at you, Francesca," she gasps, setting down the food on the dressing table and clutching her throat. "You don't look like you at all. You look absolutely beautiful," she exclaims, entirely unaware of how backhanded her compliment is. I don't mind one bit though — she's right.

I glance up at the clock on the wall and see that Shawn will be arriving with our car in less than an hour, which brings on a wave of panic. Suddenly I feel a bit claustrophobic and panicky and, not wishing to sound rude, I turn to Eduardo, Glen, Lorna and Rosa and Jessica who have just appeared to dress me and say, "Would you mind awfully if I just have five minutes on my own?"

They all reluctantly agree and shuffle out one by one, politely refusing Lorna's offer of crisps and dips on the way.

I shut the door behind them and sit on the bed in my robe. I glance across to the mirror again. With my perfect hair and my perfect make-up, I almost look like a movie star. I don't know if it's down to nerves, but suddenly I feel incredibly emotional. Who would have thought a whole year ago on that most stupendous of destiny days, when I got that call from Carrie Anne asking me if I wanted to be Caroline's personal assistant, that I would be going to the Oscars? I still can't quite believe it. I find the phone where I left it by the dressing table and dial Carrie Anne's number, knowing that Carson won't mind.

"Hello?"

"Carrie Anne, it's me, Fran."

"Babe, how are you? I'm going round to yours tonight to watch you on the red carpet. We're all so excited. How's it all going?"

"Great, thanks. Carrie Anne, thank you so, so much," I manage, desperately trying to prevent any tears from spilling on to my perfect make-up. Glen would kill me. "Thank you for everything you've done for me. You really are the most amazing friend and . . ." I don't go on, I'm too choked. But Carrie Anne doesn't answer right away and I know in that moment she truly understands how grateful I am for everything she's done for me and how much I love her.

"That's a total pleasure, babe. Now you go sock it to 'em and we'll be cheering for you. What are you wearing?"

I look across the room to where my dress is hanging up and grin.

"Something very gorgeous and very red."

The second we finish our conversation, everything starts to happen very quickly. Unable to wait any longer, Rosa and her assistant Jessica burst into the room and start laying out all my accessories, which now include a beautiful, jewelled red clutch bag that matches my dress perfectly. Then, very carefully, they help me into my dress and help me put on and fasten my diamond earrings, necklace and matching bracelet that are worth in the region of two million dollars, and to step into my red satin Jimmy Choos, which have six-inch heels and diamanté clasps. I hardly have time to look at myself properly before I hear Cameron yelling: "Daddy, Fran, Shawn's here with the limo."

It's time to go. I'm suddenly more nervous than I've ever been before in my life. I don't look like me and therefore I don't feel like me and it's all rather unnerving. My stomach is lurching, I feel slightly light-headed and my hands are clammy. Taking a deep breath and encouraged all the way by Rosa, I walk slowly out on to the landing and down the stairs, feeling just like Julia Roberts in *Pretty Woman* (the red dress bit, not the prostitute bit). Everybody is gathered at the bottom of the stairs and Lorna is the first to speak.

"Francesca, you look absolutely gorgeous. Even better than that other one who's so good-looking, that Shania Twain."

Steph laughs and comes over to me and whispers in my ear so that nobody but me can hear. "If Carson's got to have another girlfriend for the night, then I'm glad it's you. You look beautiful," and gives me a kiss on the cheek.

Cameron just says, "Wow," and Eduardo and Glen dab their eyes before both rushing over to have a last-minute fuss.

I turn to Carson, who's looking too handsome for his own good in his tux.

"Will I do?" I ask apprehensively.

He gives me one of his dazzling smiles and says, "You are full of surprises, Miss Massi," and he holds out his arm for me to take before giving Steph a little goodbye wink. She gives him a big smile and mouths, "Good luck, love you," so that Eduardo et al can't hear.

Everyone comes out to the drive to see us off and, sitting in the car with Carson in all my finery, I feel like a nervous bride on her way to church. The attack of nerves I'm having seems to be getting worse and I also seem to be developing a chronic case of Tourette's syndrome. Despite my dry mouth, I literally can't stop talking, which is unfortunate for Carson and Shawn seeing as I'm not saying anything worth listening to at all, I'm just babbling, and my language is peppered with cursing and swearing. I talk foul-mouthed rubbish nineteen to the dozen for the next ten minutes or so. Carson and Shawn just seem to take it all in their stride until at one point, after I've finished exclaiming that "I've forgotten to put any gum in my fucking bag," Carson says gently, "I hope you're not going to talk like the Osbournes all night."

I get the message, bite my lip and concentrate on being quiet for the rest of the journey.

It's not far to the Kodak Theatre at all, but as we draw closer I can understand why we had to leave so much time to get here. As soon as we are reasonably near the venue, the road becomes a sea of black-and-white limousines that sit bumper to bumper in the most glamorous traffic jam I've ever seen. Before we've even rounded the corner, a wall of sound hits us. The crowds are waiting.

Carson turns to me and winks and for the first time I register that he is nervous too.

"You OK?" I ask.

"Yeah. You?"

I nod, far too overwhelmed to say anything else. The adrenaline is now pumping for both of us. I'm feeling jittery and I just want to get out of the car now, but it seems to take forever to make any progress at all.

"Remember everything I've said, Fran. They'll find out soon enough who you are and that you worked for us, but for tonight don't give them an inch."

I nod obediently. At this rate I won't have any problem being enigmatic because, the way I feel right now, just speaking at all may be out of the question.

Eventually we make some headway and as our limo draws up I can see people straining to see who's inside. My heart races as I realize that when they spot who I'm with they're not going to be disappointed. Sure enough, the minute our door is opened and the top of Carson's head can be seen, a roar goes up from the crowd and the pandemonium heightens by at least another five notches or so.

The wave of sound is like electricity and I can feel my nerves transforming into a slightly more enjoyable kind of energy. I'm still shaking, but I'm determined that I'm going to damn well enjoy this. I take one last deep breath and Shawn winks at me in the mirror. Then, picturing Tom and hoping that he just might be watching at home, I climb elegantly out of the car. Carson gave me a poolside masterclass a couple of days ago and it pays off as I manage to avoid flashing even a hint of female anatomy. Carson gallantly takes my hand and leads me in the right direction, which I am highly grateful for as I am completely blinded by flashbulbs. I also remember something else Carson told me and I try to keep my expression fairly blank so that I'm not grimacing in too many pictures. People are shouting Carson's name from all directions and I'm pretty sure I can hear a couple of people yelling "Lady in Red, over here," but I'm far too inexperienced to know how to cope with that so I just follow Carson's lead, keep smiling and hope for the best. There's so much to take in. I'm on the red carpet. This is the Oscars. We're here; it's happening.

Just for a second I close my eyes and try to picture the scene back home. I think of my family and know that they'll be proud as punch and hardly able to believe what they're seeing. I can imagine Abbie, Sabina, Ella, Paul, Adam, Raj, Briggsy, Wayne and Carrie Anne all gaping at each other, open-mouthed, momentarily shocked by how different I look. I giggle. I'd bet good money that Briggsy has something crude to say about my dress. I wonder if Stacey is watching.

God, I hope so — her face would be a picture. Gosh, more to the point, I wonder if Caroline's watching. For the sake of whoever is with her, I do hope not. Then, lastly, I try to picture Tom, but I can't because the truth is I have no idea if he'll be watching or not, despite the fact that word will most definitely have reached him one way or another that his ex-girlfriend would be here.

I snap out of my reverie and summon up a big smile as the crowd cheer for Carson, who's squeezing my hand.

"You OK, sweetheart? You look a bit away with the fairies."

"Sorry, Carson, I'm fine," I whisper. "Actually, I'm great."

Just then I catch sight of what is being played out on the TV monitors that are dotted about. By the looks of it, mainly a steady stream of close-ups of my face. I look away, startled, and begin to realize quite how much of a big deal me being here with Carson actually is.

We pass Joan Rivers's daughter, Melissa, and as we do I hear her saying, "Who is this mystery lady with Carson Adams? Whoever she is, she will be the envy of women all over the world and I guess this finally confirms those rumours that it really is all over between him and Caroline Mason."

The fact that she is referring to me is deeply surreal so I pretend I didn't hear it and focus on Carson instead.

The way Carson handles the press is incredible and I watch him in awe. You can tell that he's a veteran of the red carpet by the way he deflects difficult questions by batting them away like flies, still managing to stay charming and always answering just enough questions to give them a decent interview.

Coming up on the long line of interrogators I spot someone from the BBC and, just ahead of them, I recognize Joan Rivers herself. My pulse has started to return to something resembling normal and I'm beginning to really enjoy myself and even to play up to the cameras a bit. The interviews aren't as worrying as I thought they might be because, standing just behind Carson, I really can't hear a word any of the reporters are saying anyway so I don't have to worry about speaking until they indicate for me to come forward so they can ask me where my dress is from. However, when we eventually reach Joan she isn't having any of it and she makes Carson bring me forward.

"So you're English, is that correct?" she rasps.

"Yes I am."

"You're the envy of every girl in the land, you know. How did you two meet?"

I look at Carson, who looks a bit nervous.

"Through friends," I say diplomatically.

"How long have you been together?"

"Oh, it's all quite new really," I offer, giving the PR a look. She gets the message and intervenes:

"One more, Joan."

"And what are you wearing?" asks Joan reluctantly, knowing that no matter what else she asks this is the thing people want to know most, and for the hundredth time that night I say, "The dress is Valentino, the shoes are Jimmy Choo and the jewellery is by Harry Winston."

As we are led away by another frazzled-looking PR, Carson squeezes my hand again. "You were great. Well done."

As we finally enter the venue a whole hour and a half after arriving, I start to take in who I've been sharing the red carpet with. There are famous people everywhere I turn and as I make my way towards the entrance of the plush auditorium, with its red velvet seats and gilt décor, I bump into Susan Sarandon and tread on her toe by mistake.

CHAPTER
THIRTY-NINE

Carson and I are seated in the second row of the auditorium and are surrounded mainly by executives and producers who worked on his film *The Reporter*. However, his co-star, Julia Roberts, is to our right, Russell Crowe is within spitting distance and Christina Ricci is directly behind me. Ever since we took our seats, a steady stream of people have come up to greet Carson and surreptitiously check me out and so far I have shaken hands with and met Robert De Niro, Brangelina, Gwyneth Paltrow and Denzel Washington to name but a few. There is quite a real chance I may wet myself.

Everybody is very friendly and highly curious about who on earth I am, and Carson has been careful to give away precisely nothing despite their digging. Then, just as Christina Ricci is leaning forward to ask Carson what happened between him and "Cas", the orchestra strikes up and hush falls upon the audience as the show begins. I have a rush of excited anticipation and I reach over and grip Carson's hand painfully hard, a gesture I'm not sure he entirely appreciates.

I try to imagine how on earth the host must be feeling right now. There can only be a handful of humans on this planet who could cope with hosting a gig of such magnitude. To carry it off with aplomb, panache and humour, as most of them do, is to be freakishly talented and confident. It'll be interesting to see how James Reddington measures up.

"Fucking hell, I'm at the pissing Oscars," I whisper excitedly to Carson, as a wave of excitement washes over me.

"You can take the girl out of Teddington . . ." he quips back wryly.

James Reddington opens the show with a song that is hilarious. He manages to incorporate verses about all the films that are nominated for best movie and makes jokes about some of the acting nominees too. I'm so carried away in the moment that it doesn't even occur to me that he may include Carson, but right at the end, of course, he does.

"*Carson Adams is nominated once again for a part where he's a reporter, but surely he's too handsome to win? Having said that, with intrigue, romance and humour the film is real fine. Julia's in it, she finds it really funny, but I don't think the same could be said for an actress called Caroline.*"

By the time he's got to his controversial punchline, James Reddington has left the stage and is practically sitting in Carson's lap and I'm highly aware that the camera is trained on all three of us. I quash a cheesy urge to wave to everyone at home and concentrate instead on studying James Reddington's sweaty brow that, close up, looks powdered and waxy.

The show rattles on at a fair old pace and it's not long before the business of prize-giving commences. Three hours later and, despite what Carson suspected, I am still not bored. How could I be when I am sitting amongst a live version of Madame Tussauds? I am, however, desperate for the toilet and I'm busy praying that if I sit still enough then the urge might go away. They do have seat-fillers for exactly these instances but there's no way I'm going now in case I miss Carson's award. Best Actor is one of the last awards given out and the competition is tough. Carson is up against Russell Crowe, Tom Hanks, Jack Nicholson and a seventeen-year-old newcomer who gave an incredible portrayal of a deaf mute in a western directed by Clint Eastwood.

After a duet of the song that won "Best Song", sung by Sting and Phil Collins, last year's best actress, Dame Judi Dench, finally comes on to make the presentation for the award that we've really been waiting for.

Carson and I exchange nervous grins.

Dame Judi gives a brief speech before introducing the clips and, despite the fact that Carson's been pretty cool about his nomination so far, as soon as his face appears on the giant screen I feel him tensing up beside me and I realize I've been naive to think that he wouldn't care at all. Suddenly it is vitally important that he wins.

The clips are over and Dame Judi opens the envelope.

"And the winner is . . . Jack Nicholson."

I spin round to look at Carson, but he's such a seasoned pro that there's not even a hint of disappointment in his expression. Instead he's smiling and looking genuinely pleased for Jack. I suppose it must slightly ease the pain knowing that you already have one of the little gold statuettes at home in your downstairs bathroom. Then again, I'm also sure that with Oscars it must be like handbags and shoes — you can never have too many. As I clap for Jack, I feel disappointed for Carson and I really hope that it doesn't put too much of a dampener on his evening.

When the curtain finally comes down an hour later, despite the fact that I really am bursting for a wee and have terrible pins and needles in my feet, I am sad that it's all over. That was the Oscars.

I've been, but — unlike the majority of the people in the room — I have been for the first and probably the last time.

It takes hours to make our way out of the auditorium due to the fact that we are constantly bumping into people who want to stop and chat to Carson and to offer him their commiserations. When we finally do get out I have to race as fast as my heels will allow me to the nearest lavatory, where there is a huge queue. It seems that movie stars have bladders just the same as us mere mortals and I wait patiently in line behind Hilary Swank and Catherine Zeta-Jones.

When I finally emerge, Carson is waiting for me and it's time to party. Needless to say, Carson has been invited to every party going but he's decided that he only wants to go to one and, judging by how many times he keeps checking his watch, he's obviously keen to get cracking.

It is somewhat of a relief to sink into the cool limo for the short journey to the party. It gives me a chance to take stock and I can finally speak to Carson properly on our own.

"Are you disappointed you didn't win?" I ask him.

"No, I'm not . . . Well, maybe just a smidgeon. I suppose I'd be lying if I said that in the back of my mind I didn't hope just a tiny bit that I might win. Still, it's not like I haven't won before. How about you? Are you having a good time?"

"Well, my feet are killing me, my jaw aches from smiling, but I can safely say I'm having the time of my life. It's amazing," I reply.

Carson gives me a sad smile. "It is, isn't it? You know, I never expected to feel sad about giving all this up, but tonight I do a bit."

My heart sinks. I can completely see why and I hope I haven't contributed to him making a decision that he might come to regret. Seeing my stricken face, he backpedals quickly.

"Don't get me wrong. I know I'm doing the right thing for myself, Cameron and Steph, and if I wasn't packing it all in I probably would have hated tonight. All the schmoozing and networking and everything can be a real bore, although I must say coming with you has been an entirely different experience to coming with Caroline. She was always nagging me to introduce her to people and breaking my balls for saying the wrong

432

thing." He leans forward to take a bottle of water out of the minibar, opens it and takes a huge gulp.

"No, I'm doing the right thing," he says, smacking his lips. "But, that said, showbusiness ain't all bad. Bottom line is, the movies do bring a lot of happiness to a lot of people and I guess I was reminded of that today, watching all those clips."

I mull this over, my mind slightly foggy from far too much champagne. "You can always change your mind in the future, Carson. I'm sure if five years down the line you want to make another film, then Steph wouldn't mind."

Carson looks at me and smiles. "As ever, Francesca, you're absolutely right."

We sit in comfortable silence for a while and then Carson turns to me and says, "Francesca, I'm sorry you're having the night of your dreams with somebody else's guy . . ." The words ". . . and not your own" hang in the air, unsaid.

I immediately feel prickles of sadness unfurling in my tummy and fight to keep them at bay.

"Carson, you're such a softie, aren't you? I'm having the night of my dreams with a wonderful friend and that's what's really important." I smile good-naturedly but, try as I might, this time my smile doesn't reach my eyes. I pull myself together.

"Besides, if I'm honest, I'm just not sure anybody is ever going to completely 'get' me," I add for no particular reason.

Carson pats my hand affectionately. "I don't think you're going to have any problems finding someone to love you, Francesca. You just need to figure out what you really want from life and you'll be fine."

Despite knowing that what he's said is absolutely true, the irony doesn't escape me that Carson is now giving me advice, when without me he would still be living in limbo with Caroline.

"Well, I'm glad you've got it all worked out, Carson," I say, and we share a bit of a laugh.

CHAPTER
FORTY

Our limo draws up outside the *Vanity Fair* party where there is a scrum of people at the door trying anything in their power to get in. I can't help but feel a bit smug as Carson and I stroll up to the front and are let in straight away, no questions asked, even if this does have absolutely nothing to do with me.

Inside, I absorb my surroundings. The party is lavish and opulent with the decor resembling all the film sets from the nominated pictures. It's all pretty spectacular-looking but at the moment the main ingredient of an amazing party, that is to say the atmosphere, is rather civilized. I don't know what I was expecting really, but I'd half hoped it would all be a bit . . . wilder? Still, the alcohol is flowing and the night is relatively young, so who knows what may happen later. On cue, a waiter approaches us with a tray of cocktails and I choose a Bellini and Carson takes a Martini. He reaches for my hand and I follow him as once again he works the room like the old pro he is, totally unfazed by all the stars who are everywhere you look. I've already spotted Drew Barrymore, Ben Stiller and Will Smith, and we've only been here for five minutes.

At one point Carson is cornered by one of the executive producers from *The Reporter*. They start to engage in conversation about people I don't know and have never heard of, so I decide to sneak off on my own.

I wander outside to the pool area where fairy lights are strewn around the branches of all the trees, making the whole place look truly magical. The air is balmy, light jazz is playing and the fountain by the pool is trickling. Everything and everyone is gorgeous. Gorgeous and well-behaved.

I take a seat and sip my cocktail while studying all the clusters of movie folk who are chatting intently, stopping only to congratulate the odd person who passes by brandishing a gold statuette. I can vividly remember Ella telling me how on her wedding day it had all gone so quickly that she always regretted not setting aside ten minutes just to take it all in and to seal the memory in her mind forever. I decide to do this now and concentrate on digesting every detail of the scene before me: the fabulous setting, the warm breeze, the twinkly lights. Stars everywhere you turn, only outnumbered by the ones above.

Suddenly I feel terribly lonely.

What on earth is wrong with me? Here I am at the most incredible event one could ever hope to go to and yet I'm still incapable of feeling entirely happy.

As ever, I'm kidding myself. I know full well I can pinpoint the second my mood shifted. It was when we were in the car and Carson alluded to Tom. I wish he hadn't, on tonight of all nights. I'm fed up of permanently thinking about Tom and wish that I could find a way to get him out of my system once and for all. For, unbeknown to Carson, not only do I know exactly how I feel about Tom but I have also figured out exactly what I want from life and, although it's taken me three decades to get there, I know for certain that I've finally arrived at the truth.

I gaze ruefully at my red satin-clad toes.

The truth is, I no longer care about fame, but I do still want to be successful at something. I do want to make a splash in one way or another and I am ambitious. I still want to wring out every drop of opportunity that comes my way and I would always prefer to regret something I've done than something I haven't. None of that has changed. You don't get a dress rehearsal for life and that has always scared the living daylights out of me and made me determined not to depend solely on another individual for my own fulfilment or happiness. But being with Tom has also made me see how amazing and indeed healthy a great relationship can be. As it turns out, being with the right person can be more inspiring than anything. It doesn't have to replace everything else in your life but can instead enhance it, complement it.

What if, in my somewhat muddled pursuit of success, I've been missing the point all along? Just because you don't spend all your time actively trying to find love, if it finds you, shouldn't you grab it with both hands? Being single is always going to be better than being in a crap relationship but, at risk of sounding terribly corny, without someone to love what does anything else actually mean?

With a sigh I realize that I must swallow my pride and ring Tom when I get back to London. After all, if I can convince him that I'm not as vacuous as he has come to believe then maybe he'll give me another chance. Of course, there's always the possibility that he's met someone else by now — but unless I ring I'll never know.

I look up and am distracted from my ponderings. There's a camera crew roaming around with a very glamorous-looking female presenter in tow. This is surprising, but I suppose it does in part explain the rather controlled atmosphere. In many ways this really is the ultimate work party and nobody wants to make a drunken fool of themselves, especially not if they might be caught on camera by a woman who has missiles for breasts. Having said that, when I think back to a few of the work parties I went to when I was working at Diamond PR, nobody was concerned about looking stupid at those; in fact, quite the opposite. One Christmas I seem to remember an ambulance had to be called for Gail from human resources who had rather over-egged the pudding and needed her stomach pumped. Not that I'm in any way suggesting that someone having their stomach pumped is a vital or even good ingredient for a successful party, but at the same time this bash could maybe do with a bit of that wanton abandonment from at least a handful of people to make it go with more of a swing. Otherwise I may be in danger of starting to feel tired and maudlin, and I don't want that to happen.

I catch a waiter's eye, give him my empty glass and exchange it for a Cosmopolitan, which I drain in one.

It seems faintly unbelievable that I am at the centre of the world that I've been so seduced by for years and years and yet suddenly all I really want to do is take my shoes off and get into bed. Everything feels rather flat now and, all of a sudden, terribly unimportant.

I get up and sway precariously in my heels. I'm a bit drunker than I thought. I spot Carson and flap at him to get his attention. I wonder if there's any chance of him wanting to go home.

He comes straight over, clearly pleased that I've given him an excuse to get away.

"Sorry about that, Fran. I got stuck. Jeez, that man was boring."

I laugh slightly harder than what he'd just said really warranted. That last Cosmopolitan was very strong.

"Are you OK, Francesca? You're not getting too hammered, are you?"

I hiccup. "No. Why?"

"Well, the night is still young and there's plenty more of the evening left to enjoy."

I get the hint. Reading between the lines, he's saying, "Can you please not turn into a member of the LA brat pack? I have my reputation to think of." Right, he's obviously in no hurry to leave so I need to get over this mood glitch. Drinking my way into a better humour could be my best option.

"Carson, can I say something without you being offended?" I say, reaching out for another cocktail from a passing tray.

"I hope so," he says, dragging another chair over to where I'm swaying on the spot. "Let's both sit down, Fran," he suggests, helping me into my seat and glancing anxiously at his watch again.

"Why do you keep checking your watch? Are you worried you're going to turn into a pumpkin or something?" I say cheekily, egged on by that last cocktail.

"No, Cinders, I'm not," he says wryly, sitting down and unbuttoning his jacket. God, he's handsome and brilliantly suave. Steph's a lucky lady, I muse, not for the first time.

"Carson?"

"Yes, Francesca?"

"This party is absolutely amazing and really beautiful . . . but don't you think that it could do with a bit of livening up?"

Carson looks amused. "Probably. But this is LA, not New York, and furthermore this is Hollywood, where it's all work and no play."

Just then a dazzling light shines in our faces. We look up, shielding our eyes with our hands and squinting to see the source. It's coming from the top of the television camera, which is currently pointing at Cameron Diaz who is being interviewed by the pool.

"E! Entertainment," explains Carson, seeing my confused expression. "They're the only cameras allowed in here."

We both watch as, clearly fed up with walking in heels, a laughing Cameron Diaz slips off her shoes. It's the only spontaneous action I have seen all night.

440

"She looks all right."

Carson looks at me questioningly.

"That Cameron, she looks like she's got a twinkle in her eye," I explain.

"Oh, she sure has," agrees Carson.

The alcohol has really gone to my head now.

"Carshon?" I say, trying and failing not to slur. "It's awfully funny this showbishness lark, you know. I mean, I will always, always love the movies, but since I've met you and Caroline I've had a real change of heart about the whole fame thing."

"And why's that?" says Carson, humouring me.

"Well, I've finally realized that fame in itself doesn't make you happy and that ambitions should be a bit more . . . well rounded."

"Well done, Einstein." Carson leans back in his chair and glances at his watch again.

I must be really boring him now, but I'm so squiffy that I don't care. I'm on a roll.

"I mean, when all is said and done, it is all marvellous and wonderfully glamorous, but there's so much bullshit involved in being a film star, isn't there? You constantly have to worry about what people think of you and it must be really tiresome having to conform to a certain ideal."

Carson shrugs, but I can tell he's amused.

"Truth be known, Carson, as far as Tom's perception of me goes, I feel as though I may have done myself a bit of a disservice too."

"Really?" This seems to interest him more than my drunken analysis of the film business and he perks up.

"Yes. You see, like everyone, obviously, I make mistakes sometimes, but deep down I think on the whole I am a good person who does have her priorities right and who would never knowingly hurt anyone. Tom thinks I'm shallow, but I'm not. I just have slightly moronic tendencies, which may qualify as annoying but doesn't make me a bad person." I'm slightly miffed to spot that Carson isn't even pretending to listen to me now and is blatantly looking over my shoulder at someone behind me. He smiles broadly at this person and gives them a small nod of the head, almost like a signal.

"Sorry, Carshon, am I being boring?"

Carson doesn't answer, but whoever's standing behind me does.

"Boring is something you could never be accused of, Francesca."

Oh . . . my . . . God.

Carson springs up from his chair, looking ridiculously pleased with himself, but I get up much, much more slowly and can't quite bring myself to turn round.

"And for the record, I've never thought of you as moronic. I do think, however, that you're clever, funny, kind, very beautiful and . . . and unable to hold your drink, judging by the way your voice is slurring."

"Tom?" I finally squeal, spinning round and practically knocking over Carson, who's grinning like a Cheshire cat.

"How on earth . . .? What the hell are you doing here? I don't understand . . . How come they let you in?"

442

"Um, I thought you were supposed to be building a case for not being shallow?" says Tom, but he's grinning like mad and looking absolutely gorgeous and wonderfully familiar and I've missed him so much I almost can't breathe.

"Oh my God, oh my God! I just can't get over it. I can't believe you're actually here. How did you . . .? How much of this is down to you, Carson?"

Carson shrugs his broad shoulders modestly.

"It's just so good to see you after all of this . . . time . . ." I trail off. My elation evaporates in a puff of realization as it occurs to me that Tom and Carson must have had this planned for a while now and that for much of that time I've been bloody miserable.

The next thing I say is in quite an angry voice. "You could have phoned, you know." Carson's face falls, as does Tom's. This wasn't the plan.

"You never even sent me so much as a lousy text and for all this time I've been thinking that you didn't care a bit and I've been so upset," I say, weeks of frustration getting the better of me, fuelled by all the drink.

Carson comes over to me and gently but firmly takes me by the hand, which is shaking like a leaf. He leads me closer to Tom and my initial delight at seeing him slowly returns.

Now that I'm a mere foot away from Tom, I take in how smart he looks. I'd bet good money that Carson has had a hand in dressing him for the evening, as he's decked out in what must be a very expensive designer tuxedo with a rather alarming cummerbund wrapped round his middle and very shiny shoes. It doesn't really suit his natural style and I can tell that he feels rather self-conscious in it. It reminds me of the first time I clapped eyes on him at Harry's wedding, when he was the only person wearing black tie. Despite myself, I start to giggle and I can't work out whether I want to hug Tom or beat him up. It's all so confusing. I still can't believe he's actually here. What does it mean?

Carson seems to think that, left to our own devices, we're never going to make any decent headway in solving our differences (he could well be right), so takes it upon himself to start giving us instructions. It's like an upmarket version of *The Jerry Springer Show*.

"Francesca. If you want to be annoyed with someone, be annoyed with me. I'm the one who persuaded Tom to wait until today to tell you how he feels. He's wanted to tell you for ages, but after speaking to you on the phone that time you sounded so angry that I said wait until the Oscars. I knew how much you were looking forward to it and I figured that Tom would be the icing on the cake, so I flew him over."

I look from a concerned Carson to an anxious-looking Tom.

"He *is* the icing on the cake," I mumble sulkily.

"Good," says Carson gently. "Jeez, thank God you're not an actress because you would be a hopeless leading lady. Now, what you're supposed to do is run into Tom's arms, kiss him and say something like, 'Ah, I don't believe it, you're here. The man of my dreams at the night of my dreams.'"

Despite myself, I laugh. "Carson, I'm English, remember? I would be more likely to bungee jump without a rope than say a line like that."

"Yeah, OK, well now you know why I don't write the scripts. But surely you can do better than 'Why didn't you bloody ring me?' " he says, laughing at his own dire attempt at an English accent.

I regard Carson with genuine affection. He's such an old softie and it's obvious that he's been envisaging a perfectly executed romantic ending ever since he master-minded this reunion. Unfortunately for him, he was never likely to get one worthy of the movies. Tom and I are both far too British to simply fall into each other's arms. We're also the opposite of smooth and slightly worried about how the other one really feels. Besides, this isn't a film, this is real life, and real life is complicated and emotions aren't always pretty. Oh, and I'm drunk.

So Tom and I stand looking at each other awkwardly, but now that I've extinguished any bad temper and my breathing has returned to normal, the joy of seeing him is taking over again. Sensing this, Tom's courage slowly returns and although we are still too self-conscious and nervous to say or do anything useful, we start to grin at each other like fools.

"Guys!!" Carson is starting to get really frustrated and looks like he'd quite like to bang our heads together.

"OK, OK," says Tom. "Sorry, Carson. Right . . . Oh God, Francesca, I had this all worked out and now it seems to have gone to pot." He takes a deep breath.

"OK, here goes. I'll start with 'I'm sorry'. I'm really, really sorry. I'm sorry that I doubted our entire relationship just because of one element of your personality. Having done nothing but think about you and what happened since December I've realized there may have been a small part of me that was fed up with always playing second fiddle to your job. Also, I understand that you have your reasons for being so intrigued by Caroline and Carson's world and I should have accepted that it was just a part of you and that we don't have to feel the same way about every single thing. You're right, I was an idiot for not ringing and I should never have got so het up about how you handled yourself with Caroline. Of course, you are more than capable of looking after yourself, I had no right to judge and I overreacted. I've thought about ringing you thousands of times, but I'm a stubborn idiot, and then for a time, to be honest, I did have trouble reconciling a couple of things you said."

I blush fiercely.

"That said, although it took a while, I eventually did. I finally 'got off my high horse' and realized I'd handled the whole argument really badly. Francesca, I've missed you like mad." He pauses and looks away.

The tension is palpable, but somewhat diluted by the fact that Carson is beaming at us both so inanely. This is very off-putting and I end up chuckling. "Carson, please stop it. You're making me laugh. You look so pleased with yourself and you're ruining the moment."

"Sorry," he says, not sounding it at all and not even remotely trying to tone down his smug grin. He orchestrated this scene so he's damn well going to enjoy it. His face only falls into a more serious and appropriate expression when he looks at Tom and realizes that he might well be in danger of blubbing.

Tom gulps. "Fran, I've missed you a horrible amount . . . and without you life has been extremely dull . . . although, come to think of it, in some ways that's actually been quite a positive thing. No emergency births, sick dogs, etc . . ."

My soppy smile begins to fade. He quickly continues.

"But more importantly, and the thing you really need to know, is that I would never have flown all the way to LA, taken a week off work, worn a Versace tuxedo with matching cummerbund and let Carson engineer this meeting if I didn't know that I'm madly in love with you, have been since the moment I met you and quite possibly will be for the rest of my days."

"Really?" Now it's my turn to feel choked.

"Yes. I care about you a ridiculous amount, which is probably why seeing Caroline being so vile to you got to me so much. I just wish I'd worked out how I felt a bit quicker. I've wasted a lot of time worrying about whether we were really compatible, whether I was exciting enough for you and whether I had left it all too long to try and win you back. By the time it had become blindingly obvious that I didn't want to be without you even for a minute, I didn't have the guts to pick up the phone. I was too worried that you wouldn't speak to me, or that you might have moved on and met

447

someone else. Have you met someone else?" he asks quizzically.

"No, I haven't."

"Oh good, that's what Carson said."

At this point Carson nods at Tom as if to say, "Hey, I told you."

Tom swallows before continuing. "I also thought that simply ringing you may have been too much of a 'run of the mill' approach for you. I know how you like things to be out of the ordinary. So when Carson suggested surprising you on Oscars night I thought, well, why not? I thought it might be worth the wait, but if you want to tell me I'm a pompous arse and to get lost, then you'd be well within your rights and I'll take it like a man."

I look at Tom. His sweet, lovely face looks tortured and everything about him makes me want to scoop him up and take him home. I know one hundred per cent what my answer is going to be.

I turn to look at Carson, who is waiting on tenterhooks. In fact, he is starting to look dangerously impatient and, if I don't hurry up and give my answer, he may throttle it out of me. Still, he was the one who wanted the big romantic ending, so that's what he's going to get and a big dramatic pause is all part of that. A pause that is pure indulgence, as I certainly don't need the time to decide anything — the truth is that the minute I saw Tom everything changed. I no longer felt hollow or empty. I was complete again and the party became the only place on earth I wanted to be, simply because he was there. I'm finally on the verge of telling

Tom all of this when, with a case of chronic bad timing, the reporter from E! Entertainment interrupts.

"Hi, Carson! Would you mind if we just filmed a quick segment for E?" she says, blinding us not just with the camera light but also her teeth.

"Um . . . now?" says Carson, with a hint of madness. "Just give me one second, please? Francesca?"

"It's OK, Carson, it's all going to be OK, and thank you so, so much," I say softly.

Having finally heard exactly what he wanted to hear, Carson breaks into a massive grin. He grabs my face with two hands and gives me a kiss on both cheeks. Then he slaps Tom on the back. "Way to go, man."

I grin from Carson back to Tom and then Tom envelopes me in the warmest, most welcome hug I've ever had. Of course, with a film crew standing so nearby we (rather frustratingly) can't do any proper snogging or make any more declarations of love, seeing as I'm meant to be with Carson, who's currently giving me a thumbs-up, seemingly satisfied that the right outcome has been achieved.

He trots happily off with the crew and, as I hug Tom, I watch Carson get into position on the other side of the pool.

"Now that they're out of earshot, will you officially put me out of my misery?" whispers Tom in my ear.

I look him square in the eye and the words finally come. "I have missed you so much, Tom. Life has been really crap with you not in it, despite the fact that loads of good things have been happening, and I'm absolutely certain that I really, really love you. I am so, so glad that you're here."

We hug again.

"Oh, and by the way," I say, drawing apart, "it looks like my book is going to be made into a film, so maybe working for Caroline wasn't a total waste of time after all."

Tom grins at me and has the good grace to turn slightly red.

"Carson told me. I think it's amazing. I think you're amazing."

I bask in his praise. I may burst with happiness.

"And by the way, Fran, do you know what really got me thinking how stupid I've been?"

"No, what?"

"*It's a Wonderful Life*. You see, I watched it over Christmas, as ever, and I couldn't help but consider how different things would be for so many people if you hadn't come into their lives, if you hadn't been born."

I wave my hand in front of my face as if to dismiss what he's saying, but Tom carries on.

"No, seriously, Fran — think about it. Without you, Carson and Caroline would still be living a ridiculous lie, Steph would be going along with it but secretly pining after a life she probably thought she couldn't ever have and poor little Cameron would still believe that Old Crone Features was his mother. Not to mention how happy you've made me and how much impact you've had on my life."

I'm unbelievably moved, but feel like I need to dilute the atmosphere now. After all, there's only so much

450

romance a girl can take at any one given time, so I grin up at his serious face. "You know what, Tom, you have a point, so will you please try and remember that next time I'm driving you mad?"

Tom laughs and, as he hugs me, a thought occurs to me. One of those thoughts that you have sometimes when you're standing on top of a high cliff.

A "what if" thought.

Usually "what if" thoughts are consigned quickly to the back of your mind where they rightfully belong, but this one isn't going anywhere.

I pull away from Tom.

"What are you up to, Fran?" he says, noticing my look of intent and suddenly feeling nervous.

"Nothing. Nothing at all," I say, with a mischievous glint in my eye. "I just think it might be time to stop talking and to show you how much I love you."

There's no more time for hesitation. I gather up my dress and do what subconsciously I've been dying to do ever since I spotted the swimming pool. Without bothering to think about the consequences or even to take my shoes off, much to the surprise of everyone around me, I charge at full pace towards the still, liquid, blue cube and jump.

And now it's almost time for you to leave me: suspended in midair, my arms hugging my knees, an expression of pure joy and freedom on my face and about to cause the biggest splash that Hollywood has ever seen. About to do what my brother would once have described as "a bomb". It's certainly about to liven up Carson's interview and in the background amongst faces that are smothered in disbelief and shock, I can just make out his beautiful face, which is wreathed in smiles and absolute approval.

Ironically, what I am about to do will achieve more notoriety than a lifetime of auditions ever could. True, I only achieve it for something silly, something funny, something that requires no talent whatsoever, but it's going to make a bloody great story for my future grandchildren.

And so it is that I soak half of Hollywood on live TV and, as I come up for air, I feel positively jubilant, unlike some of my audience who are still trying to work out how on earth they should react. But then one person at least makes up her mind and with a whoop of "Go, girl!" Cameron Diaz follows suit, hitting the water just fractionally before a liberated Carson Adams does.

The cold water sobers me up and pulls everything sharply into focus. I have never felt so exhilarated and so thrilled simply to be alive. I search for Tom and finally spot him on the sidelines, chuckling to himself as he watches the unlikely events unfold. His expression is one of adoration and pride and, as he catches my eye, we both laugh out loud. And now it seems it's his turn to surprise me, for he's loosening his dodgy cummerbund, flinging it to one side, taking a deep breath and running at full pelt towards me.

Epilogue

In a penthouse apartment far, far away from the lights of LA, in the sprawling metropolis that is New York, Caroline Mason is still tuned into E! Entertainment. She has been for the last ten hours and despite the lateness of the hour she is still watching avidly, albeit from the comfort of her bed, usually the one place she doesn't allow herself to smoke. Tonight, though, she has felt the need to bend that rule.

Leticia, who fell asleep a long while ago, is in bed next to her, lying on one side with her mouth open, snoring. Caroline knows she should put her earplugs in and try to get some shut-eye too, for she has a busy day of appointments ahead, but she can't. She's transfixed by what's going on at the Oscars, completely glued; even more so now, thanks to what's happening at the *Vanity Fair* bash.

On her forty-two-inch flat screen her ex-assistant is being helped out of a swimming pool by Tom Cruise, having just made an utter show of herself. Many of the other guests are now thronging round the pool where all the action is taking place and with gay abandon are jumping on to the bandwagon that Francesca has ridden to the party. Michael Douglas has just been pushed into the pool by Sharon Stone, who seems positively frothy with excitement, and for a worrying second it looks as if Sharon's planning on pushing Kirk in after Michael. Then she thinks better of it as it seems to dawn on her that throwing an octogenarian into a pool might not be the best plan, and she visibly calms down.

Laughing away in the pool are Cameron Diaz, Carson and, rather puzzlingly, the vet who came to see Froo Froo. The vet and Carson are roaring with laughter together and ducking each other in the pool like schoolboys. It's all very confusing.

Caroline stubs out a cigarette and considers her next move.

Next to her, on her bedside table, lies a well-thumbed script that her agent, Geoffrey, recommended that she read. The script is for a film called *Me and Miss M* and Caroline has now read it in its entirety three times and knows it is the script that has the power to make her a huge star once more. She also knows exactly who it's all about and who must have written it. Very recently she has come to the conclusion that she may have underestimated Francesca Massi in more ways than one.

Caroline examines how she feels. She wants to be disgusted by Francesca's outlandish behaviour, so from the depths of her psyche she summons up some bile. Who the hell does Francesca Massi think she is? First she writes about herself as if she is some kind of fucking saint and casts her, Caroline Mason, as a borderline witch. The next minute she's at the Oscars getting the kind of attention an ordinary girl like her simply doesn't deserve. Still not content with the havoc that she's wreaked, she then has the audacity to do the unthinkable by transforming the *Vanity Fair* party into some kind of rave.

But Caroline isn't convincing herself. She slides off the bed and pads through to the kitchen, where she opens the fridge and stares at the contents. Everything looks deeply unsatisfying.

"Fuck it," she says, as she realizes that on top of everything else Francesca has done the unspeakable and driven her to a carbohydrate craving. Caroline rummages in a cupboard, desperate to find something sweet or doughy, but the best she can come up with is a lousy cracker, which she nibbles on as she makes her way back to the bedroom. She must be unsettled because she feels rabidly hungry and just the thought of a deep-pan pepperoni pizza with extra cheese is making her salivate. She half considers ordering one but then summons up some of the determination and discipline that got her where she is today and banishes the craving from her midst.

She resumes her viewing position on the bed. Hating doing so with every fibre of her being, Caroline has to grudgingly admit that for once the party looks really fun. Even more galling, when Francesca is captured on camera again, rather than looking like a drowned rat she looks irritatingly gorgeous. She may be wet through but her red dress is clinging in all the right places, her beautiful diamonds are sparkling and she looks so happy, so alive, that for a while nobody else gets a look-in. The camera focuses on Francesca for ages and it's not surprising. She is utterly radiant.

Caroline sighs and narrows her eyes at the screen.

She wants to feel appalled and pent up with fury like she usually would. She knows how to handle feeling like that and rage would enable her to get straight on the phone to her lawyers to instruct them to sue the arse off a certain Miss Francesca Massi. However, much to her own surprise, reading *Me and Miss M* has rather taken the wind out of her sails. Seeing such uncomfortable truths in black and white has been extremely unnerving — a very strange experience and not one that she knows how to feel about. She sighs and lights another cigarette. Tomorrow she'll tell Jodie to book her in for a few extra hours with her New York therapist. That ought to help.

She sits back.

Who would have thought that a seemingly "nice girl" like Francesca would ever have the balls to inveigle her way into the Oscars, of all places, and wearing vintage Valentino to boot?

Caroline wriggles back into her pillows almost in an attempt to rid herself of what she's feeling — which is what, exactly? She can't put her finger on it, but she is certain that it's a pretty alien emotion.

And then it hits her. Francesca has stirred up something that feels horribly like pride. No matter how hard she tries to feel otherwise, what she really feels about Francesca's display at the *Vanity Fair* party is grudging admiration.

456

Finally Caroline has to reluctantly admit that, despite everything, she is a tiny bit impressed by Francesca's outrageous conduct.

It's time to acknowledge a few things.

Firstly, she knows that she won't be suing anybody over *Me and Miss M*. Scripts this good only come along once or twice in an actor's career and she would be mad not to do it. Playing Miss M would make her a star again and she will stop at nothing to get the part.

Secondly, it's absolutely imperative that no one finds out that Miss M is based on her real self. It will be very weird to play "herself", but she will have to find a way to make it work.

Lastly, and this is the point on which she has the most conviction, she knows that she hasn't seen the last of a certain Miss Massi and that their paths will most certainly cross again. She smiles to herself. This is a prospect she knows that she'll be relishing far more than Francesca will be. It is going to be a very interesting year. Savouring that thought, Caroline finally switches off the TV.

Acknowledgments

The following people all in some way, shape or form have contributed to me writing and indeed finishing this book.

Firstly, my editor, Kate Burke — thank you for your fantastic notes and for liking the song "Biology". I am utterly thrilled to be with Penguin.

The fabulous Eugenie Furniss — thanks for "weaving your magic" and for your enthusiasm and brilliance in general. Thanks to Rowan Lawton for your help and input and to anyone else at William Morris who has been involved.

A ridiculous amount of thanks are due to my amazing and very funny friend Sarah Jane Robinson. Thank you for everything you've done for me over the years, only some of which includes being my running partner in crime (as in making tea, not exercising), getting me jobs, championing this book, leading me to the inspiration behind it and a top agent to boot. You're such a star and I love you tons.

Thank you, Jonny Yeo, for not taking the easy option by not helping. If you hadn't given someone important a manuscript that they might hate, therefore risking